Maurice Leblanc

THE BEST OF LUPIN

Maurice Leblanc (1864–1941) was born in Rouen, France. He began his career as a journalist and a writer of realistic novels but became best known for the enormously popular character of Arsène Lupin, the gentlemanly thief and con artist who first appeared in a magazine story in 1905 and went on to feature in several novels and five collections of short stories. Leblanc was awarded the ribbon of the French Legion of Honor for his services to literature.

THE BEST OF
LUPIN

THE BEST OF
LUPIN

ADVENTURES OF
ARSÈNE LUPIN, GENTLEMAN-THIEF

Maurice Leblanc

Translations by
George Morehead and Alexander Teixeira de Mattos

Introduction by Martin Walker

VINTAGE CLASSICS
Vintage Books
A Division of Penguin Random House LLC
New York

FIRST VINTAGE CLASSICS EDITION 2024

Introduction copyright © 2024 by Walker and Watson Ltd.

Published in the United States by Vintage Books, a division of Penguin
Random House LLC, New York, and distributed in Canada by
Penguin Random House Canada Limited, Toronto.

Vintage is a registered trademark and Vintage Classics
and colophon are trademarks of Penguin Random House LLC.

The Library of Congress has cataloged the Vintage Classics edition as follows:
Names: Leblanc, Maurice, 1864–1941, author. | Morehead, George, translator. |
Teixera de Mattos, Alexander, 1865-1921, translator. |
Walker, Martin, [date] writer of introduction.
Title: The best of Lupin : adventures of Arsène Lupin, gentleman-thief /
Maurice Leblanc ; translations by George Morehead and
Alexander Teixera de Mattos ; introduction by Martin Walker.
Description: First Vintage classics edition. |
New York : Vintage Books, 2024. | Series: Vintage classics
Identifiers: LCCN 2023042990 (print) | LCCN 2023042991 (ebook)
Subjects: LCSH: Lupin, Arsène (Fictitious character)—Fiction. |
Leblanc, Maurice, 1864–1941—Translations into English. | Burglars—Fiction. |
LCGFT: Detective and mystery fiction. | Short stories.
Classification: LCC PQ2623.E24 B47 2024 (print) |
LCC PQ2623.E24 (ebook) | DDC 843/.912—dc23
LC record available at https://lccn.loc.gov/2023042990
LC ebook record available at https://lccn.loc.gov/2023042991

Vintage Books Trade Paperback ISBN: 978-0-593-68644-7
eBook ISBN: 978-0-593-68645-4

Book design by Christopher M. Zucker

vintagebooks.com

Printed in the United States of America
1st Printing

CONTENTS

INTRODUCTION TO THE
VINTAGE CLASSICS EDITION (2024)

Arsène Lupin stands alongside George Simenon's Maigret as one of the immortal figures of French crime fiction. He emerges in 1905 as the antihero in a serial novel by Maurice Leblanc, a young journalist from Normandy, in the French magazine *Je Sais Tout* [I Know Everything]. Lupin became an immediate global success. The first US film of his exploits, *The Gentleman Burglar*, was made in 1908. Two years later, Berlin's film studio in Germany made *Arsène Lupin contra Sherlock Holmes*. The first Japanese film, *Rupimono*, followed in 1923. The Barrymore brothers starred in an early Hollywood talkie in which Lupin goes for the *Mona Lisa*, all followed more recently by wave upon international wave of TV series, manga, comics, and video games in Korean, Japanese, Indonesian, Hindi, and most European languages.

Often compared with Sherlock Holmes, Lupin is in fact significantly different. While almost all the superstars of crime are on the right side of the law, Lupin is most of the time a criminal, a gentleman-thief. And although he has moments of public-spiritedness and personal generosity, he is no Robin Hood who can be relied on to take from the rich to give to the poor. As he declares in the splendid short story "Edith Swan-Neck":

"I may have peculiar views about other people's property;
but I assure you that it's very different when my own's at
stake. By Jove, it doesn't do to lay hands on what belongs
to me! Then I'm out for blood!"

Lupin is hard to pin down. Sometimes he is the Russian prince
Serge Rénine, with an apartment on the fashionable Boulevard
Haussmann, while in the later stories he is just as likely to play the
hard-bitten American private eye Jim Barnett, with a modest office
on the Rue Laborde. Opening a trial (from which Lupin inevitably
escapes), the judge says Lupin is widely believed to be the professor who introduced the Japanese art of jiu-jitsu to Paris, and that
he won ten thousand francs in the Grand Prix bicycle race and was
never heard of again, and before that he was the Russian student who
researched bacteriology and skin diseases at the laboratory of Doctor
Altier in the Saint-Louis hospital. And sometimes Lupin is the sworn
but admiring rival of that famous English detective Sherlock Holmes,
opening a new front in that centuries-long love-hate relationship
between the French and their neighbors across the Channel. In their
first encounter Lupin steals, but then returns, Holmes's pocket watch.

"He is possessed of a marvelous intuition . . . surpassing even that
of Sherlock Holmes himself," Sherlock Holmes admits to himself in
"The Shipwreck," one of the series of stories of their confrontation
published in 1908. "I resemble an actor whose every step and movement are directed by a stage manager . . . a superior will."

The visit of Holmes to Paris had been orchestrated by Lupin,
and as Holmes steps off the train, he sees all over Paris men carrying sandwich boards advertising THE MATCH BETWEEN SHERLOCK
HOLMES AND ARSÈNE LUPIN . . . READ THE DETAILS IN THE "ECHO
DE FRANCE" (the newspaper in which Lupin is a major shareholder).
Threats of legal action by Arthur Conan Doyle, Holmes's creator,
required Leblanc to rename the Englishman Herlock Sholmes, and
in the tales of Lupin, peace broke out. The two men agreed to a
kind of draw, or as Maurice Leblanc puts it, "The treaty of peace was
concluded."

"Must a person steal, cheat, and wrong all the time?" Lupin
demands in "The Shipwreck."

"Then you do good, also?" Sherlock Holmes asks, and his question seems genuinely curious.

"When I have the time," Lupin replies. "Besides, I find it amusing."

A master of disguise, able to change his height and build and appearance on a whim, and a genius at crafting illusions, Lupin has also (according to his creator) become something of a favorite among public opinion in Paris. One newspaper editorial, in the same short story, declares its outrage when one of Lupin's schemes leads—most unusually—to a death:

> "Let him look to himself. It would not take many exploits of this kind for him to forfeit the popularity which has not been grudged him hitherto. We have no use for Lupin, except when his rogueries are perpetrated at the expense of shady company-promoters, foreign adventurers, German barons, banks, and financial companies. And, above all, no murders! A burglar we can put up with; but a murderer, no!"

Murder, however, is one crime of which Lupin appears to be innocent. Despite the thefts, frauds, tricks, and impersonations, Lupin also seems to adhere to some moral code of his own devising that allows him to convince himself that he remains a gentleman, above all in relation to women. And in tracking down the long-lost fortune of one of the first victims of the guillotine during the Revolution over a hundred years earlier in the story "The Sign of the Shadow," Lupin contents himself with a fraction of the loot, leaving the rest to the impoverished descendants.

A mystery is not just a plot with entertaining or intriguing characters, but also something of a game between author and reader, and Leblanc is a master of that strange art: of misleading clues, the unlikely coincidence, the railway timetables that do not quite match, the footsteps in the snow that are a little too deep, and even Holmes's favorite, the dog that does not bark in the night.

In his portrayal of the gentleman crook, Leblanc again borrows from the English tradition established by Ernest William Hornung, the creator of A. J. Raffles, the classic upper-class thief who became almost as famous as Sherlock Holmes. And just as Holmes has his Dr. Watson, Hornung provided Raffles with a sidekick, Bunny Manders, and it became an open secret among their friends that Raffles and Bunny were modeled on Oscar Wilde and his lover, Lord Alfred Douglas. The connections were even more convoluted, since Hornung married Connie, one of Conan Doyle's sisters.

There was one great difference between Lupin and the two English characters, Holmes and Raffles, who between them inspired Leblanc to dream up his hero: Lupin was devoted to women. On his first adventure, aboard a ship bound for the Americas, he falls in love and escapes from prison to find his love again but wins only a fading white rose from which petals are falling. He goes through a mock wedding to save a devout countess from a forced marriage to a wealthy brute, falls for her, and she declares he is her husband "in the eyes of God" before breaking his heart by entering a nunnery.

Another of his old loves is about to lose her only child to her cruel husband, who claims to have proof that she has been unfaithful. He can then demand a divorce, take command of the child and its inheritance, and thus repair his own ruined fortunes. Lupin, under the name Horace Velmont, yet another of his many aliases, comes to the rescue when he receives a card he gave the mother many years earlier with his promise to come to her aid whenever she called.

In the guise of the private eye Jim Barnett, Lupin joins his detective friend Inspector Béchoux on a visit to the policeman's ex-wife, a ragtime singer at the Folies Bergère, whose home has been burgled of all the priceless antique furniture in her bedroom, including a bed that had belonged to Madame de Pompadour herself. Naturally, Lupin solves the case, recovers the bed, and disappears on a honeymoon trip with the ex-wife, leaving her hit number ringing in Béchoux's ears:

> *"I'm in luck, I gotta boy,*
> *Fills his momma's heart with joy—*
> *Yes, you otta see my Jim!"*

Lupin saves another woman, Hortense, from a marriage she dreads and woos her by recruiting her as his spy and aide in the fashionable beach resorts of Normandy. After solving another crime together, they are standing on a cliff top, gazing at the sea, and Lupin, in the role of Russian prince Rénine, asks what she is thinking: "I know, as certainly as I know that I exist, that you would save me, whatever the obstacles might be. There is no limit to the power of your will," says Hortense. In reply, he responds, very softly, "There is no limit to my wish to please you."

And that might be Leblanc's epigraph to his readers.

MARTIN WALKER

2023

Martin Walker is the author of a series of mystery novels set in France featuring Bruno, Chief of Police, including *To Kill a Troubadour* and *A Château Under Siege*. Bestsellers in Europe, his novels have been translated into more than fifteen languages and have sold more than six million copies worldwide. He is also the co-author of *Bruno's Cookbook: Recipes and Traditions from a French Country Kitchen*. In 2021 he was awarded Le Prix Charbonnier by the Alliance Française for services to French culture. He divides his time between Washington, D.C., and the Dordogne in France.

THE BEST OF
LUPIN

FROM ARSÈNE LUPIN:

GENTLEMAN-BURGLAR (1906)

THE ARREST OF ARSÈNE LUPIN

It was a strange ending to a voyage that had commenced in a most auspicious manner. The transatlantic steamship *La Provence* was a swift and comfortable vessel under the command of a most affable man. The passengers constituted a select and delightful society. The charm of new acquaintances and improvised amusements served to make the time pass agreeably. We enjoyed the pleasant sensation of being separated from the world, living, as it were, upon an unknown island, and consequently obliged to be sociable with each other.

Have you ever stopped to consider how much originality and spontaneity emanate from these various individuals who, on the preceding evening, did not even know each other, and who are now, for several days, condemned to lead a life of extreme intimacy, jointly defying the anger of the ocean, the terrible onslaught of the waves, the violence of the tempest and the agonizing monotony of the calm and sleepy water? Such a life becomes a sort of tragic existence, with its storms and its grandeurs, its monotony and its diversity; and that is why, perhaps, we embark upon that short voyage with mingled feelings of pleasure and fear.

But, during the past few years, a new sensation had been added to the life of the transatlantic traveler. The little floating island is now attached to the world from which it was once quite free. A bond united them, even in the very heart of the watery wastes of the Atlantic. That bond is the wireless telegraph, by means of which we receive news in the most mysterious manner. We know full well that the message is not transported by the medium of a hollow wire. No, the mystery is even more inexplicable, more romantic, and we must have recourse to the wings of the air in order to explain this new miracle. During the first day of the voyage, we felt that we were being followed, escorted, preceded even, by that distant voice, which, from time to time, whispered to one of us a few words from the receding world. Two friends spoke to me. Ten, twenty others sent gay or somber words of parting to other passengers.

On the second day, at a distance of five hundred miles from the French coast, in the midst of a violent storm, we received the following message by means of the wireless telegraph:

> "Arsène Lupin is on your vessel, first cabin, blonde hair, wound right fore-arm, traveling alone under name of R......"

At that moment, a terrible flash of lightning rent the stormy skies. The electric waves were interrupted. The remainder of the dispatch never reached us. Of the name under which Arsène Lupin was concealing himself, we knew only the initial.

If the news had been of some other character, I have no doubt that the secret would have been carefully guarded by the telegraphic operator as well as by the officers of the vessel. But it was one of those events calculated to escape from the most rigorous discretion. The same day, no one knew how, the incident became a matter of current gossip and every passenger was aware that the famous Arsène Lupin was hiding in our midst.

Arsène Lupin in our midst! the irresponsible burglar whose exploits had been narrated in all the newspapers during the past few months! the mysterious individual with whom Ganimard, our shrewdest detective, had been engaged in an implacable conflict amidst interesting and picturesque surroundings. Arsène Lupin, the eccentric gentleman who operates only in the châteaux and salons, and who, one night, entered the residence of Baron Schormann, but emerged empty-handed, leaving, however, his card on which he had scribbled these words: "Arsène Lupin, gentleman-burglar, will return when the furniture is genuine." Arsène Lupin, the man of a thousand disguises: in turn a chauffer, detective, bookmaker, Russian physician, Spanish bull-fighter, commercial traveler, robust youth, or decrepit old man.

Then consider this startling situation: Arsène Lupin was wandering about within the limited bounds of a transatlantic steamer; in that very small corner of the world, in that dining saloon, in that smoking room, in that music room! Arsène Lupin was, perhaps, this gentleman . . . or that one . . . my neighbor at the table . . . the sharer of my stateroom . . .

"And this condition of affairs will last for five days!" exclaimed Miss Nelly Underdown, next morning. "It is unbearable! I hope he will be arrested."

Then, addressing me, she added:

"And you, Monsieur d'Andrézy, you are on intimate terms with the captain; surely you know something?"

I should have been delighted had I possessed any information that would interest Miss Nelly. She was one of those magnificent creatures who inevitably attract attention in every assembly. Wealth and beauty form an irresistible combination, and Nelly possessed both.

Educated in Paris under the care of a French mother, she was now going to visit her father, the millionaire Underdown of Chicago. She was accompanied by one of her friends, Lady Jerland.

At first, I had decided to open a flirtation with her; but, in the rapidly growing intimacy of the voyage, I was soon impressed by her charming manner and my feelings became too deep and reverential for a mere flirtation. Moreover, she accepted my attentions with a certain degree of favor. She condescended to laugh at my witticisms and display an interest in my stories. Yet I felt that I had a rival in the person of a young man with quiet and refined tastes; and it struck me, at times, that she preferred his taciturn humor to my Parisian frivolity.

He formed one in the circle of admirers that surrounded Miss Nelly at the time she addressed to me the foregoing question. We were all comfortably seated in our deck-chairs. The storm of the preceding evening had cleared the sky. The weather was now delightful.

"I have no definite knowledge, mademoiselle," I replied, "but can not we, ourselves, investigate the mystery quite as well as the detective Ganimard, the personal enemy of Arsène Lupin?"

"Oh! oh! you are progressing very fast, monsieur."

"Not at all, mademoiselle. In the first place, let me ask, do you find the problem a complicated one?"

"Very complicated."

"Have you forgotten the key we hold for the solution to the problem?"

"What key?"

"In the first place, Lupin calls himself Monsieur R———."

"Rather vague information," she replied.

"Secondly, he is traveling alone."

"Does that help you?" she asked.

"Thirdly, he is blonde."

"Well?"

"Then we have only to peruse the passenger-list, and proceed by process of elimination."

I had that list in my pocket. I took it out and glanced through it. Then I remarked:

"I find that there are only thirteen men on the passenger-list whose names begin with the letter R."

"Only thirteen?"

"Yes, in the first cabin. And of those thirteen, I find that nine of them are accompanied by women, children or servants. That leaves only four who are traveling alone. First, the Marquis de Raverdan———"

"Secretary to the American Ambassador," interrupted Miss Nelly. "I know him."

"Major Rawson," I continued.

"He is my uncle," someone said.

"Mon. Rivolta."

"Here!" exclaimed an Italian, whose face was concealed beneath a heavy black beard.

Miss Nelly burst into laughter, and exclaimed: "That gentleman can scarcely be called a blonde."

"Very well, then," I said, "we are forced to the conclusion that the guilty party is the last one on the list."

"What is his name?"

"Mon. Rozaine. Does anyone know him?"

No one answered. But Miss Nelly turned to the taciturn young man, whose attentions to her had annoyed me, and said:

"Well, Monsieur Rozaine, why do you not answer?"

All eyes were now turned upon him. He was a blonde. I must confess that I myself felt a shock of surprise, and the profound silence that followed her question indicated that the others present also viewed the situation with a feeling of sudden alarm. However, the idea was an absurd one, because the gentleman in question presented an air of the most perfect innocence.

"Why do I not answer?" he said. "Because, considering my name, my position as a solitary traveler, and the color of my hair, I have already reached the same conclusion, and now think that I should be arrested."

He presented a strange appearance as he uttered these words. His thin lips were drawn closer than usual and his face was ghastly pale, whilst his eyes were streaked with blood. Of course, he was joking, yet his appearance and attitude impressed us strangely.

"But you have not the wound?" said Miss Nelly, naively. "That is true," he replied, "I lack the wound." Then he pulled up his sleeve, removing his cuff, and showed us his arm. But that action did not deceive me. He had shown us his left arm, and I was on the point of calling his attention to the fact, when another incident diverted our attention. Lady Jerland, Miss Nelly's friend, came running toward us in a state of great excitement, exclaiming:

"My jewels, my pearls! Someone has stolen them all!"

No, they were not all gone, as we soon found out. The thief had taken only part of them; a very curious thing. Of the diamond sunbursts, jeweled pendants, bracelets, and necklaces, the thief had taken, not the largest but the finest and most valuable stones. The mountings were lying upon the table. I saw them there, despoiled of their jewels, like flowers from which the beautiful colored petals had been ruthlessly plucked. And this theft must have been committed at the time Lady Jerland was taking her tea; in broad daylight, in a stateroom opening on a much frequented corridor; moreover, the thief had been obliged to force open the door of the stateroom, search for the jewel-case, which was hidden at the bottom of a hat-box, open it, select his booty, and remove it from the mountings.

Of course, all the passengers instantly reached the same conclusion; it was the work of Arsène Lupin.

That day, at the dinner table, the seats to the right and left of Rozaine remained vacant; and, during the evening, it was rumored that the captain had placed him under arrest, which information produced a feeling of safety and relief. We breathed once more. That evening, we resumed our games and dances. Miss Nelly, especially, displayed a spirit of thoughtless gayety which convinced me that if Rozaine's attentions had been agreeable to her in the beginning, she had already forgotten them. Her charm and good-humor completed my conquest. At midnight, under a bright moon, I declared my devotion with an ardor that did not seem to displease her.

But, next day, to our general amazement, Rozaine was at liberty. We learned that the evidence against him was not sufficient. He had produced documents that were perfectly regular, which showed that he was the son of a wealthy merchant of Bordeaux. Besides, his arms did not bear the slightest trace of a wound.

"Documents! Certificates of birth!" exclaimed the enemies of Rozaine, "of course, Arsène Lupin will furnish you as many as you desire. And as to the wound, he never had it, or he has removed it."

Then it was proven that, at the time of the theft, Rozaine was promenading on the deck. To which fact, his enemies replied that a man like Arsène Lupin could commit a crime without being actually present. And then, apart from all other circumstances, there remained one point which even the most skeptical could not answer: Who except Rozaine, was traveling alone, was a blonde, and bore a name beginning with R? To whom did the telegram point, if it were not Rozaine?

And when Rozaine, a few minutes before breakfast, came boldly toward our group, Miss Nelly and Lady Jerland arose and walked away.

An hour later, a manuscript circular was passed from hand to hand amongst the sailors, the stewards, and the passengers of all classes. It announced that Mon. Louis Rozaine offered a reward of ten thousand francs for the discovery of Arsène Lupin or other person in possession of the stolen jewels.

"And if no one assists me, I will unmask the scoundrel myself," declared Rozaine.

Rozaine against Arsène Lupin, or rather, according to current opinion, Arsène Lupin himself against Arsène Lupin; the contest promised to be interesting.

Nothing developed during the next two days. We saw Rozaine wandering about, day and night, searching, questioning, investigating. The captain, also, displayed commendable activity. He caused the vessel to be searched from stem to stern; ransacked every stateroom under the plausible theory that the jewels might be concealed anywhere, except in the thief's own room.

"I suppose they will find out something soon," remarked Miss Nelly to me. "He may be a wizard, but he cannot make diamonds and pearls become invisible."

"Certainly not," I replied, "but he should examine the lining of our hats and vests and everything we carry with us."

Then, exhibiting my Kodak, a 9×12 with which I had been photographing her in various poses, I added: "In an apparatus no larger than that, a person could hide all of Lady Jerland's jewels. He could pretend to take pictures and no one would suspect the game."

"But I have heard it said that every thief leaves some clue behind him."

"That may be generally true," I replied, "but there is one exception: Arsène Lupin."

"Why?"

"Because he concentrates his thoughts not only on the theft, but on all the circumstances connected with it that could serve as a clue to his identity."

"A few days ago, you were more confident."

"Yes, but since then I have seen him at work."

"And what do you think about it now?" she asked.

"Well, in my opinion, we are wasting our time."

And, as a matter of fact, the investigation had produced no result. But, in the meantime, the captain's watch had been stolen. He was furious. He quickened his efforts and watched Rozaine more closely than before. But, on the following day, the watch was found in the second officer's collar box.

This incident caused considerable astonishment, and displayed the humorous side of Arsène Lupin, burglar though he was, but dilettante as well. He combined business with pleasure. He reminded us of the author who almost died in a fit of laughter provoked by his own play. Certainly, he was an artist in his particular line of work, and whenever I saw Rozaine, gloomy and reserved, and thought of the double role that he was playing, I accorded him a certain measure of admiration.

On the following evening, the officer on deck duty heard groans emanating from the darkest corner of the ship. He approached and found a man lying there, his head enveloped in a thick gray scarf and his hands tied together with a heavy cord. It was Rozaine. He had been assaulted, thrown down and robbed. A card, pinned to his coat, bore these words: "Arsène Lupin accepts with pleasure the ten thousand francs offered by Mon. Rozaine." As a matter of fact, the stolen pocket-book contained twenty thousand francs.

Of course, some accused the unfortunate man of having simulated this attack on himself. But, apart from the fact that he could not have bound himself in that manner, it was established that the writing on the card was entirely different from that of Rozaine, but, on the contrary, resembled the handwriting of Arsène Lupin as it was reproduced in an old newspaper found on board.

Thus it appeared that Rozaine was not Arsène Lupin; but was Rozaine, the son of a Bordeaux merchant. And the presence of Arsène Lupin was once more affirmed, and that in a most alarming manner.

Such was the state of terror amongst the passengers that none would remain alone in a stateroom or wander singly in unfrequented parts of the vessel. We clung together as a matter of safety. And yet the most intimate acquaintances were estranged by a mutual feeling of distrust. Arsène Lupin was, now, anybody and everybody. Our excited imaginations attributed to him miraculous and unlimited power. We supposed him capable of assuming the most unexpected disguises; of being, by turns, the highly respectable Major Rawson or the noble Marquis de Raverdan, or even—for we no longer stopped with the accusing letter of R—or even such or such a person well known to all of us, and having wife, children, and servants.

The first wireless dispatches from America brought no news; at least, the captain did not communicate any to us. The silence was not reassuring.

Our last day on the steamer seemed interminable. We lived in constant fear of some disaster. This time, it would not be a simple theft or a comparatively harmless assault; it would be a crime, a murder. No one imagined that Arsène Lupin would confine himself to those two trifling offenses. Absolute master of the ship, the authorities powerless, he could do whatever he pleased; our property and lives were at his mercy.

Yet those were delightful hours for me, since they secured to me the confidence of Miss Nelly. Deeply moved by those startling events and being of a highly nervous nature, she spontaneously sought at my side a protection and security that I was pleased to give her. Inwardly, I blessed Arsène Lupin. Had he not been the means of bringing me and Miss Nelly closer to each other? Thanks to him, I could now indulge in delicious dreams of love and happiness—dreams that, I felt, were not unwelcome to Miss Nelly. Her smiling eyes authorized me to make them; the softness of her voice bade me hope.

As we approached the American shore, the active search for the thief was apparently abandoned, and we were anxiously awaiting the supreme moment in which the mysterious enigma would be explained. Who was Arsène Lupin? Under what name, under what disguise was the famous Arsène Lupin concealing himself? And, at last, that supreme moment arrived. If I live one hundred years, I shall not forget the slightest details of it.

"How pale you are, Miss Nelly," I said to my companion, as she leaned upon my arm, almost fainting.

"And you!" she replied, "ah! you are so changed."

"Just think! this is a most exciting moment, and I am delighted to spend it with you, Miss Nelly. I hope that your memory will sometimes revert—"

But she was not listening. She was nervous and excited. The gangway was placed in position, but, before we could use it, the uniformed customs officers came on board. Miss Nelly murmured:

"I shouldn't be surprised to hear that Arsène Lupin escaped from the vessel during the voyage."

"Perhaps he preferred death to dishonor, and plunged into the Atlantic rather than be arrested."

"Oh, do not laugh," she said.

Suddenly I started, and, in answer to her question, I said:

"Do you see that little old man standing at the bottom of the gangway?"

"With an umbrella and an olive-green coat?"

"It is Ganimard."

"Ganimard?"

"Yes, the celebrated detective who has sworn to capture Arsène Lupin. Ah! I can understand now why we did not receive any news from this side of the Atlantic. Ganimard was here! and he always keeps his business secret."

"Then you think he will arrest Arsène Lupin?"

"Who can tell? The unexpected always happens when Arsène Lupin is concerned in the affair."

"Oh!" she exclaimed, with that morbid curiosity peculiar to women, "I should like to see him arrested."

"You will have to be patient. No doubt, Arsène Lupin has already seen his enemy and will not be in a hurry to leave the steamer."

The passengers were now leaving the steamer. Leaning on his umbrella, with an air of careless indifference, Ganimard appeared to be paying no attention to the crowd that was hurrying down the gangway. The Marquis de Raverdan, Major Rawson, the Italian Rivolta, and many others had already left the vessel before Rozaine appeared. Poor Rozaine!

"Perhaps it is he, after all," said Miss Nelly to me. "What do you think?"

"I think it would be very interesting to have Ganimard and Rozaine in the same picture. You take the camera. I am loaded down."

I gave her the camera, but too late for her to use it. Rozaine was already passing the detective. An American officer, standing behind Ganimard, leaned forward and whispered in his ear. The French detective shrugged his shoulders and Rozaine passed on. Then, my God, who was Arsène Lupin?

"Yes," said Miss Nelly, aloud, "who can it be?"

Not more than twenty people now remained on board. She scrutinized them one by one, fearful that Arsène Lupin was not amongst them.

"We cannot wait much longer," I said to her.

She started toward the gangway. I followed. But we had not taken ten steps when Ganimard barred our passage.

"Well, what is it?" I exclaimed.

"One moment, monsieur. What's your hurry?"

"I am escorting mademoiselle."

"One moment," he repeated, in a tone of authority. Then, gazing into my eyes, he said:

"Arsène Lupin, is it not?"

I laughed, and replied: "No, simply Bernard d'Andrézy."

"Bernard d'Andrézy died in Macedonia three years ago."

"If Bernard d'Andrézy were dead, I should not be here. But you are mistaken. Here are my papers."

"They are his; and I can tell you exactly how they came into your possession."

"You are a fool!" I exclaimed. "Arsène Lupin sailed under the name of R—"

"Yes, another of your tricks; a false scent that deceived them at Havre. You play a good game, my boy, but this time luck is against you."

I hesitated a moment. Then he hit me a sharp blow on the right arm, which caused me to utter a cry of pain. He had struck the wound, yet unhealed, referred to in the telegram.

I was obliged to surrender. There was no alternative. I turned to Miss Nelly, who had heard everything. Our eyes met; then she glanced at the Kodak I had placed in her hands, and made a gesture that conveyed to me the impression that she understood everything. Yes, there, between the narrow folds of black leather, in the hollow center of the small object that I had taken the precaution to place in her hands before Ganimard arrested me, it was there I had deposited Rozaine's twenty thousand francs and Lady Jerland's pearls and diamonds.

Oh! I pledge my oath that, at that solemn moment, when I was in the grasp of Ganimard and his two assistants, I was perfectly indifferent to everything, to my arrest, the hostility of the people, everything except this one question: what will Miss Nelly do with the things I had confided to her?

In the absence of that material and conclusive proof, I had nothing to fear; but would Miss Nelly decide to furnish that proof? Would she betray me? Would she act the part of an enemy who cannot forgive, or that of a woman whose scorn is softened by feelings of indulgence and involuntary sympathy?

She passed in front of me. I said nothing, but bowed very low. Mingled with the other passengers, she advanced to the gangway with my Kodak in her hand. It occurred to me that she would not dare to expose me publicly, but she might do so when she reached a more private place. However, when she had passed only a few feet down the gangway, with a movement of simulated awkwardness, she let the camera fall into the water between the vessel and the pier. Then she walked down the gangway, and was quickly lost to sight in the crowd. She had passed out of my life forever.

For a moment, I stood motionless. Then, to Ganimard's great astonishment, I muttered:

"What a pity that I am not an honest man!"

Such was the story of his arrest as narrated to me by Arsène Lupin himself. The various incidents, which I shall record in writing at a later day, have established between us certain ties . . . shall I say of friendship? Yes, I venture to believe that Arsène Lupin honors me with his friendship, and that it is through friendship that he occasionally calls on me, and brings, into the silence of my library, his youthful exuberance of spirits, the contagion of his enthusiasm, and the mirth of a man for whom destiny has naught but favors and smiles.

His portrait? How can I describe him? I have seen him twenty times and each time he was a different person; even he himself said to me on one occasion: "I no longer know who I am. I cannot recognize myself in the mirror." Certainly, he was a great actor, and possessed a marvelous faculty for disguising himself. Without the slightest effort, he could adopt the voice, gestures, and mannerisms of another person.

"Why," said he, "why should I retain a definite form and feature? Why not avoid the danger of a personality that is ever the same? My actions will serve to identify me."

Then he added, with a touch of pride:

"So much the better if no one can ever say with absolute certainty: There is Arsène Lupin! The essential point is that the public may be able to refer to my work and say, without fear of mistake: Arsène Lupin did that!"

ARSÈNE LUPIN IN PRISON

There is no tourist worthy of the name who does not know the banks of the Seine, and has not noticed, in passing, the little feudal castle of the Malaquis, built upon a rock in the center of the river. An arched bridge connects it with the shore. All around it, the calm waters of the great river play peacefully amongst the reeds, and the wagtails flutter over the moist crests of the stones.

The history of the Malaquis castle is stormy like its name, harsh like its outlines. It has passed through a long series of combats, sieges, assaults, rapines, and massacres. A recital of the crimes that have been committed there would cause the stoutest heart to tremble. There are many mysterious legends connected with the castle, and they tell us of a famous subterranean tunnel that formerly led to the abbey of Jumieges and to the manor of Agnes Sorel, mistress of Charles VII.

In that ancient habitation of heroes and brigands, the Baron Nathan Cahorn now lived; or Baron Satan as he was formerly called on the Bourse, where he had acquired a fortune with incredible rapidity. The lords of Malaquis, absolutely ruined, had been obliged to sell the ancient castle at a great sacrifice. It contained an admirable collection of furniture, pictures, wood carvings, and faience. The

Baron lived there alone, attended by three old servants. No one ever enters the place. No one had ever beheld the three Rubens that he possessed, his two Watteau, his Jean Goujon pulpit, and the many other treasures that he had acquired by a vast expenditure of money at public sales.

Baron Satan lived in constant fear, not for himself, but for the treasures that he had accumulated with such an earnest devotion and with so much perspicacity that the shrewdest merchant could not say that the baron had ever erred in his taste or judgment. He loved them—his bibelots. He loved them intensely, like a miser; jealously, like a lover. Every day, at sunset, the iron gates at either end of the bridge and at the entrance to the court of honor are closed and barred. At the least touch on these gates, electric bells will ring throughout the castle.

One Thursday in September, a letter-carrier presented himself at the gate at the head of the bridge, and, as usual, it was the baron himself who partially opened the heavy portal. He scrutinized the man as minutely as if he were a stranger, although the honest face and twinkling eyes of the postman had been familiar to the baron for many years. The man laughed, as he said:

"It is only I, Monsieur le Baron. It is not another man wearing my cap and blouse."

"One can never tell," muttered the baron.

The man handed him a number of newspapers, and then said:

"And now, Monsieur le Baron, here is something new."

"Something new?"

"Yes, a letter. A registered letter."

Living as a recluse, without friends or business relations, the baron never received any letters, and the one now presented to him immediately aroused within him a feeling of suspicion and distrust. It was like an evil omen. Who was this mysterious correspondent that dared to disturb the tranquility of his retreat?

"You must sign for it, Monsieur le Baron."

He signed; then took the letter, waited until the postman had disappeared beyond the bend in the road, and, after walking nervously to and fro for a few minutes, he leaned against the parapet of the bridge and opened the envelope. It contained a sheet of paper, bearing this heading: Prison de la Santé, Paris. He looked at the signature: *Arsène Lupin*. Then he read:

> "*Monsieur le Baron:*
>
> "*There is, in the gallery in your castle, a picture of Philippe de Champaigne, of exquisite finish, which pleases me beyond measure. Your Rubens are also to my taste, as well as your smallest Watteau. In the salon to the right, I have noticed the Louis XIII cadence-table, the tapestries of Beauvais, the Empire gueridon signed 'Jacob,' and the Renaissance chest. In the salon to the left, all the cabinet full of jewels and miniatures.*
>
> "*For the present, I will content myself with those articles that can be conveniently removed. I will therefore ask you to pack them carefully and ship them to me, charges prepaid, to the station at Batignolles, within eight days, otherwise I shall be obliged to remove them myself during the night of 27 September; but, under those circumstances, I shall not content myself with the articles above mentioned.*
>
> "*Accept my apologies for any inconvenience I may cause you, and believe me to be your humble servant,*
>
> "*Arsène Lupin.*"
>
> "*P. S.—Please do not send the largest Watteau. Although you paid thirty thousand francs for it, it is only a copy, the original having been burned, under the Directoire by Barras, during a night of debauchery. Consult the memoirs of Garat.*
>
> "*I do not care for the Louis XV chatelaine, as I doubt its authenticity.*"

That letter completely upset the baron. Had it borne any other signature, he would have been greatly alarmed—but signed by Arsène Lupin!

As an habitual reader of the newspapers, he was versed in the history of recent crimes, and was therefore well acquainted with the exploits of the mysterious burglar. Of course, he knew that Lupin had been arrested in America by his enemy Ganimard and was at present incarcerated in the Prison de la Santé. But he knew also that any miracle might be expected from Arsène Lupin. Moreover, that exact knowledge of the castle, the location of the pictures and furniture, gave the affair an alarming aspect. How could he have acquired that information concerning things that no one had ever seen?

The baron raised his eyes and contemplated the stern outlines of the castle, its steep rocky pedestal, the depth of the surrounding water, and shrugged his shoulders. Certainly, there was no danger. No one in the world could force an entrance to the sanctuary that contained his priceless treasures.

No one, perhaps, but Arsène Lupin! For him, gates, walls, and drawbridges did not exist. What use were the most formidable obstacles or the most careful precautions, if Arsène Lupin had decided to effect an entrance?

That evening, he wrote to the Procurer of the Republique at Rouen. He enclosed the threatening letter and solicited aid and protection.

The reply came at once to the effect that Arsène Lupin was in custody in the Prison de la Santé, under close surveillance, with no opportunity to write such a letter, which was, no doubt, the work of some imposter. But, as an act of precaution, the Procurer had submitted the letter to an expert in handwriting, who declared that, in spite of certain resemblances, the writing was not that of the prisoner.

But the words "in spite of certain resemblances" caught the attention of the baron; in them, he read the possibility of a doubt which appeared to him quite sufficient to warrant the intervention of the law. His fears increased. He read Lupin's letter over and over again. "I shall be obliged to remove them myself." And then there was the fixed date: the night of 27 September.

To confide in his servants was a proceeding repugnant to his nature; but now, for the first time in many years, he experienced the necessity of seeking counsel with someone. Abandoned by the legal official of his own district, and feeling unable to defend himself with his own resources, he was on the point of going to Paris to engage the services of a detective.

Two days passed; on the third day, he was filled with hope and joy as he read the following item in the *Réveil de Caudebec*, a newspaper published in a neighboring town:

"We have the pleasure of entertaining in our city, at the present time, the veteran detective Mon. Ganimard who acquired a worldwide reputation by his clever capture of Arsène Lupin. He has come here for rest and recreation, and, being an enthusiastic fisherman, he threatens to capture all the fish in our river."

Ganimard! Ah, here is the assistance desired by Baron Cahorn! Who could baffle the schemes of Arsène Lupin better than Ganimard, the patient and astute detective? He was the man for the place.

The baron did not hesitate. The town of Caudebec was only six kilometers from the castle, a short distance to a man whose step was accelerated by the hope of safety.

After several fruitless attempts to ascertain the detective's address, the baron visited the office of the *Réveil*, situated on the quai. There he found the writer of the article who, approaching the window, exclaimed:

"Ganimard? Why, you are sure to see him somewhere on the quai with his fishing-pole. I met him there and chanced to read his name engraved on his rod. Ah, there he is now, under the trees."

"That little man, wearing a straw hat?"

"Exactly. He is a gruff fellow, with little to say."

Five minutes later, the baron approached the celebrated Ganimard, introduced himself, and sought to commence a conversation, but that was a failure. Then he broached the real object of his interview, and briefly stated his case. The other listened, motionless, with his attention riveted on his fishing-rod. When the baron had finished his story, the fisherman turned, with an air of profound pity, and said:

"Monsieur, it is not customary for thieves to warn people they are about to rob. Arsène Lupin, especially, would not commit such a folly."

"But—"

"Monsieur, if I had the least doubt, believe me, the pleasure of again capturing Arsène Lupin would place me at your disposal. But, unfortunately, that young man is already under lock and key."

"He may have escaped."

"No one ever escaped from the Santé."

"But, he—"

"He, no more than any other."

"Yet—"

"Well, if he escapes, so much the better. I will catch him again. Meanwhile, you go home and sleep soundly. That will do for the present. You frighten the fish."

The conversation was ended. The baron returned to the castle, reassured to some extent by Ganimard's indifference. He examined the bolts, watched the servants, and, during the next forty-eight hours, he became almost persuaded that his fears were groundless. Certainly, as Ganimard had said, thieves do not warn people they are about to rob.

The fateful day was close at hand. It was now the twenty-sixth of September and nothing had happened. But at three o'clock the bell rang. A boy brought this telegram:

"No goods at Batignolles station. Prepare everything for to-morrow night. Arsène."

This telegram threw the baron into such a state of excitement that he even considered the advisability of yielding to Lupin's demands.

However, he hastened to Caudebec. Ganimard was fishing at the same place, seated on a campstool. Without a word, he handed him the telegram.

"Well, what of it?" said the detective.

"What of it? But it is to-morrow."

"What is to-morrow?"

"The robbery! The pillage of my collections!"

Ganimard laid down his fishing-rod, turned to the baron, and exclaimed, in a tone of impatience:

"Ah! Do you think I am going to bother myself about such a silly story as that!"

"How much do you ask to pass to-morrow night in the castle?"

"Not a sou. Now, leave me alone."

"Name your own price. I am rich and can pay it."

This offer disconcerted Ganimard, who replied, calmly:

"I am here on a vacation. I have no right to undertake such work."

"No one will know. I promise to keep it secret."

"Oh! nothing will happen."

"Come! three thousand francs. Will that be enough?"

The detective, after a moment's reflection, said:

"Very well. But I must warn you that you are throwing your money out of the window."

"I do not care."

"In that case . . . but, after all, what do we know about this devil Lupin! He may have quite a numerous band of robbers with him. Are you sure of your servants?"

"My faith—"

"Better not count on them. I will telegraph for two of my men to help me. And now, go! It is better for us not to be seen together. To-morrow evening about nine o'clock."

The following day—the date fixed by Arsène Lupin—Baron Cahorn arranged all his panoply of war, furbished his weapons, and, like a sentinel, paced to and fro in front of the castle. He saw nothing, heard nothing. At half-past eight o'clock in the evening, he dismissed his servants. They occupied rooms in a wing of the building, in a retired spot, well removed from the main portion of the castle. Shortly thereafter, the baron heard the sound of approaching footsteps. It was Ganimard and his two assistants—great, powerful fellows with immense hands, and necks like bulls. After asking a few questions relating to the location of the various entrances and rooms, Ganimard carefully closed and barricaded all the doors and windows through which one could gain access to the threatened rooms. He inspected the walls, raised the tapestries, and finally installed his assistants in the central gallery which was located between the two salons.

"No nonsense! We are not here to sleep. At the slightest sound, open the windows of the court and call me. Pay attention also to the water-side. Ten meters of perpendicular rock is no obstacle to those devils."

Ganimard locked his assistants in the gallery, carried away the keys, and said to the baron:

"And now, to our post."

He had chosen for himself a small room located in the thick outer wall, between the two principal doors, and which, in former years, had been the watchman's quarters. A peep-hole opened upon the bridge; another on the court. In one corner, there was an opening to a tunnel.

"I believe you told me, Monsieur le Baron, that this tunnel is the only subterranean entrance to the castle and that it has been closed up for time immemorial?"

"Yes."

"Then, unless there is some other entrance, known only to Arsène Lupin, we are quite safe."

He placed three chairs together, stretched himself upon them, lighted his pipe and sighed:

"Really, Monsieur le Baron, I feel ashamed to accept your money for such a sinecure as this. I will tell the story to my friend Lupin. He will enjoy it immensely."

The baron did not laugh. He was anxiously listening, but heard nothing save the beating of his own heart. From time to time, he leaned over the tunnel and cast a fearful eye into its depths. He heard the clock strike eleven, twelve, one.

Suddenly, he seized Ganimard's arm. The latter leaped up, awakened from his sleep.

"Do you hear?" asked the baron, in a whisper.

"Yes."

"What is it?"

"I was snoring, I suppose."

"No, no, listen."

"Ah! yes, it is the horn of an automobile."

"Well?"

"Well! it is very improbable that Lupin would use an automobile like a battering-ram to demolish your castle. Come, Monsieur le Baron, return to your post. I am going to sleep. Good-night."

That was the only alarm. Ganimard resumed his interrupted slumbers, and the baron heard nothing except the regular snoring of his companion. At break of day, they left the room. The castle was enveloped in a profound calm; it was a peaceful dawn on the bosom of a tranquil river. They mounted the stairs, Cahorn radiant with joy, Ganimard calm as usual. They heard no sound; they saw nothing to arouse suspicion.

"What did I tell you, Monsieur le Baron? Really, I should not have accepted your offer. I am ashamed."

He unlocked the door and entered the gallery. Upon two chairs, with drooping heads and pendent arms, the detective's two assistants were asleep.

"Tonnerre de nom d'un chien!" exclaimed Ganimard. At the same moment, the baron cried out:

"The pictures! The credence!"

He stammered, choked, with arms outstretched toward the empty places, toward the denuded walls where naught remained but the useless nails and cords. The Watteau, disappeared! The Rubens, carried away! The tapestries taken down! The cabinets, despoiled of their jewels!

"And my Louis XVI candelabra! And the Regent chandelier! . . . And my twelfth-century Virgin!"

He ran from one spot to another in wildest despair. He recalled the purchase price of each article, added up the figures, counted his losses, pell-mell, in confused words and unfinished phrases. He stamped with rage; he groaned with grief. He acted like a ruined man whose only hope is suicide.

If anything could have consoled him, it would have been the stupefaction displayed by Ganimard. The famous detective did not move. He appeared to be petrified; he examined the room in a listless manner. The windows? . . . closed. The locks on the doors? . . . intact. Not a break in the ceiling; not a hole in the floor. Everything was in perfect order. The theft had been carried out methodically, according to a logical and inexorable plan.

"Arsène Lupin. . . . Arsène Lupin," he muttered.

Suddenly, as if moved by anger, he rushed upon his two assistants and shook them violently. They did not awaken.

"The devil!" he cried. "Can it be possible?"

He leaned over them and, in turn, examined them closely. They were asleep; but their response was unnatural.

"They have been drugged," he said to the baron.

"By whom?"

"By him, of course, or his men under his discretion. That work bears his stamp."

"In that case, I am lost—nothing can be done."

"Nothing," assented Ganimard.

"It is dreadful; it is monstrous."

"Lodge a complaint."

"What good will that do?"

"Oh; it is well to try it. The law has some resources."

"The law! Bah! it is useless. You represent the law, and, at this moment, when you should be looking for a clue and trying to discover something, you do not even stir."

"Discover something with Arsène Lupin! Why, my dear monsieur, Arsène Lupin never leaves any clue behind him. He leaves nothing to chance. Sometimes I think he put himself in my way and simply allowed me to arrest him in America."

"Then, I must renounce my pictures! He has taken the gems of my collection. I would give a fortune to recover them. If there is no other way, let him name his own price."

Ganimard regarded the baron attentively, as he said:

"Now, that is sensible. Will you stick to it?"

"Yes, yes. But why?"

"An idea that I have."

"What is it?"

"We will discuss it later—if the official examination does not succeed. But, not one word about me, if you wish my assistance."

He added, between his teeth:

"It is true I have nothing to boast of in this affair."

The assistants were gradually regaining consciousness with the bewildered air of people who come out of an hypnotic sleep. They opened their eyes and looked about them in astonishment. Ganimard questioned them; they remembered nothing.

"But you must have seen someone?"

"No."

"Can't you remember?"

"No, no."

"Did you drink anything?"

They considered a moment, and then one of them replied:

"Yes, I drank a little water."

"Out of that carafe?"

"Yes."

"So did I," declared the other.

Ganimard smelled and tasted it. It had no particular taste and no odor.

"Come," he said, "we are wasting our time here. One can't decide an Arsène Lupin problem in five minutes. But, morbleau! I swear I will catch him again."

The same day, a charge of burglary was duly performed by Baron Cahorn against Arsène Lupin, a prisoner in the Prison de la Santé.

||||||||||||||||||||||||||

The baron afterward regretted making the charge against Lupin when he saw his castle delivered over to the gendarmes, the procureur, the judge d'instruction, the newspaper reporters and photographers, and a throng of idle curiosity-seekers.

The affair soon became a topic of general discussion, and the name of Arsène Lupin excited the public imagination to such an extent that the newspapers filled their columns with the most fantastic stories of his exploits which found ready credence amongst their readers.

But the letter of Arsène Lupin that was published in the *Echo de France* (no once ever knew how the newspaper obtained it), that letter in which Baron Cahorn was impudently warned of the coming theft, caused considerable excitement. The most fabulous theories were advanced. Some recalled the existence of the famous subterranean tunnels, and that was the line of research pursued by the officers of the law, who searched the house from top to bottom, questioned every stone, studied the wainscoting and the chimneys, the window-frames and the girders in the ceilings. By the light of torches, they examined the immense cellars where the lords of Malaquis were wont to store their munitions and provisions. They sounded the rocky foundation to its very center. But it was all in vain. They discovered no trace of a subterranean tunnel. No secret passage existed.

But the eager public declared that the pictures and furniture could not vanish like so many ghosts. They are substantial, material things and require doors and windows for their exits and their entrances, and so do the people that remove them. "Who were those people? How did they gain access to the castle? And how did they leave it?"

The police officers of Rouen, convinced of their own impotence, solicited the assistance of the Parisian detective force. Mon. Dudouis, chief of the Sûreté, sent the best sleuths of the iron brigade. He himself spent forty-eight hours at the castle, but met with no success. Then he sent for Ganimard, whose past services had proved so useful when all else failed.

Ganimard listened, in silence, to the instructions of his superior; then, shaking his head, he said:

"In my opinion, it is useless to ransack the castle. The solution of the problem lies elsewhere."

"Where, then?"

"With Arsène Lupin."

"With Arsène Lupin! To support that theory, we must admit his intervention."

"I do admit it. In fact, I consider it quite certain."

"Come, Ganimard, that is absurd. Arsène Lupin is in prison."

"I grant you that Arsène Lupin is in prison, closely guarded; but he must have fetters on his feet, manacles on his wrists, and gag in his mouth before I change my opinion."

"Why so obstinate, Ganimard?"

"Because Arsène Lupin is the only man in France of sufficient caliber to invent and carry out a scheme of that magnitude."

"Mere words, Ganimard."

"But true ones. Look! What are they doing? Searching for subterranean passages, stones swinging on pivots, and other nonsense of that kind. But Lupin doesn't employ such old-fashioned methods. He is a modern cracksman, right up to date."

"And how would you proceed?"

"I should ask your permission to spend an hour with him."

"In his cell?"

"Yes. During the return trip from America we became very friendly, and I venture to say that if he can give me any information without compromising himself he will not hesitate to save me from incurring useless trouble."

It was shortly after noon when Ganimard entered the cell of

Arsène Lupin. The latter, who was lying on his bed, raised his head and uttered a cry of apparent joy.

"Ah! This is a real surprise. My dear Ganimard, here!"

"Ganimard himself."

"In my chosen retreat, I have felt a desire for many things, but my fondest wish was to receive you here."

"Very kind of you, I am sure."

"Not at all. You know I hold you in the highest regard."

"I am proud of it."

"I have always said: Ganimard is our best detective. He is almost— you see how candid I am!—he is almost as clever as Sherlock Holmes. But I am sorry that I cannot offer you anything better than this hard stool. And no refreshments! Not even a glass of beer! Of course, you will excuse me, as I am here only temporarily."

Ganimard smiled, and accepted the proffered seat. Then the prisoner continued:

"Mon Dieu, how pleased I am to see the face of an honest man. I am so tired of those devils of spies who come here ten times a day to ransack my pockets and my cell to satisfy themselves that I am not preparing to escape. The government is very solicitous on my account."

"It is quite right."

"Why so? I should be quite contented if they would allow me to live in my own quiet way."

"On other people's money."

"Quite so. That would be so simple. But here, I am joking, and you are, no doubt, in a hurry. So let us come to business, Ganimard. To what do I owe the honor of this visit?"

"The Cahorn affair," declared Ganimard, frankly.

"Ah! Wait, one moment. You see I have had so many affairs! First, let me fix in my mind the circumstances of this particular case. . . . Ah! yes, now I have it. The Cahorn affair, Malaquis castle, Seine-Inférieure. . . . Two Rubens, a Watteau, and a few trifling articles."

"Trifling!"

"Oh! ma foi, all that is of slight importance. But it suffices to know that the affair interests you. How can I serve you, Ganimard?"

"Must I explain to you what steps the authorities have taken in the matter?"

"Not at all. I have read the newspapers and I will frankly state that you have made very little progress."

"And that is the reason I have come to see you."

"I am entirely at your service."

"In the first place, the Cahorn affair was managed by you?"

"From A to Z."

"The letter of warning? the telegram?"

"All mine. I ought to have the receipts somewhere."

Arsène opened the drawer of a small table of plain white wood which, with the bed and stool, constituted all the furniture in his cell, and took therefrom two scraps of paper which he handed to Ganimard.

"Ah!" exclaimed the detective, in surprise, "I thought you were closely guarded and searched, and I find that you read the newspapers and collect postal receipts."

"Bah! these people are so stupid! They open the lining of my vest, they examine the soles of my shoes, they sound the walls of my cell, but they never imagine that Arsène Lupin would be foolish enough to choose such a simple hiding place."

Ganimard laughed, as he said:

"What a droll fellow you are! Really, you bewilder me. But, come now, tell me about the Cahorn affair."

"Oh! oh! not quite so fast! You would rob me of all my secrets; expose all my little tricks. That is a very serious matter."

"Was I wrong to count on your complaisance?"

"No, Ganimard, and since you insist—"

Arsène Lupin paced his cell two or three times, then, stopping before Ganimard, he asked:

"What do you think of my letter to the baron?"

"I think you were amusing yourself by playing to the gallery."

"Ah! playing to the gallery! Come, Ganimard, I thought you knew me better. Do I, Arsène Lupin, ever waste my time on such puerilities? Would I have written that letter if I could have robbed the baron without writing to him? I want you to understand that the letter was indispensable; it was the motor that set the whole machine in motion. Now, let us discuss together a scheme for the robbery of the Malaquis castle. Are you willing?"

"Yes, proceed."

"Well, let us suppose a castle carefully closed and barricaded like that of the Baron Cahorn. Am I to abandon my scheme and renounce the treasures that I covet, upon the pretext that the castle which holds them is inaccessible?"

"Evidently not."

"Should I make an assault upon the castle at the head of a band of adventurers as they did in ancient times?"

"That would be foolish."

"Can I gain admittance by stealth or cunning?"

"Impossible."

"Then there is only one way open to me. I must have the owner of the castle invite me to it,"

"That is surely an original method."

"And how easy! Let us suppose that one day the owner receives a letter warning him that a notorious burglar known as Arsène Lupin is plotting to rob him. What will he do?"

"Send a letter to the Procureur."

"Who will laugh at him, *because the said Arsène Lupin is actually in prison*. Then, in his anxiety and fear, the simple man will ask the assistance of the first-comer, will he not?"

"Very likely."

"And if he happens to read in a country newspaper that a cel-ebrated detective is spending his vacation in a neighboring town—"

"He will seek that detective."

"Of course. But, on the other hand, let us presume that, having foreseen that state of affairs, the said Arsène Lupin has requested one of his friends to visit Caudebec, make the acquaintance of the editor of the *Réveil*, a newspaper to which the baron is a subscriber, and let said editor understand that such person is the celebrated detective—then, what will happen?"

"The editor will announce in the *Réveil* the presence in Caudebec of said detective."

"Exactly; and one of two things will happen: either the fish—I mean Cahorn—will not bite, and nothing will happen; or, what is more likely, he will run and greedily swallow the bait. Thus, behold my Baron Cahorn imploring the assistance of one of my friends against me."

"Original, indeed!"

"Of course, the pseudo-detective at first refuses to give any assistance. On top of that comes the telegram from Arsène Lupin. The frightened baron rushes once more to my friend and offers him a definite sum of money for his services. My friend accepts and summons two members of our band, who, during the night, whilst Cahorn is under the watchful eye of his protector, removes certain articles by way of the window and lowers them with ropes into a nice little launch chartered for the occasion. Simple, isn't it?"

"Marvelous! Marvelous!" exclaimed Ganimard. "The boldness of the scheme and the ingenuity of all its details are beyond criticism. But who is the detective whose name and fame served as a magnet to attract the baron and draw him into your net?"

"There is only one name could do it—only one."

"And that is?"

"Arsène Lupin's personal enemy—the most illustrious Ganimard."

"I?"

"Yourself, Ganimard. And, really, it is very funny. If you go there, and the baron decides to talk, you will find that it will be your duty to arrest yourself, just as you arrested me in America. Hein! the revenge is really amusing: I cause Ganimard to arrest Ganimard."

Arsène Lupin laughed heartily. The detective, greatly vexed, bit his lips; to him the joke was quite devoid of humor. The arrival of a prison guard gave Ganimard an opportunity to recover himself. The man brought Arsène Lupin's luncheon, furnished by a neighboring restaurant. After depositing the tray upon the table, the guard retired. Lupin broke his bread, ate a few morsels, and continued:

"But, rest easy, my dear Ganimard, you will not go to Malaquis. I can tell you something that will astonish you: the Cahorn affair is on the point of being settled."

"Excuse me; I have just seen the chief of the Sûreté."

"What of that? Does Mon. Dudouis know my business better than I do myself? You will learn that Ganimard—excuse me—that the pseudo-Ganimard still remains on very good terms with the baron. The latter has authorized him to negotiate a very delicate transaction with me, and, at the present moment, in consideration of a certain sum, it is probable that the baron has recovered possession of his pictures and other treasures. And on their return, he will withdraw his complaint. Thus, there is no longer any theft, and the law must abandon the case."

Ganimard regarded the prisoner with a bewildered air.

"And how do you know all that?"

"I have just received the telegram I was expecting."

"You have just received a telegram?"

"This very moment, my dear friend. Out of politeness, I did not wish to read it in your presence. But if you will permit me—"

"You are joking, Lupin."

"My dear friend, if you will be so kind as to break that egg, you will learn for yourself that I am not joking."

Mechanically, Ganimard obeyed, and cracked the egg-shell with the blade of a knife. He uttered a cry of surprise. The shell contained nothing but a small piece of blue paper. At the request of Arsène he unfolded it. It was a telegram, or rather a portion of a telegram from which the post-marks had been removed. It read as follows:

"Contract closed. Hundred thousand balls delivered. All well."

"One hundred thousand balls?" said Ganimard.

"Yes, one hundred thousand francs. Very little, but then, you know, these are hard times. . . . And I have some heavy bills to meet. If you only knew my budget . . . living in the city comes very high."

Ganimard arose. His ill humor had disappeared. He reflected for a moment, glancing over the whole affair in an effort to discover a weak point; then, in a tone and manner that betrayed his admiration of the prisoner, he said:

"Fortunately, we do not have a dozen such as you to deal with; if we did, we would have to close up shop."

Arsène Lupin assumed a modest air, as he replied:

"Bah! a person must have some diversion to occupy his leisure hours, especially when he is in prison."

"What!" exclaimed Ganimard, "your trial, your defense, the examination—isn't that sufficient to occupy your mind?"

"No, because I have decided not to be present at my trial."

"Oh! oh!"

Arsène Lupin repeated, positively:

"I shall not be present at my trial."

"Really!"

"Ah! my dear monsieur, do you suppose I am going to rot upon the wet straw? You insult me. Arsène Lupin remains in prison just as long as it pleases him, and not one minute more."

"Perhaps it would have been more prudent if you had avoided getting there," said the detective, ironically.

"Ah! monsieur jests? Monsieur must remember that he had the honor to effect my arrest. Know then, my worthy friend, that no one, not even you, could have placed a hand upon me if a much more important event had not occupied my attention at that critical moment."

"You astonish me."

"A woman was looking at me, Ganimard, and I loved her. Do you fully understand what that means: to be under the eyes of a woman that one loves? I cared for nothing in the world but that. And that is why I am here."

"Permit me to say: you have been here a long time."

"In the first place, I wished to forget. Do not laugh; it was a delightful adventure and it is still a tender memory. Besides, I have been suffering from neurasthenia. Life is so feverish these days that it is necessary to take the 'rest cure' occasionally, and I find this spot a sovereign remedy for my tired nerves."

"Arsène Lupin, you are not a bad fellow, after all."

"Thank you," said Lupin. "Ganimard, this is Friday. On Wednesday next, at four o'clock in the afternoon, I will smoke my cigar at your house in the Rue Pergolese."

"Arsène Lupin, I will expect you."

They shook hands like two old friends who valued each other at their true worth; then the detective stepped to the door.

"Ganimard!"

"What is it?" asked Ganimard, as he turned back.

"You have forgotten your watch."

"My watch?"

"Yes, it strayed into my pocket."

He returned the watch, excusing himself.

"Pardon me . . . a bad habit. Because they have taken mine is no reason why I should take yours. Besides, I have a chronometer here that satisfies me fairly well."

He took from the drawer a large gold watch and heavy chain.

"From whose pocket did that come?" asked Ganimard.

Arsène Lupin gave a hasty glance at the initials engraved on the watch.

"J.B. . . . Who the devil can that be? . . . Ah! yes, I remember. Jules Bouvier, the judge who conducted my examination. A charming fellow! . . ."

THE ESCAPE OF ARSÈNE LUPIN

A RSÈNE LUPIN had just finished his repast and taken from his pocket an excellent cigar, with a gold hand, which he was examining with unusual care, when the door of his cell was opened. He had barely time to throw the cigar into the drawer and move away from the table. The guard entered. It was the hour for exercise.

"I was waiting for you, my dear boy," exclaimed Lupin, in his accustomed good humor.

They went out together. As soon as they had disappeared at a turn in the corridor, two men entered the cell and commenced a minute examination of it. One was Inspector Dieuzy; the other was Inspector Folenfant. They wished to verify their suspicion that Arsène Lupin was in communication with his accomplices outside of the prison. On the preceding evening, the *Grand Journal* had published these lines addressed to its court reporter:

> "*Monsieur:*
> "*In a recent article you referred to me in most unjustifiable terms. Some days before the opening of my trial I will call you to account. Arsène Lupin.*"

The handwriting was certainly that of Arsène Lupin. Consequently, he sent letters; and, no doubt, received letters. It was certain that he was preparing for that escape thus arrogantly announced by him.

The situation had become intolerable. Acting in conjunction with the examining judge, the chief of the Sûreté, Mon. Dudouis, had visited the prison and instructed the gaoler in regard to the precautions necessary to insure Lupin's safety. At the same time, he sent the two men to examine the prisoner's cell. They raised every stone, ransacked the bed, did everything customary in such a case, but they discovered nothing, and were about to abandon their investigation when the guard entered hastily and said:

"The drawer . . . look in the table-drawer. When I entered just now he was closing it."

They opened the drawer, and Dieuzy exclaimed:

"Ah! we have him this time."

Folenfant stopped him.

"Wait a moment. The chief will want to make an inventory."

"This is a very choice cigar."

"Leave it there, and notify the chief."

Two minutes later Mon. Dudouis examined the contents of the drawer. First he discovered a bundle of newspaper clippings relating to Arsène Lupin taken from the *Argus de la Presse*, then a tobacco-box, a pipe, some paper called "onion-peel," and two books. He read the titles of the books. One was an English edition of Carlyle's *Hero-worship*; the other was a charming elzevir, in modern binding, the *Manual of Epictetus*, a German translation published at Leyden in 1634. On examining the books, he found that all the pages were underlined and annotated. Were they prepared as a code for correspondence, or did they simply express the studious character of the reader? Then he examined the tobacco-box and the pipe. Finally, he took up the famous cigar with its gold band.

"Fichtre!" he exclaimed. "Our friend smokes a good cigar. It's a Henry Clay."

With the mechanical action of an habitual smoker, he placed the cigar close to his ear and squeezed it to make it crack. Immediately he uttered a cry of surprise. The cigar had yielded under the pressure of his fingers. He examined it more closely, and quickly discovered something white between the leaves of tobacco. Delicately, with the aid of a pin, he withdrew a roll of very thin paper, scarcely larger than a toothpick. It was a letter. He unrolled it, and found these words, written in a feminine handwriting:

"The basket has taken the place of the others. Eight out of ten are ready. On pressing the outer foot the plate goes downward. From twelve to sixteen every day, H-P will wait. But where? Reply at once. Rest easy; your friend is watching over you."

Mon. Dudouis reflected a moment, then said:

"It is quite clear ... the basket ... the eight compartments.... From twelve to sixteen means from twelve to four o'clock."

"But this H-P, that will wait?"

"H-P must mean automobile. H-P, horsepower, is the way they indicate strength of the motor. A twenty-four H-P is an automobile of twenty-four horsepower."

Then he rose, and asked:

"Had the prisoner finished his breakfast?"

"Yes."

"And as he has not yet read the message, which is proved by the condition of the cigar, it is probable that he had just received it."

"How?"

"In his food. Concealed in his bread or in a potato, perhaps."

"Impossible. His food was allowed to be brought in simply to trap him, but we have never found anything in it."

"We will look for Lupin's reply this evening. Detain him outside for a few minutes. I shall take this to the examining judge, and, if he agrees with me, we will have the letter photographed at once, and in an hour you can replace the letter in the drawer in a cigar similar to this. The prisoner must have no cause for suspicion."

It was not without a certain curiosity that Mon. Dudouis returned to the prison in the evening, accompanied by Inspector Dieuzy. Three empty plates were sitting on the stove in the corner.

"He has eaten?"

"Yes," replied the guard.

"Dieuzy, please cut that macaroni into very small pieces, and open that bread-roll.... Nothing?"

"No, chief."

Mon. Dudouis examined the plates, the fork, the spoon, and the knife—an ordinary knife with a rounded blade. He turned the handle to the left; then to the right. It yielded and unscrewed. The knife was hollow, and served as a hiding-place for a sheet of paper.

"Peuh!" he said, "that is not very clever for a man like Arsène. But we mustn't lose any time. You, Dieuzy, go and search the restaurant."

Then he read the note:

"I trust to you, H-P will follow at a distance every day. I will go ahead. Au revoir, dear friend."

"At last," cried Mon. Dudouis, rubbing his hands gleefully, "I think we have the affair in our own hands. A little strategy on our part, and the escape will be a success in so far as the arrest of his confederates are concerned."

"But if Arsène Lupin slips through your fingers?" suggested the guard.

"We will have a sufficient number of men to prevent that. If, however, he displays too much cleverness, ma foi, so much the worse for him! As to his band of robbers, since the chief refuses to speak, the others must."

<hr />

And, as a matter of fact, Arsène Lupin had very little to say. For several months, Mon. Jules Bouvier, the examining judge, had exerted himself in vain. The investigation had been reduced to a few uninteresting arguments between the judge and the advocate, Maître Danval, one of the leaders of the bar. From time to time, through courtesy, Arsène Lupin would speak. One day he said:

"Yes, monsieur, le judge, I quite agree with you: the robbery of the Crédit Lyonnais, the theft in the Rue de Babylone, the issue of the counterfeit bank-notes, the burglaries at the various châteaux, Armesnil, Gouret, Imblevain, Groseillers, Malaquis, all my work, monsieur, I did it all."

"Then will you explain to me—"

"It is useless. I confess everything in a lump, everything and even ten times more than you know nothing about."

Wearied by his fruitless task, the judge had suspended his examinations, but he resumed them after the two intercepted messages were brought to his attention; and regularly, at midday, Arsène Lupin was taken from the prison to the Dépôt in the prison-van with a certain number of other prisoners. They returned about three or four o'clock.

Now, one afternoon, this return trip was made under unusual conditions. The other prisoners not having been examined, it was decided to take back Arsène Lupin first, thus he found himself alone in the vehicle.

These prison-vans, vulgarly called "panniers à salade"—or salad-baskets—are divided lengthwise by a central corridor from which open ten compartments, five on either side. Each compartment is so arranged that the occupant must assume and retain a sitting posture, and, consequently, the five prisoners are seated one upon the other, and yet separated one from the other by partitions. A municipal guard, standing at one end, watches over the corridor.

Arsène was placed in the third cell on the right, and the heavy vehicle started. He carefully calculated when they left the Quai de l'Horloge, and when they passed the Palais de Justice. Then, about the center of the bridge Saint Michel, with his outer foot, that is to say, his right foot, he pressed upon the metal plate that closed his cell. Immediately something clicked, and the metal plate moved. He was able to ascertain that he was located between the two wheels.

He waited, keeping a sharp look-out. The vehicle was proceeding slowly along the Boulevard Saint Michel. At the corner of Saint Germain it stopped. A truck horse had fallen. The traffic having been interrupted, a vast throng of fiacres and omnibuses had gathered there. Arsène Lupin looked out. Another prison-van had stopped close to the one he occupied. He moved the plate still farther, put his foot on one of the spokes of the wheel, and leaped to the ground. A coachman saw him, roared with laughter, then tried to raise an outcry, but his voice was lost in the noise of the traffic that had commenced to move again. Moreover, Arsène Lupin was already far away.

He had run for a few steps; but, once upon the sidewalk, he turned and looked around; he seemed to scent the wind like a person who is uncertain which direction to take. Then, having decided, he put his hands in his pockets, and, with the careless air of an idle stroller, he proceeded up the boulevard. It was a warm, bright autumn day, and the cafés were full. He took a seat on the terrace of one of them. He ordered a bock and a package of cigarettes. He emptied his glass slowly, smoked one cigarette, and lighted a second. Then he asked the waiter to send the proprietor to him. When the proprietor came, Arsène spoke to him in a voice loud enough to be heard by everyone:

"I regret to say, monsieur, I have forgotten my pocket-book. Perhaps, on the strength of my name, you will be pleased to give me credit for a few days. I am Arsène Lupin."

The proprietor looked at him, thinking he was joking. But Arsène repeated:

"Lupin, prisoner at the Santé, but now a fugitive. I venture to assume that the name inspires you with perfect confidence in me."

And he walked away, amidst shouts of laughter, whilst the proprietor stood amazed.

Lupin strolled along the Rue Soufflot, and turned into the Rue Saint Jacques. He pursued his way slowly, smoking his cigarettes and looking into the shop-windows. At the Boulevard de Port Royal he took his bearings, discovered where he was, and then walked in the direction of the Rue de la Santé. The high forbidding walls of the prison were now before him. He pulled his hat forward to shade his face; then, approaching the sentinel, he asked:

"Is this the prison de la Santé?"

"Yes."

"I wish to regain my cell. The van left me on the way, and I would not abuse—"

"Now, young man, move along—quick!" growled the sentinel.

"Pardon me, but I must pass through that gate. And if you prevent Arsène Lupin from entering the prison it will cost you dear, my friend."

"Arsène Lupin! What are you talking about!"

"I am sorry I haven't a card with me," said Arsène, fumbling in his pockets.

The sentinel eyed him from head to foot, in astonishment. Then, without a word, he rang a bell. The iron gate was partly opened, and Arsène stepped inside. Almost immediately he encountered the keeper of the prison, gesticulating and feigning a violent anger. Arsène smiled and said:

"Come, monsieur, don't play that game with me. What! they take the precaution to carry me alone in the van, prepare a nice little obstruction, and imagine I am going to take to my heels and rejoin my friends. Well, and what about the twenty agents of the Sûreté who accompanied us on foot, in fiacres and on bicycles? No, the arrangement did not please me. I should not have got away alive. Tell me, monsieur, did they count on that?"

He shrugged his shoulders, and added:

"I beg of you, monsieur, not to worry about me. When I wish to escape I shall not require any assistance."

On the second day thereafter, the *Echo de France*, which had apparently become the official reporter of the exploits of Arsène Lupin—it was said that he was one of its principal shareholders—published a most complete account of this attempted escape. The exact wording of the messages exchanged between the prisoner and his mysterious friend, the means by which correspondence was constructed, the complicity of the police, the promenade on the Boulevard Saint Michel, the incident at the café Soufflot, everything was disclosed. It was known that the search of the restaurant and its waiters by Inspector Dieuzy had been fruitless. And the public also learned an extraordinary thing which demonstrated the infinite variety of resources that Lupin possessed: the prison-van, in which he was being carried, was prepared for the occasion and substituted by his accomplices for one of the six vans which did service at the prison.

The next escape of Arsène Lupin was not doubted by anyone. He announced it himself, in categorical terms, in a reply to Mon. Bouvier on the day following his attempted escape. The judge having made a jest about the affair, Arsène was annoyed, and, firmly eyeing the judge, he said, emphatically:

"Listen to me, monsieur! I give you my word of honor that this attempted flight was simply preliminary to my general plan of escape."

"I do not understand," said the judge.

"It is not necessary that you should understand."

And when the judge, in the course of that examination which was reported at length in the columns of the *Echo de France*, when the judge sought to resume his investigation, Arsène Lupin exclaimed, with an assumed air of lassitude:

"Mon Dieu, Mon Dieu, what's the use! All these questions are of no importance!"

"What! No importance?" cried the judge.

"No; because I shall not be present at the trial."

"You will not be present?"

"No; I have fully decided on that, and nothing will change my mind."

Such assurance combined with the inexplicable indiscretions that Arsène committed every day served to annoy and mystify the officers of the law. There were secrets known only to Arsène Lupin; secrets that he alone could divulge. But for what purpose did he reveal them? And how?

Arsène Lupin was changed to another cell. The judge closed his preliminary investigation. No further proceedings were taken in his case for a period of two months, during which time Arsène was seen almost constantly lying on his bed with his face turned toward the wall. The changing of his cell seemed to discourage him. He refused to see his advocate. He exchanged only a few necessary words with his keepers.

During the fortnight preceding his trial, he resumed his vigorous life. He complained of want of air. Consequently, early every morning he was allowed to exercise in the courtyard, guarded by two men.

Public curiosity had not died out; every day it expected to be regaled with news of his escape; and, it is true, he had gained a considerable amount of public sympathy by reason of his verve, his gayety, his diversity, his inventive genius, and the mystery of his life. Arsène Lupin must escape. It was his inevitable fate. The public expected it, and was surprised that the event had been delayed so long. Every morning the Préfect of Police asked his secretary:

"Well, has he escaped yet?"

"No, Monsieur le Préfect."

"To-morrow, probably."

And, on the day before the trial, a gentleman called at the office of the *Grand Journal*, asked to see the court reporter, threw his card in the reporter's face, and walked rapidly away. These words were written on the card: "Arsène Lupin always keeps his promises."

It was under these conditions that the trial commenced. An enormous crowd gathered at the court. Everybody wished to see the famous Arsène Lupin. They had a gleeful anticipation that the prisoner would play some audacious pranks upon the judge. Advocates and magistrates, reporters and men of the world, actresses and society women were crowded together on the benches provided for the public.

It was a dark, somber day, with a steady downpour of rain. Only a dim light pervaded the courtroom, and the spectators caught a very indistinct view of the prisoner when the guards brought him in. But his heavy, shambling walk, the manner in which he dropped into his seat, and his passive, stupid appearance were not at all prepossessing. Several times his advocate—one of Mon. Danval's assistants—spoke to him, but he simply shook his head and said nothing.

The clerk read the indictment, then the judge spoke:

"Prisoner at the bar, stand up. Your name, age, and occupation?"

Not receiving any reply, the judge repeated:

"Your name? I ask you your name?"

A thick, slow voice muttered:

"Baudru, Désiré."

A murmur of surprise pervaded the courtroom. But the judge proceeded:

"Baudru, Désiré? Ah! a new alias! Well, as you have already assumed a dozen different names and this one is, no doubt, as imaginary as the others, we will adhere to the name of Arsène Lupin, by which you are more generally known."

The judge referred to his notes, and continued:

"For, despite the most diligent search, your past history remains unknown. Your case is unique in the annals of crime. We know not whom you are, whence you came, your birth and breeding—all is a mystery to us. Three years ago you appeared in our midst as Arsène Lupin, presenting to us a strange combination of intelligence and perversion, immorality and generosity. Our knowledge of your life prior to that date is vague and problematical. It may be that the man called Rostat who, eight years ago, worked with Dickson, the prestidigitator, was none other than Arsène Lupin. It is probable that the Russian student who, six years ago, attended the laboratory of Doctor Altier at the Saint-Louis Hospital, and who often astonished the doctor by the ingenuity of his hypotheses on subjects of bacteriology and the boldness of his experiments in diseases of the skin, was none other than Arsène Lupin. It is probable, also, that Arsène Lupin was the professor who introduced the Japanese art of jiu-jitsu to the Parisian public. We have some reason to believe that Arsène Lupin was the bicyclist who won the Grand Prix de l'Exposition, received his ten thousand francs, and was never heard of again. Arsène Lupin may have been, also, the person who saved so many lives through the little dormer-window at the Charity Bazaar; and, at the same time, picked their pockets."

The judge paused for a moment, then continued:

"Such is that epoch which seems to have been utilized by you in a thorough preparation for the warfare you have since waged against society; a methodical apprenticeship in which you developed your strength, energy and skill to the highest point possible. Do you acknowledge the accuracy of these facts?"

During this discourse the prisoner had stood balancing himself, first on one foot, then on the other, with shoulders stooped and arms inert. Under the strongest light one could observe his extreme thinness, his hollow cheeks, his projecting cheek-bones, his earthen-colored face dotted with small red spots and framed in a rough, straggling beard. Prison life had caused him to age and wither. He had lost the youthful face and elegant figure we had seen portrayed so often in the newspapers.

It appeared as if he had not heard the question propounded by the judge. Twice it was repeated to him. Then he raised his eyes, seemed to reflect, then, making a desperate effort, he murmured:

"Baudru, Désiré."

The judge smiled, as he said:

"I do not understand the theory of your defense, Arsène Lupin. If you are seeking to avoid responsibility for your crimes on the ground of imbecility, such a line of defense is open to you. But I shall proceed with the trial and pay no heed to your vagaries."

He then narrated at length the various thefts, swindles, and forgeries charged against Lupin. Sometimes he questioned the prisoner, but the latter simply grunted or remained silent. The examination of witnesses commenced. Some of the evidence given was immaterial; other portions of it seemed more important, but through all of it there ran a vein of contradictions and inconsistencies. A wearisome obscurity enveloped the proceedings, until Detective Ganimard was called as a witness; then interest was revived.

From the beginning the actions of the veteran detective appeared strange and unaccountable. He was nervous and ill at ease. Several times he looked at the prisoner, with obvious doubt and anxiety. Then, with his hands resting on the rail in front of him, he recounted the events in which he had participated, including his pursuit of the prisoner across Europe and his arrival in America. He was listened to with great avidity, as his capture of Arsène Lupin was well known to everyone through the medium of the press. Toward the close of his testimony, after referring to his conversations with Arsène Lupin, he stopped, twice, embarrassed and undecided. It was apparent that he was possessed of some thought which he feared to utter. The judge said to him, sympathetically:

"If you are ill, you may retire for the present."

"No, no, but—"

He stopped, looked sharply at the prisoner, and said:

"I ask permission to scrutinize the prisoner at closer range. There is some mystery about him that I must solve."

He approached the accused man, examined him attentively for several minutes, then returned to the witness-stand, and, in an almost solemn voice, he said:

"I declare, on oath, that the prisoner now before me is not Arsène Lupin."

A profound silence followed the statement. The judge, nonplussed for a moment, exclaimed:

"Ah! What do you mean? That is absurd!"

The detective continued:

"At first sight there is a certain resemblance, but if you carefully consider the nose, the mouth, the hair, the color of skin, you will see that it is not Arsène Lupin. And the eyes! Did he ever have those alcoholic eyes!"

"Come, come, witness! What do you mean? Do you pretend to say that we are trying the wrong man?"

"In my opinion, yes. Arsène Lupin has, in some manner, contrived to put this poor devil in his place, unless this man is a willing accomplice."

This dramatic dénouement caused much laughter and excitement amongst the spectators. The judge adjourned the trial, and sent for Mon. Bouvier, the gaoler, and guards employed in the prison.

When the trial was resumed, Mon. Bouvier and the gaoler examined the accused and declared that there was only a very slight resemblance between the prisoner and Arsène Lupin.

"Well, then!" exclaimed the judge, "who is this man? Where does he come from? What is he in prison for?"

Two of the prison-guards were called and both of them declared that the prisoner was Arsène Lupin. The judged breathed once more.

But one of the guards then said:

"Yes, yes, I think it is he."

"What!" cried the judge, impatiently, "you *think* it is he! What do you mean by that?"

"Well, I saw very little of the prisoner. He was placed in my charge in the evening and, for two months, he seldom stirred, but laid on his bed with his face to the wall."

"What about the time prior to those two months?"

"Before that he occupied a cell in another part of the prison. He was not in cell 24."

Here the head gaoler interrupted, and said:

"We changed him to another cell after his attempted escape."

"But you, monsieur, you have seen him during those two months?"

"I had no occasion to see him. He was always quiet and orderly."

"And this prisoner is not Arsène Lupin?"

"No."

"Then who is he?" demanded the judge.

"I do not know."

"Then we have before us a man who was substituted for Arsène Lupin, two months ago. How do you explain that?"

"I cannot."

In absolute despair, the judge turned to the accused and addressed him in a conciliatory tone:

"Prisoner, can you tell me how, and since when, you became an inmate of the Prison de la Santé?"

The engaging manner of the judge was calculated to disarm the mistrust and awaken the understanding of the accused man. He tried to reply. Finally, under clever and gentle questioning, he succeeded in framing a few phrases from which the following story was gleaned: Two months ago he had been taken to the Dépôt, examined and released. As he was leaving the building, a free man, he was seized by two guards and placed in the prison-van. Since then he had occupied cell 24. He was contented there, plenty to eat, and he slept well—so he did not complain.

All that seemed probable; and, amidst the mirth and excitement of the spectators, the judge adjourned the trial until the story could be investigated and verified.

⁕⁕⁕⁕⁕⁕⁕⁕⁕⁕⁕⁕⁕⁕

The following facts were at once established by an examination of the prison records: Eight weeks before a man named Baudru Désiré had slept at the Dépôt. He was released the next day, and left the Dépôt at two o'clock in the afternoon. On the same day at two o'clock, having been examined for the last time, Arsène Lupin left the Dépôt in a prison-van.

Had the guards made a mistake? Had they been deceived by the resemblance and carelessly substituted this man for their prisoner?

Another question suggested itself: Had the substitution been arranged in advance? In that event Baudru must have been an accomplice and must have caused his own arrest for the express purpose of taking Lupin's place. But then, by what miracle had such a plan, based on a series of improbable chances, been carried to success?

Baudru Désiré was turned over to the anthropological service; they had never seen anything like him. However, they easily traced his past history. He was known at Courbevois, at Asnières and at Levallois. He lived on alms and slept in one of those ragpicker's huts near the barrier de Ternes. He had disappeared from there a year ago.

Had he been enticed away by Arsène Lupin? There was no evidence to that effect. And even if that was so, it did not explain the flight of the prisoner. That still remained a mystery. Amongst twenty theories which sought to explain it, not one was satisfactory. Of the escape itself, there was no doubt; an escape that was incomprehensible, sensational, in which the public, as well as the officers of the law, could detect a carefully prepared plan, a combination of circumstances marvelously dove-tailed, whereof the dénouement fully justified the confident prediction of Arsène Lupin: "I shall not be present at my trial."

After a month of patient investigation, the problem remained unsolved. The poor devil of a Baudru could not be kept in prison indefinitely, and to place him on trial would be ridiculous. There was no charge against him. Consequently, he was released; but the chief of the Sûreté resolved to keep him under surveillance. This idea originated with Ganimard. From his point of view there was neither complicity nor chance. Baudru was an instrument upon which Arsène Lupin had played with his extraordinary skill. Baudru, when set at liberty, would lead them to Arsène Lupin or, at least, to some of his accomplices. The two inspectors, Folenfant and Dieuzy, were assigned to assist Ganimard.

One foggy morning in January the prison gates opened and Baudru Désiré stepped forth—a free man. At first he appeared to be quite embarrassed, and walked like a person who has no precise idea whither he is going. He followed the Rue de la Santé and the Rue Saint Jacques. He stopped in front of an old-clothes shop, removed his jacket and his vest, sold his vest on which he realized a few sous; then, replacing his jacket, he proceeded on his way. He crossed the Seine. At the Châtelet an omnibus passed him. He wished to enter it, but there was no place. The controller advised him to secure a number, so he entered the waiting-room.

Ganimard called to his two assistants, and, without removing his eyes from the waiting room, he said to them:

"Stop a carriage . . . no, two. That will be better. I will go with one of you, and we will follow him."

The men obeyed. Yet Baudru did not appear. Ganimard entered the waiting-room. It was empty.

"Idiot that I am!" he muttered, "I forgot there was another exit."

There was an interior corridor extending from the waiting-room to the Rue Saint Martin. Ganimard rushed through it and arrived just in time to observe Baudru upon the top of the Batignolles-Jardin de Plates omnibus as it was turning the corner of the Rue de Rivoli. He ran and caught the omnibus. But he had lost his two assistants. He must continue the pursuit alone. In his anger he was inclined to seize the man by the collar without ceremony. Was it not with premeditation and by means of an ingenious ruse that his pretended imbecile had separated him from his assistants?

He looked at Baudru. The latter was asleep on the bench, his head rolling from side to side, his mouth half-opened, and an incredible expression of stupidity on his blotched face. No, such an adversary was incapable of deceiving old Ganimard. It was a stroke of luck—nothing more.

At the Galleries-Lafayette, the man leaped from the omnibus and took the La Muette tramway, following the Boulevard Haussmann and the Avenue Victor Hugo. Baudru alighted at La Muette station; and, with a nonchalant air, strolled into the Bois de Boulogne.

He wandered through one path after another, and sometimes retraced his steps. What was he seeking? Had he any definite object? At the end of an hour, he appeared to be faint from fatigue, and, noticing a bench, he sat down. The spot, not far from Auteuil, on the edge of a pond hidden amongst the trees, was absolutely deserted. After the lapse of another half-hour, Ganimard became impatient and resolved to speak to the man. He approached and took a seat beside Baudru, lighted a cigarette, traced some figures in the sand with the end of his cane, and said:

"It's a pleasant day."

No response. But, suddenly the man burst into laughter, a happy, mirthful laugh, spontaneous and irresistible. Ganimard felt his hair stand on end in horror and surprise. It was that laugh, that infernal laugh he knew so well!

With a sudden movement, he seized the man by the collar and looked at him with a keen, penetrating gaze; and found that he no longer saw the man Baudru. To be sure, he saw Baudru; but, at the same time, he saw the other, the real man, Lupin. He discovered the intense life in the eyes, he filled up the shrunken features, he perceived the real flesh beneath the flabby skin, the real mouth through the grimaces that deformed it. Those were the eyes and mouth of the other, and especially his keen, alert, mocking expression, so clear and youthful!

"Arsène Lupin, Arsène Lupin," he stammered.

Then, in a sudden fit of rage, he seized Lupin by the throat and tried to hold him down. In spite of his fifty years, he still possessed unusual strength, whilst his adversary was apparently in a weak condition. But the struggle was a brief one. Arsène Lupin made only a slight movement, and, as suddenly as he had made the attack, Ganimard released his hold. His right arm fell inert, useless.

"If you had taken lessons in jiu-jitsu at the Quai des Orfèvres," said Lupin, "you would know that that blow is called udi-shi-ghi in Japanese. A second more, and I would have broken your arm and that would have been just what you deserve. I am surprised that you, an old friend whom I respect and before whom I voluntarily expose my incognito, should abuse my confidence in that violent manner. It is unworthy—Ah! What's the matter?"

Ganimard did not reply. That escape for which he deemed himself responsible—was it not he, Ganimard, who, by his sensational evidence, had led the court into serious error? That escape appeared to him like a dark cloud on his professional career. A tear rolled down his cheek to his gray moustache.

"Oh! mon Dieu, Ganimard, don't take it to heart. If you had not spoken, I would have arranged for someone else to do it. I couldn't allow poor Baudru Désiré to be convicted."

"Then," murmured Ganimard, "it was you that was there? And now you are here?"

"It is I, always I, only I."

"Can it be possible?"

"Oh, it is not the work of a sorcerer. Simply, as the judge remarked at the trial, the apprenticeship of a dozen years that equips a man to cope successfully with all the obstacles in life."

"But your face? Your eyes?"

"You can understand that if I worked eighteen months with Doctor Altier at the Saint-Louis hospital, it was not out of love for the work. I considered that he, who would one day have the honor of calling himself Arsène Lupin, ought to be exempt from the ordinary laws governing appearance and identity. Appearance? That can be modified at will. For instance, a hypodermic injection of paraffine will puff up the skin at the desired spot. Pyrogallic acid will change your skin to that of an Indian. The juice of the greater celandine will adorn you with the most beautiful eruptions and tumors. Another chemical affects the growth of your beard and hair; another changes the tone of your voice. Add to that two months of dieting in cell 24; exercises repeated a thousand times to enable me to hold my features in a certain grimace, to carry my head at a certain inclination, and adapt my back and shoulders to a stooping posture. Then five drops of atropine in the eyes to make them haggard and wild, and the trick is done."

"I do not understand how you deceived the guards."

"The change was progressive. The evolution was so gradual that they failed to notice it."

"But Baudru Désiré?"

"Baudru exists. He is a poor, harmless fellow whom I met last year; and, really, he bears a certain resemblance to me. Considering my arrest as a possible event, I took charge of Baudru and studied the points wherein we differed in appearance with a view to correct them in my own person. My friends caused him to remain at the Dépôt overnight, and to leave there next day about the same hour as I did— a coincidence easily arranged. Of course, it was necessary to have a record of his detention at the Dépôt in order to establish the fact that such a person was a reality; otherwise, the police would have sought elsewhere to find out my identity. But, in offering to them this excellent Baudru, it was inevitable, you understand, inevitable that they would seize upon him, and, despite the insurmountable difficulties of a substitution, they would prefer to believe in a substitution than confess their ignorance."

"Yes, yes, of course," said Ganimard.

"And then," exclaimed Arsène Lupin, "I held in my hands a trump-card: an anxious public watching and waiting for my escape. And that is the fatal error into which you fell, you and the others, in the course of that fascinating game pending between me and the officers of the law wherein the stake was my liberty. And you supposed that I was playing to the gallery; that I was intoxicated with my success. I, Arsène Lupin, guilty of such weakness! Oh, no! And, no longer ago than the Cahorn affair, you said: 'When Arsène Lupin cries from the housetops that he will escape, he has some object in view.' But, sapristi, you must understand that in order to escape I must create, in advance, a public belief in that escape, a belief amounting to an article of faith, an absolute conviction, a reality as glittering as the sun. And I did create that belief that Arsène Lupin would escape, that Arsène Lupin would not be present at his trial. And when you gave your evidence and said: 'That man is not Arsène Lupin,' everybody was prepared to believe you. Had one person doubted it, had anyone uttered this simple restriction: Suppose it is Arsène Lupin?— from that moment, I was lost. If anyone had scrutinized my face, not imbued with the idea that I was not Arsène Lupin, as you and the others did at my trial, but with the idea that I might be Arsène Lupin; then, despite all my precautions, I should have been recognized. But I had no fear. Logically, psychologically, no one could entertain the idea that I was Arsène Lupin."

He grasped Ganimard's hand.

"Come, Ganimard, confess that on the Wednesday after our conversation in the prison de la Santé, you expected me at your house at four o'clock, exactly as I said I would go."

"And your prison-van?" said Ganimard, evading the question.

"A bluff! Some of my friends secured that old unused van and wished to make the attempt. But I considered it impractical without the concurrence of a number of unusual circumstances. However, I found it useful to carry out that attempted escape and give it the widest publicity. An audaciously planned escape, though not completed, gave to the succeeding one the character of reality simply by anticipation."

"So that the cigar . . ."

"Hollowed by myself, as well as the knife."

"And the letters?"

"Written by me."

"And the mysterious correspondent?"

"Did not exist."

Ganimard reflected a moment, then said:

"When the anthropological service had Baudru's case under consideration, why did they not perceive that his measurements coincided with those of Arsène Lupin?"

"My measurements are not in existence."

"Indeed!"

"At least, they are false. I have given considerable attention to that question. In the first place, the Bertillon system records the visible marks of identification—and you have seen that they are not infallible—and, after that, the measurements of the head, the fingers, the ears, etc. Of course, such measurements are more or less infallible."

"Absolutely."

"No; but it costs money to get around them. Before we left America, one of the employees of the service there accepted so much money to insert false figures in my measurements. Consequently, Baudru's measurements should not agree with those of Arsène Lupin."

After a short silence, Ganimard asked:

"What are you going to do now?"

"Now," replied Lupin, "I am going to take a rest, enjoy the best of food and drink and gradually recover my former healthy condition. It is all very well to become Baudru or some other person, on occasion, and to change your personality as you do your shirt, but you soon grow weary of the change. I feel exactly as I imagine the man who lost his shadow must have felt, and I shall be glad to be Arsène Lupin once more."

He walked to and fro for a few minutes, then, stopping in front of Ganimard, he said:

"You have nothing more to say, I suppose?"

"Yes. I should like to know if you intend to reveal the true state of facts connected with your escape. The mistake that I made—"

"Oh! no one will ever know that it was Arsène Lupin who was discharged. It is to my own interest to surround myself with mystery, and therefore I shall permit my escape to retain its almost miraculous character. So, have no fear on that score, my dear friend. I shall say nothing. And now, good-bye. I am going out to dinner this evening, and have only sufficient time to dress."

"I though you wanted a rest."

"Ah! there are duties to society that one cannot avoid. To-morrow, I shall rest."

"Where do you dine to-night?"

"With the British Ambassador!"

THE MYSTERIOUS TRAVELER

The evening before, I had sent my automobile to Rouen by the highway. I was to travel to Rouen by rail, on my way to visit some friends that live on the banks of the Seine.

At Paris, a few minutes before the train started, seven gentlemen entered my compartment; five of them were smoking. No matter that the journey was a short one, the thought of traveling with such a company was not agreeable to me, especially as the car was built on the old model, without a corridor. I picked up my overcoat, my newspapers, and my time-table, and sought refuge in a neighboring compartment.

It was occupied by a lady, who, at sight of me, made a gesture of annoyance that did not escape my notice, and she leaned toward a gentleman who was standing on the step and was, no doubt, her husband. The gentleman scrutinized me closely, and, apparently, my appearance did not displease him, for he smiled as he spoke to his wife with the air of one who reassures a frightened child. She smiled also, and gave me a friendly glance as if she now understood that I was one of those gallant men with whom a woman can remain shut up for two hours in a little box, six feet square, and have nothing to fear.

Her husband said to her:

"I have an important appointment, my dear, and cannot wait any longer. Adieu."

He kissed her affectionately and went away. His wife threw him a few kisses and waved her handkerchief. The whistle sounded, and the train started.

At that precise moment, and despite the protests of the guards, the door was opened, and a man rushed into our compartment. My companion, who was standing and arranging her luggage, uttered a cry of terror and fell upon the seat. I am not a coward—far from it—but I confess that such intrusions at the last minute are always disconcerting. They have a suspicious, unnatural aspect.

However, the appearance of the new arrival greatly modified the unfavorable impression produced by his precipitant action. He was correctly and elegantly dressed, wore a tasteful cravat, correct gloves, and his face was refined and intelligent. But, where the devil had I seen that face before? Because, beyond all possible doubt, I had seen it. And yet the memory of it was so vague and indistinct that I felt it would be useless to try to recall it at that time.

Then, directing my attention to the lady, I was amazed at the pallor and anxiety I saw in her face. She was looking at her neighbor—they occupied seats on the same side of the compartment—with an expression of intense alarm, and I perceived that one of her trembling hands was slowly gliding toward a little traveling bag that was lying on the seat about twenty inches from her. She finished by seizing it and nervously drawing it to her. Our eyes met, and I read in hers so much anxiety and fear that I could not refrain from speaking to her:

"Are you ill, madame? Shall I open the window?"

Her only reply was a gesture indicating that she was afraid of our companion. I smiled, as her husband had done, shrugged my shoulders, and explained to her, in pantomime, that she had nothing to fear, that I was there, and, besides, the gentleman appeared to be a very harmless individual. At that moment, he turned toward us, scrutinized both of us from head to foot, then settled down in his corner and paid us no more attention.

After a short silence, the lady, as if she had mustered all her energy to perform a desperate act, said to me, in an almost inaudible voice:

"Do you know who is on our train?"

"Who?"

"He . . . he . . . I assure you . . ."

"Who is he?"

"Arsène Lupin!"

She had not taken her eyes off our companion, and it was to him rather than to me that she uttered the syllables of that disquieting name. He drew his hat over his face. Was that to conceal his agitation or, simply, to arrange himself for sleep? Then I said to her:

"Yesterday, through contumacy, Arsène Lupin was sentenced to twenty years' imprisonment at hard labor. Therefore it is improbable that he would be so imprudent, to-day, as to show himself in public. Moreover, the newspapers have announced his appearance in Turkey since his escape from the Santé."

"But he is on this train at the present moment," the lady proclaimed, with the obvious intention of being heard by our companion; "my husband is one of the directors in the penitentiary service, and it was the stationmaster himself who told us that a search was being made for Arsène Lupin."

"They may have been mistaken—"

"No; he was seen in the waiting-room. He bought a first-class ticket for Rouen."

"He has disappeared. The guard at the waiting-room door did not see him pass, and it is supposed that he had got into the express that leaves ten minutes after us."

"In that case, they will be sure to catch him."

"Unless, at the last moment, he leaped from that train to come here, into our train . . . which is quite probable . . . which is almost certain."

"If so, he will be arrested just the same; for the employees and guards would no doubt observe his passage from one train to the other, and, when we arrive at Rouen, they will arrest him there."

"Him—never! He will find some means of escape."

"In that case, I wish him 'bon voyage.'"

"But, in the meantime, think what he may do!"

"What?"

"I don't know. He may do anything."

She was greatly agitated, and, truly, the situation justified, to some extent, her nervous excitement. I was impelled to say to her:

"Of course, there are many strange coincidences, but you need have no fear. Admitting that Arsène Lupin is on this train, he will not commit any indiscretion; he will be only too happy to escape the peril that already threatens him."

My words did not reassure her, but she remained silent for a time. I unfolded my newspapers and read reports of Arsène Lupin's trial, but, as they contained nothing that was new to me, I was not greatly interested. Moreover, I was tired and sleepy. I felt my eyelids close and my head drop.

"But, monsieur, you are not going to sleep!"

She seized my newspaper, and looked at me with indignation.

"Certainly not," I said.

"That would be very imprudent."

"Of course," I assented.

I struggled to keep awake. I looked through the window at the landscape and the fleeting clouds, but in a short time all that became confused and indistinct; the image of the nervous lady and the drowsy gentleman were effaced from my memory, and I was buried in the soothing depths of a profound sleep. The tranquility of my response was soon disturbed by disquieting dreams, wherein a creature that had played the part and bore the name of Arsène Lupin held an important place. He appeared to me with his back laden with articles of value; he leaped over walls, and plundered castles. But the outlines of that creature, who was no longer Arsène Lupin, assumed a more definite form. He came toward me, growing larger and larger, leaped into the compartment with incredible agility, and landed squarely on my chest. With a cry of fright and pain, I awoke. The man, the traveler, our companion, with his knee on my breast, held me by the throat.

My sight was very indistinct, for my eyes were suffused with blood. I could see the lady, in a corner of the compartment, convulsed with fright. I tried even not to resist. Besides, I did not have the strength. My temples throbbed; I was almost strangled. One minute more, and I would have breathed my last. The man must have realized it, for he relaxed his grip, but did not remove his hand. Then he took a cord, in which he had prepared a slipknot, and tied my wrists together. In an instant, I was bound, gagged, and helpless.

Certainly, he accomplished the trick with an ease and skill that revealed the hand of a master; he was, no doubt, a professional thief. Not a word, not a nervous movement; only coolness and audacity. And I was there, lying on the bench, bound like a mummy, I—Arsène Lupin!

It was anything but a laughing matter, and yet, despite the gravity of the situation, I keenly appreciated the humor and irony that it involved. Arsène Lupin seized and bound like a novice! robbed as if I were an unsophisticated rustic—for, you must understand, the scoundrel had deprived me of my purse and wallet! Arsène Lupin, a victim, duped, vanquished. . . . What an adventure!

The lady did not move. He did not even notice her. He contented himself with picking up her traveling-bag that had fallen to the floor and taking from it the jewels, purse, and gold and silver trinkets that it contained. The lady opened her eyes, trembled with fear, drew the rings from her fingers and handed them to the man as if she wished to spare him unnecessary trouble. He took the rings and looked at her. She swooned.

Then, quite unruffled, he resumed his seat, lighted a cigarette, and proceeded to examine the treasure that he had acquired. The examination appeared to give him perfect satisfaction.

But I was not so well satisfied. I do not speak of the twelve thousand francs of which I had been unduly deprived: that was only a temporary loss, because I was certain that I would recover possession of that money after a very brief delay, together with the important papers contained in my wallet: plans, specifications, addresses, lists of correspondents, and compromising letters. But, for the moment, a more immediate and more serious question troubled me: How would this affair end? What would be the outcome of this adventure?

As you can imagine, the disturbance created by my passage through the Saint-Lazare station has not escaped my notice. Going to visit friends who knew me under the name of Guillaume Berlat, and amongst whom my resemblance to Arsène Lupin was a subject of many innocent jests, I could not assume a disguise, and my presence had been remarked. So, beyond question, the commissary of police at Rouen, notified by telegraph, and assisted by numerous agents, would be awaiting the train, would question all suspicious passengers, and proceed to search the cars.

Of course, I had foreseen all that, but it had not disturbed me, as I was certain that the police of Rouen would not be any shrewder than the police of Paris and that I could escape recognition; would it not be sufficient for me to carelessly display my card as "député," thanks to which I had inspired complete confidence in the gate-keeper at Saint-Lazare?—But the situation was greatly changed. I was no longer free. It was impossible to attempt one of my usual tricks. In one of the compartments, the commissary of police would find Mon. Arsène Lupin, bound hand and foot, as docile as a lamb, packed up, all ready to be dumped into a prison-van. He would have simply to accept delivery of the parcel, the same as if it were so much merchandise or a basket of fruit and vegetables. Yet, to avoid that shameful dénouement, what could I do?—bound and gagged, as I was? And the train was rushing on toward Rouen, the next and only station.

Another problem was presented, in which I was less interested, but the solution of which aroused my professional curiosity. What were the intentions of my rascally companion? Of course, if I had been alone, he could, on our arrival at Rouen, leave the car slowly and fearlessly. But the lady? As soon as the door of the compartment should be opened, the lady, now so quiet and humble, would scream and call for help. That was the dilemma that perplexed me! Why had he not reduced her to a helpless condition similar to mine? That would have given him ample time to disappear before his double crime was discovered.

He was still smoking, with his eyes fixed upon the window that was now being streaked with drops of rain. Once he turned, picked up my time-table, and consulted it.

The lady had to feign a continued lack of consciousness in order to deceive the enemy. But fits of coughing, provoked by the smoke, exposed her true condition. As to me, I was very uncomfortable, and very tired. And I meditated; I plotted.

The train was rushing on, joyously, intoxicated with its own speed. Saint Etienne! . . . At that moment, the man arose and took two steps toward us, which caused the lady to utter a cry of alarm and fall into a genuine swoon. What was the man about to do? He lowered the window on our side. A heavy rain was now falling, and, by a gesture, the man expressed his annoyance at his not having an umbrella or an overcoat. He glanced at the rack. The lady's umbrella was there. He took it. He also took my overcoat and put it on.

We were now crossing the Seine. He turned up the bottoms of his trousers, then leaned over and raised the exterior latch of the door. Was he going to throw himself upon the track? At that speed, it would have been instant death. We now entered a tunnel. The man opened the door half-way and stood on the upper step. What folly! The darkness, the smoke, the noise, all gave a fantastic appearance to his actions. But suddenly, the train diminished its speed. A moment later it increased its speed, then slowed up again. Probably, some repairs were being made in that part of the tunnel which obliged the trains to diminish their speed, and the man was aware of the fact. He immediately stepped down to the lower step, closed the door behind him, and leaped to the ground. He was gone.

The lady immediately recovered her wits, and her first act was to lament the loss of her jewels. I gave her an imploring look. She understood, and quickly removed the gag that stifled me. She wished to untie the cords that bound me, but I prevented her.

"No, no, the police must see everything exactly as it stands. I want them to see what the rascal did to us."

"Suppose I pull the alarm-bell?"

"Too late. You should have done that when he made the attack on me."

"But he would have killed me. Ah! monsieur, didn't I tell you that he was on this train. I recognized him from his portrait. And now he has gone off with my jewels."

"Don't worry. The police will catch him."

"Catch Arsène Lupin! Never."

"That depends on you, madame. Listen. When we arrive at Rouen, be at the door and call. Make a noise. The police and the railway employees will come. Tell what you have seen: the assault made on me and the flight of Arsène Lupin. Give a description of him—soft hat, umbrella—yours—gray overcoat . . ."

"Yours," said she.

"What! mine? Not at all. It was his. I didn't have any."

"It seems to me he didn't have one when he came in."

"Yes, yes . . . unless the coat was one that someone had forgotten and left in the rack. At all events, he had it when he went away, and that is the essential point. A gray overcoat—remember! . . . Ah! I forgot. You must tell your name, first thing you do. Your husband's official position will stimulate the zeal of the police."

We arrived at the station. I gave her some further instructions in a rather imperious tone:

"Tell them my name—Guillaume Berlat. If necessary, say that you know me. That will save time. We must expedite the preliminary investigation. The important thing is the pursuit of Arsène Lupin. Your jewels, remember! Let there be no mistake. Guillaume Berlat, a friend of your husband."

"I understand. . . . Guillaume Berlat."

She was already calling and gesticulating. As soon as the train stopped, several men entered the compartment. The critical moment had come.

Panting for breath, the lady exclaimed:

"Arsène Lupin . . . he attacked us . . . he stole my jewels . . . I am Madame Renaud . . . my husband is a director of the penitentiary service. . . . Ah! here is my brother, Georges Ardelle, director of the Crédit Rouennais . . . you must know . . ."

She embraced a young man who had just joined us, and whom the commissary saluted. Then she continued, weeping:

"Yes, Arsène Lupin . . . while monsieur was sleeping, he seized him by the throat . . . Mon. Berlat, a friend of my husband."

The commissary asked:

"But where is Arsène Lupin?"

"He leaped from the train, when passing through the tunnel."

"Are you sure that it was he?"

"Am I sure! I recognized him perfectly. Besides, he was seen at the Saint-Lazare station. He wore a soft hat—"

"No, a hard felt, like that," said the commissary, pointing to my hat.

"He had a soft hat, I am sure," repeated Madame Renaud, "and a gray overcoat."

"Yes, that is right," replied the commissary, "the telegram says he wore a gray overcoat with a black velvet collar."

"Exactly, a black velvet collar," exclaimed Madame Renaud, triumphantly.

I breathed freely. Ah! the excellent friend I had in that little woman.

The police agents had now released me. I bit my lips until they ran blood. Stooping over, with my handkerchief over my mouth, an attitude quite natural in a person who has remained for a long time in an uncomfortable position, and whose mouth shows the bloody marks of the gag, I addressed the commissary, in a weak voice:

"Monsieur, it was Arsène Lupin. There is no doubt about that. If we make haste, he can be caught yet. I think I may be of some service to you."

The railway car in which the crime occurred was detached from the train to serve as a mute witness at the official investigation. The train continued on its way to Havre. We were then conducted to the station-master's office through a crowd of curious spectators.

Then, I had a sudden access of doubt and discretion. Under some pretext or other, I must gain my automobile, and escape. To remain there was dangerous. Something might happen; for instance, a telegram from Paris, and I would be lost.

Yes, but what about my thief? Abandoned to my own resources, in an unfamiliar country, I could not hope to catch him.

"Bah! I must make the attempt," I said to myself. "It may be a difficult game, but an amusing one, and the stake is well worth the trouble."

And when the commissary asked us to repeat the story of the robbery, I exclaimed:

"Monsieur, really, Arsène Lupin is getting the start of us. My automobile is waiting in the courtyard. If you will be so kind as to use it, we can try . . ."

The commissary smiled, and replied:

"The idea is a good one; so good, indeed, that it is already being carried out. Two of my men have set out on bicycles. They have been gone for some time."

"Where did they go?"

"To the entrance of the tunnel. There, they will gather evidence, secure witnesses, and follow on the track of Arsène Lupin."

I could not refrain from shrugging my shoulders, as I replied:

"Your men will not secure any evidence or any witnesses."

"Really!"

"Arsène Lupin will not allow anyone to see him emerge from the tunnel. He will take the first road—"

"To Rouen, where we will arrest him."

"He will not go to Rouen."

"Then he will remain in the vicinity, where his capture will be even more certain."

"He will not remain in the vicinity."

"Oh! oh! And where will he hide?"

I looked at my watch, and said:

"At the present moment, Arsène Lupin is prowling around the station at Darnétal. At ten fifty, that is, in twenty-two minutes from now, he will take the train that goes from Rouen to Amiens."

"Do you think so? How do you know it?"

"Oh! it is quite simple. While we were in the car, Arsène Lupin consulted my railway guide. Why did he do it? Was there, not far from the spot where he disappeared, another line of railway, a station upon that line, and a train stopping at that station? On consulting my railway guide, I found such to be the case."

"Really, monsieur," said the commissary, "that is a marvelous deduction. I congratulate you on your skill."

I was now convinced that I had made a mistake in displaying so much cleverness. The commissary regarded me with astonishment, and I thought a slight suspicion entered his official mind. . . . Oh! scarcely that, for the photographs distributed broadcast by the police department were too imperfect; they presented an Arsène Lupin so different from the one he had before him, that he could not possibly recognize me by it. But, all the same, he was troubled, confused and ill-at-ease.

"Mon Dieu! nothing stimulates the comprehension so much as the loss of a pocket-book and the desire to recover it. And it seems to me that if you will give me two of your men, we may be able . . ."

"Oh! I beg of you, monsieur le commissaire," cried Madame Renaud, "listen to Mon. Berlat."

The intervention of my excellent friend was decisive. Pronounced by her, the wife of an influential official, the name of Berlat became really my own, and gave me an identity that no mere suspicion could affect. The commissary arose, and said:

"Believe me, Monsieur Berlat, I shall be delighted to see you succeed. I am as much interested as you are in the arrest of Arsène Lupin."

He accompanied me to the automobile, and introduced two of his men, Honoré Massol and Gaston Delivet, who were assigned to assist me. My chauffer cranked up the car and I took my place at the wheel. A few seconds later, we left the station. I was saved.

Ah! I must confess that in rolling over the boulevards that surrounded the old Norman city, in my swift thirty-five horsepower Moreau-Lepton, I experienced a deep feeling of pride, and the motor responded, sympathetically to my desires. At right and left, the trees flew past us with startling rapidity, and I, free, out of danger, had simply to arrange my little personal affairs with the two honest representatives of the Rouen police who were sitting behind me. Arsène Lupin was going in search of Arsène Lupin!

Modest guardians of social order—Gaston Delivet and Honoré Massol—how valuable was your assistance! What would I have done without you? Without you, many times, at the cross-roads, I might have taken the wrong route! Without you, Arsène Lupin would have made a mistake, and the other would have escaped!

But the end was not yet. Far from it. I had yet to capture the thief and recover the stolen papers. Under no circumstances must my two acolytes be permitted to see those papers, much less to seize them. That was a point that might give me some difficulty.

We arrived at Darnétal three minutes after the departure of the train. True, I had the consolation of learning that a man wearing a gray overcoat with a black velvet collar had taken the train at the station. He had bought a second-class ticket for Amiens. Certainly, my début as detective was a promising one.

Delivet said to me:

"The train is express, and the next stop is Montérolier-Buchy in nineteen minutes. If we do not reach there before Arsène Lupin, he can proceed to Amiens, or change for the train going to Clères, and, from that point, reach Dieppe or Paris."

"How far to Montérolier?"

"Twenty-three kilometers."

"Twenty-three kilometers in nineteen minutes. . . . We will be there ahead of him."

We were off again! Never had my faithful Moreau-Repton

responded to my impatience with such ardor and regularity. It participated in my anxiety. It indorsed my determination. It comprehended my animosity against that rascally Arsène Lupin. The knave! The traitor!

"Turn to the right," cried Delivet, "then to the left."

We fairly flew, scarcely touching the ground. The mile-stones looked like little timid beasts that vanished at our approach. Suddenly, at a turn of the road, we saw a vortex of smoke. It was the Northern Express. For a kilometer, it was a struggle, side by side, but an unequal struggle in which the issue was certain. We won the race by twenty lengths.

In three seconds we were on the platform standing before the second-class carriages. The doors were opened, and some passengers alighted, but not my thief. We made a search through the compartments. No sign of Arsène Lupin.

"Sapristi!" I cried, "he must have recognized me in the automobile as we were racing, side by side, and he leaped from the train."

"Ah! there he is now! crossing the track."

I started in pursuit of the man, followed by my two acolytes, or rather followed by one of them, for the other, Massol, proved himself to be a runner of exceptional speed and endurance. In a few moments, he had made an appreciable gain upon the fugitive. The man noticed it, leaped over a hedge, scampered across a meadow, and entered a thick grove. When we reached this grove, Massol was waiting for us. He went no farther, for fear of losing us.

"Quite right, my dear friend," I said. "After such a run, our victim must be out of wind. We will catch him now."

I examined the surroundings with the idea of proceeding alone in the arrest of the fugitive, in order to recover my papers, concerning which the authorities would doubtless ask many disagreeable questions. Then I returned to my companions, and said:

"It is all quite easy. You, Massol, take your place at the left; you, Delivet, at the right. From there, you can observe the entire posterior line of the bush, and he cannot escape without you seeing him, except by that ravine, and I shall watch it. If he does not come out voluntarily, I will enter and drive him out toward one or the other of you. You have simply to wait. Ah! I forgot: in case I need you, a pistol shot."

Massol and Delivet walked away to their respective posts. As soon as they had disappeared, I entered the grove with the greatest precaution so as to be neither seen nor heard. I encountered dense thickets, through which narrow paths had been cut, but the overhanging boughs compelled me to adopt a stooping posture. One of these paths led to a clearing in which I found footsteps upon the wet grass. I followed them; they led me to the foot of a mound which was surmounted by a deserted, dilapidated hovel.

"He must be there," I said to myself. "It is a well-chosen retreat."

I crept cautiously to the side of the building. A slight noise informed me that he was there; and, then, through an opening, I saw him. His back was turned toward me. In two bounds, I was upon him. He tried to fire a revolver that he held in his hand. But he had no time. I threw him to the ground, in such a manner that his arms were beneath him, twisted and helpless, whilst I held him down with my knee on his breast.

"Listen, my boy," I whispered in his ear. "I am Arsène Lupin. You are to deliver over to me, immediately and gracefully, my pocket-book and the lady's jewels, and, in return therefore, I will save you from the police and enroll you amongst my friends. One word: yes or no?"

"Yes," he murmured.

"Very good. Your escape, this morning, was well planned. I congratulate you."

I arose. He fumbled in his pocket, drew out a large knife and tried to strike me with it.

"Imbecile!" I exclaimed.

With one hand, I parried the attack; with the other, I gave him a sharp blow on the carotid artery. He fell—stunned!

In my pocket-book, I recovered my papers and bank-notes. Out of curiosity, I took his. Upon an envelope, addressed to him, I read his name: Pierre Onfrey. It startled me. Pierre Onfrey, the assassin of the Rue Lafontaine at Auteuil! Pierre Onfrey, he who had cut the throats of Madame Delbois and her two daughters. I leaned over him. Yes, those were the features which, in the compartment, had evoked in me the memory of a face I could not then recall.

But time was passing. I placed in an envelope two bank-notes of one hundred francs each, with a card bearing these words: "Arsène Lupin to his worthy colleagues Honoré Massol and Gaston Delivet, as a slight token of his gratitude." I placed it in a prominent spot in the room, where they would be sure to find it. Beside it, I placed Madame Renaud's handbag. Why could I not return it to the lady who had befriended me? I must confess that I had taken from it everything that possessed any interest or value, leaving there only a shell comb, a stick of rouge Dorin for the lips, and an empty purse. But, you know, business is business. And then, really, her husband is engaged in such a dishonorable vocation!

The man was becoming conscious. What was I to do? I was unable to save him or condemn him. So I took his revolver and fired a shot in the air.

"My two acolytes will come and attend to his case," I said to myself, as I hastened away by the road through the ravine. Twenty minutes later, I was seated in my automobile.

At four o'clock, I telegraphed to my friends at Rouen that an unexpected event would prevent me from making my promised visit. Between ourselves, considering what my friends must now know, my visit is postponed indefinitely. A cruel disillusion for them!

At six o'clock I was in Paris. The evening newspapers informed me that Pierre Onfrey had been captured at last.

Next day,—let us not despise the advantages of judicious advertising—the *Echo de France* published this sensational item:

"Yesterday, near Buchy, after numerous exciting incidents, Arsène Lupin effected the arrest of Pierre Onfrey. The assassin of the rue Lafontaine had robbed Madame Renaud, wife of the director in the penitentiary service, in a railway carriage on the Paris-Havre line. Arsène Lupin restored to Madame Renaud the hand-bag that contained her jewels, and gave a generous recompense to the two detectives who had assisted him in making that dramatic arrest."

THE QUEEN'S NECKLACE

Two or three times each year, on occasions of unusual importance, such as the halls at the Austrian Embassy or the soirees of Lady Billingstone, the Countess de Dreux-Soubise wore upon her white shoulders "The Queen's Necklace."

It was, indeed, the famous necklace, the legendary necklace that Bohmer and Bassenge, court jewelers, had made for Madame Du Barry; the veritable necklace that the Cardinal de Rohan-Soubise intended to give to Marie-Antoinette, Queen of France; and the same that the adventuress Jeanne de Valois, Countess de la Motte, had pulled to pieces one evening in February, 1785, with the aid of her husband and their accomplice, Rétaux de Villette.

To tell the truth, the mounting alone was genuine. Rétaux de Villette had kept it, whilst the Count de la Motte and his wife scattered to the four winds of heaven the beautiful stones so carefully chosen by Bohmer. Later, he sold the mounting to Gaston de Dreux-Soubise, nephew and heir of the Cardinal, who re-purchased the few diamonds that remained in the possession of the English jeweler, Jeffreys; supplemented them with other stones of the same size but of much inferior quality, and thus restored the marvelous necklace to the form in which it had come from the hands of Bohmer and Bassenge.

For nearly a century, the house of Dreux-Soubise had prided itself upon the possession of this historic jewel. Although adverse circumstances had greatly reduced their fortune, they preferred to curtail their household expenses rather than part with this relic of royalty. More particularly, the present count clung to it as a man clings to the home of his ancestors. As a matter of prudence, he had rented a safety-deposit box at the Crédit Lyonnais in which to keep it. He went for it himself on the afternoon of the day on which his wife wished to wear it, and he, himself, carried it back next morning.

On this particular evening, at the reception given at the Palais de Castille, the countess achieved a remarkable success; and King Christian, in whose honor the fête was given, commented on her grace and beauty. The thousand facets of the diamond sparkled and shone like flames of fire about her shapely neck and shoulders, and it is safe to say that none but she could have borne the weight of such an ornament with so much ease and grace.

This was a double triumph, and the Count de Dreux was highly elated when they returned to their chamber in the old house of the faubourg Saint-Germain. He was proud of his wife, and quite as proud, perhaps, of the necklace that had conferred added luster to his noble house for generations. His wife, also, regarded the necklace with an almost childish vanity, and it was not without regret that she removed it from her shoulders and handed it to her husband who admired it as passionately as if he had never seen it before. Then, having placed it in its case of red leather, stamped with the Cardinal's arms, he passed into an adjoining room which was simply an alcove or cabinet that had been cut off from their chamber, and which could be entered only by means of a door at the foot of their bed. As he had done on previous occasions, he hid it on a high shelf amongst hat-boxes and piles of linen. He closed the door, and retired.

Next morning, he arose about nine o'clock, intending to go to the Crédit Lyonnais before breakfast. He dressed, drank a cup of coffee, and went to the stables to give his orders. The condition of one of the horses worried him. He caused it to be exercised in his presence. Then he returned to his wife, who had not yet left the chamber. Her maid was dressing her hair. When her husband entered, she asked:

"Are you going out?"

"Yes, as far as the bank."

"Of course. That is wise."

He entered the cabinet; but, after a few seconds, and without any sign of astonishment, he asked:

"Did you take it, my dear?"

"What? . . . No, I have not taken anything."

"You must have moved it."

"Not at all. I have not even opened that door."

He appeared at the door, disconcerted, and stammered, in a scarcely intelligible voice:

"You haven't. . . . It wasn't you? . . . Then . . ."

She hastened to his assistance, and, together, they made a thorough search, throwing the boxes to the floor and overturning the piles of linen. Then the count said, quite discouraged:

"It is useless to look any more. I put it here, on this shelf."

"You must be mistaken."

"No, no, it was on this shelf—nowhere else."

They lighted a candle, as the room was quite dark, and then carried out all the linen and other articles that the room contained. And, when the room was emptied, they confessed, in despair, that the famous necklace had disappeared. Without losing time in vain lamentations, the countess notified the commissary of police, Mon. Valorbe, who came at once, and, after hearing their story, inquired of the count:

"Are you sure that no one passed through your chamber during the night?"

"Absolutely sure, as I am a very light sleeper. Besides, the chamber door was bolted, and I remember unbolting it this morning when my wife rang for her maid."

"And there is no other entrance to the cabinet?"

"None."

"No windows?"

"Yes, but it is closed up."

"I will look at it."

Candles were lighted, and Mon. Valorbe observed at once that the lower half of the window was covered by a large press which was, however, so narrow that it did not touch the casement on either side.

"On what does this window open?"

"A small inner court."

"And you have a floor above this?"

"Two; but, on a level with the servant's floor, there is a close grating over the court. That is why this room is so dark."

When the press was moved, they found that the window was fastened, which would not have been the case if anyone had entered that way.

"Unless," said the count, "they went out through our chamber."

"In that case, you would have found the door unbolted."

The commissary considered the situation for a moment, then asked the countess:

"Did any of your servants know that you wore the necklace last evening?"

"Certainly; I didn't conceal the fact. But nobody knew that it was hidden in that cabinet."

"No one?"

"No one . . . unless . . ."

"Be quite sure, madam, as it is a very important point."

She turned to her husband, and said:

"I was thinking of Henriette."

"Henriette? She didn't know where we kept it."

"Are you sure?"

"Who is this woman Henriette?" asked Mon. Valorbe.

"A school-mate, who was disowned by her family for marrying beneath her. After her husband's death, I furnished an apartment in this house for her and her son. She is clever with her needle and has done some work for me."

"What floor is she on?"

"Same as ours . . . at the end of the corridor . . . and I think . . . the window of her kitchen . . ."

"Opens on this little court, does it not?"

"Yes, just opposite ours."

Mon. Valorbe then asked to see Henriette. They went to her apartment; she was sewing, whilst her son Raoul, about six years old, was sitting beside her, reading. The commissary was surprised to see the wretched apartment that had been provided for the woman. It consisted of one room without a fireplace, and a very small room that served as a kitchen. The commissary proceeded to question her. She appeared to be overwhelmed on learning of the theft. Last evening she had herself dressed the countess and placed the necklace upon her shoulders.

"Good God!" she exclaimed, "it can't be possible!"

"And you have no idea? Not the least suspicion? Is it possible that the thief may have passed through your room?"

She laughed heartily, never supposing that she could be an object of suspicion.

"But I have not left my room. I never go out. And, perhaps, you have not seen?"

She opened the kitchen window, and said:

"See, it is at least three meters to the ledge of the opposite window."

"Who told you that we supposed the theft might have been committed in that way?"

"But . . . the necklace was in the cabinet, wasn't it?"

"How do you know that?"

"Why, I have always known that it was kept there at night. It had been mentioned in my presence."

Her face, though still young, bore unmistakable traces of sorrow and resignation. And it now assumed an expression of anxiety as if some danger threatened her. She drew her son toward her. The child took her hand, and kissed it affectionately.

When they were alone again, the count said to the commissary:

"I do not suppose you suspect Henriette. I can answer for her. She is honesty itself."

"I quite agree with you," replied Mon. Valorbe. "At most, I thought there might have been an unconscious complicity. But I confess that even that theory must be abandoned, as it does not help solve the problem now before us."

The commissary of police abandoned the investigation, which was now taken up and completed by the examining judge. He questioned the servants, examined the condition of the bolt, experimented with the opening and closing of the cabinet window, and explored the little court from top to bottom. All was in vain. The bolt was intact. The window could not be opened or closed from the outside.

The inquiries especially concerned Henriette, for, in spite of everything, they always turned in her direction. They made a thorough investigation of her past life, and ascertained that, during the last three years, she had left the house only four times, and her business, on those occasions, was satisfactorily explained. As a matter of fact, she acted as chambermaid and seamstress to the countess, who treated her with great strictness and even severity.

At the end of a week, the examining judge had secured no more definite information than the commissary of police. The judge said:

"Admitting that we know the guilty party, which we do not, we are confronted by the fact that we do not know how the theft was committed. We are brought face to face with two obstacles: a door and a window—both closed and fastened. It is thus a double mystery. How could anyone enter, and, moreover, how could anyone escape, leaving behind him a bolted door and a fastened window?"

At the end of four months, the secret opinion of the judge was that the count and countess, being hard pressed for money, which was their normal condition, had sold the Queen's Necklace. He closed the investigation.

The loss of the famous jewel was a severe blow to the Dreux-Soubise. Their credit being no longer propped up by the reserve fund that such a treasure constituted, they found themselves confronted by more exacting creditors and money-lenders. They were obliged to cut down to the quick, to sell or mortgage every article that possessed any commercial value. In brief, it would have been their ruin, if two large legacies from some distant relatives had not saved them.

Their pride also suffered a downfall, as if they had lost a quartering from their escutcheon. And, strange to relate, it was upon her former schoolmate, Henriette, that the countess vented her spleen. Toward her, the countess displayed the most spiteful feelings, and even openly accused her. First, Henriette was relegated to the servants' quarters, and, next day, discharged.

For some time, the count and countess passed an uneventful life. They traveled a great deal. Only one incident of record occurred during that period. Some months after the departure of Henriette, the countess was surprised when she received and read the following letter, signed by Henriette:

"Madame,"

"I do not know how to thank you; for it was you, was it not, who sent me that? It could not have been anyone else. No one but you knows where I live. If I am wrong, excuse me, and accept my sincere thanks for your past favors . . ."

What did the letter mean? The present or past favors of the countess consisted principally of injustice and neglect. Why, then, this letter of thanks?

When asked for an explanation, Henriette replied that she had received a letter, through the mails, enclosing two bank-notes of one thousand francs each. The envelope, which she enclosed with her reply, bore the Paris post-mark, and was addressed in a handwriting that was obviously disguised. Now, whence came those two thousand francs? Who had sent them? And why had they sent them?

Henriette received a similar letter and a like sum of money twelve months later. And a third time; and a fourth; and each year for a period of six years, with this difference, that in the fifth and sixth years the sum was doubled. There was another difference: the post-office authorities having seized one of the letters under the pretext that it was not registered, the last two letters were duly sent according to the postal regulations, the first dated from Saint-Germain, the other from Suresnes. The writer signed the first one, "Anquety"; and the other, "Péchard." The addresses that he gave were false.

At the end of six years, Henriette died, and the mystery remained unsolved.

||||||||||||||||||||||||

All these events are known to the public. The case was one of those which excite public interest, and it was a strange coincidence that this necklace, which had caused such a great commotion in France at the close of the eighteenth century, should create a similar commotion a century later. But what I am about to relate is known only to the parties directly interested and a few others from whom the count exacted a promise of secrecy. As it is probable that some day or other that promise will be broken, I have no hesitation in rending the veil and thus disclosing the key to the mystery, the explanation of the letter published in the morning papers two days ago; an extraordinary letter which increased, if possible, the mists and shadows that envelope this inscrutable drama.

Five days ago, a number of guests were dining with the Count de Dreux-Soubise. There were several ladies present, including his two nieces and his cousin, and the following gentlemen: the president of Essaville, the deputy Bochas, the chevalier Floriani, whom the count had known in Sicily, and General Marquis de Rouzières, an old club friend.

After the repast, coffee was served by the ladies, who gave the gentlemen permission to smoke their cigarettes, provided they would not desert the salon. The conversation was general, and finally one of the guests chanced to speak of celebrated crimes. And that gave the Marquis de Rouzières, who delighted to tease the count, an opportunity to mention the affair of the Queen's Necklace, a subject that the count detested.

Each one expressed his own opinion of the affair; and, of course, their various theories were not only contradictory but impossible.

"And you, monsieur," said the countess to the chevalier Floriani, "what is your opinion?"

"Oh! I—I have no opinion, madame."

All the guests protested; for the chevalier had just related in an entertaining manner various adventures in which he had participated with his father, a magistrate at Palermo, and which established his judgment and taste in such manners.

"I confess," said he, "I have sometimes succeeded in unraveling mysteries that the cleverest detectives have renounced; yet I do not claim to be Sherlock Holmes. Moreover, I know very little about the affair of the Queen's Necklace."

Everybody now turned to the count, who was thus obliged, quite unwillingly, to narrate all the circumstances connected with the theft. The chevalier listened, reflected, asked a few questions, and said:

"It is very strange . . . at first sight, the problem appears to be a very simple one."

The count shrugged his shoulders. The others drew closer to the chevalier, who continued, in a dogmatic tone:

"As a general rule, in order to find the author of a crime or a theft, it is necessary to determine how that crime or theft was committed, or, at least, how it could have been committed. In the present case, nothing is more simple, because we are face to face, not with several theories, but with one positive fact, that is to say: the thief could only enter by the chamber door or the window of the cabinet. Now, a person cannot open a bolted door from the outside. Therefore, he must have entered through the window."

"But it was closed and fastened, and we found it fastened afterward," declared the count.

"In order to do that," continued Floriani, without heeding the interruption, "he had simply to construct a bridge, a plank, or a ladder, between the balcony of the kitchen and the ledge of the window, and as the jewel-case—"

"But I repeat that the window was fastened," exclaimed the count, impatiently.

This time, Floriani was obliged to reply. He did so with the greatest tranquility, as if the objection was the most insignificant affair in the world.

"I will admit that it was; but is there not a transom in the upper part of the window?"

"How do you know that?"

"In the first place, that was customary in houses of that date; and, in the second place, without such a transom, the theft cannot be explained."

"Yes, there is one, but it was closed, the same as the window. Consequently, we did not pay attention to it."

"That was a mistake; for, if you had examined it, you would have found that it had been opened."

"But how?"

"I presume that, like all others, it opens by means of a wire with a ring on the lower end."

"Yes, but I do not see—"

"Now, through a hole in the window, a person could, by the aid of some instrument, let us say a poker with a hook at the end, grip the ring, pull down, and open the transom."

The count laughed and said:

"Excellent! excellent! Your scheme is very cleverly constructed, but you overlook one thing, monsieur, there is no hole in the window."

"There was a hole."

"Nonsense, we would have seen it."

"In order to see it, you must look for it, and no one has looked. The hole is there; it must be there, at the side of the window, in the putty. In a vertical direction, of course."

The count arose. He was greatly excited. He paced up and down the room, two or three times, in a nervous manner; then, approaching Floriani, said:

"Nobody has been in that room since; nothing has been changed."

"Very well, monsieur, you can easily satisfy yourself that my explanation is correct."

"It does not agree with the facts established by the examining judge. You have seen nothing, and yet you contradict all that we have seen and all that we know."

Floriani paid no attention to the count's petulance. He simply smiled and said:

"Mon Dieu, monsieur, I submit my theory; that is all. If I am mistaken, you can easily prove it."

"I will do so at once . . . I confess that your assurance—"

The count muttered a few more words; then suddenly rushed to the door and passed out. Not a word was uttered in his absence; and this profound silence gave the situation an air of almost tragic importance. Finally, the count returned. He was pale and nervous. He said to his friends, in a trembling voice:

"I beg your pardon . . . the revelations of the chevalier were so unexpected . . . I should never have thought . . ."

His wife questioned him, eagerly:

"Speak . . . what is it?"

He stammered: "The hole is there, at the very spot, at the side of the window—"

He seized the chevalier's arm, and said to him in an imperious tone:

"Now, monsieur, proceed. I admit that you are right so far, but now . . . that is not all . . . go on . . . tell us the rest of it."

Floriani disengaged his arm gently, and, after a moment, continued:

"Well, in my opinion, this is what happened. The thief, knowing that the countess was going to wear the necklace that evening, had prepared his gangway or bridge during your absence. He watched you through the window and saw you hide the necklace. Afterward, he cut the glass and pulled the ring."

"Ah! but the distance was so great that it would be impossible for him to reach the window-fastening through the transom."

"Well, then, if he could not open the window by reaching through the transom, he must have crawled through the transom."

"Impossible; it is too small. No man could crawl through it."

"Then it was not a man," declared Floriani.

"What!"

"If the transom is too small to admit a man, it must have been a child."

"A child!"

"Did you not say that your friend Henriette had a son?"

"Yes; a son named Raoul."

"Then, in all probability, it was Raoul who committed the theft."

"What proof have you of that?"

"What proof! Plenty of it. . . . For instance—"

He stopped, and reflected for a moment, then continued:

"For instance, that gangway or bridge. It is improbable that the child could have brought it in from outside the house and carried it away again without being observed. He must have used something close at hand. In the little room used by Henriette as a kitchen, were there not some shelves against the wall on which she placed her pans and dishes?"

"Two shelves, to the best of my memory."

"Are you sure that those shelves are really fastened to the wooden brackets that support them? For, if they are not, we could be justified in presuming that the child removed them, fastened them together, and thus formed his bridge. Perhaps, also, since there was a stove, we might find the bent poker that he used to open the transom."

Without saying a word, the count left the room; and, this time, those present did not feel the nervous anxiety they had experienced the first time. They were confident that Floriani was right, and no one was surprised when the count returned and declared:

"It was the child. Everything proves it."

"You have seen the shelves and the poker?"

"Yes. The shelves have been unnailed, and the poker is there yet."

But the countess exclaimed:

"You had better say it was his mother. Henriette is the guilty party. She must have compelled her son—"

"No," declared the chevalier, "the mother had nothing to do with it."

"Nonsense! they occupied the same room. The child could not have done it without the mother's knowledge."

"True, they lived in the same room, but all this happened in the adjoining room, during the night, while the mother was asleep."

"And the necklace?" said the count. "It would have been found amongst the child's things."

"Pardon me! He had been out. That morning, on which you found him reading, he had just come from school, and perhaps the commissary of police, instead of wasting his time on the innocent mother, would have been better employed in searching the child's desk amongst his school-books."

"But how do you explain those two thousand francs that Henriette received each year? Are they not evidence of her complicity?"

"If she had been an accomplice, would she have thanked you for that money? And then, was she not closely watched? But the child, being free, could easily go to a neighboring city, negotiate with some dealer, and sell him one diamond or two diamonds, as he might wish, upon condition that the money should be sent from Paris, and that proceeding could be repeated from year to year."

An indescribable anxiety oppressed the Dreux-Soubise and their guests. There was something in the tone and attitude of Floriani—something more than the chevalier's assurance which, from the beginning, had so annoyed the count. There was a touch of irony, that seemed rather hostile than sympathetic. But the count affected to laugh, as he said:

"All that is very ingenious and interesting, and I congratulate you upon your vivid imagination."

"No, not at all," replied Floriani, with the utmost gravity, "I imagine nothing. I simply describe the events as they must have occurred."

"But what do you know about them?"

"What you yourself have told me. I picture to myself the life of the mother and child down there in the country; the illness of the mother, the schemes of and inventions of the child to sell the precious stones in order to save his mother's life, or, at least, soothe her dying moments. Her illness overcomes her. She dies. Years roll on. The child becomes a man; and then—and now I will give my imagination a free rein—let us suppose that the man feels a desire to return to the home of his childhood, that he does so, and that he meets there certain people who suspect and accuse his mother . . . do you realize the sorrow and anguish of such an interview in the very house wherein the original drama was played?"

His words seemed to echo for a few seconds in the ensuing silence, and one could read upon the faces of the Count and Countess de Dreux a bewildered effort to comprehend his meaning and, at the same time, the fear and anguish of such a comprehension. The count spoke at last, and said:

"Who are you, monsieur?"

"I? The chevalier Floriani, whom you met at Palermo, and whom you have been gracious enough to invite to your house on several occasions."

"Then what does this story mean?"

"Oh! nothing at all! It is simply a pastime, so far as I am concerned. I endeavor to depict the pleasure that Henriette's son, if he still lives, would have in telling you that he was the guilty party, and that he did it because his mother was unhappy, as she was on the point of losing the place of a . . . servant, by which she lived, and because the child suffered at sight of his mother's sorrow."

He spoke with suppressed emotion, rose partially, and inclined toward the countess. There could be no doubt that the chevalier Floriani was Henriette's son. His attitude and words proclaimed it. Besides, was it not his obvious intention and desire to be recognized as such?

The count hesitated. What action would he take against the audacious guest? Ring? Provoke a scandal? Unmask the man who had once robbed him? But that was a long time ago! And who would believe that absurd story about the guilty child? No; better far to accept the situation, and pretend not to comprehend the true meaning of it. So the count, turning to Floriani, exclaimed:

"Your story is very curious, very entertaining; I enjoyed it much.

But what do you think has become of this young man, this model son? I hope he has not abandoned the career in which he made such a brilliant début."

"Oh! certainly not."

"After such a début! To steal the Queen's Necklace at six years of age; the celebrated necklace that was coveted by Marie-Antoinette!"

"And to steal it," remarked Floriani, falling in with the count's mood, "without costing him the slightest trouble, without anyone thinking to examine the condition of the window, or to observe that the window-sill was too clean—that window-sill which he had wiped in order to efface the marks he had made in the thick dust. We must admit that it was sufficient to turn the head of a boy at that age. It was all so easy. He had simply to desire the thing, and reach out his hand to get it."

"And he reached out his hand."

"Both hands," replied the chevalier, laughing.

His companions received a shock. What mystery surrounded the life of the so-called Floriani? How wonderful must have been the life of that adventurer, a thief at six years of age, and who, to-day, in search of excitement or, at most, to gratify a feeling of resentment, had come to brave his victim in her own house, audaciously, foolishly, and yet with all the grace and delicacy of a courteous guest!

He arose and approached the countess to bid her adieu. She recoiled, unconsciously. He smiled.

"Oh! Madame, you are afraid of me! Did I pursue my role of parlor-magician a step too far?"

She controlled herself, and replied, with her accustomed ease:

"Not at all, monsieur. The legend of that dutiful son interested me very much, and I am pleased to know that my necklace had such a brilliant destiny. But do you not think that the son of that woman, that Henriette, was the victim of hereditary influence in the choice of his vocation?"

He shuddered, feeling the point, and replied:

"I am sure of it; and, moreover, his natural tendency to crime must have been very strong or he would have been discouraged."

"Why so?"

"Because, as you must know, the majority of the diamonds were false. The only genuine stones were the few purchased from the English jeweler, the others having been sold, one by one, to meet the cruel necessities of life."

"It was still the Queen's Necklace, monsieur," replied the countess, haughtily, "and that is something that he, Henriette's son, could not appreciate."

"He was able to appreciate, madame, that, whether true or false, the necklace was nothing more that an object of parade, an emblem of senseless pride."

The count made a threatening gesture, but his wife stopped him.

"Monsieur," she said, "if the man to whom you allude has the slightest sense of honor—"

She stopped, intimidated by Floriani's cool manner.

"If that man has the slightest sense of honor," he repeated.

She felt that she would not gain anything by speaking to him in that manner, and in spite of her anger and indignation, trembling as she was from humiliated pride, she said to him, almost politely:

"Monsieur, the legend says that Rétaux de Villette, when in possession of the Queen's Necklace, did not disfigure the mounting. He understood that the diamonds were simply the ornament, the accessory, and that the mounting was the essential work, the creation of the artist, and he respected it accordingly. Do you think that this man had the same feeling?"

"I have no doubt that the mounting still exists. The child respected it."

"Well, monsieur, if you should happen to meet him, will you tell him that he unjustly keeps possession of a relic that is the property and pride of a certain family, and that, although the stones have been removed, the Queen's Necklace still belongs to the house of Dreux-Soubise. It belongs to us as much as our name or our honor."

The chevalier replied, simply:

"I shall tell him, madame."

He bowed to her, saluted the count and the other guests, and departed.

Four days later, the Countess de Dreux found upon the table in her chamber a red leather case bearing the Cardinal's arms. She opened it, and found the Queen's Necklace.

But as all things must, in the life of a man who strives for unity and logic, converge toward the same goal—and as a little advertising never does any harm—on the following day, the *Echo de France* published these sensational lines:

> "The Queen's Necklace, the famous historical jewelry stolen from the family of Dreux-Soubise, has been recovered by Arsène Lupin, who hastened to restore it to its rightful owner. We cannot too highly commend such a delicate and chivalrous act."

THE BLACK PEARL

A violent ringing of the bell awakened the concierge of number nine, Avenue Hoche. She pulled the doorstring, grumbling:

"I thought everybody was in. It must be three o'clock!"

"Perhaps it is someone for the doctor," muttered her husband.

At that moment, a voice inquired:

"Doctor Harel . . . what floor?"

"Third floor, left. But the doctor won't go out at night."

"He must go to-night."

The visitor entered the vestibule, ascended to the first floor, the second, the third, and, without stopping at the doctor's door, he continued to the fifth floor. There, he tried two keys. One of them fitted the lock.

"Ah! good!" he murmured, "that simplifies the business wonderfully. But before I commence work I had better arrange for my retreat. Let me see . . . have I had sufficient time to rouse the doctor and be dismissed by him? Not yet . . . a few minutes more."

At the end of ten minutes, he descended the stairs, grumbling noisily about the doctor. The concierge opened the door for him and heard it click behind him. But the door did not lock, as the man had quickly inserted a piece of iron in the lock in such a manner that the bolt could not enter. Then, quietly, he entered the house again, unknown to the concierge. In case of alarm, his retreat was assured. Noiselessly, he ascended to the fifth floor once more. In the ante-chamber, by the light of his electric lantern, he placed his hat and overcoat on one of the chairs, took a seat on another, and covered his heavy shoes with felt slippers.

"Ouf! Here I am—and how simple it was! I wonder why more people do not adopt the profitable and pleasant occupation of bur-glar. With a little care and reflection, it becomes a most delightful profession. Not too quiet and monotonous, of course, as it would then become wearisome."

He unfolded a detailed plan of the apartment.

"Let me commence by locating myself. Here, I see the vestibule in which I am sitting. On the street front, the drawing-room, the bou-doir, and dining-room. Useless to waste any time there, as it appears that the countess has a deplorable taste . . . not a bibelot of any value! . . . Now, let's get down to business! . . . Ah! here is a corridor; it must lead to the bed chambers. At a distance of three meters, I should come to the door of the wardrobe-closet which connects with the chamber of the countess." He folded his plan, extinguished his lan-tern, and proceeded down the corridor, counting his distance, thus:

"One meter . . . two meters . . . three meters . . . Here is the door. . . . Mon Dieu, how easy it is! Only a small, simple bolt now separates me from the chamber, and I know that the bolt is located exactly one meter, forty-three centimeters, from the floor. So that, thanks to a small incision I am about to make, I can soon get rid of the bolt."

He drew from his pocket the necessary instruments. Then the fol-lowing idea occurred to him:

"Suppose, by chance, the door is not bolted. I will try it first."

He turned the knob, and the door opened.

"My brave Lupin, surely fortune favors you. . . . What's to be done now? You know the situation of the rooms; you know the place in which the countess hides the black pearl. Therefore, in order to secure the black pearl, you have simply to be more silent than silence, more invisible than darkness itself."

Arsène Lupin was employed fully a half-hour in opening the second door—a glass door that led to the countess's bedchamber. But he accomplished it with so much skill and precaution, that even had the countess been awake, she would not have heard the slightest sound. According to the plan of the rooms, that he holds, he has merely to pass around a reclining chair and, beyond that, a small table close to the bed. On the table, there was a box of letter-paper, and the black pearl was concealed in that box. He stooped and crept cautiously over the carpet, following the outlines of the reclining-chair. When he reached the extremity of it, he stopped in order to repress the throbbing of his heart. Although he was not moved by any sense of fear, he found it impossible to overcome the nervous anxiety that one usually feels in the midst of profound silence. That circumstance astonished him, because he had passed through many more solemn moments without the slightest trace of emotion. No danger threatened him. Then why did his heart throb like an alarm-bell? Was it that sleeping woman who affected him? Was it the proximity of another pulsating heart?

He listened, and thought he could discern the rhythmical breathing of a person asleep. It gave him confidence, like the presence of a friend. He sought and found the armchair; then, by slow, cautious movements, advanced toward the table, feeling ahead of him with outstretched arm. His right had touched one of the feet of the table. Ah! now, he had simply to rise, take the pearl, and escape. That was fortunate, as his heart was leaping in his breast like a wild beast, and made so much noise that he feared it would waken the countess. By a powerful effort of the will, he subdued the wild throbbing of his heart, and was about to rise from the floor when his left hand encountered, lying on the floor, an object which he recognized as a candlestick—an overturned candlestick. A moment later, his hand encountered another object: a clock—one of those small traveling clocks, covered with leather.

Well! What had happened? He could not understand. That candlestick, that clock; why were those articles not in their accustomed places? Ah! what had happened in the dread silence of the night?

Suddenly a cry escaped him. He had touched—oh! some strange, unutterable thing! "No! no!" he thought, "it cannot be. It is some fantasy of my excited brain." For twenty seconds, thirty seconds, he remained motionless, terrified, his forehead bathed with perspiration, and his fingers still retained the sensation of that dreadful contact.

Making a desperate effort, he ventured to extend his arm again. Once more, his hand encountered that strange, unutterable thing. He felt it. He must feel it and find out what it is. He found that it was hair, human hair, and a human face; and that face was cold, almost icy.

However frightful the circumstances may be, a man like Arsène Lupin controls himself and commands the situation as soon as he learns what it is. So, Arsène Lupin quickly brought his lantern into use. A woman was lying before him, covered with blood. Her neck and shoulders were covered with gaping wounds. He leaned over her and made a closer examination. She was dead.

"Dead! Dead!" he repeated, with a bewildered air.

He stared at those fixed eyes, that grim mouth, that livid flesh, and that blood—all that blood which had flowed over the carpet and congealed there in thick, black spots. He arose and turned on the electric lights. Then he beheld all the marks of a desperate struggle. The bed was in a state of great disorder. On the floor, the candlestick, and the clock, with the hands pointing to twenty minutes after eleven; then, further away, an overturned chair; and, everywhere, there was blood, spots of blood and pools of blood.

"And the black pearl?" he murmured.

The box of letter-paper was in its place. He opened it, eagerly. The jewel-case was there, but it was empty.

"Fichtre!" he muttered. "You boasted of your good fortune much too soon, my friend Lupin. With the countess lying cold and dead, and the black pearl vanished, the situation is anything but pleasant. Get out of here as soon as you can, or you may get into serious trouble."

Yet, he did not move.

"Get out of here? Yes, of course. Any person would, except Arsène Lupin. He has something better to do. Now, to proceed in an orderly way. At all events, you have a clear conscience. Let us suppose that you are the commissary of police and that you are proceeding to make an inquiry concerning this affair——Yes, but in order to do that, I require a clearer brain. Mine is muddled like a ragout."

He tumbled into an armchair, with his clenched hands pressed against his burning forehead.

⸺⸺⸺⸺⸺

The murder of the Avenue Hoche is one of those which have recently surprised and puzzled the Parisian public, and, certainly, I should never have mentioned the affair if the veil of mystery had not been removed by Arsène Lupin himself. No one knew the exact truth of the case.

Who did not know—from having met her in the Bois—the fair Léotine Zalti, the once-famous cantatrice, wife and widow of the Count d'Andillot; the Zalti, whose luxury dazzled all Paris some twenty years ago; the Zalti who acquired an European reputation for the magnificence of her diamonds and pearls? It was said that she wore upon her shoulders the capital of several banking houses and the gold mines of numerous Australian companies. Skillful jewelers worked for Zalti as they had formerly wrought for kings and queens. And who does not remember the catastrophe in which all that wealth was swallowed up? Of all that marvelous collection, nothing remained except the famous black pearl. The black pearl! That is to say a fortune, if she had wished to part with it.

But she preferred to keep it, to live in a commonplace apartment with her companion, her cook, and a man-servant, rather than sell that inestimable jewel. There was a reason for it; a reason she was not afraid to disclose: the black pearl was the gift of an emperor! Almost ruined, and reduced to the most mediocre existence, she remained faithful to the companion of her happy and brilliant youth. The black pearl never left her possession. She wore it during the day, and, at night, concealed it in a place known to her alone.

All these facts, being republished in the columns of the public press, served to stimulate curiosity; and, strange to say, but quite obvious to those who have the key to the mystery, the arrest of the presumed assassin only complicated the question and prolonged the excitement. Two days later, the newspapers published the following item:

"Information has reached us of the arrest of Victor Danègre, the servant of the Countess d'Andillot. The evidence against him is clear and convincing. On the silken sleeve of his liveried waistcoat, which chief detective Dudouis found in his garret between the mattresses of his bed, several spots of blood were discovered. In addition, a cloth-covered button was missing from that garment, and this button was found beneath the bed of the victim.

"It is supposed that, after dinner, in place of going to his own room, Danègre slipped into the wardrobe-closet, and, through the glass door, had seen the countess hide the precious black pearl. This is simply a theory, as yet unverified by any evidence. There is, also, another obscure point. At seven o'clock in the morning, Danègre went to the tobacco-shop on the Boulevard de Courcelles; the concierge and the shop-keeper both affirm this fact. On the other hand, the countess's companion and cook, who sleep at the end of the hall, both declare that, when they arose at eight o'clock, the door of the antechamber and the door of the kitchen were locked. These two persons have been in the service of the countess for twenty years, and are above suspicion. The question is: How did Danègre leave the apartment? Did he have another key? These are matters that the police will investigate."

As a matter of fact, the police investigation threw no light on the mystery. It was learned that Victor Danègre was a dangerous criminal, a drunkard, and a debauchee. But, as they proceeded with the investigation, the mystery deepened and new complications arose. In the first place, a young woman, Mlle. De Sinclèves, the cousin and sole heiress of the countess, declared that the countess, a month before her death, had written a letter to her and in it described the manner in which the black pearl was concealed. The letter disappeared the day after she received it. Who had stolen it?

Again, the concierge related how she had opened the door for a person who had inquired for Doctor Harel. On being questioned, the doctor testified that no one had rung his bell. Then who was that person? An accomplice?

The theory of an accomplice was thereupon adopted by the press and public, and also by Ganimard, the famous detective.

"Lupin is at the bottom of this affair," he said to the judge.

"Bah!" exclaimed the judge, "you have Lupin on the brain. You see him everywhere."

"I see him everywhere, because he is everywhere."

"Say rather that you see him every time you encounter something you cannot explain. Besides, you overlook the fact that the crime was committed at twenty minutes past eleven in the evening, as is shown by the clock, while the nocturnal visit, mentioned by the concierge, occurred at three o'clock in the morning."

Officers of the law frequently form a hasty conviction as to the guilt of a suspected person, and then distort all subsequent discoveries to conform to their established theory. The deplorable antecedents of Victor Danègre, habitual criminal, drunkard, and rake, influenced the judge, and despite the fact that nothing new was discovered in corroboration of the early clues, his official opinion remained firm and unshaken. He closed his investigation, and, a few weeks later, the trial commenced. It proved to be slow and tedious. The judge was listless, and the public prosecutor presented the case in a careless manner. Under those circumstances, Danègre's counsel had an easy task. He pointed out the defects and inconsistencies of the case for the prosecution, and argued that the evidence was quite insufficient to convict the accused. Who had made the key, the indispensable key without which Danègre, on leaving the apartment, could not have locked the door behind him? Who had ever seen such a key, and what had become of it? Who had seen the assassin's knife, and where is it now?

"In any event," argued the prisoner's counsel, "the prosecution must prove, beyond any reasonable doubt, that the prisoner committed the murder. The prosecution must show that the mysterious individual who entered the house at three o'clock in the morning is not the guilty party. To be sure, the clock indicated eleven o'clock. But what of that? I contend, that proves nothing. The assassin could turn the hands of the clock to any hour he pleased, and thus deceive us in regard to the exact hour of the crime."

Victor Danègre was acquitted.

He left the prison on Friday about dusk in the evening, weak and depressed by his six months' imprisonment. The inquisition, the solitude, the trial, the deliberations of the jury, combined to fill him with a nervous fear. At night, he had been afflicted with terrible nightmares and haunted by weird visions of the scaffold. He was a mental and physical wreck.

Under the assumed name of Anatole Dufour, he rented a small room on the heights of Montmartre, and lived by doing odd jobs wherever he could find them. He led a pitiful existence. Three times, he obtained regular employment, only to be recognized and then discharged. Sometimes, he had an idea that men were following him—detectives, no doubt, who were seeking to trap and denounce him. He could almost feel the strong hand of the law clutching him by the collar.

One evening, as he was eating his dinner at a neighboring restaurant, a man entered and took a seat at the same table. He was a person about forty years of age, and wore a frock-coat of doubtful cleanliness. He ordered soup, vegetables, and a bottle of wine. After he had finished his soup, he turned his eyes on Danègre, and gazed at him intently. Danègre winced. He was certain that this was one of the men who had been following him for several weeks. What did he want? Danègre tried to rise, but failed. His limbs refused to support him. The man poured himself a glass of wine, and then filled Danègre's glass. The man raised his glass, and said:

"To your health, Victor Danègre."

Victor started in alarm, and stammered:

"I! . . . I! . . . no, no . . . I swear to you . . ."

"You will swear what? That you are not yourself? The servant of the countess?"

"What servant? My name is Dufour. Ask the proprietor."

"Yes, Anatole Dufour to the proprietor of this restaurant, but Victor Danègre to the officers of the law."

"That's not true! Someone has lied to you."

The new-comer took a card from his pocket and handed it to Victor, who read on it: "Grimaudan, ex-inspector of the detective force. Private business transacted." Victor shuddered as he said:

"You are connected with the police?"

"No, not now, but I have a liking for the business and I continue to work at it in a manner more—profitable. From time to time I strike upon a golden opportunity—such as your case presents."

"My case?"

"Yes, yours. I assure you it is a most promising affair, provided you are inclined to be reasonable."

"But if I am not reasonable?"

"Oh! my good fellow, you are not in a position to refuse me anything I may ask."

"What is it . . . you want?" stammered Victor, fearfully.

"Well, I will inform you in a few words. I am sent by Mademoiselle de Sinclèves, the heiress of the Countess d'Andillot."

"What for?"

"To recover the black pearl."

"Black pearl?"

"That you stole."

"But I haven't got it."

"You have it."

"If I had, then I would be the assassin."

"You are the assassin."

Danègre showed a forced smile.

"Fortunately for me, monsieur, the Assizecourt was not of your opinion. The jury returned an unanimous verdict of acquittal. And when a man has a clear conscience and twelve good men in his favor—"

The ex-inspector seized him by the arm and said:

"No fine phrases, my boy. Now, listen to me and weigh my words carefully. You will find they are worthy of your consideration. Now, Danègre, three weeks before the murder, you abstracted the cook's key to the servants' door, and had a duplicate key made by a locksmith named Outard, 244 Rue Oberkampf."

"It's a lie—it's a lie!" growled Victor. "No person has seen that key. There is no such key."

"Here it is."

After a silence, Grimaudan continued:

"You killed the countess with a knife purchased by you at the Bazar de la Republique on the same day as you ordered the duplicate key. It has a triangular blade with a groove running from end to end."

"That is all nonsense. You are simply guessing at something you don't know. No one ever saw the knife."

"Here it is."

Victor Danègre recoiled. The ex-inspector continued:

"There are some spots of rust upon it. Shall I tell you how they came there?"

"Well! . . . you have a key and a knife. Who can prove that they belong to me?"

"The locksmith, and the clerk from whom you bought the knife. I have already refreshed their memories, and, when you confront them, they cannot fail to recognize you."

His speech was dry and hard, with a tone of firmness and precision. Danègre was trembling with fear, and yet he struggled desperately to maintain an air of indifference.

"Is that all the evidence you have?"

"Oh! no, not at all. I have plenty more. For instance, after the crime, you went out the same way you had entered. But, in the center of the wardrobe-room, being seized by some sudden fear, you leaned against the wall for support."

"How do you know that? No one could know such a thing," argued the desperate man.

"The police know nothing about it, of course. They never think of lighting a candle and examining the walls. But if they had done so, they would have found on the white plaster a faint red spot, quite distinct, however, to trace in it the imprint of your thumb which you had pressed against the wall while it was wet with blood. Now, as you are well aware, under the Bertillon system, thumb-marks are one of the principal means of identification."

Victor Danègre was livid; great drops of perspiration rolled down his face and fell upon the table. He gazed, with a wild look, at the strange man who had narrated the story of his crime as faithfully as if he had been an invisible witness to it. Overcome and powerless, Victor bowed his head. He felt that it was useless to struggle against this marvelous man. So he said:

"How much will you give me, if I give you the pearl?"

"Nothing."

"Oh! you are joking! Or do you mean that I should give you an article worth thousands and hundreds of thousands and get nothing in return?"

"You will get your life. Is that nothing?"

The unfortunate man shuddered. Then Grimaudan added, in a milder tone:

"Come, Danègre, that pearl has no value in your hands. It is quite impossible for you to sell it; so what is the use of your keeping it?"

"There are pawnbrokers . . . and, some day, I will be able to get something for it."

"But that day may be too late."

"Why?"

"Because by that time you may be in the hands of the police, and, with the evidence that I can furnish—the knife, the key, the thumb-mark—what will become of you?"

Victor rested his head on his hands and reflected. He felt that he was lost, irremediably lost, and, at the same time, a sense of weariness and depression overcame him. He murmured, faintly:

"When must I give it to you?"

"To-night—within an hour."

"If I refuse?"

"If you refuse, I shall post this letter to the Procureur of the Republic; in which letter Mademoiselle de Sinclèves denounces you as the assassin."

Danègre poured out two glasses of wine which he drank in rapid succession, then, rising, said:

"Pay the bill, and let us go. I have had enough of the cursed affair."

Night had fallen. The two men walked down the Rue Lepic and followed the exterior boulevards in the direction of the Place de l'Etoile. They pursued their way in silence; Victor had a stooping carriage and a dejected face. When they reached the Parc Monceau, he said:

"We are near the house."

"Parbleu! You only left the house once, before your arrest, and that was to go to the tobacco-shop."

"Here it is," said Danègre, in a dull voice.

They passed along the garden wall of the countess's house, and crossed a street on a corner of which stood the tobacco-shop. A few steps further on, Danègre stopped; his limbs shook beneath him, and he sank to a bench.

"Well! what now?" demanded his companion.

"It is there."

"Where? Come, now, no nonsense!"

"There—in front of us."

"Where?"

"Between two paving-stones."

"Which?"

"Look for it."

"Which stones?"

Victor made no reply.

"Ah; I see!" exclaimed Grimaudan, "you want me to pay for the information."

"No . . . but . . . I am afraid I will starve to death."

"So! that is why you hesitate. Well, I'll not be hard on you. How much do you want?"

"Enough to buy a steerage pass to America."

"All right."

"And a hundred francs to keep me until I get work there."

"You shall have two hundred. Now, speak."

"Count the paving-stones to the right from the sewer-hole. The pearl is between the twelfth and thirteenth."

"In the gutter?"

"Yes, close to the sidewalk."

Grimaudan glanced around to see if anyone were looking. Some tramcars and pedestrians were passing. But, bah, they will not suspect anything. He opened his pocketknife and thrust it between the twelfth and thirteenth stones.

"And if it is not there?" he said to Victor.

"It must be there, unless someone saw me stoop down and hide it."

Could it be possible that the back pearl had been cast into the mud and filth of the gutter to be picked up by the first comer? The black pearl—a fortune!

"How far down?" he asked.

"About ten centimeters."

He dug up the wet earth. The point of his knife struck something.

He enlarged the hole with his finger. Then he abstracted the black pearl from its filthy hiding-place.

"Good! Here are your two hundred francs. I will send you the ticket for America."

On the following day, this article was published in the *Echo de France*, and was copied by the leading newspapers throughout the world:

"Yesterday, the famous black pearl came into the possession of Arsène Lupin, who recovered it from the murderer of the Countess d'Andillot. In a short time, facsimiles of that precious jewel will be exhibited in London, St. Petersburg, Calcutta, Buenos Ayres, and New York.

"Arsène Lupin will be pleased to consider all propositions submitted to him through his agents."

iIIIIIIIIIIIIIIIIIIIIIII

"And that is how crime is always punished and virtue rewarded," said Arsène Lupin, after he had told me the foregoing history of the black pearl.

"And that is how you, under the assumed name of Grimaudan, ex-inspector of detectives, were chosen by fate to deprive the criminal of the benefit of his crime."

"Exactly. And I confess that the affair gives me infinite satisfaction and pride. The forty minutes that I passed in the apartment of the Countess d'Andillot, after learning of her death, were the most thrilling and absorbing moments of my life. In those forty minutes, involved as I was in a most dangerous plight, I calmly studied the scene of the murder and reached the conclusion that the crime must have been committed by one of the house servants. I also decided that, in order to get the pearl, that servant must be arrested, and so I left the waistcoat button; it was necessary, also, for me to hold some convincing evidence of his guilt, so I carried away the knife which I found upon the floor, and the key which I found in the lock. I closed and locked the door, and erased the finger-marks from the plaster in the wardrobe-closet. In my opinion, that was one of those flashes—"

"Of genius," I said, interrupting.

"Of genius, if you wish. But, I flatter myself, it would not have occurred to the average mortal. To frame, instantly, the two elements of the problem—an arrest and an acquittal; to make use of the formidable machinery of the law to crush and humble my victim, and reduce him to a condition in which, when free, he would be certain to fall into the trap I was laying for him!"

"Poor devil—"

"Poor devil, do you say? Victor Danègre, the assassin! He might have descended to the lowest depths of vice and crime, if he had retained the black pearl. Now, he lives! Think of that: Victor Danègre is alive!"

"And you have the black pearl."

He took it out of one of the secret pockets of his wallet, examined it, gazed at it tenderly, and caressed it with loving fingers, and sighed, as he said:

"What cold Russian prince, what vain and foolish rajah may some day possess this priceless treasure! Or, perhaps, some American millionaire is destined to become the owner of this morsel of exquisite beauty that once adorned the fair bosom of Leontine Zalti, the Countess d'Andillot."

SHERLOCK HOLMES ARRIVES TOO LATE

"It is really remarkable, Velmont, what a close resemblance you bear to Arsène Lupin!"

"How do you know?"

"Oh! like everyone else, from photographs, no two of which are alike, but each of them leaves the impression of a face . . . something like yours."

Horace Velmont displayed some vexation.

"Quite so, my dear Devanne. And, believe me, you are not the first one who has noticed it."

"It is so striking," persisted Devanne, "that if you had not been recommended to me by my cousin d'Estevan, and if you were not the celebrated artist whose beautiful marine views I so admire, I have no doubt I should have warned the police of your presence in Dieppe."

This sally was greeted with an outburst of laughter. The large dining-hall of the Château de Thibermesnil contained on this occasion, besides Velmont, the following guests: Father Gélis, the parish priest, and a dozen officers whose regiments were quartered in the vicinity and who had accepted the invitation of the banker Georges Devanne and his mother. One of the officers then remarked:

"I understand that an exact description of Arsène Lupin has been furnished to all the police along this coast since his daring exploit on the Paris-Havre express."

"I suppose so," said Devanne. "That was three months ago; and a week later, I made the acquaintance of our friend Velmont at the casino, and, since then, he has honored me with several visits—an agreeable preamble to a more serious visit that he will pay me one of these days—or, rather, one of these nights."

This speech evoked another round of laughter, and the guests then passed into the ancient "Hall of the Guards," a vast room with a high ceiling, which occupied the entire lower part of the Tour Guillaume—William's Tower—and wherein Georges Devanne had collected the incomparable treasures which the lords of Thibermesnil had accumulated through many centuries. It contained ancient chests, credences, andirons, and chandeliers. The stone walls were overhung with magnificent tapestries. The deep embrasures of the four windows were furnished with benches, and the Gothic windows were composed of small panes of colored glass set in a leaden frame. Between the door and the window to the left stood an immense bookcase of Renaissance style, on the pediment of which, in letters of gold, was the word "Thibermesnil," and, below it, the proud family device: "Fais ce que veulx" (Do what thou wishest). When the guests had lighted their cigars, Devanne resumed the conversation.

"And remember, Velmont, you have no time to lose; in fact, to-night is the last chance you will have."

"How so?" asked the painter, who appeared to regard the affair as a joke. Devanne was about to reply, when his mother mentioned to him to keep silent, but the excitement of the occasion and a desire to interest his guests urged him to speak.

"Bah!" he murmured. "I can tell it now. It won't do any harm."

The guests drew closer, and he commenced to speak with the satisfied air of a man who has an important announcement to make.

"To-morrow afternoon at four o'clock, Sherlock Holmes, the famous English detective, for whom such a thing as mystery does not exist; Sherlock Holmes, the most remarkable solver of enigmas the world has ever known, that marvelous man who would seem to be the creation of a romantic novelist—Sherlock Holmes will be my guest!"

Immediately, Devanne was the target of numerous eager questions.

"Is Sherlock Holmes really coming?" "Is it so serious as that?" "Is Arsène Lupin really in this neighborhood?"

"Arsène Lupin and his band are not far away. Besides the robbery of the Baron Cahorn, he is credited with the thefts at Montigny, Gruchet, and Crasville. And now it is my turn."

"Has he sent you a warning, as he did to Baron Cahorn?"

"No," replied Devanne, "he can't work the same trick twice."

"What then?"

"I will show you."

He rose, and pointing to a small empty space between the two enormous folios on one of the shelves of the bookcase, he said:

"There used to be a book there—a book of the sixteenth century entitled *Chronique de Thibermesnil*, which contained the history of the castle since its construction by Duke Rollo on the site of a former feudal fortress. There were three engraved plates in the book; one of which was a general view of the whole estate; another, the plan of the buildings; and the third—I call your attention to it, particularly—the third was the sketch of a subterranean passage, an entrance to which is outside the first line of ramparts, while the other end of the passage is here, in this very room. Well, that book disappeared a month ago."

"The deuce!" said Velmont, "that looks bad. But it doesn't seem to be a sufficient reason for sending for Sherlock Holmes."

"Certainly, that was not sufficient in itself, but another incident happened that gives the disappearance of the book a special significance. There was another copy of this book in the National Library at Paris, and the two books differed in certain details relating to the subterranean passage; for instance, each of them contained drawings and annotations, not printed, but written in ink and more or less effaced. I knew those facts, and I knew that the exact location of the passage could be determined only by a comparison of the two books. Now, the day after my book disappeared, the book was called for in the National Library by a reader who carried it away, and no one knows how the theft was effected."

The guests uttered many exclamations of surprise.

"Certainly, the affair looks serious," said one.

"Well, the police investigated the matter, and, as usual, discovered no clue whatever."

"They never do, when Arsène Lupin is concerned in it."

"Exactly; and so I decided to ask the assistance of Sherlock Holmes, who replied that he was ready and anxious to enter the lists with Arsène Lupin."

"What glory for Arsène Lupin!" said Velmont. "But if our national thief, as they call him, has no evil designs on your castle, Sherlock Holmes will have his trip in vain."

"There are other things that will interest him, such as the discovery of the subterranean passage."

"But you told us that one end of the passage was outside the ramparts and the other was in this very room!"

"Yes, but in what part of the room? The line which represents the passage on the charts ends here, with a small circle marked with the letters 'T.G.,' which no doubt stand for 'Tour Guillaume.' But the tower is round, and who can tell the exact spot at which the passage touches the tower?"

Devanne lighted a second cigar and poured himself a glass of Benedictine. His guests pressed him with questions and he was pleased to observe the interest that his remarks had created. Then he continued:

"The secret is lost. No one knows it. The legend is to the effect that the former lords of the castle transmitted the secret from father to son on their deathbeds, until Geoffroy, the last of the race, was beheaded during the Revolution in his nineteenth year."

"That is over a century ago. Surely, someone has looked for it since that time?"

"Yes, but they failed to find it. After I purchased the castle, I made a diligent search for it, but without success. You must remember that this tower is surrounded by water and connected with the castle only by a bridge; consequently, the passage must be underneath the old moat. The plan that was in the book in the National Library showed a series of stairs with a total of forty-eight steps, which indicates a depth of more than ten meters. You see, the mystery lies within the walls of this room, and yet I dislike to tear them down."

"Is there nothing to show where it is?"

"Nothing."

"Mon. Devanne, we should turn our attention to the two quotations," suggested Father Gélis.

"Oh!" exclaimed Mon. Devanne, laughing, "our worthy father is fond of reading memoirs and delving into the musty archives of the castle. Everything relating to Thibermesnil interests him greatly. But the quotations that he mentions only serve to complicate the mystery. He has read somewhere that two kings of France have known the key to the puzzle."

"Two kings of France! Who were they?"

"Henry the Fourth and Louis the Sixteenth. And the legend runs like this: On the eve of the battle of Arques, Henry the Fourth spent the night in this castle. At eleven o'clock in the evening, Louise de Tancarville, the prettiest woman in Normandy, was brought into the castle through the subterranean passage by Duke Edgard, who, at the same time, informed the king of the secret passage. Afterward, the king confided the secret to his minister Sully, who, in turn, relates the story in his book, *Royales Economies d'Etat*, without making any comment upon it, but linking with it this incomprehensible sentence: 'Turn one eye on the bee that shakes, the other eye will lead to God!'"

After a brief silence, Velmont laughed and said:

"Certainly, it doesn't throw a dazzling light upon the subject."

"No; but Father Gélis claims that Sully concealed the key to the mystery in this strange sentence in order to keep the secret from the secretaries to whom he dictated his memoirs."

"That is an ingenious theory," said Velmont.

"Yes, and it may be nothing more; I cannot see that it throws any light on the mysterious riddle."

"And was it also to receive the visit of a lady that Louis the Sixteenth caused the passage to be opened?"

"I don't know," said Mon. Devanne. "All I can say is that the king stopped here one night in 1784, and that the famous Iron Casket found in the Louvre contained a paper bearing these words in the king's own writing: 'Thibermesnil 3-4-11.'"

Horace Velmont laughed heartily, and exclaimed:

"At last! And now that we have the magic key, where is the man who can fit it to the invisible lock?"

"Laugh as much as you please, monsieur," said Father Gélis, "but I am confident the solution is contained in those two sentences, and some day we will find a man able to interpret them."

"Sherlock Holmes is the man," said Mon. Devanne, "unless Arsène Lupin gets ahead of him. What is your opinion, Velmont?"

Velmont arose, placed his hand on Devanne's shoulder, and declared:

"I think that the information furnished by your book and the book of the National Library was deficient in a very important detail which you have now supplied. I thank you for it."

"What is it?"

"The missing key. Now that I have it, I can go to work at once," said Velmont.

"Of course; without losing a minute," said Devanne, smiling.

"Not even a second!" replied Velmont. "To-night, before the arrival of Sherlock Holmes, I must plunder your castle."

"You have no time to lose. Oh! by the way, I can drive you over this evening."

"To Dieppe?"

"Yes. I am going to meet Monsieur and Madame d'Androl and a young lady of their acquaintance who are to arrive by the midnight train."

Then addressing the officers, Devanne added: "Gentlemen, I shall expect to see all of you at breakfast to-morrow."

The invitation was accepted. The company dispersed, and a few moments later Devanne and Velmont were speeding toward Dieppe in an automobile. Devanne dropped the artist in front of the Casino, and proceeded to the railway station. At twelve o'clock his friends alighted from the train. A half hour later the automobile was at the entrance to the castle. At one o'clock, after a light supper, they retired. The lights were extinguished, and the castle was enveloped in the darkness and silence of the night.

The moon appeared through a rift in the clouds, and filled the drawing-room with its bright white light. But only for a moment. Then the moon again retired behind its ethereal draperies, and darkness and silence reigned supreme. No sound could be heard, save the monotonous ticking of the clock. It struck two, and then continued its endless repetitions of the seconds. Then, three o'clock.

Suddenly, something clicked, like the opening and closing of a signal-disc that warns the passing train. A thin stream of light flashed to every corner of the room, like an arrow that leaves behind it a trail of light. It shot forth from the central fluting of a column that supported the pediment of the bookcase. It rested for a moment on the panel opposite like a glittering circle of burnished silver, then flashed in all directions like a guilty eye that scrutinizes every shadow. It disappeared for a short time, but burst forth again as a whole section of the bookcase revolved on a pivot and disclosed a large opening like a vault.

A man entered, carrying an electric lantern. He was followed by a second man, who carried a coil of rope and various tools. The leader inspected the room, listened a moment, and said:

"Call the others."

Then eight men, stout fellows with resolute faces, entered the room, and immediately commenced to remove the furnishings. Arsène Lupin passed quickly from one piece of furniture to another, examined each, and, according to its size or artistic value, he directed his men to take it or leave it. If ordered to be taken, it was carried to the gaping mouth of the tunnel, and ruthlessly thrust into the bowels of the earth. Such was the fate of six armchairs, six small Louis XV chairs, a quantity of Aubusson tapestries, some candelabra, paintings by Fragonard and Nattier, a bust by Houdon, and some statuettes. Sometimes, Lupin would linger before a beautiful chest or a superb picture, and sigh:

"That is too heavy . . . too large . . . what a pity!"

In forty minutes the room was dismantled; and it had been accomplished in such an orderly manner and with as little noise as if the various articles had been packed and wadded for the occasion.

Lupin said to the last man who departed by way of the tunnel:

"You need not come back. You understand, that as soon as the auto-van is loaded, you are to proceed to the grange at Roquefort."

"But you, patron?"

"Leave me the motor-cycle."

When the man had disappeared, Arsène Lupin pushed the section of the bookcase back into its place, carefully effaced the traces of the men's footsteps, raised a portière, and entered a gallery, which was the only means of communication between the tower and the castle. In the center of this gallery there was a glass cabinet which had attracted Lupin's attentions. It contained a valuable collection of watches, snuff-boxes, rings, chatelaines, and miniatures of rare and beautiful workmanship. He forced the lock with a small jimmy, and experienced a great pleasure in handling those gold and silver ornaments, those exquisite and delicate works of art.

He carried a large linen bag, specially prepared for the removal of such knick-knacks. He filled it. Then he filled the pockets of his coat, waistcoat, and trousers. And he was just placing over his left arm a number of pearl reticules when he heard a slight sound. He listened. No, he was not deceived. The noise continued. Then he remembered that, at one end of the gallery, there was a stairway leading to an unoccupied apartment, but which was probably occupied that night by the young lady whom Mon. Devanne had brought from Dieppe with his other visitors.

Immediately he extinguished his lantern, and had scarcely gained the friendly shelter of a window-embrasure, when the door at the top of the stairway was opened and a feeble light illuminated the gallery. He could feel—for, concealed by a curtain, he could not see—that a woman was cautiously descending the upper steps of the stairs. He hoped she would come no closer. Yet, she continued to descend, and even advanced some distance into the room. Then she uttered a faint cry. No doubt she had discovered the broken and dismantled cabinet.

She advanced again. Now he could smell the perfume, and hear the throbbing of her heart as she drew closer to the window where he was concealed. She passed so close that her skirt brushed against the window-curtain, and Lupin felt that she suspected the presence of another, behind her, in the shadow, within reach of her hand. He thought: "She is afraid. She will go away." But she did not go. The candle, that she carried in her trembling hand, grew brighter. She turned, hesitated a moment, appeared to listen, then suddenly drew aside the curtain.

They stood face to face. Arsène was astounded. He murmured, involuntarily:

"You—you—mademoiselle."

It was Miss Nelly. Miss Nelly! his fellow passenger on the transatlantic steamer, who had been the subject of his dreams on that memorable voyage, who had been a witness to his arrest, and who, rather than betray him, had dropped into the water the Kodak in which he had concealed the bank-notes and diamonds. Miss Nelly! that charming creature, the memory of whose face had sometimes cheered, sometimes saddened the long hours of imprisonment.

It was such an unexpected encounter that brought them face to face in that castle at that hour of the night, that they could not move, nor utter a word; they were amazed, hypnotized, each at the sudden apparition of the other. Trembling with emotion, Miss Nelly staggered to a seat. He remained standing in front of her.

Gradually, he realized the situation and conceived the impression he must have produced at that moment with his arms laden with knick-knacks, and his pockets and a linen sack overflowing with plunder. He was overcome with confusion, and he actually blushed to find himself in the position of a thief caught in the act. To her, henceforth, he was a thief, a man who puts his hand in another's pocket, who steals into houses and robs people while they sleep.

A watch fell upon the floor; then another. These were followed by other articles which slipped from his grasp one by one. Then, actuated by a sudden decision, he dropped the other articles into an armchair, emptied his pockets, and unpacked his sack. He felt very uncomfortable in Nelly's presence, and stepped toward her with the intention of speaking to her, but she shuddered, rose quickly, and fled toward the salon. The portière closed behind her. He followed her. She was standing trembling and amazed at the sight of the devastated room. He said to her, at once:

"To-morrow, at three o'clock, everything will be returned. The furniture will be brought back."

She made no reply, so he repeated:

"I promise it. To-morrow, at three o'clock. Nothing in the world could induce me to break that promise. . . . To-morrow, at three o'clock."

Then followed a long silence that he dared not break, whilst the agitation of the young girl caused him a feeling of genuine regret. Quietly, without a word, he turned away, thinking: "I hope she will go away. I can't endure her presence." But the young girl suddenly spoke, and stammered:

"Listen . . . footsteps . . . I hear someone . . ."

He looked at her with astonishment. She seemed to be over-whelmed by the thought of approaching peril.

"I don't hear anything," he said.

"But you must go—you must escape!"

"Why should I go?"

"Because—you must. Oh! do not remain here another minute. Go!"

She ran, quickly, to the door leading to the gallery and listened. No, there was no one there. Perhaps the noise was outside. She waited a moment, then returned reassured.

But Arsène Lupin had disappeared.

As soon as Mon. Devanne was informed of the pillage of his castle, he said to himself: It was Velmont who did it, and Velmont is Arsène Lupin. That theory explained everything, and there was no other plausible explanation. And yet the idea seemed preposterous. It was ridiculous to suppose that Velmont was anyone else than Velmont, the famous artist, and club-fellow of his cousin d'Estevan. So, when the captain of the gendarmes arrived to investigate the affair, Devanne did not even think of mentioning his absurd theory.

Throughout the forenoon there was a lively commotion at the castle. The gendarmes, the local police, the chief of police from Dieppe, the villagers, all circulated to and fro in the halls, examining every nook and corner that was open to their inspection. The approach of the maneuvering troops, the rattling fire of the musketry, added to the picturesque character of the scene.

The preliminary search furnished no clue. Neither the doors nor windows showed any signs of having been disturbed. Consequently, the removal of the goods must have been effected by means of the secret passage. Yet, there were no indications of footsteps on the floor, nor any unusual marks upon the walls.

Their investigations revealed, however, one curious fact that denoted the whimsical character of Arsène Lupin: the famous Chronique of the sixteenth century had been restored to its accustomed place in the library and, beside it, there was a similar book, which was none other than the volume stolen from the National Library.

At eleven o'clock the military officers arrived. Devanne welcomed them with his usual gayety; for, no matter how much chagrin he might suffer from the loss of his artistic treasures, his great wealth enabled him to bear his loss philosophically. His guests, Monsieur and Madame d'Androl and Miss Nelly, were introduced; and it was then noticed that one of the expected guests had not arrived. It was Horace Velmont. Would he come? His absence had awakened the suspicions of Mon. Devanne. But at twelve o'clock he arrived. Devanne exclaimed:

"Ah! here you are!"

"Why, am I not punctual?" asked Velmont.

"Yes, and I am surprised that you are . . . after such a busy night! I suppose you know the news?"

"What news?"

"You have robbed the castle."

"Nonsense!" exclaimed Velmont, smiling.

"Exactly as I predicted. But, first escort Miss Underdown to the dining-room. Mademoiselle, allow me—"

He stopped, as he remarked the extreme agitation of the young girl. Then, recalling the incident, he said:

"Ah! of course, you met Arsène Lupin on the steamer, before his arrest, and you are astonished at the resemblance. Is that it?"

She did not reply. Velmont stood before her, smiling. He bowed. She took his proffered arm. He escorted her to her place, and took his seat opposite her. During the breakfast, the conversation related exclusively to Arsène Lupin, the stolen goods, the secret passage, and Sherlock Holmes. It was only at the close of the repast, when the conversation had drifted to other subjects, that Velmont took any part in it. Then he was, by turns, amusing and grave, talkative and pensive. And all his remarks seemed to be directed to the young girl. But she, quite absorbed, did not appear to hear them.

Coffee was served on the terrace overlooking the court of honor and the flower garden in front of the principal façade. The regimental band played on the lawn, and scores of soldiers and peasants wandered through the park.

Miss Nelly had not forgotten, for one moment, Lupin's solemn promise: "To-morrow, at three o'clock, everything will be returned."

At three o'clock! And the hands of the great clock in the right wing of the castle now marked twenty minutes to three. In spite of herself, her eyes wandered to the clock every minute. She also watched Velmont, who was calmly swinging to and fro in a comfortable rocking chair.

Ten minutes to three!... Five minutes to three!... Nelly was impatient and anxious. Was it possible that Arsène Lupin would carry out his promise at the appointed hour, when the castle, the courtyard, and the park were filled with people, and at the very moment when the officers of the law were pursuing their investigations? And yet... Arsène Lupin had given her his solemn promise. "It will be exactly as he said," thought she, so deeply was she impressed with the authority, energy, and assurance of that remarkable man. To her, it no longer assumed the form of a miracle, but, on the contrary, a natural incident that must occur in the ordinary course of events. She blushed, and turned her head.

Three o'clock! The great clock struck slowly: one . . . two . . . three. . . . Horace Velmont took out his watch, glanced at the clock, then returned the watch to his pocket. A few seconds passed in silence; and then the crowd in the courtyard parted to give passage to two wagons, that had just entered the park-gate, each drawn by two horses. They were army-wagons, such as are used for the transportation of provisions, tents, and other necessary military stores. They stopped in front of the main entrance, and a commissary-sergeant leaped from one of the wagons and inquired for Mon. Devanne. A moment later, that gentleman emerged from the house, descended the steps, and, under the canvas covers of the wagons, beheld his furniture, pictures, and ornaments carefully packaged and arranged.

When questioned, the sergeant produced an order that he had received from the officer of the day. By that order, the second company of the fourth battalion were commanded to proceed to the crossroads of Halleux in the forest of Arques, gather up the furniture and other articles deposited there, and deliver same to Monsieur Georges Devanne, owner of the Thibermesnil castle, at three o'clock. Signed: Col. Beauvel.

"At the crossroads," explained the sergeant, "we found everything ready, lying on the grass, guarded by some passers-by. It seemed very strange, but the order was imperative."

One of the officers examined the signature. He declared it a forgery; but a clever imitation. The wagons were unloaded, and the goods restored to their proper places in the castle.

During this commotion, Nelly had remained alone at the extreme end of the terrace, absorbed by confused and distracted thoughts. Suddenly, she observed Velmont approaching her. She would have avoided him, but the balustrade that surrounded the terrace cut off her retreat. She was cornered. She could not move. A gleam of sunshine, passing through the scant foliage of a bamboo, lighted up her beautiful golden hair. Someone spoke to her in a low voice:

"Have I not kept my promise?"

Arsène Lupin stood close to her. No one else was near. He repeated, in a calm, soft voice:

"Have I not kept my promise?"

He expected a word of thanks, or at least some slight movement that would betray her interest in the fulfillment of his promise. But she remained silent.

Her scornful attitude annoyed Arsène Lupin; and he realized the vast distance that separated him from Miss Nelly, now that she had learned the truth. He would gladly have justified himself in her eyes, or at least pleaded extenuating circumstances, but he perceived the absurdity and futility of such an attempt. Finally, dominated by a surging flood of memories, he murmured:

"Ah! how long ago that was! You remember the long hours on the deck of the *Provence*. Then, you carried a rose in your hand, a white rose like the one you carry to-day. I asked you for it. You pretended you did not hear me. After you had gone away, I found the rose—forgotten, no doubt—and I kept it."

She made no reply. She seemed to be far away. He continued:

"In memory of those happy hours, forget what you have learned since. Separate the past from the present. Do not regard me as the man you saw last night, but look at me, if only for a moment, as you did in those far-off days when I was Bernard d'Andrezy, for a short time. Will you, please?"

She raised her eyes and looked at him as he had requested. Then, without saying a word, she pointed to a ring he was wearing on his forefinger. Only the ring was visible; but the setting, which was turned toward the palm of his hand, consisted of a magnificent ruby. Arsène Lupin blushed. The ring belonged to Georges Devanne. He smiled bitterly, and said:

"You are right. Nothing can be changed. Arsène Lupin is now and always will be Arsène Lupin. To you, he cannot be even so much as a memory. Pardon me . . . I should have known that any attention I may now offer you is simply an insult. Forgive me."

He stepped aside, hat in hand. Nelly passed before him. He was inclined to detain her and beseech her forgiveness. But his courage failed, and he contented himself by following her with his eyes, as he had done when she descended the gangway to the pier at New York. She mounted the steps leading to the door, and disappeared within the house. He saw her no more.

A cloud obscured the sun. Arsène Lupin stood watching the imprints of her tiny feet in the sand. Suddenly, he gave a start. Upon the box which contained the bamboo, beside which Nelly had been standing, he saw the rose, the white rose which he had desired but dared not ask for. Forgotten, no doubt—it, also! But how—designedly or through distraction? He seized it eagerly. Some of its petals fell to the ground. He picked them up, one by one, like precious relics.

"Come!" he said to himself, "I have nothing more to do here. I must think of my safety, before Sherlock Holmes arrives."

<hr />

The park was deserted, but some gendarmes were stationed at the park-gate. He entered a grove of pine trees, leaped over the wall, and, as a short cut to the railroad station, followed a path across the fields. After walking about ten minutes, he arrived at a spot where the road grew narrower and ran between two steep banks. In this ravine, he met a man traveling in the opposite direction. It was a man about fifty years of age, tall, smooth-shaven, and wearing clothes of a foreign cut. He carried a heavy cane, and a small satchel was strapped across his shoulder. When they met, the stranger spoke, with a slight English accent:

"Excuse me, monsieur, is this the way to the castle?"

"Yes, monsieur, straight ahead, and turn to the left when you come to the wall. They are expecting you."

"Ah!"

"Yes, my friend Devanne told us last night that you were coming, and I am delighted to be the first to welcome you. Sherlock Holmes has no more ardent admirer than . . . myself."

There was a touch of irony in his voice that he quickly regretted, for Sherlock Holmes scrutinized him from head to foot with such a keen, penetrating eye that Arsène Lupin experienced the sensation of being seized, imprisoned, and registered by that look more thoroughly and precisely than he had ever been by a camera.

"My negative is taken now," he thought, "and it will be useless to use a disguise with that man. He would look right through it. But, I wonder, has he recognized me?"

They bowed to each other as if about to part. But, at that moment, they heard a sound of horses' feet, accompanied by a clinking of steel. It was the gendarmes. The two men were obliged to draw back against the embankment, amongst the brushes, to avoid the horses. The gendarmes passed by, but, as they followed each other at a considerable distance, they were several minutes in doing so. And Lupin was thinking:

"It all depends on that question: has he recognized me? If so, he will probably take advantage of the opportunity. It is a trying situation."

When the last horseman had passed, Sherlock Holmes stepped forth and brushed the dust from his clothes. Then, for a moment, he and Arsène Lupin gazed at each other; and, if a person could have seen them at that moment, it would have been an interesting sight, and memorable as the first meeting of two remarkable men, so strange, so powerfully equipped, both of superior quality, and destined by fate, through their peculiar attributes, to hurl themselves one at the other like two equal forces that nature opposes, one against the other, in the realms of space.

Then the Englishman said: "Thank you, monsieur."

"You are quite welcome," replied Arsène Lupin.

They parted. Lupin went toward the railway station, and Sherlock Holmes continued on his way to the castle.

The local officers had given up the investigation after several hours of fruitless efforts, and the people at the castle were awaiting the arrival of the English detective with a lively curiosity. At first sight, they were a little disappointed on account of his commonplace appearance, which differed so greatly from the pictures they had formed of him in their own minds. He did not in any way resemble the romantic hero, the mysterious and diabolical personage that the name of Sherlock Holmes had evoked in their imaginations. However, Mon. Devanne exclaimed with much gusto:

"Ah! monsieur, you are here! I am delighted to see you. It is a long-deferred pleasure. Really, I scarcely regret what has happened, since it affords me the opportunity to meet you. But, how did you come?"

"By the train."

"But I sent my automobile to meet you at the station."

"An official reception, eh? with music and fireworks! Oh! no, not for me. That is not the way I do business," grumbled the Englishman.

This speech disconcerted Devanne, who replied, with a forced smile:

"Fortunately, the business has been greatly simplified since I wrote to you."

"In what way?"

"The robbery took place last night."

"If you had not announced my intended visit, it is probable the robbery would not have been committed last night."

"When, then?"

"To-morrow, or some other day."

"And in that case?"

"Lupin would have been trapped," said the detective.

"And my furniture?"

"Would not have been carried away."

"Ah! but my goods are here. They were brought back at three o'clock."

"By Lupin."

"By two army-wagons."

Sherlock Holmes put on his cap and adjusted his satchel. Devanne exclaimed, anxiously:

"But, monsieur, what are you going to do?"

"I am going home."

"Why?"

"Your goods have been returned; Arsène Lupin is far away—there is nothing for me to do."

"Yes, there is. I need your assistance. What happened yesterday, may happen again to-morrow, as we do not know how he entered, or how he escaped, or why, a few hours later, he returned the goods."

"Ah! you don't know—"

The idea of a problem to be solved quickened the interest of Sherlock Holmes.

"Very well, let us make a search—at once—and alone, if possible."

Devanne understood, and conducted the Englishman to the salon. In a dry, crisp voice, in sentences that seemed to have been prepared in advance, Holmes asked a number of questions about the events of the preceding evening, and enquired also concerning the guests and the members of the household. Then he examined the two volumes of the *Chronique*, compared the plans of the subterranean passage, requested a repetition of the sentences discovered by Father Gélis, and then asked:

"Was yesterday the first time you have spoken those two sentences to anyone?"

"Yes."

"You had never communicated then to Horace Velmont?"

"No."

"Well, order the automobile. I must leave in an hour."

"In an hour?"

"Yes; within that time, Arsène Lupin solved the problem that you placed before him."

"I . . . placed before him—"

"Yes, Arsène Lupin or Horace Velmont—same thing."

"I thought so. Ah! the scoundrel!"

"Now, let us see," said Holmes, "last night at ten o'clock, you furnished Lupin with the information that he lacked, and that he had been seeking for many weeks. During the night, he found time to solve the problem, collect his men, and rob the castle. I shall be quite as expeditious."

He walked from end to end of the room, in deep thought, then sat down, crossed his long legs, and closed his eyes.

Devanne waited, quite embarrassed. Thought he: "Is the man asleep? Or is he only meditating?" However, he left the room to give some orders, and when he returned he found the detective on his knees scrutinizing the carpet at the foot of the stairs in the gallery.

"What is it?" he enquired.

"Look . . . there . . . spots from a candle."

"You are right—and quite fresh."

"And you will also find them at the top of the stairs, and around the cabinet that Arsène Lupin broke into, and from which he took the bibelots that he afterward placed in this armchair."

"What do you conclude from that?"

"Nothing. These facts would doubtless explain the cause for the restitution, but that is a side issue that I cannot wait to investigate. The main question is the secret passage. First, tell me, is there a chapel some two or three hundred meters from the castle?"

"Yes, a ruined chapel, containing the tomb of Duke Rollo."

"Tell your chauffeur to wait for us near that chapel."

"My chauffeur hasn't returned. If he had, they would have informed me. Do you think the secret passage runs to the chapel? What reason have—"

"I would ask you, monsieur," interrupted the detective, "to furnish me with a ladder and a lantern."

"What! do you require a ladder and a lantern?"

"Certainly, or I shouldn't have asked for them."

Devanne, somewhat disconcerted by this crude logic, rang the bell. The two articles were given with the sternness and precision of military commands.

"Place the ladder against the bookcase, to the left of the word Thibermesnil."

Devanne placed the ladder as directed, and the Englishman continued:

"More to the left . . . to the right . . . There! . . . Now, climb up. . . . All the letters are in relief, aren't they?"

"Yes."

"First, turn the letter I one way or the other."

"Which one? There are two of them."

"The first one."

Devanne took hold of the letter, and exclaimed:

"Ah! yes, it turns toward the right. Who told you that?"

Sherlock Holmes did not reply to the question, but continued his directions:

"Now, take the letter B. Move it back and forth as you would a bolt."

Devanne did so, and, to his great surprise, it produced a clicking sound.

"Quite right," said Holmes. "Now, we will go to the other end of the word Thibermesnil, try the letter I, and see if it will open like a wicket."

With a certain degree of solemnity, Devanne seized the letter. It opened, but Devanne fell from the ladder, for the entire section of the bookcase, lying between the first and last letters of the words, turned on a pivot and disclosed the subterranean passage.

Sherlock Holmes said, coolly:

"You are not hurt?"

"No, no," said Devanne, as he rose to his feet, "not hurt, only bewildered. I can't understand now . . . those letters turn . . . the secret passage opens . . ."

"Certainly. Doesn't that agree exactly with the formula given by Sully? Turn one eye on the bee that shakes, the other eye will lead to God."

"But Louis the Sixteenth?" asked Devanne.

"Louis the Sixteenth was a clever locksmith. I have read a book he wrote about combination locks. It was a good idea on the part of the owner of Thibermesnil to show His Majesty a clever bit of mechanism. As an aid to his memory, the king wrote: 3-4-11, that is to say, the third, fourth, and eleventh letters of the word."

"Exactly. I understand that. It explains how Lupin got out of the room, but it does not explain how he entered. And it is certain he came from the outside."

Sherlock Holmes lighted his lantern, and stepped into the passage.

"Look! All the mechanism is exposed here, like the works of a clock, and the reverse side of the letters can be reached. Lupin worked the combination from this side—that is all."

"What proof is there of that?"

"Proof? Why, look at that puddle of oil. Lupin foresaw that the wheels would require oiling."

"Did he know about the other entrance?"

"As well as I know it," said Holmes. "Follow me."

"Into that dark passage?"

"Are you afraid?"

"No, but are you sure you can find the way out?"

"With my eyes closed."

At first, they descended twelve steps, then twelve more, and, farther on, two other flights of twelve steps each. Then they walked through a long passageway, the brick walls of which showed the marks of successive restorations, and, in spots, were dripping with water. The earth, also, was very damp.

"We are passing under the pond," said Devanne, somewhat nervously.

At last, they came to a stairway of twelve steps, followed by three others of twelve steps each, which they mounted with difficulty, and then found themselves in a small cavity cut in the rock. They could go no further.

"The deuce!" muttered Holmes, "nothing but bare walls. This is provoking."

"Let us go back," said Devanne. "I have seen enough to satisfy me."

But the Englishman raised his eye and uttered a sigh of relief. There, he saw the same mechanism and the same word as before. He had merely to work the three letters. He did so, and a block of granite swung out of place. On the other side, this granite block formed the tombstone of Duke Rollo, and the word "Thibermesnil" was engraved on it in relief. Now, they were in the little ruined chapel, and the detective said:

"The other eye leads to God; that means, to the chapel."

"It is marvelous!" exclaimed Devanne, amazed at the clairvoyance and vivacity of the Englishman. "Can it be possible that those few words were sufficient for you?"

"Bah!" declared Holmes, "they weren't even necessary. In the chart in the book of the National Library, the drawing terminates at the left, as you know, in a circle, and at the right, as you do not know, in a cross. Now, that cross must refer to the chapel in which we now stand."

Poor Devanne could not believe his ears. It was all so new, so novel to him. He exclaimed:

"It is incredible, miraculous, and yet of a childish simplicity! How is it that no one has ever solved the mystery?"

"Because no one has ever united the essential elements, that is to say, the two books and the two sentences. No one, but Arsène Lupin and myself."

"But, Father Gélis and I knew all about those things, and, likewise—"

Holmes smiled, and said:

"Monsieur Devanne, everybody cannot solve riddles."

"I have been trying for ten years to accomplish what you did in ten minutes."

"Bah! I am used to it."

They emerged from the chapel, and found an automobile.

"Ah! there's an auto waiting for us."

"Yes, it is mine," said Devanne.

"Yours? You said your chauffeur hadn't returned."

They approached the machine, and Mon. Devanne questioned the chauffeur:

"Edouard, who gave you orders to come here?"

"Why, it was Monsieur Velmont."

"Mon. Velmont? Did you meet him?"

"Near the railway station, and he told me to come to the chapel."

"To come to the chapel! What for?"

"To wait for you, monsieur, and your friend."

Devanne and Holmes exchanged looks, and Mon. Devanne said:

"He knew the mystery would be a simple one for you. It is a delicate compliment."

A smile of satisfaction lighted up the detective's serious features for a moment. The compliment pleased him. He shook his head, as he said:

"A clever man! I knew that when I saw him."

"Have you seen him?"

"I met him a short time ago—on my way from the station."

"And you knew it was Horace Velmont—I mean, Arsène Lupin?"

"That is right. I wonder how it came—"

"No, but I supposed it was—from a certain ironical speech he made."

"And you allowed him to escape?"

"Of course I did. And yet I had everything on my side, such as five gendarmes who passed us."

"Sacrebleu!" cried Devanne. "You should have taken advantage of the opportunity."

"Really, monsieur," said the Englishman, haughtily, "when I encounter an adversary like Arsène Lupin, I do not take advantage of chance opportunities, I create them."

But time pressed, and since Lupin had been so kind as to send the automobile, they resolved to profit by it. They seated themselves in the comfortable limousine; Edouard took his place at the wheel, and away they went toward the railway station. Suddenly, Devanne's eyes fell upon a small package in one of the pockets of the carriage.

"Ah! what is that? A package! Whose is it? Why, it is for you."

"For me?"

"Yes, it is addressed: Sherlock Holmes, from Arsène Lupin."

The Englishman took the package, opened it, and found that it contained a watch.

"Ah!" he exclaimed, with an angry gesture.

"A watch," said Devanne. "How did it come there?"

The detective did not reply.

"Oh! it is your watch! Arsène Lupin returns your watch! But, in order to return it, he must have taken it. Ah! I see! He took your watch! That is a good one! Sherlock Holmes's watch stolen by Arsène Lupin! Mon Dieu! that is funny! Really . . . you must excuse me . . . I can't help it."

He roared with laughter, unable to control himself. After which, he said, in a tone of earnest conviction:

"A clever man, indeed!"

The Englishman never moved a muscle. On the way to Dieppe,

he never spoke a word, but fixed his gaze on the flying landscape. His silence was terrible, unfathomable, more violent than the wildest rage. At the railway station, he spoke calmly, but in a voice that impressed one with the vast energy and will power of that famous man. He said:

"Yes, he is a clever man, but some day I shall have the pleasure of placing on his shoulder the hand I now offer to you, Monsieur Devanne. And I believe that Arsène Lupin and Sherlock Holmes will meet again some day. Yes, the world is too small—we will meet—we must meet—and then—"

FROM ARSÈNE LUPIN VERSUS

HERLOCK SHOLMES* (1908)

* After his first published story featuring a parodic version of Sherlock Holmes, "Sherlock Holmes Arrives Too Late," prompted a threat of legal action from Arthur Conan Doyle, Leblanc changed the character's name to Herlock Sholmes in his next book; we have restored the original spelling in this edition. The two stories reproduced here form one connected episode.

THE JEWISH LAMP

Sherlock Holmes and Watson were sitting in front of the fire-place, in comfortable armchairs, with the feet extended toward the grateful warmth of a glowing coke fire.

Holmes's pipe, a short brier with a silver band, had gone out. He knocked out the ashes, filled it, lighted it, pulled the skirts of his dressing-gown over his knees, and drew from his pipe great puffs of smoke, which ascended toward the ceiling in scores of shadow rings.

Watson gazed at him, as a dog lying curled up on a rug before the fire might look at his master, with great round eyes which have no hope other than to obey the least gesture of his owner. Was the master going to break the silence? Would he reveal to Watson the subject of his reverie and admit his satellite into the charmed realm of his thoughts?

When Holmes had maintained his silent attitude for some time, Watson ventured to speak:

"Everything seems quiet now. Not the shadow of a case to occupy our leisure moments."

Holmes did not reply, but the rings of smoke emitted by Holmes were better formed, and Watson observed that his companion drew considerable pleasure from that trifling fact—an indication that the great man was not absorbed in any serious meditation. Watson, discouraged, arose and went to the window.

The lonely street extended between the gloomy façades of grimy houses, unusually gloomy this morning by reason of a heavy downfall of rain. A cab passed; then another. Watson made an entry of their numbers in his memorandum-book. One never knows!

"Ah!" he exclaimed, "the postman."

The man entered, shown in by the servant.

"Two registered letters, sir . . . if you will sign, please?"

Holmes signed the receipts, accompanied the man to the door, and was opening one of the letters as he returned.

"It seems to please you," remarked Watson, after a moment's silence.

"This letter contains a very interesting proposition. You are anxious for a case—here's one. Read——"

Watson read:

"Monsieur,

"I desire the benefit of your services and experience. I have been the victim of a serious theft, and the investigation has as yet been unsuccessful. I am sending to you by this mail a number of newspapers which will inform you of the affair, and if you will undertake the case, I will place my house at your disposal and ask you to fill in the enclosed check, signed by me, for whatever sum you require for your expenses.

"Kindly reply by telegraph, and much oblige,

"Your humble servant,
"Baron Victor d'Imblevalle,
"18 Rue Murillo, Paris."

"Ah!" exclaimed Holmes, "that sounds good . . . a little trip to Paris . . . and why not, Watson? Since my famous duel with Arsène Lupin, I have not had an excuse to go there. I should be pleased to visit the capital of the world under less strenuous conditions."

He tore the check into four pieces and, while Watson, whose arm had not yet regained its former strength, uttered bitter words against Paris and the Parisians, Holmes opened the second envelope. Immediately, he made a gesture of annoyance, and a wrinkle appeared on his forehead during the reading of the letter; then, crushing the paper into a ball, he threw it, angrily, on the floor.

"Well! What's the matter?" asked Watson, anxiously.

He picked up the ball of paper, unfolded it, and read, with increasing amazement:

> "My Dear Monsieur:
>   "You know full well the admiration I have for you and the interest I take in your renown. Well, believe me, when I warn you to have nothing whatever to do with the case on which you have just now been called to Paris. Your intervention will cause much harm; your efforts will produce a most lamentable result; and you will be obliged to make a public confession of your defeat.
>   "Having a sincere desire to spare you such humiliation, I implore you, in the name of the friendship that unites us, to remain peacefully reposing at your own fireside.
>   "My best wishes to Monsieur Watson, and, for yourself, the sincere regards of your devoted
>
>   Arsène Lupin."

"Arsène Lupin!" repeated Watson, astounded.

Holmes struck the table with his fist, and exclaimed:

"Ah! he is pestering me already, the fool! He laughs at me as if I were a schoolboy! The public confession of my defeat! Didn't I force him to disgorge the blue diamond?"

"I tell you—he's afraid," suggested Watson.

"Nonsense! Arsène Lupin is not afraid, and this taunting letter proves it."

"But how did he know that the Baron d'Imblevalle had written to you?"

"What do I know about it? You do ask some stupid questions, my boy."

"I thought . . . I supposed——"

"What? That I am a clairvoyant? Or a sorcerer?"

"No, but I have seen you do some marvelous things."

"No person can perform *marvelous* things. I no more than you. I reflect, I deduct, I conclude—that is all; but I do not divine. Only fools divine."

Watson assumed the attitude of a whipped cur, and resolved not to make a fool of himself by trying to divine why Holmes paced the room with quick, nervous strides. But when Holmes rang for the servant and ordered his valise, Watson thought that he was in possession of a material fact which gave him the right to reflect, deduct, and conclude that his associate was about to take a journey. The same mental operation permitted him to assert, with almost mathematical exactness:

"Holmes, you are going to Paris."

"Possibly."

"And Lupin's affront impels you to go, rather than the desire to assist the Baron d'Imblevalle."

"Possibly."

"Holmes, I shall go with you."

"Ah; ah! my old friend," exclaimed Holmes, interrupting his walking, "you are not afraid that your right arm will meet the same fate as your left?"

"What can happen to me? You will be there."

"That's the way to talk, Watson. We will show that clever Frenchman that he made a mistake when he threw his glove in our faces. Be quick, Watson, we must catch the first train."

"Without waiting for the papers the baron has sent you?"

"What good are they?"

"I will send a telegram."

"No; if you do that, Arsène Lupin will know of my arrival. I wish to avoid that. This time, Watson, we must fight under cover."

|||||||||||||||||||||||

That afternoon, the two friends embarked at Dover. The passage was a delightful one. In the train from Calais to Paris, Holmes had three hours sound sleep, while Watson guarded the door of the compartment.

Holmes awoke in good spirits. He was delighted at the idea of another duel with Arsène Lupin, and he rubbed his hands with the satisfied air of a man who looks forward to a pleasant vacation.

"At last!" exclaimed Watson, "we are getting to work again."

And he rubbed his hands with the same satisfied air.

At the station, Holmes took the wraps and, followed by Watson, who carried the valises, he gave up his tickets and started off briskly.

"Fine weather, Watson . . . Blue sky and sunshine! Paris is giving us a royal reception."

"Yes, but what a crowd!"

"So much the better, Watson, we will pass unnoticed. No one will recognize us in such a crowd."

"Is this Monsieur Holmes?"

He stopped, somewhat puzzled. Who the deuce could thus address him by his name? A woman stood beside him; a young girl whose simple dress outlined her slender form and whose pretty face had a sad and anxious expression. She repeated her enquiry:

"You are Monsieur Holmes?"

As he still remained silent, as much from confusion as from a habit of prudence, the girl asked a third time:

"Have I the honor of addressing Monsieur Holmes?"

"What do you want?" he replied, testily, considering the incident a suspicious one.

"You must listen to me, Monsieur Holmes, as it is a serious matter. I know that you are going to the Rue Murillo."

"What do you say?"

"I know . . . I know . . . Rue Murillo . . . number 18. Well, you must not go . . . no, you must not. I assure you that you will regret it. Do not think that I have any interest in the matter. I do it because it is right . . . because my conscience tells me to do it."

Holmes tried to get away, but she persisted:

"Oh! I beg of you, don't neglect my advice. . . . Ah! if I only knew how to convince you! Look at me! Look into my eyes! They are sincere . . . they speak the truth."

She gazed at Holmes, fearlessly but innocently, with those beautiful eyes, serious and clear, in which her very soul seemed to be reflected.

Watson nodded his head, as he said:

"Mademoiselle looks honest."

"Yes," she implored, "and you must have confidence——"

"I have confidence in you, mademoiselle," replied Watson.

"Oh, how happy you make me! And so has your friend? I feel it . . . I am sure of it! What happiness! Everything will be all right now! . . . What a good idea of mine! . . . Ah! yes, there is a train for Calais in twenty minutes. You will take it. . . . Quick, follow me . . . you must come this way . . . there is just time."

She tried to drag them along. Holmes seized her arm, and in as gentle a voice as he could assume, said to her:

"Excuse me, mademoiselle, if I cannot yield to your wishes, but I never abandon a task that I have once undertaken."

"I beseech you . . . I implore you. . . . Ah if you could only understand!"

Holmes passed outside and walked away at a quick pace. Watson said to the girl:

"Have no fear . . . he will be in at the finish. He never faded yet."

And he ran to overtake Holmes.

SHERLOCK HOLMES—ARSÈNE LUPIN.

These words, in great black letters, met their gaze as soon as they left the railway station. A number of sandwich-men were parading through the street, one behind the other, carrying heavy canes with iron ferrules with which they struck the pavement in harmony, and, on their backs, they carried large posters, on which one could read the following notice:

THE MATCH BETWEEN SHERLOCK HOLMES AND ARSÈNE LUPIN. ARRIVAL OF THE ENGLISH CHAMPION. THE GREAT DETECTIVE ATTACKS THE MYSTERY OF

THE RUE MURILLO. READ THE DETAILS IN THE "ECHO
DE FRANCE."

Watson shook his head, and said:

"Look at that, Holmes, and we thought we were traveling incognito! I shouldn't be surprised to find the republican guard waiting for us at the Rue Murillo to give us an official reception with toasts and champagne."

"Watson, when you get funny, you get beastly funny," growled Holmes.

Then he approached one of the sandwich-men with the obvious intention of seizing him in his powerful grip and crushing him, together with his infernal sign-board. There was quite a crowd gathered about the men, reading the notices, and joking and laughing.

Repressing a furious access of rage, Holmes said to the man:

"When did they hire you?"

"This morning."

"How long have you been parading?"

"About an hour."

"But the boards were ready before that?"

"Oh, yes, they were ready when we went to the agency this morning."

So then it appears that Arsène Lupin had foreseen that he, Holmes, would accept the challenge. More than that, the letter written by Lupin showed that he was eager for the fray and that he was prepared to measure swords once more with his formidable rival. Why? What motive could Arsène Lupin have in renewing the struggle?

Holmes hesitated for a moment. Lupin must be very confident of his success to show so much insolence in advance; and was not he, Holmes, falling into a trap by rushing into the battle at the first call for help?

However, he called a carriage.

"Come, Watson! . . . Driver, 18 Rue Murillo!" he exclaimed, with an outburst of his accustomed energy. With distended veins and clenched fists, as if he were about to engage in a boxing bout, he jumped into the carriage.

The Rue Murillo is bordered with magnificent private residences, the rear of which overlook the Parc Monceau. One of the most pretentious of these houses is number 18, owned and occupied by the Baron d'Imblevalle and furnished in a luxurious manner consistent with the owner's taste and wealth. There was a courtyard in front of the house, and, in the rear, a garden well filled with trees whose branches mingle with those of the park.

After ringing the bell, the two Englishmen were admitted, crossed the courtyard, and were received at the door by a footman who showed them into a small parlor facing the garden in the rear of the house. They sat down and, glancing about, made a rapid inspection of the many valuable objects with which the room was filled.

"Everything very choice," murmured Watson, "and in the best of taste. It is a safe deduction to make that those who had the leisure to collect these articles must now be at least fifty years of age."

The door opened, and the Baron d'Imblevalle entered, followed by his wife. Contrary to the deduction made by Watson, they were both quite young, of elegant appearance, and vivacious in speech and action. They were profuse in their expressions of gratitude.

"So kind of you to come! Sorry to have caused you so much trouble! The theft now seems of little consequence, since it has procured us this pleasure."

"How charming these French people are!" thought Watson, evolving one of his commonplace deductions.

"But time is money," exclaimed the baron, "especially your time, Monsieur Holmes. So I will come to the point. Now, what do you think of the affair? Do you think you can succeed in it?"

"Before I can answer that I must know what it is about."

"I thought you knew."

"No; so I must ask you for full particulars, even to the smallest detail. First, what is the nature of the case?"

"A theft."

"When did it take place?"

"Last Saturday," replied the baron, "or, at least, some time during Saturday night or Sunday morning."

"That was six days ago. Now, you can tell me all about it."

"In the first place, monsieur, I must tell you that my wife and I, conforming to the manner of life that our position demands, go out very little. The education of our children, a few receptions, and the care and decoration of our house—such constitutes our life; and nearly all our evenings are spent in this little room, which is my wife's boudoir, and in which we have gathered a few artistic objects. Last Saturday night, about eleven o'clock, I turned off the electric lights, and my wife and I retired, as usual, to our room."

"Where is your room?"

"It adjoins this. That is the door. Next morning, that is to say, Sunday morning, I arose quite early. As Suzanne, my wife, was still asleep, I passed into the boudoir as quietly as possible so as not to wake her. What was my astonishment when I found that window open—as we had left it closed the evening before!"

"A servant——"

"No one enters here in the morning until we ring. Besides, I always take the precaution to bolt the second door which communicates with the antechamber. Therefore, the window must have been opened from the outside. Besides, I have some evidence of that: the second pane of glass from the right—close to the fastening—had been cut."

"And what does that window overlook?"

"As you can see for yourself, it opens on a little balcony, surrounded by a stone railing. Here, we are on the first floor, and you can see the garden behind the house and the iron fence which separates it from the Parc Monceau. It is quite certain that the thief came through the park, climbed the fence by the aid of a ladder, and thus reached the terrace below the window."

"That is quite certain, you say?"

"Well, in the soft earth on either side of the fence, they found the two holes made by the bottom of the ladder, and two similar holes can be seen below the window. And the stone railing of the balcony shows two scratches which were doubtless made by the contact of the ladder."

"Is the Parc Monceau closed at night?"

"No; but if it were, there is a house in course of erection at number 14, and a person could enter that way."

Sherlock Holmes reflected for a few minutes, and then said:

"Let us come down to the theft. It must have been committed in this room?"

"Yes; there was here, between that twelfth century Virgin and that tabernacle of chased silver, a small Jewish lamp. It has disappeared."

"And is that all?"

"That is all."

"Ah!... And what is a Jewish lamp?"

"One of those copper lamps used by the ancient Jews, consisting of a standard which supported a bowl containing the oil, and from this bowl projected several burners intended for the wicks."

"Upon the whole, an object of small value."

"No great value, of course. But this one contained a secret hiding-place in which we were accustomed to place a magnificent jewel, a chimera in gold, set with rubies and emeralds, which was of great value."

"Why did you hide it there?"

"Oh! I can't give any reason, monsieur, unless it was an odd fancy to utilize a hiding-place of that kind."

"Did anyone know it?"

"No."

"No one—except the thief," said Holmes. "Otherwise he would not have taken the trouble to steal the lamp."

"Of course. But how could he know it, as it was only by accident that the secret mechanism of the lamp was revealed to us."

"A similar accident has revealed it to someone else . . . a servant . . . or an acquaintance. But let us proceed: I suppose the police have been notified?"

"Yes. The examining magistrate has completed his investigation. The reporter-detectives attached to the leading newspapers have also made their investigations. But, as I wrote to you, it seems to me the mystery will never be solved."

Holmes arose, went to the window, examined the casement, the balcony, the terrace, studied the scratches on the stone railing with his magnifying-glass, and then requested Mon. d'Imblevalle to show him the garden.

Outside, Holmes sat down in a rattan chair and gazed at the roof of the house in a dreamy way. Then he walked over to the two little wooden boxes with which they had covered the holes made in the ground by the bottom of the ladder with a view of preserving them intact. He raised the boxes, kneeled on the ground, scrutinized the holes, and made some measurements. After making a similar examination of the holes near the fence, he and the baron returned to the boudoir where Madame d'Imblevalle was waiting for them. After a short silence Holmes said:

"At the very outset of your story, baron, I was surprised at the very simple methods employed by the thief. To raise a ladder, cut a window-pane, select a valuable article, and walk out again—no, that is not the way such things are done. All that is too plain, too simple."

"Well, what do you think?"

"That the Jewish lamp was stolen under the direction of Arsène Lupin."

"Arsène Lupin!" exclaimed the baron.

"Yes, but he did not do it himself, as no one came from the outside. Perhaps a servant descended from the upper floor by means of a waterspout that I noticed when I was in the garden."

"What makes you think so?"

"Arsène Lupin would not leave this room empty-handed."

"Empty-handed! But he had the lamp."

"But that would not have prevented his taking that snuff-box, set with diamonds, or that opal necklace. When he leaves anything, it is because he can't carry it away."

"But the marks of the ladder outside?"

"A false scent. Placed there simply to avert suspicion."

"And the scratches on the balustrade?"

"A farce! They were made with a piece of sandpaper. See, here are scraps of the paper that I picked up in the garden."

"And what about the marks made by the bottom of the ladder?"

"Counterfeit! Examine the two rectangular holes below the window, and the two holes near the fence. They are of a similar form, but I find that the two holes near the house are closer to each other than the two holes near the fence. What does that fact suggest? To me, it suggested that the four holes were made by a piece of wood prepared for the purpose."

"The better proof would be the piece of wood itself."

"Here it is," said Holmes, "I found it in the garden, under the box of a laurel tree."

The baron bowed to Holmes in recognition of his skill. Only forty minutes had elapsed since the Englishman had entered the house, and he had already exploded all the theories theretofore formed, and which had been based on what appeared to be obvious and undeniable facts. But what now appeared to be the real facts of the case rested upon a more solid foundation, to-wit, the astute reasoning of a Sherlock Holmes.

"The accusation which you make against one of our household is a very serious matter," said the baroness. "Our servants have been with us a long time and none of them would betray our trust."

"If none of them has betrayed you, how can you explain the fact that I received this letter on the same day and by the same mail as the letter you wrote to me?"

He handed to the baroness the letter that he had received from Arsène Lupin. She exclaimed, in amazement:

"Arsène Lupin! How could he know?"

"Did you tell anyone that you had written to me?"

"No one," replied the baron. "The idea occurred to us the other evening at the dinner-table."

"Before the servants?"

"No, only our two children. Oh! no . . . Sophie and Henriette had left the table, hadn't they, Suzanne?"

Madame d'Imblevalle, after a moment's reflection, replied:

"Yes, they had gone to Mademoiselle."

"Mademoiselle?" queried Holmes.

"The governess, Mademoiselle Alice Demun."

"Does she take her meals with you?"

"No. Her meals are served in her room."

Watson had an idea. He said:

"The letter written to my friend Sherlock Holmes was posted?"

"Of course."

"Who posted it?"

"Dominique, who has been my valet for twenty years," replied the baron. "Any search in that direction would be a waste of time."

"One never wastes his time when engaged in a search," said Watson, sententiously.

This preliminary investigation now ended, and Holmes asked permission to retire.

At dinner, an hour later, he saw Sophie and Henriette, the two children of the family, one was six and the other eight years of age. There was very little conversation at the table. Holmes responded to the friendly advances of his hosts in such a curt manner that they were soon reduced to silence. When the coffee was served, Holmes swallowed the contents of his cup, and rose to take his leave.

At that moment, a servant entered with a telephone message addressed to Holmes. He opened it, and read:

> *"You have my enthusiastic admiration. The results attained by you in so short a time are simply marvelous. I am dismayed.*
>
> *"Arsène Lupin."*

Holmes made a gesture of indignation and handed the message to the baron, saying:

"What do you think now, monsieur? Are the walls of your house furnished with eyes and ears?"

"I don't understand it," said the baron, in amazement.

"Nor do I; but I do understand that Lupin has knowledge of everything that occurs in this house. He knows every movement, every word. There is no doubt of it. But how does he get his information? That is the first mystery I have to solve, and when I know that I will know everything."

That night, Watson retired with the clear conscience of a man who has performed his whole duty and thus acquired an undoubted right to sleep and repose. So he fell asleep very quickly, and was soon enjoying the most delightful dreams in which he pursued Lupin and captured him single-handed; and the sensation was so vivid and exciting that it woke him from his sleep. Someone was standing at his bedside. He seized his revolver, and cried:

"Don't move, Lupin, or I'll fire."

"The deuce! Watson, what do you mean?"

"Oh! it is you, Holmes. Do you want me?"

"I want to show you something. Get up."

Holmes led him to the window, and said:

"Look! . . . on the other side of the fence . . ."

"In the park?"

"Yes. What do you see?"

"I don't see anything."

"Yes, you do see something."

"Ah! of course, a shadow . . . two of them."

"Yes, close to the fence. See, they are moving. Come, quick!"

Quickly they descended the stairs, and reached a room which opened into the garden. Through the glass door they could see the two shadowy forms in the same place.

"It is very strange," said Holmes, "but it seems to me I can hear a noise inside the house."

"Inside the house? Impossible! Everybody is asleep."

"Well, listen——"

At that moment a low whistle came from the other side of the fence, and they perceived a dim light which appeared to come from the house.

"The baron must have turned on the light in his room. It is just above us."

"That must have been the noise you heard," said Watson. "Perhaps they are watching the fence also."

Then there was a second whistle, softer than before.

"I don't understand it; I don't understand," said Holmes, irritably.

"No more do I," confessed Watson.

Holmes turned the key, drew the bolt, and quietly opened the door. A third whistle, louder than before, and modulated to another form. And the noise above their heads became more pronounced. Holmes said:

"It seems to be on the balcony outside the boudoir window."

He put his head through the half-opened door, but immediately recoiled, with a stifled oath. Then Watson looked. Quite close to them there was a ladder, the upper end of which was resting on the balcony.

"The deuce!" said Holmes, "there is someone in the boudoir. That is what we heard. Quick, let us remove the ladder."

But at that instant a man slid down the ladder and ran toward the spot where his accomplices were waiting for him outside the fence. He carried the ladder with him. Holmes and Watson pursued the man and overtook him just as he was placing the ladder against the fence. From the other side of the fence two shots were fired.

"Wounded?" cried Holmes.

"No," replied Watson.

Watson seized the man by the body and tried to hold him, but the man turned and plunged a knife into Watson's breast. He uttered a groan, staggered, and fell.

"Damnation!" muttered Holmes, "if they have killed him I will kill them."

He laid Watson on the grass and rushed toward the ladder. Too late—the man had climbed the fence and, accompanied by his confederates, had fled through the bushes.

"Watson, Watson, it is not serious, hein? Merely a scratch."

The house door opened, and Monsieur d'Imblevalle appeared, followed by the servants, carrying candles.

"What's the matter?" asked the baron. "Is Monsieur Watson wounded?"

"Oh! it's nothing—a mere scratch," repeated Holmes, trying to deceive himself.

The blood was flowing profusely, and Watson's face was livid. Twenty minutes later the doctor ascertained that the point of the knife had penetrated to within an inch and a half of the heart.

"An inch and a half of the heart! Watson always was lucky!" said Holmes, in an envious tone.

"Lucky . . . lucky . . ." muttered the doctor.

"Of course! Why, with his robust constitution he will soon be out again."

"Six weeks in bed and two months of convalescence."

"Not more?"

"No, unless complications set in."

"Oh! the devil! what does he want complications for?"

Fully reassured, Holmes joined the baron in the boudoir. This time the mysterious visitor had not exercised the same restraint. Ruthlessly, he had laid his vicious hand upon the diamond snuff-box, upon the opal necklace, and, in a general way, upon everything that could find a place in the greedy pockets of an enterprising burglar.

The window was still open; one of the window-panes had been neatly cut; and, in the morning, a summary investigation showed that the ladder belonged to the house then in course of construction.

"Now, you can see," said Mon. d'Imblevalle, with a touch of irony, "it is an exact repetition of the affair of the Jewish lamp."

"Yes, if we accept the first theory adopted by the police."

"Haven't you adopted it yet? Doesn't this second theft shatter your theory in regard to the first?"

"It only confirms it, monsieur."

"That is incredible! You have positive evidence that last night's theft was committed by an outsider, and yet you adhere to your theory that the Jewish lamp was stolen by someone in the house."

"Yes, I am sure of it."

"How do you explain it?"

"I do not explain anything, monsieur; I have established two facts which do not appear to have any relation to each other, and yet I am seeking the missing link that connects them."

His conviction seemed to be so earnest and positive that the baron submitted to it, and said:

"Very well, we will notify the police——"

"Not at all!" exclaimed the Englishman, quickly, "not at all! I intend to ask for their assistance when I need it—but not before."

"But the attack on your friend?"

"That's of no consequence. He is only wounded. Secure the license of the doctor. I shall be responsible for the legal side of the affair."

<hr />

The next two days proved uneventful. Yet Holmes was investigating the case with a minute care, and with a sense of wounded pride resulting from that audacious theft, committed under his nose, in spite of his presence and beyond his power to prevent it. He made a thorough investigation of the house and garden, interviewed the servants, and paid lengthy visits to the kitchen and stables. And, although his efforts were fruitless, he did not despair.

"I will succeed," he thought, "and the solution must be sought within the walls of this house. This affair is quite different from that of the blonde Lady, where I had to work in the dark, on unknown ground. This time I am on the battlefield itself. The enemy is not the elusive and invisible Lupin, but the accomplice, in flesh and blood, who lives and moves within the confines of this house. Let me secure the slightest clue and the game is mine!"

That clue was furnished to him by accident.

On the afternoon of the third day, when he entered a room located above the boudoir, which served as a study for the children, he found Henriette, the younger of the two sisters. She was looking for her scissors.

"You know," she said to Holmes, "I make papers like that you received the other evening."

"The other evening?"

"Yes, just as dinner was over, you received a paper with marks on it . . . you know, a telegram. . . . Well, I make them, too."

She left the room. To anyone else these words would seem to be nothing more than the insignificant remark of a child, and Holmes himself listened to them with a distracted air and continued his investigation. But, suddenly, he ran after the child, and overtook her at the head of the stairs. He said to her:

"So you paste stamps and marks on papers?"

Henriette, very proudly, replied:

"Yes, I cut them out and paste them on."

"Who taught you that little game?"

"Mademoiselle . . . my governess . . . I have seen her do it often. She takes words out of the newspapers and pastes them——"

"What does she make out of them?"

"Telegrams and letters that she sends away."

Sherlock Holmes returned to the study, greatly puzzled by the information and seeking to draw from it a logical deduction. There was a pile of newspapers on the mantel. He opened them and found that many words and, in some places, entire lines had been cut out. But, after reading a few of the words which preceded or followed, he decided that the missing words had been cut out at random—probably by the child. It was possible that one of the newspapers had been cut by mademoiselle; but how could he assure himself that such was the case?

Mechanically, Holmes turned over the school-books on the table; then others which were lying on the shelf of a bookcase. Suddenly he uttered a cry of joy. In a corner of the bookcase, under a pile of old exercise books, he found a child's alphabet-book, in which the letters were ornamented with pictures, and on one of the pages of that book he discovered a place where a word had been removed. He examined it. It was a list of the days of the week. Monday, Tuesday, Wednesday, etc. The word "Saturday" was missing. Now, the theft of the Jewish lamp had occurred on a Saturday night.

Holmes experienced that slight fluttering of the heart which always announced to him, in the clearest manner, that he had discovered the road which leads to victory. That ray of truth, that feeling of certainty, never deceived him.

With nervous fingers he hastened to examine the balance of the book. Very soon he made another discovery. It was a page composed of capital letters, followed by a line of figures. Nine of those letters and three of those figures had been carefully cut out. Holmes made a list of the missing letters and figures in his memorandum book, in alphabetical and numerical order, and obtained the following result:

CDEHNOPEZ—237.

"Well! at first sight, it is a rather formidable puzzle," he murmured, "but, by transposing the letters and using all of them, is it possible to form one, two, or three complete words?"

Holmes tried it, in vain.

Only one solution seemed possible; it constantly appeared before him, no matter which way he tried to juggle the letters, until, at length, he was satisfied it was the true solution, since it harmonized with the logic of the facts and the general circumstances of the case.

As that page of the book did not contain any duplicate letters it was probable, in fact quite certain, that the words he could form from those letters would be incomplete, and that the original words had been completed with letters taken from other pages. Under those conditions he obtained the following solution, errors and omissions excepted:

REPOND Z—CH—237.

The first word was quite clear: répondez [reply], a letter E is missing because it occurs twice in the word, and the book furnished only one letter of each kind.

As to the second incomplete word, no doubt it formed, with the aid of the number 237, an address to which the reply was to be sent. They appointed Saturday as the time, and requested a reply to be sent to the address CH. 237.

Or, perhaps, CH. 237 was an address for a letter to be sent to the "general delivery" of some post-office, or, again, they might form a part of some incomplete word. Holmes searched the book once more, but did not discover that any other letters had been removed. Therefore, until further orders, he decided to adhere to the foregoing interpretation.

Henriette returned and observed what he was doing.

"Amusing, isn't it?"

"Yes, very amusing," he replied. "But, have you any other papers?... Or, rather, words already cut out that I can paste?"

"Papers?... No... And Mademoiselle wouldn't like it."

"Mademoiselle?"

"Yes, she has scolded me already."

"Why?"

"Because I have told you some things... and she says that a person should never tell things about those they love."

"You are quite right."

Henriette was delighted to receive his approbation, in fact so highly pleased that she took from a little silk bag that was pinned to her dress some scraps of cloth, three buttons, two cubes of sugar, and, lastly, a piece of paper which she handed to Holmes.

"See, I give it to you just the same."

It was the number of a cab—8,279.

"Where did this number come from?"

"It fell out of her pocket-book."

"When?"

"Sunday, at mass, when she was taking out some sous for the collection."

"Exactly! And now I shall tell you how to keep from being scolded again. Do not tell Mademoiselle that you saw me."

Holmes then went to Mon. d'Imblevalle and questioned him in regard to Mademoiselle. The baron replied, indignantly:

"Alice Demun! How can you imagine such a thing? It is utterly impossible!"

"How long has she been in your service?"

"Only a year, but there is no one in the house in whom I have greater confidence."

"Why have I not seen her yet?"

"She has been away for a few days."

"But she is here now."

"Yes; since her return she has been watching at the bedside of your friend. She has all the qualities of a nurse … gentle … thoughtful … Monsieur Watson seems much pleased …"

"Ah!" said Holmes, who had completely neglected to inquire about his friend. After a moment's reflection he asked:

"Did she go out on Sunday morning?"

"The day after the theft?"

"Yes."

The baron called his wife and asked her. She replied:

"Mademoiselle went to the eleven o'clock mass with the children, as usual."

"But before that?"

"Before that? No. … Let me see! … I was so upset by the theft … but I remember now that, on the evening before, she asked permission to go out on Sunday morning … to see a cousin who was passing through Paris, I think. But, surely, you don't suspect her?"

"Of course not … but I would like to see her."

He went to Watson's room. A woman dressed in a gray cloth dress, as in the hospitals, was bending over the invalid, giving him a drink.

When she turned her face Holmes recognized her as the young girl who had accosted him at the railway station.

Alice Demun smiled sweetly; her great serious, innocent eyes showed no sign of embarrassment. The Englishman tried to speak, muttered a few syllables, and stopped. Then she resumed her work, acting quite naturally under Holmes's astonished gaze, moved the bottles, unrolled and rolled cotton bandages, and again regarded Holmes with her charming smile of pure innocence.

He turned on his heels, descended the stairs, noticed Mon. d'Imblevalle's automobile in the courtyard, jumped into it, and went to Levallois, to the office of the cab company whose address was printed on the paper he had received from Henriette. The man who had driven carriage number 8,279 on Sunday morning not being there, Holmes dismissed the automobile and waited for the man's return. He told Holmes that he had picked up a woman in the vicinity of the Parc Monceau, a young woman dressed in black, wearing a heavy veil, and, apparently, quite nervous.

"Did she have a package?"

"Yes, quite a long package."

"Where did you take her?"

"Avenue des Ternes, corner of the Place Saint-Ferdinand. She remained there about ten minutes, and then returned to the Parc Monceau."

"Could you recognize the house in the Avenue des Ternes?"

"Parbleu! Shall I take you there?"

"Presently. First take me to 36 Quai des Orfevres."

At the police office he saw Detective Ganimard.

"Monsieur Ganimard, are you at liberty?"

"If it has anything to do with Lupin—no!"

"It has something to do with Lupin."

"Then I do not go."

"What! you surrender——"

"I bow to the inevitable. I am tired of the unequal struggle, in which we are sure to be defeated. Lupin is stronger than I am—stronger than the two of us; therefore, we must surrender."

"I will not surrender."

"He will make you, as he has all others."

"And you would be pleased to see it—eh, Ganimard?"

"At all events, it is true," said Ganimard, frankly. "And since you are determined to pursue the game, I will go with you."

Together they entered the carriage and were driven to the Avenue des Ternes. Upon their order the carriage stopped on the other side of the street, at some distance from the house, in front of a little café, on the terrace of which the two men took seats amongst the shrubbery. It was commencing to grow dark.

"Waiter," said Holmes, "some writing material."

He wrote a note, recalled the waiter, and gave him the letter with instructions to deliver it to the concierge of the house which he pointed out.

In a few minutes the concierge stood before them. Holmes asked him if, on the Sunday morning, he had seen a young woman dressed in black.

"In black? Yes, about nine o'clock. She went to the second floor."

"Have you seen her often?"

"No, but for some time—well, during the last few weeks, I have seen her almost every day."

"And since Sunday?"

"Only once . . . until to-day."

"What! Did she come to-day?"

"She is here now."

"Here now?"

"Yes, she came about ten minutes ago. Her carriage is standing in the Place Saint-Ferdinand, as usual. I met her at the door."

"Who is the occupant of the second floor?"

"There are two: a modiste, Mademoiselle Langeais, and a gentleman who rented two furnished rooms a month ago under the name of Bresson."

"Why do you say 'under the name'?"

"Because I have an idea that it is an assumed name. My wife takes care of his rooms, and . . . well, there are not two shirts there with the same initials."

"Is he there much of the time?"

"No; he is nearly always out. He has not been here for three days."

"Was he here on Saturday night?"

"Saturday night?... Let me think.... Yes, Saturday night, he came in and stayed all night."

"What sort of a man is he?"

"Well, I can scarcely answer that. He is so changeable. He is, by turns, big, little, fat, thin ... dark and light. I do not always recognize him."

Ganimard and Holmes exchanged looks.

"That is he, all right," said Ganimard.

"Ah!" said the concierge, "there is the girl now."

Mademoiselle had just emerged from the house and was walking toward her carriage in the Place Saint-Ferdinand.

"And there is Monsieur Bresson."

"Monsieur Bresson? Which is he?"

"The man with the parcel under his arm."

"But he is not looking after the girl. She is going to her carriage alone."

"Yes, I have never seen them together."

The two detectives had arisen. By the light of the street-lamps they recognized the form of Arsène Lupin, who had started off in a direction opposite to that taken by the girl.

"Which will you follow?" asked Ganimard.

"I will follow him, of course. He's the biggest game."

"Then I will follow the girl," proposed Ganimard.

"No, no," said Holmes, quickly, who did not wish to disclose the girl's identity to Ganimard, "I know where to find her. Come with me."

They followed Lupin at a safe distance, taking care to conceal themselves as well as possible amongst the moving throng and behind the newspaper kiosks. They found the pursuit an easy one, as he walked steadily forward without turning to the right or left, but with a slight limp in the right leg, so slight as to require the keen eye of a professional observer to detect it. Ganimard observed it, and said:

"He is pretending to be lame. Ah! if we could only collect two or three policemen and pounce on our man! We run a chance to lose him."

But they did not meet any policemen before they reached the Porte des Ternes, and, having passed the fortifications, there was no prospect of receiving any assistance.

"We had better separate," said Holmes, "as there are so few people on the street."

They were now on the Boulevard Victor-Hugo. They walked one on each side of the street, and kept well in the shadow of the trees. They continued thus for twenty minutes, when Lupin turned to the left and followed the Seine. Very soon they saw him descend to the edge of the river. He remained there only a few seconds, but they could not observe his movements. Then Lupin retraced his steps. His pursuers concealed themselves in the shadow of a gateway. Lupin passed in front of them. His parcel had disappeared. And as he walked away another man emerged from the shelter of a house and glided amongst the trees.

"He seems to be following him also," said Holmes, in a low voice.

The pursuit continued, but was now embarrassed by the presence of the third man. Lupin returned the same way, passed through the Porte des Ternes, and re-entered the house in the Avenue des Ternes.

The concierge was closing the house for the night when Ganimard presented himself.

"Did you see him?"

"Yes," replied the concierge, "I was putting out the gas on the landing when he closed and bolted his door."

"Is there any person with him?"

"No; he has no servant. He never eats here."

"Is there a servants' stairway?"

"No."

Ganimard said to Holmes:

"I had better stand at the door of his room while you go for the commissary of police in the Rue Demours."

"And if he should escape during that time?" said Holmes.

"While I am here! He can't escape."

"One to one, with Lupin, is not an even chance for you."

"Well, I can't force the door. I have no right to do that, especially at night."

Holmes shrugged his shoulders and said:

"When you arrest Lupin no one will question the methods by which you made the arrest. However, let us go up and ring, and see what happens then."

They ascended to the second floor. There was a double door at the left of the landing. Ganimard rang the bell. No reply. He rang again. Still no reply.

"Let us go in," said Holmes.

"All right, come on," replied Ganimard.

Yet, they stood still, irresolute. Like people who hesitate when they ought to accomplish a decisive action they feared to move, and it seemed to them impossible that Arsène Lupin was there, so close to them, on the other side of that fragile door that could be broken down by one blow of the fist. But they knew Lupin too well to suppose that he would allow himself to be trapped in that stupid manner. No, no—a thousand times, no—Lupin was no longer there. Through the adjoining houses, over the roofs, by some conveniently prepared exit, he must have already made his escape, and, once more, it would only be Lupin's shadow that they would seize.

They shuddered as a slight noise, coming from the other side of the door, reached their ears. Then they had the impression, amounting almost to a certainty, that he was there, separated from them by that frail wooden door, and that he was listening to them, that he could hear them.

What was to be done? The situation was a serious one. In spite of their vast experience as detectives, they were so nervous and excited that they thought they could hear the beating of their own hearts. Ganimard questioned Holmes by a look. Then he struck the door a violent blow with his fist. Immediately they heard the sound of footsteps, concerning which there was no attempt at concealment.

Ganimard shook the door. Then he and Holmes, uniting their efforts, rushed at the door, and burst it open with their shoulders. Then they stood still, in surprise. A shot had been fired in the adjoining room. Another shot, and the sound of a falling body.

When they entered they saw the man lying on the floor with his face toward the marble mantel. His revolver had fallen from his hand. Ganimard stooped and turned the man's head. The face was covered with blood, which was flowing from two wounds, one in the cheek, the other in the temple.

"You can't recognize him for blood."

"No matter!" said Holmes. "It is not Lupin."

"How do you know? You haven't even looked at him."

"Do you think that Arsène Lupin is the kind of a man that would kill himself?" asked Holmes, with a sneer.

"But we thought we recognized him outside."

"We thought so, because the wish was father to the thought. That man has us bewitched."

"Then it must be one of his accomplices."

"The accomplices of Arsène Lupin do not kill themselves."

"Well, then, who is it?"

They searched the corpse. In one pocket Sherlock Holmes found an empty pocket-book; in another Ganimard found several louis. There were no marks of identification on any part of his clothing. In a trunk and two valises they found nothing but wearing apparel. On the mantel there was a pile of newspapers. Ganimard opened them. All of them contained articles referring to the theft of the Jewish lamp.

An hour later, when Ganimard and Holmes left the house, they had acquired no further knowledge of the strange individual who had been driven to suicide by their untimely visit.

Who was he? Why had he killed himself? What was his connection with the affair of the Jewish lamp? Who had followed him on his return from the river? The situation involved many complex questions—many mysteries——

|||||||||||||||||||||||||||||

Sherlock Holmes went to bed in a very bad humor. Early next morning he received the following telephonic message:

"Arsène Lupin has the honor to inform you of his tragic death in the person of Monsieur Bresson, and requests the honor of your presence at the funeral service and burial, which will be held at the public expense on Thursday, 25 June."

THE SHIPWRECK

That's what I don't like, Watson," said Sherlock Holmes, after he had read Arsène Lupin's message; "that is what exasperates me in this affair—to feel that the cunning, mocking eye of that fellow follows me everywhere. He sees everything; he knows everything; he reads my inmost thoughts; he even foresees my slightest movement. Ah! he is possessed of a marvelous intuition, far surpassing that of the most instinctive woman, yes, surpassing even that of Sherlock Holmes himself. Nothing escapes him. I resemble an actor whose every step and movement are directed by a stage manager; who says this and does that in obedience to a superior will. That is my position. Do you understand, Watson?"

Certainly Watson would have understood if his faculties had not been deadened by the profound slumber of a man whose temperature varies between one hundred and one hundred and three degrees. But whether he heard or not was a matter of no consequence to Sherlock Holmes, who continued:

"I have to concentrate all my energy and bring all my resources into action in order to make the slightest progress. And, fortunately for me, those petty annoyances are like so many pricks from a needle and serve only to stimulate me. As soon as the heat of the wound is appeased and the shock to my vanity has subsided I say to myself: 'Amuse yourself, my dear fellow, but remember that he who laughs last laughs best. Sooner or later you will betray yourself.' For you know, Watson, it was Lupin himself, who, by his first dispatch and the observation that it suggested to little Henriette, disclosed to me the secret of his correspondence with Alice Demun. Have you forgotten that circumstance, dear boy?"

But Watson was asleep; and Holmes, pacing to and fro, resumed his speech:

"And, now, things are not in a bad shape; a little obscure, perhaps, but the light is creeping in. In the first place, I must learn all about Monsieur Bresson. Ganimard and I will visit the bank of the river, at the spot where Bresson threw away the package, and the particular role of that gentleman will be known to me. After that the game will be played between me and Alice Demun. Rather a light-weight opponent, hein, Watson? And do you not think that I will soon know the phrase represented by the letters clipped from the alphabet-book, and what the isolated letters—the 'C' and the 'H'—mean? That is all I want to know, Watson."

Mademoiselle entered at that moment, and, observing Holmes gesticulating, she said, in her sweetest manner:

"Monsieur Holmes, I must scold you if you waken my patient. It isn't nice of you to disturb him. The doctor has ordered absolute rest."

He looked at her in silence, astonished, as on their first meeting, at her wonderful self-possession.

"Why do you look at me so, Monsieur Holmes? . . . You seem to be trying to read my thoughts. . . . No? . . . Then what is it?"

She questioned him with the most innocent expression on her pretty face and in her frank blue eyes. A smile played upon her lips; and she displayed so much unaffected candor that the Englishman almost lost his temper. He approached her and said, in a low voice:

"Bresson killed himself last night."

She affected not to understand him; so he repeated:

"Bresson killed himself yesterday . . ."

She did not show the slightest emotion; she acted as if the matter did not concern or interest her in any way.

"You have been informed," said Holmes, displaying his annoyance.

"Otherwise, the news would have caused you to start, at least. Ah! you are stronger than I expected. But what's the use of your trying to conceal anything from me?"

He picked up the alphabet-book, which he had placed on a convenient table, and, opening it at the mutilated page, said:

"Will you tell me the order in which the missing letters should be arranged in order to express the exact wording of the message you sent to Bresson four days before the theft of the Jewish lamp?"

"The order? . . . Bresson? . . . the theft of the Jewish lamp?"

She repeated the words slowly, as if trying to grasp their meaning. He continued:

"Yes. Here are the letters employed . . . on this bit of paper. . . . What did you say to Bresson?"

"The letters employed . . . what did I say . . ."

Suddenly she burst into laughter:

"Ah! that is it! I understand! I am an accomplice in the crime! There is a Monsieur Bresson who stole the Jewish lamp and who has now committed suicide. And I am the friend of that gentleman. Oh! how absurd you are!"

"Whom did you go to see last night on the second floor of a house in the Avenue des Ternes?"

"Who? My modiste, Mademoiselle Langeais. Do you suppose that my modiste and my friend Monsieur Bresson are the same person?"

Despite all he knew, Holmes was now in doubt. A person can feign terror, joy, anxiety, in fact all emotions; but a person cannot feign absolute indifference or light, careless laughter. Yet he continued to question her:

"Why did you accost me the other evening at the Northern Railway station? And why did you entreat me to leave Paris immediately without investigating this theft?"

"Ah! you are too inquisitive, Monsieur Holmes," she replied, still laughing in the most natural manner. "To punish you I will tell you nothing, and, besides, you must watch the patient while I go to the pharmacy on an urgent message. Au revoir."

She left the room.

"I am beaten . . . by a girl," muttered Holmes. "Not only did I get nothing out of her but I exposed my hand and put her on her guard."

And he recalled the affair of the blue diamond and his first interview with Clotilde Destange. Had not the blonde Lady met his question with the same unruffled serenity, and was he not once more face to face with one of those creatures who, under the protection and influence of Arsène Lupin, maintain the utmost coolness in the face of a terrible danger?

"Holmes . . . Holmes . . ."

It was Watson who called him. Holmes approached the bed, and, leaning over, said:

"What's the matter, Watson? Does your wound pain you?"

Watson's lips moved, but he could not speak. At last, with a great effort, he stammered:

"No . . . Holmes . . . it is not she . . . that is impossible——"

"Come, Watson, what do you know about it? I tell you that it is she! It is only when I meet one of Lupin's creatures, prepared and instructed by him, that I lose my head and make a fool of myself. . . . I bet you that within an hour Lupin will know all about our interview. Within an hour? What am I saying? . . . Why, he may know already. The visit to the pharmacy . . . urgent message. All nonsense! . . . She has gone to telephone to Lupin."

Holmes left the house hurriedly, went down the Avenue de Messine, and was just in time to see Mademoiselle enter a pharmacy. Ten minutes later she emerged from the shop carrying some small packages and a bottle wrapped in white paper. But she had not proceeded far, when she was accosted by a man who, with hat in hand and an obsequious air, appeared to be asking for charity. She stopped, gave him something, and proceeded on her way.

"She spoke to him," said the Englishman to himself.

If not a certainty, it was at least an intuition, and quite sufficient to cause him to change his tactics. Leaving the girl to pursue her own course, he followed the suspected mendicant, who walked slowly to the Avenue des Ternes and lingered for a long time around the house in which Bresson had lived, sometimes raising his eyes to the windows of the second floor and watching the people who entered the house.

At the end of an hour he climbed to the top of a tramcar going in the direction of Neuilly. Holmes followed and took a seat behind the man, and beside a gentleman who was concealed behind the pages of a newspaper. At the fortifications the gentleman lowered the paper, and Holmes recognized Ganimard, who thereupon whispered, as he pointed to the man in front:

"It is the man who followed Bresson last night. He has been watching the house for an hour."

"Anything new in regard to Bresson?" asked Holmes.

"Yes, a letter came to his address this morning."

"This morning? Then it was posted yesterday before the sender could know of Bresson's death."

"Exactly. It is now in the possession of the examining magistrate. But I read it. It says: *He will not accept any compromise. He wants everything—the first thing as well as those of the second affair. Otherwise he will proceed.*"

"There is no signature," added Ganimard. "It seems to me those few lines won't help us much."

"I don't agree with you, Monsieur Ganimard. To me those few lines are very interesting."

"Why so? I can't see it."

"For reasons that are personal to me," replied Holmes, with the indifference that he frequently displayed toward his colleague.

The tramcar stopped at the Rue de Château, which was the terminus. The man descended and walked away quietly. Holmes followed at so short a distance that Ganimard protested, saying:

"If he should turn around he will suspect us."

"He will not turn around."

"How do you know?"

"He is an accomplice of Arsène Lupin, and the fact that he walks in that manner, with his hands in his pockets, proves, in the first place, that he knows he is being followed and, in the second place, that he is not afraid."

"But I think we are keeping too close to him."

"Not too close to prevent his slipping through our fingers. He is too sure of himself."

"Ah! Look there! In front of that café there are two of the bicycle police. If I summon them to our assistance, how can the man slip through our fingers?"

"Well, our friend doesn't seem to be worried about it. In fact, he is asking for their assistance himself."

"Mon Dieu!" exclaimed Ganimard, "he has a nerve."

The man approached the two policemen just as they were mounting their bicycles. After a few words with them he leaped on a third bicycle, which was leaning against the wall of the café, and rode away at a fast pace, accompanied by the two policemen.

"Hein! one, two, three, and away!" growled Holmes. "And through whose agency, Monsieur Ganimard? Two of your colleagues. . . . Ah! but Arsène Lupin has a wonderful organization! Bicycle policemen in his service! . . . I told you our man was too calm, too sure of himself."

"Well, then," said Ganimard, quite vexed, "what are we to do now? It is easy enough to laugh! Anyone can do that."

"Come, come, don't lose your temper! We will get our revenge. But, in the meantime, we need reinforcements."

"Folenfant is waiting for me at the end of the Avenue de Neuilly."

"Well, go and get him and join me later. I will follow our fugitive."

Holmes followed the bicycle tracks, which were plainly visible in the dust of the road as two of the machines were furnished with striated tires. Very soon he ascertained that the tracks were leading him to the edge of the Seine, and that the three men had turned in the direction taken by Bresson on the preceding evening. Thus he arrived at the gateway where he and Ganimard had concealed themselves, and, a little farther on, he discovered a mingling of the bicycle tracks which showed that the men had halted at that spot. Directly opposite there was a little point of land which projected into the river and, at the extremity thereof, an old boat was moored.

It was there that Bresson had thrown away the package, or, rather, had dropped it. Holmes descended the bank and saw that the declivity was not steep and the water quite shallow, so it would be quite easy to recover the package, provided the three men had not forestalled him.

"No, that can't be," he thought, "they have not had time. A quarter of an hour at the most. And yet, why did they come this way?"

A fisherman was seated on the old boat. Holmes asked him:

"Did you see three men on bicycles a few minutes ago?"

The fisherman made a negative gesture. But Holmes insisted:

"Three men who stopped on the road just on top of the bank?"

The fisherman rested his pole under his arm, took a memorandum book from his pocket, wrote on one of the pages, tore it out, and handed it to Holmes. The Englishman gave a start of surprise. In the middle of the paper which he held in his hand he saw the series of letters cut from the alphabet-book:

CDEHNOPRZEO—237.

The man resumed his fishing, sheltered from the sun by a large straw hat, with his coat and vest lying beside him. He was intently watching the cork attached to his line as it floated on the surface of the water.

There was a moment of silence—solemn and terrible.

"Is it he?" conjectured Holmes, with an anxiety that was almost pitiful. Then the truth burst upon him:

"It is he! It is he! No one else could remain there so calmly, without the slightest display of anxiety, without the least fear of what might happen. And who else would know the story of those mysterious letters? Alice had warned him by means of her messenger."

Suddenly the Englishman felt that his hand—that his own hand had involuntarily seized the handle of his revolver, and that his eyes were fixed on the man's back, a little below the neck. One movement, and the drama would be finished; the life of the strange adventurer would come to a miserable end.

The fisherman did not stir.

Holmes nervously toyed with his revolver, and experienced a wild desire to fire it and end everything; but the horror of such an act was repugnant to his nature. Death would be certain and would end all.

"Ah!" he thought, "let him get up and defend himself. If he doesn't, so much the worse for him. One second more . . . and I fire . . ."

But a sound of footsteps behind him caused him to turn his head. It was Ganimard coming with some assistants.

Then, quickly changing his plans, Holmes leaped into the boat, which was broken from its moorings by his sudden action; he pounced upon the man and seized him around the body. They rolled to the bottom of the boat together.

"Well, now!" exclaimed Lupin, struggling to free himself, "what does this mean? When one of us has conquered the other, what good will it do? You will not know what to do with me, nor I with you. We will remain here like two idiots."

The two oars slipped into the water. The boat drifted into the stream.

"Good Lord, what a fuss you make! A man of your age ought to know better! You act like a child."

Lupin succeeded in freeing himself from the grasp of the detective, who, thoroughly exasperated and ready to kill, put his hand in his pocket. He uttered an oath: Lupin had taken his revolver. Then he knelt down and tried to capture one of the lost oars in order to regain the shore, while Lupin was trying to capture the other oar in order to drive the boat down the river.

"It's gone! I can't reach it," said Lupin. "But it's of no consequence. If you get your oar I can prevent your using it. And you could do the same to me. But, you see, that is the way in this world, we act without any purpose or reason, as our efforts are in vain since Fate decides everything. Now, don't you see, Fate is on the side of his friend Lupin. The game is mine! The current favors me!"

The boat was slowly drifting down the river.

"Look out!" cried Lupin, quickly.

Someone on the bank was pointing a revolver. Lupin stooped, a shot was fired; it struck the water beyond the boat. Lupin burst into laughter.

"God bless me! It's my friend Ganimard! But it was very wrong of you to do that, Ganimard. You have no right to shoot except in self-defense. Does poor Lupin worry you so much that you forget yourself? . . . Now, be good, and don't shoot again! . . . If you do you will hit our English friend."

He stood behind Holmes, facing Ganimard, and said:

"Now, Ganimard, I am ready! Aim for his heart! . . . Higher! . . . A little to the left. . . . Ah! you missed that time . . . deuced bad shot. . . . Try again. . . . Your hand shakes, Ganimard. . . . Now, once more . . . one, two, three, fire! . . . Missed! . . . Parbleu! the authorities furnish you with toy-pistols."

Lupin drew a long revolver and fired without taking aim. Ganimard put his hand to his hat: the bullet had passed through it.

"What do you think of that, Ganimard? Ah! that's a real revolver! A genuine English bulldog. It belongs to my friend, Sherlock Holmes."

And, with a laugh, he threw the revolver to the shore, where it landed at Ganimard's feet.

Holmes could not withhold a smile of admiration. What a torrent of youthful spirits! And how he seemed to enjoy himself! It appeared as if the sensation of peril caused him a physical pleasure; and this extraordinary man had no other purpose in life than to seek for dangers simply for the amusement it afforded him in avoiding them.

Many people had now gathered on the banks of the river, and Ganimard and his men followed the boat as it slowly floated down the stream. Lupin's capture was a mathematical certainty.

"Confess, old fellow," said Lupin, turning to the Englishman, "that you would not exchange your present position for all the gold in the Transvaal! You are now in the first row of the orchestra chairs! But, in the first place, we must have the prologue . . . after which we can leap, at one bound, to the fifth act of the drama, which will represent the capture or escape of Arsène Lupin. Therefore, I am going to ask you a plain question, to which I request a plain answer—a simple yes or no. Will you renounce this affair? At present I can repair the damage you have done; later it will be beyond my power. Is it a bargain?"

"No."

Lupin's face showed his disappointment and annoyance. He continued:

"I insist. More for your sake than my own, I insist, because I am certain you will be the first to regret your intervention. For the last time, yes or no?"

"No."

Lupin stooped down, removed one of the boards in the bottom of the boat, and, for some minutes, was engaged in a work the nature of which Holmes could not discern. Then he arose, seated himself beside the Englishman, and said:

"I believe, monsieur, that we came to the river to-day for the same purpose: to recover the object which Bresson threw away. For my part I had invited a few friends to join me here, and I was on the point of making an examination of the bed of the river when my friends announced your approach. I confess that the news did not surprise me, as I have been notified every hour concerning the progress of your investigation. That was an easy matter. Whenever anything occurred in the Rue Murillo that might interest me, simply a ring on the telephone and I was informed."

He stopped. The board that he had displaced in the bottom of the boat was rising and water was working into the boat all around it.

"The deuce! I didn't know how to fix it. I was afraid this old boat would leak. You are not afraid, monsieur?"

Holmes shrugged his shoulders. Lupin continued:

"You will understand then, in those circumstances, and knowing in advance that you would be more eager to seek a battle than I would be to avoid it, I assure you I was not entirely displeased to enter into a contest of which the issue is quite certain, since I hold all the trump cards in my hand. And I desired that our meeting should be given the widest publicity in order that your defeat may be universally known, so that another Countess de Crozon or another Baron d'Imblevalle may not be tempted to solicit your aid against me. Besides, my dear monsieur——"

He stopped again and, using his half-closed hands as a lorgnette, he scanned the banks of the river.

"Mon Dieu! they have chartered a superb boat, a real war-vessel, and see how they are rowing. In five minutes they will be along-side, and I am lost. Monsieur Holmes, a word of advice; you seize me, bind me, and deliver me to the officers of the law. Does that program please you? . . . Unless, in the meantime, we are shipwrecked, in which event we can do nothing but prepare our wills. What do you think?"

They exchanged looks. Holmes now understood Lupin's scheme: he had scuttled the boat. And the water was rising. It had reached the soles of their boots. Then it covered their feet; but they did not move. It was half-way to their knees. The Englishman took out his tobacco, rolled a cigarette, and lighted it. Lupin continued to talk:

"But do not regard that offer as a confession of my weakness. I surrender to you in a battle in which I can achieve a victory in order to avoid a struggle upon a field not of my own choosing. In so doing I recognize the fact that Holmes is the only enemy I fear, and announce my anxiety that Holmes will not be diverted from my track. I take this opportunity to tell you these things since fate has accorded me the honor of a conversation with you. I have only one regret; it is that our conversation should have occurred while we are taking a foot-bath ... a situation that is lacking in dignity, I must confess. ... What did I say? A foot-bath? It is worse than that."

The water had reached the board on which they were sitting, and the boat was gradually sinking.

Holmes, smoking his cigarette, appeared to be calmly admiring the scenery. For nothing in the world, while face to face with that man who, while threatened by dangers, surrounded by a crowd, followed by a posse of police, maintained his equanimity and good humor, for nothing in the world would he, Holmes, display the slightest sign of nervousness.

Each of them looked as if he might say: Should a person be disturbed by such trifles? Are not people drowned in a river every day? Is it such an unusual event as to deserve special attention? One chatted, whilst the other dreamed; both concealing their wounded pride beneath a mask of indifference.

One minute more and the boat will sink. Lupin continued his chatter:

"The important thing to know is whether we will sink before or after the arrival of the champions of the law. That is the main question. As to our shipwreck, that is a fore-gone conclusion. Now, monsieur, the hour has come in which we must make our wills. I give, devise, and bequeath all my property to Sherlock Holmes, a citizen of England, for his own use and benefit. But, mon Dieu, how quickly the champions of the law are approaching! Ah! the brave fellows! It is a pleasure to watch them. Observe the precision of the oars! Ah! is it you, Brigadier Folenfant? Bravo! The idea of a war-vessel is an excellent one. I commend you to your superiors, Brigadier Folenfant. ... Do you wish a medal? You shall have it. And your comrade Dieuzy, where is he? ... Ah! yes, I think I see him on the left bank of the river at the head of a hundred natives. So that, if I escape shipwreck, I shall be captured on the left by Dieuzy and his natives, or, on the right, by Ganimard and the populace of Neuilly. An embarrassing dilemma!"

The boat entered an eddy; it swung around and Holmes caught hold of the oarlocks. Lupin said to him:

"Monsieur, you should remove your coat. You will find it easier to swim without a coat. No? You refuse? Then I shall put on my own."

He donned his coat, buttoned it closely, the same as Holmes, and said:

"What a discourteous man you are! And what a pity that you should be so stubborn in this affair, in which, of course, you display your strength, but, oh! so vainly! really, you mar your genius——"

"Monsieur Lupin," interrupted Holmes, emerging from his silence, "you talk too much, and you frequently err through excess of confidence and through your frivolity."

"That is a severe reproach."

"Thus, without knowing it, you furnished me, only a moment ago, with the information I required."

"What! you required some information and you didn't tell me?"

"I had no occasion to ask you for it—you volunteered it. Within three hours I can deliver the key of the mystery to Monsieur d'Imblevalle. That is the only reply——"

He did not finish the sentence. The boat suddenly sank, taking both of the men down with it. It emerged immediately, with its keel in the air. Shouts were heard on either bank, succeeded by an anxious moment of silence. Then the shouts were renewed: one of the shipwrecked party had come to the surface.

It was Sherlock Holmes. He was an excellent swimmer, and struck out, with powerful strokes, for Folenfant's boat.

"Courage, Monsieur Holmes," shouted Folenfant; "we are here. Keep it up . . . we will get you . . . a little more, Monsieur Holmes . . . catch the rope."

The Englishman seized the rope they had thrown to him. But, while they were hauling him into the boat, he heard a voice behind him, saying:

"The key of the mystery, monsieur, yes, you shall have it. I am astonished that you haven't got it already. What then? What good will it do you? By that time you will have lost the battle . . ."

Now comfortably installed astride the keel of the boat, Lupin continued his speech with solemn gestures, as if he hoped to convince his adversary.

"You must understand, my dear Holmes, there is nothing to be done, absolutely nothing. You find yourself in the deplorable position of a gentleman——"

"Surrender, Lupin!" shouted Folenfant.

"You are an ill-bred fellow, Folenfant, to interrupt me in the middle of a sentence. I was saying——"

"Surrender, Lupin!"

"Oh! parbleu! Brigadier Folenfant, a man surrenders only when he is in danger. Surely, you do not pretend to say that I am in any danger."

"For the last time, Lupin, I call on you to surrender."

"Brigadier Folenfant, you have no intention of killing me; you may wish to wound me since you are afraid I may escape. But if by chance the wound prove mortal? Just think of your remorse! It would embitter your old age."

The shot was fired.

Lupin staggered, clutched at the keel of the boat for a moment, then let go and disappeared.

⁜

It was exactly three o'clock when the foregoing events transpired. Precisely at six o'clock, as he had foretold, Sherlock Holmes, dressed in trousers that were too short and a coat that was too small, which he had borrowed from an innkeeper at Neuilly, wearing a cap and a flannel shirt, entered the boudoir in the Rue Murillo, after having sent word to Monsieur and Madame d'Imblevalle that he desired an interview.

They found him walking up and down the room. And he looked so ludicrous in his strange costume that they could scarcely suppress their mirth. With pensive air and stooped shoulders, he walked like an automaton from the window to the door and from the door to the window, taking each time the same number of steps, and turning each time in the same manner.

He stopped, picked up a small ornament, examined it mechanically, and resumed his walk. At last, planting himself before them, he asked:

"Is Mademoiselle here?"

"Yes, she is in the garden with the children."

"I wish Mademoiselle to be present at this interview."

"Is it necessary——"

"Have a little patience, monsieur. From the facts I am going to present to you, you will see the necessity for her presence here."

"Very well. Suzanne, will you call her?"

Madame d'Imblevalle arose, went out, and returned almost immediately, accompanied by Alice Demun. Mademoiselle, who was a trifle paler than usual, remained standing, leaning against a table, and without even asking why she had been called. Holmes did not look at her, but, suddenly turning toward Monsieur d'Imblevalle, he said, in a tone which did not admit of a reply:

"After several days' investigation, monsieur, I must repeat what I told you when I first came here: the Jewish lamp was stolen by someone living in the house."

"The name of the guilty party?"

"I know it."

"Your proof?"

"I have sufficient to establish that fact."

"But we require more than that. We desire the restoration of the stolen goods."

"The Jewish lamp? It is in my possession."

"The opal necklace? The snuff-box?"

"The opal necklace, the snuff-box, and all the goods stolen on the second occasion are in my possession."

Holmes delighted in these dramatic dialogues, and it pleased him to announce his victories in that curt manner. The baron and his wife were amazed, and looked at Holmes with a silent curiosity, which was the highest praise.

He related to them, very minutely, what he had done during those three days. He told of his discovery of the alphabet-book, wrote upon a sheet of paper the sentence formed by the missing letters, then related the journey of Bresson to the bank of the river and the suicide of the adventurer, and, finally, his struggle with Lupin, the shipwreck, and the disappearance of Lupin. When he had finished, the baron said, in a low voice:

"Now, you have told us everything except the name of the guilty party. Whom do you accuse?"

"I accuse the person who cut the letters from the alphabet-book, and communicated with Arsène Lupin by means of those letters."

"How do you know that such correspondence was carried on with Arsène Lupin?"

"My information comes from Lupin himself."

He produced a piece of paper that was wet and crumpled. It was the page which Lupin had torn from his memorandum-book, and upon which he had written the phrase.

"And you will notice," said Holmes, with satisfaction, "that he was not obliged to give me that sheet of paper, and, in that way, disclose his identity. Simple childishness on his part, and yet it gave me exactly the information I desired."

"What was it?" asked the baron. "I don't understand."

Holmes took a pencil and made a fresh copy of the letters and figures.

"CDEHNOPRZEO—237."

"Well?" said the baron; "it is the formula you showed me yourself."

"No. If you had turned and returned that formula in every way, as I have done, you would have seen at first glance that this formula is not like the first one."

"In what respect do they differ?"

"This one has two more letters—an E and an O."

"Really; I hadn't noticed that."

"Join those two letters to the C and the H which remained after forming the word 'répondez,' and you will agree with me that the only possible word is ECHO."

"What does that mean?"

"It refers to the *Echo de France*, Lupin's newspaper, his official organ, the one in which he publishes his communications. Reply in the *Echo de France*, in the personal advertisements, under number 237. That is the key to the mystery, and Arsène Lupin was kind enough to furnish it to me. I went to the newspaper office."

"What did you find there?"

"I found the entire story of the relations between Arsène Lupin and his accomplice."

Holmes produced seven newspapers which he opened at the fourth page and pointed to the following lines:

1. Ars. Lup. Lady implores protection. 540.
2. 540. Awaiting particulars. A. L.
3. A. L. Under domin. enemy. Lost.
4. 540. Write address. Will make investigation.
5. A. L. Murillo.
6. 540. Park three o'clock. Violets.
7. 237. Understand. Sat. Will be Sun. morn. park.

"And you call that the whole story!" exclaimed the baron.

"Yes, and if you will listen to me for a few minutes, I think I can convince you. In the first place, a lady who signs herself 540 implores the protection of Arsène Lupin, who replies by asking for particulars. The lady replies that she is under the domination of an enemy—who is Bresson, no doubt—and that she is lost if someone does not come to her assistance. Lupin is suspicious and does not yet venture to appoint an interview with the unknown woman, demands the address, and proposes to make an investigation. The lady hesitates for four days—look at the dates—finally, under stress of circumstances and influenced by Bresson's threats, she gives the name of the street—Murillo. Next day, Arsène Lupin announces that he will be in the Park Monceau at three o'clock, and asks his unknown correspondent to wear a bouquet of violets as a means of identification. Then there is a lapse of eight days in the correspondence. Arsène Lupin and the lady do not require to correspond through the newspaper now, as they see each other or write directly. The scheme is arranged in this way: in order to satisfy Bresson's demands, the lady is to carry off the Jewish lamp. The date is not yet fixed. The lady who, as a matter of prudence, corresponds by means of letters cut out of a book, decides on Saturday and adds: *Reply Echo 237*. Lupin replies that it is understood and that he will be in the park on Sunday morning. Sunday morning, the theft takes place."

"Really, that is an excellent chain of circumstantial evidence and every link is complete," said the baron.

"The theft has taken place," continued Holmes. "The lady goes out on Sunday morning, tells Lupin what she has done, and carries the Jewish lamp to Bresson. Everything occurs then exactly as Lupin had foreseen. The officers of the law, deceived by an open window, four holes in the ground, and two scratches on the balcony railing, immediately advance the theory that the theft was committed by a burglar. The lady is safe."

"Yes, I confess the theory was a logical one," said the baron. "But the second theft——"

"The second theft was provoked by the first. The newspapers having related how the Jewish lamp had disappeared, someone conceived the idea of repeating the crime and carrying away what had been left. This time, it was not a simulated theft, but a real one, a genuine burglary, with ladders and other paraphernalia——"

"Lupin, of course——"

"No. Lupin does not act so stupidly. He doesn't fire at people for trifling reasons."

"Then, who was it?"

"Bresson, no doubt, and unknown to the lady whom he had menaced. It was Bresson who entered here; it was Bresson that I pursued; it was Bresson who wounded poor Watson."

"Are you sure of it?"

"Absolutely. One of Bresson's accomplices wrote to him yesterday, before his suicide, a letter which proves that negotiations were pending between this accomplice and Lupin for the restitution of all the articles stolen from your house. Lupin demanded everything, *'the first thing* (that is, the Jewish lamp) *as well as those of the second affair.'* Moreover, he was watching Bresson. When the latter returned from the river last night, one of Lupin's men followed him as well as we."

"What was Bresson doing at the river?"

"Having been warned of the progress of my investigations——"

"Warned! by whom?"

"By the same lady, who justly feared that the discovery of the Jewish lamp would lead to the discovery of her own adventure. Thereupon, Bresson, having been warned, made into a package all the things that could compromise him and threw them into a place where he thought he could get them again when the danger was past. It was after his return, tracked by Ganimard and myself, having, no doubt, other sins on his conscience, that he lost his head and killed himself."

"But what did the package contain?"

"The Jewish lamp and your other ornaments."

"Then, they are not in your possession?"

"Immediately after Lupin's disappearance, I profited by the bath he had forced upon me, went to the spot selected by Bresson, where I found the stolen articles wrapped in some soiled linen. They are there, on the table."

Without a word, the baron cut the cord, tore open the wet linen, picked out the lamp, turned a screw in the foot, then divided the bowl of the lamp which opened in two equal parts and there he found the golden chimera, set with rubies and emeralds.

It was intact.

|||||||||||||||||||||||||

There was in that scene, so natural in appearance and which consisted of a simple exposition of facts, something which rendered it frightfully tragic—it was the formal, direct, irrefutable accusation that Holmes launched in each of his words against Mademoiselle. And it was also the impressive silence of Alice Demun.

During that long, cruel accumulation of accusing circumstances heaped one upon another, not a muscle of her face had moved, not a trace of revolt or fear had marred the serenity of her limpid eyes. What were her thoughts? And, especially, what was she going to say at the solemn moment when it would become necessary for her to speak and defend herself in order to break the chain of evidence that Sherlock Holmes had so cleverly woven around her?

That moment had come, but the girl was silent.

"Speak! Speak!" cried Mon. d'Imblevalle.

She did not speak. So he insisted:

"One word will clear you. One word of denial, and I will believe you."

That word, she would not utter.

The baron paced to and fro in his excitement; then, addressing Holmes, he said:

"No, monsieur, I cannot believe it, I do not believe it. There are impossible crimes! and this is opposed to all I know and to all that I have seen during the past year. No, I cannot believe it."

He placed his hand on the Englishman's shoulder, and said:

"But you yourself, monsieur, are you absolutely certain that you are right?"

Holmes hesitated, like a man on whom a sudden demand is made and cannot frame an immediate reply. Then he smiled, and said:

"Only the person whom I accuse, by reason of her situation in your house, could know that the Jewish lamp contained that magnificent jewel."

"I cannot believe it," repeated the baron.

"Ask her."

It was, really, the very thing he would not have done, blinded by the confidence the girl had inspired in him. But he could no longer refrain from doing it. He approached her and, looking into her eyes, said:

"Was it you, mademoiselle? Was it you who took the jewel? Was it you who corresponded with Arsène Lupin and committed the theft?"

"It was I, monsieur," she replied.

She did not drop her head. Her face displayed no sign of shame or fear.

"Is it possible?" murmured Mon. d'Imblevalle. "I would never have believed it. . . . You are the last person in the world that I would have suspected. How did you do it?"

"I did it exactly as Monsieur Holmes has told it. On Saturday night I came to the boudoir, took the lamp, and, in the morning I carried it . . . to that man."

"No," said the baron; "what you pretend to have done is impossible."

"Impossible—why?"

"Because, in the morning I found the door of the boudoir bolted."

She blushed, and looked at Holmes as if seeking his counsel. Holmes was astonished at her embarrassment. Had she nothing to say? Did the confessions, which had corroborated the report that he, Holmes, had made concerning the theft of the Jewish lamp, merely serve to mask a lie? Was she misleading them by a false confession?

The baron continued:

"That door was locked. I found the door exactly as I had left it the night before. If you entered by that door, as you pretend, someone must have opened it from the interior—that is to say, from the boudoir or from our chamber. Now, there was no one inside these two rooms . . . there was no one except my wife and myself."

Holmes bowed his head and covered his face with his hands in order to conceal his emotion. A sudden light had entered his mind, that startled him and made him exceedingly uncomfortable. Everything was revealed to him, like the sudden lifting of a fog from the morning landscape. He was annoyed as well as ashamed, because his deductions were fallacious and his entire theory was wrong.

Alice Demun was innocent!

Alice Demun was innocent. That proposition explained the embarrassment he had experienced from the beginning in directing the terrible accusation against that young girl. Now, he saw the truth; he knew it. After a few seconds, he raised his head, and looked at Madame d'Imblevalle as naturally as he could. She was pale—with that unusual pallor which invades us in the relentless moments of our lives. Her hands, which she endeavored to conceal, were trembling as if stricken with palsy.

"One minute more," thought Holmes, "and she will betray herself."

He placed himself between her and her husband in the desire to avert the awful danger which, *through his fault,* now threatened that man and woman. But, at sight of the baron, he was shocked to the very center of his soul. The same dreadful idea had entered the mind of Monsieur d'Imblevalle. The same thought was at work in the brain of the husband. He understood, also! He saw the truth!

In desperation, Alice Demun hurled herself against the implacable truth, saying:

"You are right, monsieur. I made a mistake. I did not enter by this door. I came through the garden and the vestibule . . . by aid of a ladder——"

It was a supreme effort of true devotion. But a useless effort! The words rang false. The voice did not carry conviction, and the poor girl no longer displayed those clear, fearless eyes and that natural air of innocence which had served her so well. Now, she bowed her head—vanquished.

The silence became painful. Madame d'Imblevalle was waiting for her husband's next move, overwhelmed with anxiety and fear. The baron appeared to be struggling against the dreadful suspicion, as if he would not submit to the overthrow of his happiness. Finally, he said to his wife:

"Speak! Explain!"

"I have nothing to tell you," she replied, in a very low voice, and with features drawn by anguish.

"So, then . . . Mademoiselle . . ."

"Mademoiselle saved me . . . through devotion . . . through affection . . . and accused herself . . ."

"Saved you from what? From whom?"

"From that man."

"Bresson?"

"Yes; it was I whom he held in fear by threats. . . . I met him at one of my friends' . . . and I was foolish enough to listen to him. Oh! there was nothing that you cannot pardon. But I wrote him two letters . . . letters which you will see. . . . I had to buy them back . . . you know how. . . . Oh! have pity on me! . . . I have suffered so much!"

"You! You! Suzanne!"

He raised his clenched fists, ready to strike her, ready to kill her. But he dropped his arms, and murmured:

"You, Suzanne . . . You! . . . Is it possible?"

By short detached sentences, she related the heartrending story, her dreadful awakening to the infamy of the man, her remorse, her fear, and she also told of Alice's devotion; how the young girl divined the sorrow of her mistress, wormed a confession out of her, wrote to Lupin, and devised the scheme of the theft in order to save her from Bresson.

"You, Suzanne, you," repeated Monsieur d'Imblevalle, bowed with grief and shame. . . . "How could you?"

On the same evening, the steamer *City of London*, which plies between Calais and Dover, was gliding slowly over the smooth sea. The night was dark; the wind was fainter than a zephyr. The majority of the passengers had retired to their cabins; but a few, more intrepid, were promenading on the deck or sleeping in large rocking-chairs, wrapped in their traveling-rugs. One could see, here and there, the light of a cigar, and one could hear, mingled with the soft murmur of the breeze, the faint sound of voices which were carefully subdued to harmonize with the deep silence of the night.

One of the passengers, who had been pacing to and fro upon the deck, stopped before a woman who was lying on a bench, scrutinized her, and, when she moved a little, he said:

"I thought you were asleep, Mademoiselle Alice."

"No, Monsieur Holmes, I am not sleepy. I was thinking."

"Of what? If I may be so bold as to inquire?"

"I was thinking of Madame d'Imblevalle. She must be very unhappy. Her life is ruined."

"Oh! no, no," he replied quickly. "Her mistake was not a serious one. Monsieur d'Imblevalle will forgive and forget it. Why, even before we left, his manner toward her had softened."

"Perhaps . . . but he will remember it for a long time . . . and she will suffer a great deal."

"You love her?"

"Very much. It was my love for her that gave me strength to smile when I was trembling from fear, that gave me courage to look in your face when I desired to hide from your sight."

"And you are sorry to leave her?"

"Yes, very sorry. I have no relatives, no friends—but her."

"You will have friends," said the Englishman, who was affected by her sorrow. "I have promised that. I have relatives . . . and some influence. I assure you that you will have no cause to regret coming to England."

"That may be, monsieur, but Madame d'Imblevalle will not be there."

Sherlock Holmes resumed his promenade upon the deck. After a few minutes, he took a seat near his traveling companion, filled his pipe, and struck four matches in a vain effort to light it. Then, as he had no more matches, he arose and said to a gentleman who was sitting near him:

"May I trouble you for a match?"

The gentleman opened a box of matches and struck one. The flame lighted up his face. Holmes recognized him—it was Arsène Lupin.

If the Englishman had not given an almost imperceptible movement of surprise, Lupin would have supposed that his presence on board had been known to Holmes, so well did he control his feelings and so natural was the easy manner in which he extended his hand to his adversary.

"How's the good health, Monsieur Lupin?"

"Bravo!" exclaimed Lupin, who could not repress a cry of admiration at the Englishman's sang-froid.

"Bravo? and why?"

"Why? Because I appear before you like a ghost, only a few hours after you saw me drowned in the Seine; and through pride—a quality that is essentially English—you evince not the slightest surprise. You greet me as a matter of course. Ah! I repeat: Bravo! Admirable!"

"There is nothing remarkable about it. From the manner in which you fell from the boat, I knew very well that you fell voluntarily, and that the bullet had not touched you."

"And you went away without knowing what had become of me?"

"What had become of you? Why, I knew that. There were at least five hundred people on the two banks of the river within a space of half-a-mile. If you escaped death, your capture was certain."

"And yet I am here."

"Monsieur Lupin, there are two men in the world at whom I am never astonished: in the first place, myself—and then, Arsène Lupin." The treaty of peace was concluded.

If Holmes had not been successful in his contests with Arsène Lupin; if Lupin remained the only enemy whose capture he must never hope to accomplish; if, in the course of their struggles, he had not always displayed a superiority, the Englishman had, none the less, by means of his extraordinary intuition and tenacity, succeeded in recovering the Jewish lamp as well as the blue diamond. This time, perhaps, the finish had not been so brilliant, especially from the stand-point of the public spectators, since Holmes was obliged to maintain a discreet silence in regard to the circumstances in which the Jewish lamp had been recovered, and to announce that he did not know the name of the thief. But as man to man, Arsène Lupin against Sherlock Holmes, detective against burglar, there was neither victor nor vanquished. Each of them had won corresponding victories.

Therefore they could now converse as courteous adversaries who had lain down their arms and held each other in high regard.

At Holmes's request, Arsène Lupin related the strange story of his escape.

"If I may dignify it by calling it an escape," he said. "It was so simple! My friends were watching for me, as I had asked them to meet me there to recover the Jewish lamp. So, after remaining a good half-hour under the overturned boat, I took advantage of an occasion when Folenfant and his men were searching for my dead body along the bank of the river, to climb on top of the boat. Then my friends simply picked me up as they passed by in their motor-boat, and we sailed away under the staring eyes of an astonished multitude, including Ganimard and Folenfant."

"Very good," exclaimed Holmes, "very neatly played. And now you have some business in England?"

"Yes, some accounts to square up. . . . But I forgot . . . what about Monsieur d'Imblevalle?"

"He knows everything."

"Ah! my dear Holmes, what did I tell you? The wrong is now irreparable. Would it not have been better to have allowed me to carry out the affair in my own way? In a day or two more, I should have recovered the stolen goods from Bresson, restored them to Monsieur d'Imblevalle, and those two honest citizens would have lived together in peace and happiness ever after. Instead of that——"

"Instead of that," said Holmes, sneeringly, "I have mixed the cards and sown the seeds of discord in the bosom of a family that was under your protection."

"Mon Dieu! of course, I was protecting them. Must a person steal, cheat, and wrong all the time?"

"Then you do good, also?"

"When I have the time. Besides, I find it amusing. Now, for instance, in our last adventure, I found it extremely diverting that I should be the good genius seeking to help and save unfortunate mortals, while you were the evil genius who dispensed only despair and tears."

"Tears! Tears!" protested Holmes.

"Certainly! The d'Imblevalle household is demolished, and Alice Demun weeps."

"She could not remain any longer. Ganimard would have discovered her some day, and, through her, reached Madame d'Imblevalle."

"Quite right, monsieur; but whose fault is it?"

Two men passed by. Holmes said to Lupin, in a friendly tone:

"Do you know those gentlemen?"

"I thought I recognized one of them as the captain of the steamer."

"And the other?"

"I don't know."

"It is Austin Gilett, who occupies in London a position similar to that of Monsieur Dudouis in Paris."

"Ah! how fortunate! Will you be so kind as to introduce me? Monsieur Dudouis is one of my best friends, and I shall be delighted to say as much of Monsieur Austin Gilett."

The two gentlemen passed again.

"And if I should take you at your word, Monsieur Lupin?" said Holmes, rising, and seizing Lupin's wrist with a hand of iron.

"Why do you grasp me so tightly, monsieur? I am quite willing to follow you."

In fact, he allowed himself to be dragged along without the least resistance. The two gentlemen were disappearing from sight. Holmes quickened his pace. His finger-nails even sank into Lupin's flesh.

"Come! Come!" he exclaimed, with a sort of feverish haste, in harmony with his action. "Come! quicker than that."

But he stopped suddenly. Alice Demun was following them.

"What are you doing, Mademoiselle? You need not come. You must not come!"

It was Lupin who replied:

"You will notice, monsieur, that she is not coming of her own free will. I am holding her wrist in the same tight grasp that you have on mine."

"Why?"

"Because I wish to present her also. Her part in the affair of the Jewish lamp is much more important than mine. Accomplice of Arsène Lupin, accomplice of Bresson, she has a right to tell her adventure with the Baroness d'Imblevalle—which will deeply interest Monsieur Gilett as an officer of the law. And by introducing her also, you will have carried your gracious intervention to the very limit, my dear Holmes."

The Englishman released his hold on his prisoner's wrist. Lupin liberated Mademoiselle.

They stood looking at each other for a few seconds, silently and motionless. Then Holmes returned to the bench and sat down, followed by Lupin and the girl.

After a long silence, Lupin said:

"You see, monsieur, whatever we may do, we will never be on the same side. You are on one side of the fence; I am on the other. We can exchange greetings, shake hands, converse a moment, but the fence is always there. You will remain Sherlock Holmes, detective, and I, Arsène Lupin, gentleman-burglar. And Sherlock Holmes will ever obey, more or less spontaneously, with more or less propriety, his instinct as a detective, which is to pursue the burglar and run him down, if possible. And Arsène Lupin, in obedience to his burglarious instinct, will always be occupied in avoiding the reach of the detective, and making sport of the detective, if he can do it. And, this time, he can do it. Ha-ha-ha!"

He burst into a loud laugh, cunning, cruel, and odious.

Then, suddenly becoming serious, he addressed. Alice Demun:

"You may be sure, mademoiselle, even when reduced to the last extremity, I shall not betray you. Arsène Lupin never betrays anyone—especially those whom he loves and admires. And, may I be permitted to say, I love and admire the brave, dear woman you have proved yourself to be."

He took from his pocket a visiting card, tore it in two, gave one-half of it to the girl, as he said, in a voice shaken with emotion:

"If Monsieur Holmes's plans for you do not succeed, mademoiselle, go to Lady Strongborough—you can easily find her address— and give her that half of the card, and, at the same time, say to her: *Faithful friend*. Lady Strongborough will show you the true devotion of a sister."

"Thank you," said the girl; "I shall see her to-morrow."

"And now, Monsieur Holmes," exclaimed Lupin, with the satisfied air of a gentleman who has fulfilled his duty, "I will say good-night. We will not land for an hour yet, so I will get that much rest."

He lay down on the bench, with his hands beneath his head.

In a short time the high cliffs of the English coast loomed up in the increasing light of a new-born day. The passengers emerged from the cabins and crowded the deck, eagerly gazing on the approaching shore. Austin Gilett passed by, accompanied by two men whom Holmes recognized as sleuths from Scotland Yard.

Lupin was asleep, on his bench.

FROM THE CONFESSIONS OF
ARSÈNE LUPIN (1912)

TWO HUNDRED THOUSAND FRANCS REWARD! . . .

L upin," I said, "tell me something about yourself."
"Why, what would you have me tell you? Everybody knows
my life!" replied Lupin, who lay drowsing on the sofa in my study.

"Nobody knows it!" I protested. "People know from your letters in
the newspapers that you were mixed up in this case, that you started
that case. But the part which you played in it all, the plain facts of the
story, the upshot of the mystery: these are things of which they know
nothing."

"Pooh! A heap of uninteresting twaddle!"

"What! Your present of fifty thousand francs to Nicolas Dugrival's wife! Do you call that uninteresting? And what about the way in
which you solved the puzzle of the three pictures?"

Lupin laughed:

"Yes, that was a queer puzzle, certainly. I can suggest a title for you
if you like: what do you say to *The Sign of the Shadow*?"

"And your successes in society and with the fair sex?" I continued. "The dashing Arsène's love-affairs! . . . And the clue to your
good actions? Those chapters in your life to which you have so often
alluded under the names of *The Wedding-ring*, *Shadowed by Death*,

and so on! . . . Why delay these confidences and confessions, my dear Lupin? . . . Come, do what I ask you! . . ."

It was at the time when Lupin, though already famous, had not yet fought his biggest battles; the time that preceded the great adventures of *The Hollow Needle* and *813*. He had not yet dreamt of annexing the accumulated treasures of the French Royal House nor of changing the map of Europe under the Kaiser's nose: he contented himself with milder surprises and humbler profits, making his daily effort, doing evil from day to day and doing a little good as well, naturally and for the love of the thing, like a whimsical and compassionate Don Quixote.

He was silent; and I insisted:

"Lupin, I wish you would!"

To my astonishment, he replied:

"Take a sheet of paper, old fellow, and a pencil."

I obeyed with alacrity, delighted at the thought that he at last meant to dictate to me some of those pages which he knows how to clothe with such vigour and fancy, pages which I, unfortunately, am obliged to spoil with tedious explanations and boring developments.

"Are you ready?" he asked.

"Quite."

"Write down, 20, 1, 11, 5, 14, 15."

"What?"

"Write it down, I tell you."

He was now sitting up, with his eyes turned to the open window and his fingers rolling a Turkish cigarette. He continued:

"Write down, 21, 14, 14, 5 . . ."

He stopped. Then he went on:

"3, 5, 19, 19 . . ."

And, after a pause:

"5, 18, 25 . . ."

Was he mad? I looked at him hard and, presently, I saw that his eyes were no longer listless, as they had been a little before, but keen and attentive and that they seemed to be watching, somewhere, in space, a sight that apparently captivated them.

Meanwhile, he dictated, with intervals between each number:

"18, 9, 19, 11, 19 . . ."

There was hardly anything to be seen through the window but a patch of blue sky on the right and the front of the building opposite, an old private house, whose shutters were closed as usual. There was nothing particular about all this, no detail that struck me as new among those which I had had before my eyes for years . . .

"1, 2 . . ."

And suddenly I understood . . . or rather I thought I understood, for how could I admit that Lupin, a man so essentially level-headed under his mask of frivolity, could waste his time upon such childish nonsense? What he was counting was the intermittent flashes of a ray of sunlight playing on the dingy front of the opposite house, at the height of the second floor!

"15, 22 . . ." said Lupin.

The flash disappeared for a few seconds and then struck the house again, successively, at regular intervals, and disappeared once more.

I had instinctively counted the flashes and I said, aloud:

"5 . . ."

"Caught the idea? I congratulate you!" he replied, sarcastically.

He went to the window and leant out, as though to discover the exact direction followed by the ray of light. Then he came and lay on the sofa again, saying:

"It's your turn now. Count away!"

The fellow seemed so positive that I did as he told me. Besides, I could not help confessing that there was something rather curious about the ordered frequency of those gleams on the front of the house opposite, those appearances and disappearances, turn and turn about, like so many flash signals.

They obviously came from a house on our side of the street, for the sun was entering my windows slantwise. It was as though someone were alternately opening and shutting a casement, or, more likely, amusing himself by making sunlight flashes with a pocket-mirror.

"It's a child having a game!" I cried, after a moment or two, feeling a little irritated by the trivial occupation that had been thrust upon me.

"Never mind, go on!"

And I counted away. . . . And I put down rows of figures. . . . And the sun continued to play in front of me, with mathematical precision.

"Well?" said Lupin, after a longer pause than usual.

"Why, it seems finished. . . . There has been nothing for some minutes . . ."

We waited and, as no more light flashed through space, I said, jestingly:

"My idea is that we have been wasting our time. A few figures on paper: a poor result!"

Lupin, without stirring from his sofa, rejoined:

"Oblige me, old chap, by putting in the place of each of those numbers the corresponding letter of the alphabet. Count A as 1, B as 2, and so on. Do you follow me?"

"But it's idiotic!"

"Absolutely idiotic, but we do such a lot of idiotic things in this life.... One more or less, you know!..."

I sat down to this silly work and wrote out the first letters:

"Take no ..."

I broke off in surprise:

"Words!" I exclaimed. "Two English words meaning..."

"Go on, old chap."

And I went on and the next letters formed two more words, which I separated as they appeared. And, to my great amazement, a complete English sentence lay before my eyes.

"Done?" asked Lupin, after a time.

"Done!... By the way, there are mistakes in the spelling..."

"Never mind those and read it out, please.... Read slowly."

Thereupon I read out the following unfinished communication, which I will set down as it appeared on the paper in front of me:

"Take no unnecessery risks. Above all, avoid atacks, approach ennemy with great prudance and ..."

I began to laugh:

"And there you are! *Fiat lux!* We're simply dazed with light! But, after all, Lupin, confess that this advice, dribbled out by a kitchen-maid, doesn't help you much!"

Lupin rose, without breaking his contemptuous silence, and took the sheet of paper.

I remembered soon after that, at this moment, I happened to look at the clock. It was eighteen minutes past five.

Lupin was standing with the paper in his hand; and I was able at my ease to watch, on his youthful features, that extraordinary mobility of expression which baffles all observers and constitutes his great strength and his chief safeguard. By what signs can one hope to identify a face which changes at pleasure, even without the help of make-up, and whose every transient expression seems to be the final, definite expression? . . . By what signs? There was one which I knew well, an invariable sign: Two little crossed wrinkles that marked his forehead whenever he made a powerful effort of concentration. And I saw it at that moment, saw the tiny tell-tale cross, plainly and deeply scored.

He put down the sheet of paper and muttered:

"Child's play!"

The clock struck half-past five.

"What!" I cried. "Have you succeeded? . . . In twelve minutes? . . ."

He took a few steps up and down the room, lit a cigarette, and said:

"You might ring up Baron Repstein, if you don't mind, and tell him I shall be with him at ten o'clock this evening."

"Baron Repstein?" I asked. "The husband of the famous baroness?"

"Yes."

"Are you serious?"

"Quite serious."

Feeling absolutely at a loss, but incapable of resisting him, I opened the telephone-directory and unhooked the receiver. But, at that moment, Lupin stopped me with a peremptory gesture and said, with his eyes on the paper, which he had taken up again:

"No, don't say anything. . . . It's no use letting him know. . . . There's something more urgent . . . a queer thing that puzzles me. . . . Why on earth wasn't the last sentence finished? Why is the sentence . . ."

He snatched up his hat and stick:

"Let's be off. If I'm not mistaken, this is a business that requires immediate solution; and I don't believe I *am* mistaken."

He put his arm through mine, as we went down the stairs, and said:

"I know what everybody knows. Baron Repstein, the company-promoter and racing-man, whose colt Etna won the Derby and the Grand Prix this year, has been victimized by his wife. The wife, who was well known for her fair hair, her dress, and her extravagance, ran away a fortnight ago, taking with her a sum of three million francs, stolen from her husband, and quite a collection of diamonds, pearls, and jewelry which the Princesse de Berny had placed in her hands and which she was supposed to buy. For two weeks the police have been pursuing the baroness across France and the continent: an easy job, as she scatters gold and jewels wherever she goes. They think they have her every moment. Two days ago, our champion detective, the egregious Ganimard, arrested a visitor at a big hotel in Belgium, a woman against whom the most positive evidence seemed to be heaped up. On enquiry, the lady turned out to be a notorious chorus-girl called Nelly Darbal. As for the baroness, she has vanished. The baron, on his side, has offered a reward of two hundred thousand francs to whosoever finds his wife. The money is in the hands of a solicitor. Moreover, he has sold his racing-stud, his house on the Boulevard Haussmann and his country-seat of Roquencourt in one lump, so that he may indemnify the Princesse de Berny for her loss."

"And the proceeds of the sale," I added, "are to be paid over at once. The papers say that the princess will have her money to-morrow. Only, frankly, I fail to see the connection between this story, which you have told very well, and the puzzling sentence . . ."

Lupin did not condescend to reply.

We had been walking down the street in which I live and had passed some four or five houses, when he stepped off the pavement and began to examine a block of flats, not of the latest construction, which looked as if it contained a large number of tenants:

"According to my calculations," he said, "this is where the signals came from, probably from that open window."

"On the third floor?"

"Yes."

He went to the portress and asked her:

"Does one of your tenants happen to be acquainted with Baron Repstein?"

"Why, of course!" replied the woman. "We have M. Lavernoux

here, such a nice gentleman; he is the baron's secretary and agent. I look after his flat."

"And can we see him?"

"See him? . . . The poor gentleman is very ill."

"Ill?"

"He's been ill a fortnight . . . ever since the trouble with the baroness. . . . He came home the next day with a temperature and took to his bed."

"But he gets up, surely?"

"Ah, that I can't say!"

"How do you mean, you can't say?"

"No, his doctor won't let anyone into his room. He took my key from me."

"Who did?"

"The doctor. He comes and sees to his wants, two or three times a day. He left the house only twenty minutes ago . . . an old gentleman with a grey beard and spectacles. . . . Walks quite bent. . . . But where are you going, sir?"

"I'm going up, show me the way," said Lupin, with his foot on the stairs. "It's the third floor, isn't it, on the left?"

"But I mustn't!" moaned the portress, running after him. "Besides, I haven't the key . . . the doctor . . ."

They climbed the three flights, one behind the other. On the landing, Lupin took a tool from his pocket and, disregarding the woman's protests, inserted it in the lock. The door yielded almost immediately. We went in.

At the back of a small dark room we saw a streak of light filtering through a door that had been left ajar. Lupin ran across the room and, on reaching the threshold, gave a cry:

"Too late! Oh, hang it all!"

The portress fell on her knees, as though fainting.

I entered the bedroom, in my turn, and saw a man lying half-dressed on the carpet, with his legs drawn up under him, his arms contorted and his face quite white, an emaciated, fleshless face, with the eyes still staring in terror and the mouth twisted into a hideous grin.

"He's dead," said Lupin, after a rapid examination.

"But why?" I exclaimed. "There's not a trace of blood!"

"Yes, yes, there is," replied Lupin, pointing to two or three drops that showed on the chest, through the open shirt. "Look, they must have taken him by the throat with one hand and pricked him to the heart with the other. I say, 'pricked,' because really the wound can't be seen. It suggests a hole made by a very long needle."

He looked on the floor, all round the corpse. There was nothing to attract his attention, except a little pocket-mirror, the little mirror with which M. Lavernoux had amused himself by making the sunbeams dance through space.

But, suddenly, as the portress was breaking into lamentations and calling for help, Lupin flung himself on her and shook her:

"Stop that! . . . Listen to me . . . you can call out later. . . . Listen to me and answer me. It is most important. M. Lavernoux had a friend living in this street, had he not? On the same side, to the right? An intimate friend?"

"Yes."

"A friend whom he used to meet at the café in the evening and with whom he exchanged the illustrated papers?"

"Yes."

"Was the friend an Englishman?"

"Yes."

"What's his name?"

"Mr. Hargrove."

"Where does he live?"

"At No. 92 in this street."

"One word more: had that old doctor been attending him long?"

"No. I did not know him. He came on the evening when M. Lavernoux was taken ill."

Without another word, Lupin dragged me away once more, ran down the stairs and, once in the street, turned to the right, which took us past my flat again. Four doors further, he stopped at No. 92, a small, low-storied house, of which the ground-floor was occupied by the proprietor of a dram-shop, who stood smoking in his doorway, next to the entrance-passage. Lupin asked if Mr. Hargrove was at home.

"Mr. Hargrove went out about half an hour ago," said the publican. "He seemed very much excited and took a taxi-cab, a thing he doesn't often do."

"And you don't know . . ."

"Where he was going? Well, there's no secret about it. He shouted it loud enough! 'Prefecture of Police' is what he said to the driver . . ."

Lupin was himself just hailing a taxi, when he changed his mind; and I heard him mutter:

"What's the good? He's got too much start of us . . ."

He asked if anyone called after Mr. Hargrove had gone.

"Yes, an old gentleman with a grey beard and spectacles. He went up to Mr. Hargrove's, rang the bell, and went away again."

"I am much obliged," said Lupin, touching his hat.

He walked away slowly without speaking to me, wearing a thoughtful air. There was no doubt that the problem struck him as very difficult, and that he saw none too clearly in the darkness through which he seemed to be moving with such certainty.

He himself, for that matter, confessed to me:

"These are cases that require much more intuition than reflection. But this one, I may tell you, is well worth taking pains about."

We had now reached the boulevards. Lupin entered a public reading-room and spent a long time consulting the last fortnight's newspapers. Now and again, he mumbled:

"Yes . . . yes . . . of course . . . it's only a guess, but it explains everything. . . . Well, a guess that answers every question is not far from being the truth . . ."

It was now dark. We dined at a little restaurant and I noticed that Lupin's face became gradually more animated. His gestures were more decided. He recovered his spirits, his liveliness. When we left, during the walk which he made me take along the Boulevard Haussmann, toward Baron Repstein's house, he was the real Lupin of the great occasions, the Lupin who had made up his mind to go in and win.

We slackened our pace just short of the Rue de Courcelles. Baron Repstein lived on the left-hand side, between this street and the Faubourg Saint-Honoré, in a three-storied private house of which we could see the front, decorated with columns and caryatides.

"Stop!" said Lupin, suddenly.

"What is it?"

"Another proof to confirm my supposition . . ."

"What proof? I see nothing."

"I do. . . . That's enough . . ."

He turned up the collar of his coat, lowered the brim of his soft hat, and said:

"By Jove, it'll be a stiff fight! Go to bed, my friend. I'll tell you about my expedition to-morrow . . . if it doesn't cost me my life."

"What are you talking about?"

"Oh, I know what I'm saying! I'm risking a lot. First of all, getting arrested, which isn't much. Next, getting killed, which is worse. But . . ." He gripped my shoulder. "But there's a third thing I'm risking, which is getting hold of two millions. . . . And, once I possess a capital of two millions, I'll show people what I can do! Good-night, old chap, and, if you never see me again . . ." He spouted Musset's lines:

> *Plant a willow by my grave,*
> *The weeping willow that I love . . ."*

I walked away. Three minutes later—I am continuing the narrative as he told it to me next day—three minutes later, Lupin rang at the door of the Hôtel Repstein.

"Is monsieur le baron at home?"

"Yes," replied the butler, examining the intruder with an air of surprise, "but monsieur le baron does not see people as late as this."

"Does monsieur le baron know of the murder of M. Lavernoux, his land-agent?"

"Certainly."

"Well, please tell monsieur le baron that I have come about the murder and that there is not a moment to lose."

A voice called from above:

"Show the gentleman up, Antoine."

In obedience to this peremptory order, the butler led the way to the first floor. In an open doorway stood a gentleman whom Lupin recognized from his photograph in the papers as Baron Repstein, husband of the famous baroness and owner of Etna, the horse of the year.

He was an exceedingly tall, square-shouldered man. His clean-shaven face wore a pleasant, almost smiling expression, which was not affected by the sadness of his eyes. He was dressed in a well-cut morning-coat, with a tan waistcoat and a dark tie fastened with a pearl pin, the value of which struck Lupin as considerable.

He took Lupin into his study, a large, three-windowed room, lined with book-cases, sets of pigeonholes, an American desk, and a safe. And he at once asked, with ill-concealed eagerness:

"Do you know anything?"

"Yes, monsieur le baron."

"About the murder of that poor Lavernoux?"

"Yes, monsieur le baron, and about madame le baronne also."

"Do you really mean it? Quick, I entreat you . . ."

He pushed forward a chair. Lupin sat down and began:

"Monsieur le baron, the circumstances are very serious. I will be brief."

"Yes, do, please."

"Well, monsieur le baron, in a few words, it amounts to this: five or six hours ago, Lavernoux, who, for the last fortnight, had been kept in a sort of enforced confinement by his doctor, Lavernoux—how shall I put it?—telegraphed certain revelations by means of signals which were partly taken down by me and which put me on the track of this case. He himself was surprised in the act of making this communication and was murdered."

"But by whom? By whom?"

"By his doctor."

"Who is this doctor?"

"I don't know. But one of M. Lavernoux's friends, an Englishman called Hargrove, the friend, in fact, with whom he was communicating, is bound to know and is also bound to know the exact and complete meaning of the communication, because, without waiting for the end, he jumped into a motor-cab and drove to the Prefecture of Police."

"Why? Why? . . . And what is the result of that step?"

"The result, monsieur le baron, is that your house is surrounded. There are twelve detectives under your windows. The moment the sun rises, they will enter in the name of the law and arrest the criminal."

"Then is Lavernoux's murderer concealed in my house? Who is he? One of the servants? But no, for you were speaking of a doctor! . . ."

"I would remark, monsieur le baron, that when this Mr. Hargrove went to the police to tell them of the revelations made by his friend Lavernoux, he was not aware that his friend Lavernoux was going to be murdered. The step taken by Mr. Hargrove had to do with something else . . ."

"With what?"

"With the disappearance of madame la baronne, of which he knew the secret, thanks to the communication made by Lavernoux."

"What! They know at last! They have found the baroness! Where is she? And the jewels? And the money she robbed me of?"

Baron Repstein was talking in a great state of excitement. He rose and, almost shouting at Lupin, cried:

"Finish your story, sir! I can't endure this suspense!"

Lupin continued, in a slow and hesitating voice: "The fact is . . . you see . . . it is rather difficult to explain . . . for you and I are looking at the thing from a totally different point of view."

"I don't understand."

"And yet you ought to understand, monsieur le baron. . . . We begin by saying—I am quoting the newspapers—by saying, do we not, that Baroness Repstein knew all the secrets of your business and that she was able to open not only that safe over there, but also the one at the Crédit Lyonnais in which you kept your securities locked up?"

"Yes."

"Well, one evening, a fortnight ago, while you were at your club, Baroness Repstein, who, unknown to yourself, had converted all those securities into cash, left this house with a traveling-bag, containing your money and all the Princesse de Berny's jewels?"

"Yes."

"And, since then, she has not been seen?"

"No."

"Well, there is an excellent reason why she has not been seen."

"What reason?"

"This, that Baroness Repstein has been murdered . . ."

"Murdered! . . . The baroness! . . . But you're mad!"

"Murdered . . . and probably that same evening."

"I tell you again, you are mad! How can the baroness have been murdered, when the police are following her tracks, so to speak, step by step?"

"They are following the tracks of another woman."

"What woman?"

"The murderer's accomplice."

"And who is the murderer?"

"The same man who, for the last fortnight, knowing that Lavernoux, through the situation which he occupied in this house, had discovered the truth, kept him imprisoned, forced him to silence, threatened him, terrorized him; the same man who, finding Lavernoux in the act of communicating with a friend, made away with him in cold blood by stabbing him to the heart."

"The doctor, therefore?"

"Yes."

"But who is this doctor? Who is this malevolent genius, this infernal being who appears and disappears, who slays in the dark and whom nobody suspects?"

"Can't you guess?"

"No."

"And do you want to know?"

"Do I want to know? . . . Why, speak, man, speak! . . . You know where he is hiding?"

"Yes."

"In this house?"

"Yes."

"And it is he whom the police are after?"

"Yes."

"And I know him?"

"Yes."

"Who is it?"

"You!"

"I! . . ."

Lupin had not been more than ten minutes with the baron; and the duel was commencing. The accusation was hurled, definitely, violently, implacably.

Lupin repeated:

"You yourself, got up in a false beard and a pair of spectacles, bent in two, like an old man. In short, you, Baron Repstein; and it is you for a very good reason, of which nobody has thought, which is that, if it was not you who contrived the whole plot, the case becomes inexplicable. Whereas, taking you as the criminal, you as murdering the baroness in order to get rid of her and run through those millions with another woman, you as murdering Lavernoux, your agent, in order to suppress an unimpeachable witness, oh, then the whole case is explained! Well, is it pretty clear? And are not you yourself convinced?"

The baron, who, throughout this conversation, had stood bending over his visitor, waiting for each of his words with feverish avidity, now drew himself up and looked at Lupin as though he undoubtedly had to do with a madman. When Lupin had finished speaking, the baron stepped back two or three paces, seemed on the point of uttering words which he ended by not saying, and then, without taking his eyes from his strange visitor, went to the fireplace and rang the bell.

Lupin did not make a movement. He waited smiling.

The butler entered. His master said:

"You can go to bed, Antoine. I will let this gentleman out."

"Shall I put out the lights, sir?"

"Leave a light in the hall."

Antoine left the room and the baron, after taking a revolver from his desk, at once came back to Lupin, put the weapon in his pocket, and said, very calmly:

"You must excuse this little precaution, sir. I am obliged to take it in case you should be mad, though that does not seem likely. No, you are not mad. But you have come here with an object which I fail to grasp; and you have sprung upon me an accusation of so astounding a character that I am curious to know the reason. I have experienced so much disappointment and undergone so much suffering that an outrage of this kind leaves me indifferent. Continue, please."

His voice shook with emotion and his sad eyes seemed moist with tears.

Lupin shuddered. Had he made a mistake? Was the surmise which his intuition had suggested to him and which was based upon a frail groundwork of slight facts, was this surmise wrong?

His attention was caught by a detail: through the opening in the baron's waistcoat he saw the point of the pin fixed in the tie and was thus able to realize the unusual length of the pin. Moreover, the gold stem was triangular and formed a sort of miniature dagger, very thin and very delicate, yet formidable in an expert hand.

And Lupin had no doubt but that the pin attached to that magnificent pearl was the weapon which had pierced the heart of the unfortunate M. Lavernoux.

He muttered:

"You're jolly clever, monsieur le baron!"

The other, maintaining a rather scornful gravity, kept silence, as though he did not understand and as though waiting for the explanation to which he felt himself entitled. And, in spite of everything, this impassive attitude worried Arsène Lupin. Nevertheless, his conviction was so profound and, besides, he had staked so much on the adventure that he repeated:

"Yes, jolly clever, for it is evident that the baroness only obeyed your orders in realizing your securities and also in borrowing the princess's jewels on the pretense of buying them. And it is evident that the person who walked out of your house with a bag was not your wife, but an accomplice, that chorus-girl probably, and that it is your chorus-girl who is deliberately allowing herself to be chased across the continent by our worthy Ganimard. And I look upon the trick as marvelous. What does the woman risk, seeing that it is the baroness who is being looked for? And how could they look for any other woman than the baroness, seeing that you have promised a reward of two hundred thousand francs to the person who finds the baroness? . . . Oh, that two hundred thousand francs lodged with a solicitor: what a stroke of genius! It has dazzled the police! It has thrown dust in the eyes of the most clear-sighted! A gentleman who lodges two hundred thousand francs with a solicitor is a gentleman who speaks the truth. . . . So they go on hunting the baroness! And they leave you quietly to settle your affairs, to sell your stud and your two houses to the highest bidder and to prepare your fight! Heavens, what a joke!"

The baron did not wince. He walked up to Lupin and asked, without abandoning his imperturbable coolness:

"Who are you?"

Lupin burst out laughing.

"What can it matter who I am? Take it that I am an emissary of fate, looming out of the darkness for your destruction!"

He sprang from his chair, seized the baron by the shoulder, and jerked out:

"Yes, for your destruction, my bold baron! Listen to me! Your wife's three millions, almost all the princess's jewels, the money you received to-day from the sale of your stud and your real estate: it's all there, in your pocket, or in that safe. Your flight is prepared. Look, I can see the leather of your portmanteau behind that hanging. The papers on your desk are in order. This very night, you would have done a guy. This very night, disguised beyond recognition, after taking all your precautions, you would have joined your chorus-girl, the creature for whose sake you have committed murder, that same Nelly Darbal, no doubt, whom Ganimard arrested in Belgium. But for one sudden, unforeseen obstacle: the police, the twelve detectives who, thanks to Lavernoux's revelations, have been posted under your windows. They've cooked your goose, old chap! . . . Well, I'll save you. A word through the telephone; and, by three or four o'clock in the morning, twenty of my friends will have removed the obstacle, polished off the twelve detectives, and you and I will slip away quietly. My conditions? Almost nothing; a trifle to you: we share the millions and the jewels. Is it a bargain?"

He was leaning over the baron, thundering at him with irresistible energy. The baron whispered:

"I'm beginning to understand. It's blackmail . . ."

"Blackmail or not, call it what you please, my boy, but you've got to go through with it and do as I say. And don't imagine that I shall give way at the last moment. Don't say to yourself, 'Here's a gentleman whom the fear of the police will cause to think twice. If I run a big risk in refusing, he also will be risking the handcuffs, the cells, and the rest of it, seeing that we are both being hunted down like wild beasts.' That would be a mistake, monsieur le baron. I can always get out of it. It's a question of yourself, of yourself alone. . . . Your money or your life, my lord! Share and share alike . . . if not, the scaffold! Is it a bargain?"

A quick movement. The baron released himself, grasped his revolver, and fired.

But Lupin was prepared for the attack, the more so as the baron's face had lost its assurance and gradually, under the slow impulse of rage and fear, acquired an expression of almost bestial ferocity that heralded the rebellion so long kept under control.

He fired twice. Lupin first flung himself to one side and then dived at the baron's knees, seized him by both legs, and brought him to the ground. The baron freed himself with an effort. The two enemies rolled over in each other's grip; and a stubborn, crafty, brutal, savage struggle followed.

Suddenly, Lupin felt a pain at his chest:

"You villain!" he yelled. "That's your Lavernoux trick; the tie-pin!"

Stiffening his muscles with a desperate effort, he overpowered the baron and clutched him by the throat victorious at last and omnipotent.

"You ass!" he cried. "If you hadn't shown your cards, I might have thrown up the game! You have such a look of the honest man about you! But what a biceps, my lord! . . . I thought for a moment. . . . But it's all over, now! . . . Come, my friend, hand us the pin and look cheerful. . . . No, that's what I call pulling a face. . . . I'm holding you too tight, perhaps? My lord's at his last gasp? . . . Come, be good! . . . That's it, just a wee bit of string round the wrists; do you allow me? . . . Why, you and I are agreeing like two brothers! It's touching! . . . At heart, you know, I'm rather fond of you. . . . And now, my bonnie lad, mind yourself! And a thousand apologies! . . ."

Half raising himself, with all his strength he caught the other a terrible blow in the pit of the stomach. The baron gave a gurgle and lay stunned and unconscious.

"That comes of having a deficient sense of logic, my friend," said Lupin. "I offered you half your money. Now I'll give you none at all . . . provided I know where to find any of it. For that's the main thing. Where has the beggar hidden his dust? In the safe? By George, it'll be a tough job! Luckily, I have all the night before me . . ."

He began to feel in the baron's pockets, came upon a bunch of keys, first made sure that the portmanteau behind the curtain held no papers or jewels, and then went to the safe.

But, at that moment, he stopped short: he heard a noise somewhere. The servants? Impossible. Their attics were on the top floor.

He listened. The noise came from below. And, suddenly, he understood: the detectives, who had heard the two shots, were banging at the front door, as was their duty, without waiting for daybreak. Then an electric bell rang, which Lupin recognized as that in the hall:

"By Jupiter!" he said. "Pretty work! Here are these jokers coming . . . and just as we were about to gather the fruits of our laborious efforts! Tut, tut, Lupin, keep cool! What's expected of you? To open a safe, of which you don't know the secret, in thirty seconds. That's a mere trifle to lose your head about! Come, all you have to do is to discover the secret! How many letters are there in the word? Four?"

He went on thinking, while talking and listening to the noise outside. He double-locked the door of the outer room and then came back to the safe:

"Four ciphers. . . . Four letters . . . four letters. . . . Who can lend me a hand? . . . Who can give me just a tiny hint? . . . Who? Why, Lavernoux, of course! That good Lavernoux, seeing that he took the trouble to indulge in optical telegraphy at the risk of his life. . . . Lord, what a fool I am! . . . Why, of course, why, of course, that's it! . . . By Jove, this is too exciting! . . . Lupin, you must count ten and suppress that distracted beating of your heart. If not, it means bad work."

He counted ten and, now quite calm, knelt in front of the safe. He turned the four knobs with careful attention. Next, he examined the bunch of keys, selected one of them, then another, and attempted, in vain, to insert them in the lock:

"There's luck in odd numbers," he muttered, trying a third key. "Victory! This is the right one! Open Sesame, good old Sesame, open!"

The lock turned. The door moved on its hinges. Lupin pulled it to him, after taking out the bunch of keys:

"The millions are ours," he said. "Baron, I forgive you!"

And then he gave a single bound backward, hiccoughing with fright. His legs staggered beneath him. The keys jingled together in his fevered hand with a sinister sound. And, for twenty, for thirty seconds, despite the din that was being raised and the electric bells that kept ringing through the house, he stood there, wild-eyed, gazing at the most horrible, the most abominable sight: a woman's body, half-dressed, bent in two in the safe, crammed in, like an over-large parcel . . . and fair hair hanging down . . . and blood . . . clots of blood . . . and livid flesh, blue in places, decomposing, flaccid . . .

"The baroness!" he gasped. "The baroness! . . . Oh, the monster! . . ."

He roused himself from his torpor, suddenly, to spit in the murderer's face and pound him with his heels:

"Take that, you wretch! . . . Take that, you villain! . . . And, with it, the scaffold, the bran-basket! . . ."

Meanwhile, shouts came from the upper floors in reply to the detectives' ringing. Lupin heard footsteps scurrying down the stairs. It was time to think of beating a retreat.

In reality, this did not trouble him greatly. During his conversation with the baron, the enemy's extraordinary coolness had given him the feeling that there must be a private outlet. Besides, how could the baron have begun the fight, if he were not sure of escaping the police?

Lupin went into the next room. It looked out on the garden. At the moment when the detectives were entering the house, he flung his legs over the balcony and let himself down by a rain-pipe. He walked round the building. On the opposite side was a wall lined with shrubs. He slipped in between the shrubs and the wall and at once found a little door which he easily opened with one of the keys on the bunch. All that remained for him to do was to walk across a yard and pass through the empty rooms of a lodge; and in a few moments he found himself in the Rue du Faubourg Saint-Honoré. Of course—and this he had reckoned on—the police had not provided for this secret outlet.

⁞⁞⁞⁞⁞⁞⁞⁞⁞⁞⁞⁞⁞⁞⁞⁞⁞⁞⁞⁞⁞

"Well, what do you think of Baron Repstein?" cried Lupin, after giving me all the details of that tragic night. "What a dirty scoundrel! And how it teaches one to distrust appearances! I swear to you, the fellow looked a thoroughly honest man!"

"But what about the millions?" I asked. "The princess's jewels?"

"They were in the safe. I remember seeing the parcel."

"Well?"

"They are there still."

"Impossible!"

"They are, upon my word! I might tell you that I was afraid of the detectives, or else plead a sudden attack of delicacy. But the truth is simpler . . . and more prosaic: the smell was too awful! . . ."

"What?"

"Yes, my dear fellow, the smell that came from that safe . . . from that coffin. . . . No, I couldn't do it . . . my head swam. . . . Another second and I should have been ill. . . . Isn't it silly? . . . Look, this is all I got from my expedition: the tie-pin. . . . The bed-rock value of the pearl is thirty thousand francs. . . . But all the same, I feel jolly well annoyed. What a sell!"

"One more question," I said. "The word that opened the safe!"

"Well?"

"How did you guess it?"

"Oh, quite easily! In fact, I am surprised that I didn't think of it sooner."

"Well, tell me."

"It was contained in the revelations telegraphed by that poor Lavernoux."

"What?"

"Just think, my dear chap, the mistakes in spelling . . ."

"The mistakes in spelling?"

"Why, of course! They were deliberate. Surely, you don't imagine that the agent, the private secretary of the baron—who was a company-promoter, mind you, and a racing-man—did not know English better than to spell 'necessery' with an 'e,' 'atack' with one 't,' 'ennemy' with two 'n's,' and 'prudance' with an 'a'! The thing struck me at once. I put the four letters together and got 'Etna,' the name of the famous horse."

"And was that one word enough?"

"Of course! It was enough to start with, to put me on the scent of the Repstein case, of which all the papers were full, and, next, to make me guess that it was the key-word of the safe, because, on the one hand, Lavernoux knew the gruesome contents of the safe and, on the other, he was denouncing the baron. And it was in the same way that I was led to suppose that Lavernoux had a friend in the street, that they both frequented the same café, that they amused themselves by working out the problems and cryptograms in the illustrated papers and that they had contrived a way of exchanging telegrams from window to window."

"That makes it all quite simple!" I exclaimed.

"Very simple. And the incident once more shows that, in the discovery of crimes, there is something much more valuable than the examination of facts, than observations, deductions, inferences, and all that stuff and nonsense. What I mean is, as I said before, intuition . . . intuition and intelligence. . . . And Arsène Lupin, without boasting, is deficient in neither one nor the other! . . ."

THE WEDDING-RING

Yvonne d'Origny kissed her son and told him to be good:
"You know your grandmother d'Origny is not very found of
children. Now that she has sent for you to come and see her, you must
show her what a sensible little boy you are." And, turning to the governess, "Don't forget, Fräulein, to bring him home immediately after
dinner. . . . Is monsieur still in the house?"

"Yes, madame, monsieur le comte is in his study."

As soon as she was alone, Yvonne d'Origny walked to the window
to catch a glimpse of her son as he left the house. He was out in the
street in a moment, raised his head, and blew her a kiss, as was his
custom every day. Then the governess took his hand with, as Yvonne
remarked to her surprise, a movement of unusual violence. Yvonne
leant further out of the window and, when the boy reached the corner of the boulevard, she suddenly saw a man step out of a motor-car
and go up to him. The man, in whom she recognized Bernard, her
husband's confidential servant, took the child by the arm, made both
him and the governess get into the car, and ordered the chauffeur to
drive off.

The whole incident did not take ten seconds.

Yvonne, in her trepidation, ran to her bedroom, seized a wrap, and went to the door. The door was locked; and there was no key in the lock.

She hurried back to the boudoir. The door of the boudoir also was locked.

Then, suddenly, the image of her husband appeared before her, that gloomy face which no smile ever lit up, those pitiless eyes in which, for years, she had felt so much hatred and malice.

"It's he . . . it's he!" she said to herself. "He has taken the child. . . . Oh, it's horrible!"

She beat against the door with her fists, with her feet, then flew to the mantelpiece and pressed the bell fiercely.

The shrill sound rang through the house from top to bottom. The servants would be sure to come. Perhaps a crowd would gather in the street. And, impelled by a sort of despairing hope, she kept her finger on the button.

A key turned in the lock. . . . The door was flung wide open. The count appeared on the threshold of the boudoir. And the expression of his face was so terrible that Yvonne began to tremble.

He entered the room. Five or six steps separated him from her. With a supreme effort, she tried to stir, but all movement was impossible; and, when she attempted to speak, she could only flutter her lips and emit incoherent sounds. She felt herself lost. The thought of death unhinged her. Her knees gave way beneath her and she sank into a huddled heap, with a moan.

The count rushed at her and seized her by the throat:

"Hold your tongue . . . don't call out!" he said, in a low voice. "That will be best for you! . . ."

Seeing that she was not attempting to defend herself, he loosened his hold of her and took from his pocket some strips of canvas ready rolled and of different lengths. In a few minutes, Yvonne was lying on a sofa, with her wrists and ankles bound and her arms fastened close to her body.

It was now dark in the boudoir. The count switched on the electric light and went to a little writing-desk where Yvonne was accustomed to keep her letters. Not succeeding in opening it, he picked the lock with a bent wire, emptied the drawers, and collected all the contents into a bundle, which he carried off in a cardboard file:

"Waste of time, eh?" he grinned. "Nothing but bills and letters of no importance. . . . No proof against you. . . . Tah! I'll keep my son for all that; and I swear before Heaven that I will not let him go!"

As he was leaving the room, he was joined, near the door, by his man Bernard. The two stopped and talked, in a low voice; but Yvonne heard these words spoken by the servant:

"I have had an answer from the working jeweler. He says he holds himself at my disposal."

And the count replied:

"The thing is put off until twelve o'clock midday, to-morrow. My mother has just telephoned to say that she could not come before."

Then Yvonne heard the key turn in the lock and the sound of steps going down to the ground-floor, where her husband's study was.

She long lay inert, her brain reeling with vague, swift ideas that burnt her in passing, like flames. She remembered her husband's infamous behavior, his humiliating conduct to her, his threats, his plans for a divorce; and she gradually came to understand that she was the victim of a regular conspiracy, that the servants had been sent away until the following evening by their master's orders, that the governess had carried off her son by the count's instructions and with Bernard's assistance, that her son would not come back, and that she would never see him again.

"My son!" she cried. "My son! . . ."

Exasperated by her grief, she stiffened herself, with every nerve, with every muscle tense, to make a violent effort. And she was astonished to find that her right hand, which the count had fastened too hurriedly, still retained a certain freedom.

Then a mad hope invaded her; and, slowly, patiently, she began the work of self-deliverance.

It was long in the doing. She needed a deal of time to widen the knot sufficiently and a deal of time afterward, when the hand was released, to undo those other bonds which tied her arms to her body and those which fastened her ankles.

Still, the thought of her son sustained her; and the last shackle fell as the clock struck eight. She was free!

She was no sooner on her feet than she flew to the window and flung back the latch, with the intention of calling the first passer-by. At that moment a policeman came walking along the pavement. She leant out. But the brisk evening air, striking her face, calmed her. She thought of the scandal, of the judicial investigation, of the cross-examination, of her son. O Heaven! What could she do to get him back? How could she escape? The count might appear at the least sound. And who knew but that, in a moment of fury . . . ?

She shivered from head to foot, seized with a sudden terror. The horror of death mingled, in her poor brain, with the thought of her son; and she stammered, with a choking throat:

"Help! . . . Help! . . ."

She stopped and said to herself, several times over, in a low voice, "Help! . . . Help! . . ." as though the word awakened an idea, a memory within her, and as though the hope of assistance no longer seemed to her impossible. For some minutes she remained absorbed in deep meditation, broken by fears and starts. Then, with an almost mechanical series of movements, she put out her arm to a little set of shelves hanging over the writing-desk, took down four books, one after the other, turned the pages with a distraught air, replaced them, and ended by finding, between the pages of the fifth, a visiting-card on which her eyes spelt the name:

HORACE VELMONT,

followed by an address written in pencil:

CERCLE DE LA RUE ROYALE.

And her memory conjured up the strange thing which that man had said to her, a few years before, in that same house, on a day when she was at home to her friends:

"If ever a danger threatens you, if you need help, do not hesitate; post this card, which you see me put into this book; and, whatever the hour, whatever the obstacles, I will come."

With what a curious air he had spoken these words and how well he had conveyed the impression of certainty, of strength, of unlimited power, of indomitable daring!

Abruptly, unconsciously, acting under the impulse of an irresistible determination, the consequences of which she refused to anticipate, Yvonne, with the same automatic gestures, took a pneumatic-delivery envelope, slipped in the card, sealed it, directed it to "Horace Velmont, Cercle de la Rue Royale," and went to the open window. The policeman was walking up and down outside. She flung out the envelope, trusting to fate. Perhaps it would be picked up, treated as a lost letter, and posted.

She had hardly completed this act when she realized its absurdity. It was mad to suppose that the message would reach the address and madder still to hope that the man to whom she was sending could come to her assistance, "whatever the hour, whatever the obstacles."

A reaction followed which was all the greater inasmuch as the effort had been swift and violent. Yvonne staggered, leant against a chair, and, losing all energy, let herself fall.

The hours passed by, the dreary hours of winter evenings when nothing but the sound of carriages interrupts the silence of the street. The clock struck, pitilessly. In the half-sleep that numbed her limbs, Yvonne counted the strokes. She also heard certain noises, on different floors of the house, which told her that her husband had dined, that he was going up to his room, that he was going down again to his study. But all this seemed very shadowy to her; and her torpor was such that she did not even think of lying down on the sofa, in case he should come in . . .

The twelve strokes of midnight. . . . Then half-past twelve . . . then one. . . . Yvonne thought of nothing, awaiting the events which were preparing and against which rebellion was useless. She pictured her son and herself as one pictures those beings who have suffered much and who suffer no more and who take each other in their loving arms. But a nightmare shattered this dream. For now those two beings were to be torn asunder; and she had the awful feeling, in her delirium, that she was crying and choking . . .

She leapt from her seat. The key had turned in the lock. The count was coming, attracted by her cries. Yvonne glanced round for a weapon with which to defend herself. But the door was pushed back quickly and, astounded, as though the sight that presented itself before her eyes seemed to her the most inexplicable prodigy, she stammered:

"You! . . . You! . . ."

A man was walking up to her, in dress-clothes, with his opera-hat and cape under his arm, and this man, young, slender, and elegant, she had recognized as Horace Velmont.

"You!" she repeated.

He said, with a bow:

"I beg your pardon, madame, but I did not receive your letter until very late."

"Is it possible? Is it possible that this is you . . . that you were able to . . . ?"

He seemed greatly surprised:

"Did I not promise to come in answer to your call?"

"Yes . . . but . . ."

"Well, here I am," he said, with a smile.

He examined the strips of canvas from which Yvonne had succeeded in freeing herself and nodded his head, while continuing his inspection:

"So those are the means employed? The Comte d'Origny, I presume? . . . I also saw that he locked you in. . . . But then the pneumatic letter? . . . Ah, through the window! . . . How careless of you not to close it!"

He pushed both sides to. Yvonne took fright:

"Suppose they hear!"

"There is no one in the house. I have been over it."

"Still . . ."

"Your husband went out ten minutes ago."

"Where is he?"

"With his mother, the Comtesse d'Origny."

"How do you know?"

"Oh, it's very simple! He was rung up by telephone and I awaited the result at the corner of this street and the boulevard. As I expected, the count came out hurriedly, followed by his man. I at once entered, with the aid of special keys."

He told this in the most natural way, just as one tells a meaningless anecdote in a drawing-room. But Yvonne, suddenly seized with fresh alarm, asked:

"Then it's not true? . . . His mother is not ill? . . . In that case, my husband will be coming back . . ."

"Certainly, the count will see that a trick has been played on him and in three quarters of an hour at the latest . . ."

"Let us go. . . . I don't want him to find me here. . . . I must go to my son . . ."

"One moment . . ."

"One moment! . . . But don't you know that they have taken him from me? . . . That they are hurting him, perhaps? . . ."

With set face and feverish gestures, she tried to push Velmont back. He, with great gentleness, compelled her to sit down and, leaning over her in a respectful attitude, said, in a serious voice:

"Listen, madame, and let us not waste time, when every minute is valuable. First of all, remember this: we met four times, six years ago. . . . And, on the fourth occasion, when I was speaking to you, in the drawing-room of this house, with too much—what shall I say?—with too much feeling, you gave me to understand that my visits were no longer welcome. Since that day I have not seen you. And, nevertheless, in spite of all, your faith in me was such that you kept the card which I put between the pages of that book and, six years later, you send for me and none other. That faith in me I ask you to continue. You must obey me blindly. Just as I surmounted every obstacle to come to you, so I will save you, whatever the position may be."

Horace Velmont's calmness, his masterful voice, with the friendly intonation, gradually quieted the countess. Though still very weak, she gained a fresh sense of ease and security in that man's presence.

"Have no fear," he went on. "The Comtesse d'Origny lives at the other end of the Bois de Vincennes. Allowing that your husband finds a motor-cab, it is impossible for him to be back before a quarter-past three. Well, it is twenty-five to three now. I swear to take you away at three o'clock exactly and to take you to your son. But I will not go before I know everything."

"What am I to do?" she asked.

"Answer me and very plainly. We have twenty minutes. It is enough. But it is not too much."

"Ask me what you want to know."

"Do you think that the count had any . . . any murderous intentions?"

"No."

"Then it concerns your son?"

"Yes."

"He is taking him away, I suppose, because he wants to divorce you and marry another woman, a former friend of yours, whom you have turned out of your house. Is that it? Oh, I entreat you, answer me frankly! These are facts of public notoriety, and your hesitation, your scruples, must all cease, now that the matter concerns your son. So your husband wished to marry another woman?"

"Yes."

"The woman has no money. Your husband, on his side, has gambled away all his property and has no means beyond the allowance which he receives from his mother, the Comtesse d'Origny, and the income of a large fortune which your son inherited from two of your uncles. It is this fortune which your husband covets and which he would appropriate more easily if the child were placed in his hands. There is only one way: divorce. Am I right?"

"Yes."

"And what has prevented him until now is your refusal?"

"Yes, mine and that of my mother-in-law, whose religious feelings are opposed to divorce. The Comtesse d'Origny would only yield in case . . ."

"In case . . . ?"

"In case they could prove me guilty of shameful conduct."

Velmont shrugged his shoulders:

"Therefore he is powerless to do anything against you or against your son. Both from the legal point of view and from that of his own interests, he stumbles against an obstacle which is the most insurmountable of all: the virtue of an honest woman. And yet, in spite of everything, he suddenly shows fight."

"What do you mean?"

"I mean that, if a man like the count, after so many hesitations and in the face of so many difficulties, risks so doubtful an adventure, it must be because he thinks he has command of weapons . . ."

"What weapons?"

"I don't know. But they exist . . . or else he would not have begun by taking away your son."

Yvonne gave way to her despair:

"Oh, this is horrible! . . . How do I know what he may have done, what he may have invented?"

"Try and think. . . . Recall your memories. . . . Tell me, in this desk which he has broken open, was there any sort of letter which he could possibly turn against you?"

"No . . . only bills and addresses . . ."

"And, in the words he used to you, in his threats, is there nothing that allows you to guess?"

"Nothing."

"Still . . . still," Velmont insisted, "there must be something." And he continued, "Has the count a particularly intimate friend . . . in whom he confides?"

"No."

"Did anybody come to see him yesterday?"

"No, nobody."

"Was he alone when he bound you and locked you in?"

"At that moment, yes."

"But afterward?"

"His man, Bernard, joined him near the door and I heard them talking about a working jeweler . . ."

"Is that all?"

"And about something that was to happen the next day, that is, to-day, at twelve o'clock, because the Comtesse d'Origny could not come earlier."

Velmont reflected:

"Has that conversation any meaning that throws a light upon your husband's plans?"

"I don't see any."

"Where are your jewels?"

"My husband has sold them all."

"You have nothing at all left?"

"No."

"Not even a ring?"

"No," she said, showing her hands, "none except this."

"Which is your wedding-ring?"

"Which is my . . . wedding- . . ."

She stopped, nonplussed. Velmont saw her flush as she stammered:

"Could it be possible?... But no... no... he doesn't know..."

Velmont at once pressed her with questions and Yvonne stood silent, motionless, anxious-faced. At last, she replied, in a low voice:

"This is not my wedding-ring. One day, long ago, it dropped from the mantelpiece in my bedroom, where I had put it a minute before and, hunt for it as I might, I could not find it again. So I ordered another, without saying anything about it ... and this is the one, on my hand..."

"Did the real ring bear the date of your wedding?"

"Yes ... the 23rd of October."

"And the second?"

"This one has no date."

He perceived a slight hesitation in her and a confusion which, in point of fact, she did not try to conceal.

"I implore you," he exclaimed, "don't hide anything from me.... You see how far we have gone in a few minutes, with a little logic and calmness.... Let us go on, I ask you as a favor."

"Are you sure," she said, "that it is necessary?"

"I am sure that the least detail is of importance and that we are nearly attaining our object. But we must hurry. This is a crucial moment."

"I have nothing to conceal," she said, proudly raising her head. "It was the most wretched and the most dangerous period of my life. While suffering humiliation at home, outside I was surrounded with attentions, with temptations, with pitfalls, like any woman who is seen to be neglected by her husband. Then I remembered: before my marriage, a man had been in love with me. I had guessed his unspoken love; and he has died since. I had the name of that man engraved inside the ring; and I wore it as a talisman. There was no love in me, because I was the wife of another. But, in my secret heart, there was a memory, a sad dream, something sweet and gentle that protected me..."

She had spoken slowly, without embarrassment, and Velmont did not doubt for a second that she was telling the absolute truth. He kept silent; and she, becoming anxious again, asked:

"Do you suppose ... that my husband ...?"

He took her hand and, while examining the plain gold ring, said:

"The puzzle lies here. Your husband, I don't know how, knows of the substitution of one ring for the other. His mother will be here at twelve o'clock. In the presence of witnesses, he will compel you to take off your ring; and, in this way, he will obtain the approval of his mother and, at the same time, will be able to obtain his divorce, because he will have the proof for which he was seeking."

"I am lost!" she moaned. "I am lost!"

"On the contrary, you are saved! Give me that ring ... and presently he will find another there, another which I will send you, to reach you before twelve, and which will bear the date of the 23rd of October. So ..."

He suddenly broke off. While he was speaking, Yvonne's hand had turned ice-cold in his; and, raising his eyes, he saw that the young woman was pale, terribly pale:

"What's the matter? I beseech you ..."

She yielded to a fit of mad despair:

"This is the matter, that I am lost! ... This is the matter, that I can't get the ring off! It has grown too small for me! ... Do you understand? ... It made no difference and I did not give it a thought.... But to-day ... this proof ... this accusation.... Oh, what torture! ... Look ... it forms part of my finger ... it has grown into my flesh ... and I can't ... I can't ..."

She pulled at the ring, vainly, with all her might, at the risk of injuring herself. But the flesh swelled up around the ring; and the ring did not budge.

"Oh!" she cried, seized with an idea that terrified her. "I remember ... the other night ... a nightmare I had. ... It seemed to me that someone entered my room and caught hold of my hand. ... And I could not wake up.... It was he! It was he! He had put me to sleep, I was sure of it ... and he was looking at the ring.... And presently he will pull it off before his mother's eyes.... Ah, I understand everything: that working jeweler! ... He will cut it from my hand to-morrow.... You see, you see ... I am lost! ..."

She hid her face in her hands and began to weep. But, amid the silence, the clock struck once ... and twice ... and yet once more. And Yvonne drew herself up with a jerk:

"There he is!" she cried. "He is coming! ... It is three o'clock! ... Let us go! ..."

She grabbed at her cloak and ran to the door . . . Velmont barred the way and, in a masterful tone:

"You shall not go!"

"My son . . . I want to see him, to take him back . . ."

"You don't even know where he is!"

"I want to go."

"You shall not go! . . . It would be madness . . ."

He took her by the wrists. She tried to release herself; and Velmont had to employ a little force to overcome her resistance. In the end, he succeeded in getting her back to the sofa, then in laying her at full length and, at once, without heeding her lamentations, he took the canvas strips and fastened her wrists and ankles:

"Yes," he said, "It would be madness! Who would have set you free? Who would have opened that door for you? An accomplice? What an argument against you and what a pretty use your husband would make of it with his mother! . . . And, besides, what's the good? To run away means accepting divorce . . . and what might that not lead to? . . . You must stay here . . ."

She sobbed:

"I'm frightened . . . I'm frightened . . . this ring burns me. . . . Break it. . . . Take it away. . . . Don't let him find it!"

"And if it is not found on your finger, who will have broken it? Again an accomplice. . . . No, you must face the music . . . and face it boldly, for I answer for everything. . . . Believe me . . . I answer for everything. . . . If I have to tackle the Comtesse d'Origny bodily and thus delay the interview. . . . If I had to come myself before noon . . . it is the real wedding-ring that shall be taken from your finger—that I swear!—and your son shall be restored to you."

Swayed and subdued, Yvonne instinctively held out her hands to the bonds. When he stood up, she was bound as she had been before.

He looked round the room to make sure that no trace of his visit remained. Then he stooped over the countess again and whispered:

"Think of your son and, whatever happens, fear nothing. . . . I am watching over you."

She heard him open and shut the door of the boudoir and, a few minutes later, the hall-door.

At half-past three, a motor-cab drew up. The door downstairs was slammed again; and, almost immediately after, Yvonne saw her husband hurry in, with a furious look in his eyes. He ran up to her, felt to see if she was still fastened and, snatching her hand, examined the ring. Yvonne fainted . . .

||||||||||||||||||||||||||

She could not tell, when she woke, how long she had slept. But the broad light of day was filling the boudoir; and she perceived, at the first movement which she made, that her bonds were cut. Then she turned her head and saw her husband standing beside her, looking at her:

"My son . . . my son . . ." she moaned. "I want my son . . ."

He replied, in a voice of which she felt the jeering insolence:

"Our son is in a safe place. And, for the moment, it's a question not of him, but of you. We are face to face with each other, probably for the last time, and the explanation between us will be a very serious one. I must warn you that it will take place before my mother. Have you any objection?"

Yvonne tried to hide her agitation and answered:

"None at all."

"Can I send for her?"

"Yes. Leave me, in the meantime. I shall be ready when she comes."

"My mother is here."

"Your mother is here?" cried Yvonne, in dismay, remembering Horace Vermont's promise.

"What is there to astonish you in that?"

"And is it now . . . is it at once that you want to . . . ?"

"Yes."

"Why? . . . Why not this evening? . . . Why not to-morrow?"

"To-day and now," declared the count. "A rather curious incident happened in the course of last night, an incident which I cannot account for and which decided me to hasten the explanation. Don't you want something to eat first?"

"No . . . no . . ."

"Then I will go and fetch my mother."

He turned to Yvonne's bedroom. Yvonne glanced at the clock. It marked twenty-five minutes to eleven!

"Ah!" she said, with a shiver of fright.

Twenty-five minutes to eleven! Horace Velont would not save her and nobody in the world and nothing in the world would save her, for there was no miracle that could place the wedding-ring upon her finger.

The count, returning with the Comtesse d'Origny, asked her to sit down. She was a tall, lank, angular woman, who had always displayed a hostile feeling to Yvonne. She did not even bid her daughter-in-law good-morning, showing that her mind was made up as regards the accusation:

"I don't think," she said, "that we need speak at length. In two words, my son maintains . . ."

"I don't maintain, mother," said the count, "I declare. I declare on my oath that, three months ago, during the holidays, the upholsterer, when laying the carpet in this room and the boudoir, found the wedding-ring which I gave my wife lying in a crack in the floor. Here is the ring. The date of the 23rd of October is engraved inside."

"Then," said the countess, "the ring which your wife carries . . ."

"That is another ring, which she ordered in exchange for the real one. Acting on my instructions, Bernard, my man, after long searching, ended by discovering in the outskirts of Paris, where he now lives, the little jeweler to whom she went. This man remembers perfectly and is willing to bear witness that his customer did not tell him to engrave a date, but a name. He has forgotten the name, but the man who used to work with him in his shop may be able to remember it. This working jeweler has been informed by letter that I required his services and he replied yesterday, placing himself at my disposal. Bernard went to fetch him at nine o'clock this morning. They are both waiting in my study."

He turned to his wife:

"Will you give me that ring of your own free will?"

"You know," she said, "from the other night, that it won't come off my finger."

"In that case, can I have the man up? He has the necessary implements with him."

"Yes," she said, in a voice faint as a whisper.

She was resigned. She conjured up the future as in a vision: the scandal, the decree of divorce pronounced against herself, the custody of the child awarded to the father; and she accepted this, thinking that she would carry off her son, that she would go with him to the ends of the earth and that the two of them would live alone together and happy . . .

Her mother-in-law said:

"You have been very thoughtless, Yvonne."

Yvonne was on the point of confessing to her and asking for her protection. But what was the good? How could the Comtesse d'Origny possibly believe her innocent? She made no reply.

Besides, the count at once returned, followed by his servant and by a man carrying a bag of tools under his arm.

And the count said to the man:

"You know what you have to do?"

"Yes," said the workman. "It's to cut a ring that's grown too small. . . . That's easily done. . . . A touch of the nippers . . ."

"And then you will see," said the count, "if the inscription inside the ring was the one you engraved."

Yvonne looked at the clock. It was ten minutes to eleven. She seemed to hear, somewhere in the house, a sound of voices raised in argument; and, in spite of herself, she felt a thrill of hope. Perhaps Velmont has succeeded. . . . But the sound was renewed; and she perceived that it was produced by some costermongers passing under her window and moving farther on.

It was all over. Horace Velmont had been unable to assist her. And she understood that, to recover her child, she must rely upon her own strength, for the promises of others are vain.

She made a movement of recoil. She had felt the workman's heavy hand on her hand; and that hateful touch revolted her.

The man apologized, awkwardly. The count said to his wife:

"You must make up your mind, you know."

Then she put out her slim and trembling hand to the workman, who took it, turned it over, and rested it on the table, with the palm upward. Yvonne felt the cold steel. She longed to die, then and there; and, at once attracted by that idea of death, she thought of the poisons which she would buy and which would send her to sleep almost without her knowing it.

The operation did not take long. Inserted on the slant, the little steel pliers pushed back the flesh, made room for themselves, and bit the ring. A strong effort . . . and the ring broke. The two ends had only to be separated to remove the ring from the finger. The workman did so.

The count exclaimed, in triumph:

"At last! Now we shall see! . . . The proof is there! And we are all witnesses . . ."

He snatched up the ring and looked at the inscription. A cry of amazement escaped him. The ring bore the date of his marriage to Yvonne: "23rd of October"! . . .

We were sitting on the terrace at Monte Carlo. Lupin finished his story, lit a cigarette, and calmly puffed the smoke into the blue air.

I said:

"Well?"

"Well what?"

"Why, the end of the story . . ."

"The end of the story? But what other end could there be?"

"Come . . . you're joking . . ."

"Not at all. Isn't that enough for you? The countess is saved. The count, not possessing the least proof against her, is compelled by his mother to forego the divorce and to give up the child. That is all. Since then, he has left his wife, who is living happily with her son, a fine lad of sixteen."

"Yes . . . yes . . . but the way in which the countess was saved?"

Lupin burst out laughing:

"My dear old chap"—Lupin sometimes condescends to address me in this affectionate manner—"my dear old chap, you may be rather smart at relating my exploits, but, by Jove, you do want to have the i's dotted for you! I assure you, the countess did not ask for explanations!"

"Very likely. But there's no pride about me," I added, laughing. "Dot those i's for me, will you?"

He took out a five-franc piece and closed his hand over it.

"What's in my hand?"

"A five-franc piece."

He opened his hand. The five-franc piece was gone.

"You see how easy it is! A working jeweler, with his nippers, cuts a ring with a date engraved upon it: 23rd of October. It's a simple little trick of sleight-of-hand, one of many which I have in my bag. By Jove, I didn't spend six months with Dickson, the conjurer, for nothing!"

"But then . . . ?"

"Out with it!"

"The working jeweler?"

"Was Horace Velmont! Was good old Lupin! Leaving the countess at three o'clock in the morning, I employed the few remaining minutes before the husband's return to have a look round his study. On the table I found the letter from the working jeweler. The letter gave me the address. A bribe of a few louis enabled me to take the workman's place; and I arrived with a wedding-ring ready cut and engraved. Hocus-pocus! Pass! . . . The count couldn't make head or tail of it."

"Splendid!" I cried. And I added, a little chaffingly, in my turn, "But don't you think that you were humbugged a bit yourself, on this occasion?"

"Oh! And by whom, pray?"

"By the countess?"

"In what way?"

"Hang it all, that name engraved as a talisman! . . . The mysterious Adonis who loved her and suffered for her sake! . . . All that story seems very unlikely; and I wonder whether, Lupin though you be, you did not just drop upon a pretty love-story, absolutely genuine and . . . none too innocent."

Lupin looked at me out of the corner of his eye:

"No," he said.

"How do you know?"

"If the countess made a misstatement in telling me that she knew that man before her marriage—and that he was dead—and if she really did love him in her secret heart, I, at least, have a positive proof that it was an ideal love and that he did not suspect it."

"And where is the proof?"

"It is inscribed inside the ring which I myself broke on the countess's finger . . . and which I carry on me. Here it is. You can read the name she had engraved on it."

He handed me the ring. I read:

"Horace Velmont."

There was a moment of silence between Lupin and myself; and, noticing it, I also observed on his face a certain emotion, a tinge of melancholy.

I resumed:

"What made you tell me this story . . . to which you have often alluded in my presence?"

"What made me . . . ?"

He drew my attention to a woman, still exceedingly handsome, who was passing on a young man's arm. She saw Lupin and bowed.

"It's she," he whispered. "She and her son."

"Then she recognized you?"

"She always recognizes me, whatever my disguise."

"But since the burglary at the Château de Thibermesnil, the police have identified the two names of Arsène Lupin and Horace Velmont."

"Yes."

"Therefore she knows who you are."

"Yes."

"And she bows to you?" I exclaimed, in spite of myself.

He caught me by the arm and, fiercely:

"Do you think that I am Lupin to her? Do you think that I am a burglar in her eyes, a rogue, a cheat? . . . Why, I might be the lowest of miscreants, I might be a murderer even . . . and still she would bow to me!"

"Why? Because she loved you once?"

"Rot! That would be an additional reason, on the contrary, why she should now despise me."

"What then?"

"I am the man who gave her back her son!"

THE SIGN OF THE SHADOW

"I received your telegram and here I am," said a gentleman with a grey moustache, who entered my study, dressed in a dark-brown frock-coat and a wide-brimmed hat, with a red ribbon in his buttonhole. "What's the matter?"

Had I not been expecting Arsène Lupin, I should certainly never have recognized him in the person of this old half-pay officer:

"What's the matter?" I echoed. "Oh, nothing much: a rather curious coincidence, that's all. And, as I know that you would just as soon clear up a mystery as plan one . . ."

"Well?"

"You seem in a great hurry!"

"I am . . . unless the mystery in question is worth putting myself out for. So let us get to the point."

"Very well. Just begin by casting your eye on this little picture, which I picked up, a week or two ago, in a grimy old shop on the other side of the river. I bought it for the sake of its Empire frame, with the palm-leaf ornaments on the moldings . . . for the painting is execrable."

"Execrable, as you say," said Lupin, after he had examined it, "but the subject itself is rather nice. That corner of an old courtyard, with its rotunda of Greek columns, its sun-dial and its fish-pond and that ruined well with the Renascence roof and those stone steps and stone benches: all very picturesque."

"And genuine," I added. "The picture, good or bad, has never been taken out of its Empire frame. Besides, it is dated. . . . There, in the left-hand bottom corner: those red figures, 15. 4. 2, which obviously stand for 15 April, 1802."

"I dare say . . . I dare say. . . . But you were speaking of a coincidence and, so far, I fail to see . . ."

I went to a corner of my study, took a telescope, fixed it on its stand, and pointed it, through the open window, at the open window of a little room facing my flat, on the other side of the street. And I asked Lupin to look through it.

He stooped forward. The slanting rays of the morning sun lit up the room opposite, revealing a set of mahogany furniture, all very simple, a large bed and a child's bed hung with cretonne curtains.

"Ah!" cried Lupin, suddenly. "The same picture!"

"Exactly the same!" I said. "And the date: do you see the date, in red? 15. 4. 2."

"Yes, I see. . . . And who lives in that room?"

"A lady . . . or, rather, a workwoman, for she has to work for her living . . . needlework, hardly enough to keep herself and her child."

"What is her name?"

"Louise d'Ernemont. . . . From what I hear, she is the great-granddaughter of a farmer-general who was guillotined during the Terror."

"Yes, on the same day as André Chénier," said Lupin. "According to the memoirs of the time, this d'Ernemont was supposed to be a very rich man." He raised his head and said, "It's an interesting story. . . . Why did you wait before telling me?"

"Because this is the 15th of April."

"Well?"

"Well, I discovered yesterday—I heard them talking about it in the porter's box—that the 15th of April plays an important part in the life of Louise d'Ernemont."

"Nonsense!"

"Contrary to her usual habits, this woman who works every day of her life, who keeps her two rooms tidy, who cooks the lunch which her little girl eats when she comes home from the parish school . . . this woman, on the 15th of April, goes out with the child at ten o'clock in the morning and does not return until nightfall. And this has happened for years and in all weathers. You must admit that there is something queer about this date which I find on an old picture, which is inscribed on another, similar picture and which controls the annual movements of the descendant of d'Ernemont the farmer-general."

"Yes, it's curious . . . you're quite right," said Lupin, slowly. "And don't you know where she goes to?"

"Nobody knows. She does not confide in a soul. As a matter of fact, she talks very little."

"Are you sure of your information?"

"Absolutely. And the best proof of its accuracy is that here she comes."

A door had opened at the back of the room opposite, admitting a little girl of seven or eight, who came and looked out of the window. A lady appeared behind her, tall, good-looking still, and wearing a sad and gentle air. Both of them were ready and dressed, in clothes which were simple in themselves, but which pointed to a love of neatness and a certain elegance on the part of the mother.

"You see," I whispered, "they are going out."

And presently the mother took the child by the hand and they left the room together.

Lupin caught up his hat:

"Are you coming?"

My curiosity was too great for me to raise the least objection. I went downstairs with Lupin.

As we stepped into the street, we saw my neighbor enter a baker's shop. She bought two rolls and placed them in a little basket which her daughter was carrying and which seemed already to contain some other provisions. Then they went in the direction of the outer boulevards and followed them as far as the Place de l'Étoile, where they turned down the Avenue Kléber to walk toward Passy.

Lupin strolled silently along, evidently obsessed by a train of thought which I was glad to have provoked. From time to time, he uttered a sentence which showed me the thread of his reflections; and I was able to see that the riddle remained as much a mystery to him as to myself.

Louise d'Ernemont, meanwhile, had branched off to the left, along the Rue Raynouard, a quiet old street in which Franklin and Balzac once lived, one of those streets which, lined with old-fashioned houses and walled gardens, give you the impression of being in a country-town. The Seine flows at the foot of the slope which the street crowns; and a number of lanes run down to the river.

My neighbor took one of these narrow, winding, deserted lanes. The first building, on the right, was a house the front of which faced the Rue Raynouard. Next came a moss-grown wall, of a height above the ordinary, supported by buttresses and bristling with broken glass.

Half-way along the wall was a low, arched door. Louise d'Ernemont stopped in front of this door and opened it with a key which seemed to us enormous. Mother and child entered and closed the door.

"In any case," said Lupin, "she has nothing to conceal, for she has not looked round once . . ."

He had hardly finished his sentence when we heard the sound of footsteps behind us. It was two old beggars, a man and a woman, tattered, dirty, squalid, covered in rags. They passed us without paying the least attention to our presence. The man took from his wallet a key similar to my neighbor's and put it into the lock. The door closed behind them.

And, suddenly, at the top of the lane, came the noise of a motor-car stopping. . . . Lupin dragged me fifty yards lower down, to a corner in which we were able to hide. And we saw coming down the lane, carrying a little dog under her arm, a young and very much over-dressed woman, wearing a quantity of jewelry, a young woman whose eyes were too dark, her lips too red, her hair too fair. In front of the door, the same performance, with the same key. . . . The lady and the dog disappeared from view.

"This promises to be most amusing," said Lupin, chuckling. "What earthly connection can there be between those different people?"

There hove in sight successively two elderly ladies, lean and rather poverty-stricken in appearance, very much alike, evidently sisters; a footman in livery; an infantry corporal; a fat gentleman in a soiled and patched jacket-suit; and, lastly, a workman's family, father, mother, and four children, all six of them pale and sickly, looking like people who never eat their fill. And each of the newcomers carried a basket or string-bag filled with provisions.

"It's a picnic!" I cried.

"It grows more and more surprising," said Lupin, "and I sha'n't be satisfied till I know what is happening behind that wall."

To climb it was out of the question. We also saw that it finished, at the lower as well as at the upper end, at a house none of whose windows overlooked the enclosure which the wall contained.

During the next hour, no one else came along.

We vainly cast about for a stratagem; and Lupin, whose fertile brain had exhausted every possible expedient, was about to go in search of a ladder, when, suddenly, the little door opened and one of the workman's children came out.

The boy ran up the lane to the Rue Raynouard. A few minutes later he returned, carrying two bottles of water, which he set down on the pavement to take the big key from his pocket.

By that time Lupin had left me and was strolling slowly along the wall. When the child, after entering the enclosure, pushed back the door Lupin sprang forward and stuck the point of his knife into the staple of the lock. The bolt failed to catch; and it became an easy matter to push the door ajar.

"That's done the trick!" said Lupin.

He cautiously put his hand through the doorway and then, to my great surprise, entered boldly. But, on following his example, I saw that, ten yards behind the wall, a clump of laurels formed a sort of curtain which allowed us to come up unobserved.

Lupin took his stand right in the middle of the clump. I joined him and, like him, pushed aside the branches of one of the shrubs. And the sight which presented itself to my eyes was so unexpected that I was unable to suppress an exclamation, while Lupin, on his side, muttered, between his teeth:

"By Jupiter! This is a funny job!"

We saw before us, within the confined space that lay between the two windowless houses, the identical scene represented in the old picture which I had bought at a second-hand dealer's!

The identical scene! At the back, against the opposite wall, the same Greek rotunda displayed its slender columns. In the middle, the same stone benches topped a circle of four steps that ran down to a fish-pond with moss-grown flags. On the left, the same well raised its wrought-iron roof; and, close at hand, the same sun-dial showed its slanting gnomon and its marble face.

The identical scene! And what added to the strangeness of the sight was the memory, obsessing Lupin and myself, of that date of the 15th of April, inscribed in a corner of the picture, and the thought that this very day was the 15th of April and that sixteen or seventeen people, so different in age, condition, and manners, had chosen the 15th of April to come together in this forgotten corner of Paris!

All of them, at the moment when we caught sight of them, were sitting in separate groups on the benches and steps; and all were eating. Not very far from my neighbor and her daughter, the workman's family and the beggar couple were sharing their provisions; while the footman, the gentleman in the soiled suit, the infantry corporal, and the two lean sisters were making a common stock of their sliced ham, their tins of sardines, and their gruyère cheese.

The lady with the little dog alone, who had brought no food with her, sat apart from the others, who made a show of turning their backs upon her. But Louise d'Ernemont offered her a sandwich, whereupon her example was followed by the two sisters; and the corporal at once began to make himself as agreeable to the young person as he could.

It was now half-past one. The beggar-man took out his pipe, as did the fat gentleman; and, when they found that one had no tobacco and the other no matches, their needs soon brought them together. The men went and smoked by the rotunda and the women joined them. For that matter, all these people seemed to know one another quite well.

They were at some distance from where we were standing, so that we could not hear what they said. However, we gradually perceived that the conversation was becoming animated. The young person with the dog, in particular, who by this time appeared to be in great request, indulged in much voluble talk, accompanying her words with many gestures, which set the little dog barking furiously.

But, suddenly, there was an outcry, promptly followed by shouts of rage; and one and all, men and women alike, rushed in disorder toward the well. One of the workman's brats was at that moment coming out of it, fastened by his belt to the hook at the end of the rope; and the three other urchins were drawing him up by turning the handle. More active than the rest, the corporal flung himself upon him; and forthwith the footman and the fat gentleman seized hold of him also, while the beggars and the lean sisters came to blows with the workman and his family.

In a few seconds the little boy had not a stitch left on him beyond his shirt. The footman, who had taken possession of the rest of the clothes, ran away, pursued by the corporal, who snatched away the boy's breeches, which were next torn from the corporal by one of the lean sisters.

"They are mad!" I muttered, feeling absolutely at sea.

"Not at all, not at all," said Lupin.

"What! Do you mean to say that you can make head or tail of what is going on?"

He did not reply. The young lady with the little dog, tucking her pet under her arm, had started running after the child in the shirt, who uttered loud yells. The two of them raced round the laurel-clump in which we stood hidden; and the brat flung himself into his mother's arms.

At long last, Louise d'Ernemont, who had played a conciliatory part from the beginning, succeeded in allaying the tumult. Everybody sat down again; but there was a reaction in all those exasperated people and they remained motionless and silent, as though worn out with their exertions.

And time went by. Losing patience and beginning to feel the pangs of hunger, I went to the Rue Raynouard to fetch something to eat, which we divided while watching the actors in the incomprehensible comedy that was being performed before our eyes. They hardly stirred. Each minute that passed seemed to load them with increasing melancholy; and they sank into attitudes of discouragement, bent their backs more and more and sat absorbed in their meditations.

The afternoon wore on in this way, under a grey sky that shed a dreary light over the enclosure.

"Are they going to spend the night here?" I asked, in a bored voice.

But, at five o'clock or so, the fat gentleman in the soiled jacket-suit took out his watch. The others did the same and all, watch in hand, seemed to be anxiously awaiting an event of no little importance to themselves. The event did not take place, for, in fifteen or twenty minutes, the fat gentleman gave a gesture of despair, stood up, and put on his hat.

Then lamentations broke forth. The two lean sisters and the workman's wife fell upon their knees and made the sign of the cross. The lady with the little dog and the beggar-woman kissed each other and sobbed; and we saw Louise d'Ernemont pressing her daughter sadly to her.

"Let's go," said Lupin.

"You think it's over?"

"Yes; and we have only just time to make ourselves scarce."

We went out unmolested. At the top of the lane, Lupin turned to the left and, leaving me outside, entered the first house in the Rue Raynouard, the one that backed on to the enclosure.

After talking for a few seconds to the porter, he joined me and we stopped a passing taxi-cab:

"No. 34 Rue de Turin," he said to the driver.

The ground-floor of No. 34 was occupied by a notary's office; and we were shown in, almost without waiting, to Maître Valandier, a smiling, pleasant-spoken man of a certain age.

Lupin introduced himself by the name of Captain Jeanniot, retired from the army. He said that he wanted to build a house to his own liking and that someone had suggested to him a plot of ground situated near the Rue Raynouard.

"But that plot is not for sale," said Maître Valandier.

"Oh, I was told . . ."

"You have been misinformed, I fear."

The lawyer rose, went to a cupboard, and returned with a picture which he showed us. I was petrified. It was the same picture which I had bought, the same picture that hung in Louise d'Ernemont's room.

"This is a painting," he said, "of the plot of ground to which you refer. It is known as the Clos d'Ernemont."

"Precisely."

"Well, this close," continued the notary, "once formed part of a large garden belonging to d'Ernemont, the farmer-general, who was executed during the Terror. All that could be sold has been sold, piece-meal, by the heirs. But this last plot has remained and will remain in their joint possession ... unless ..."

The notary began to laugh.

"Unless what?" asked Lupin.

"Well, it's quite a romance, a rather curious romance, in fact. I often amuse myself by looking through the voluminous documents of the case."

"Would it be indiscreet, if I asked ... ?"

"Not at all, not at all," declared Maître Valandier, who seemed delighted, on the contrary, to have found a listener for his story. And, without waiting to be pressed, he began: "At the outbreak of the Revolution, Louis Agrippa d'Ernemont, on the pretense of join-ing his wife, who was staying at Geneva with their daughter Pauline, shut up his mansion in the Faubourg Saint-Germain, dismissed his servants and, with his son Charles, came and took up his abode in his pleasure-house at Passy, where he was known to nobody except an old and devoted serving-woman. He remained there in hiding for three years and he had every reason to hope that his retreat would not be discovered, when, one day, after luncheon, as he was having a nap, the old servant burst into his room. She had seen, at the end of the street, a patrol of armed men who seemed to be making for the house. Louis d'Ernemont got ready quickly and, at the moment when the men were knocking at the front door, disappeared through the door that led to the garden, shouting to his son, in a scared voice, to keep them talking, if only for five minutes. He may have intended to escape and found the outlets through the garden watched. In any case, he returned in six or seven minutes, replied very calmly to the questions put to him, and raised no difficulty about accompanying the men. His son Charles, although only eighteen years of age, was arrested also."

"When did this happen?" asked Lupin.

"It happened on the 26th day of Germinal, Year II, that is to say, on the ..."

Maître Valandier stopped, with his eyes fixed on a calendar that hung on the wall, and exclaimed:

"Why, it was on this very day! This is the 15th of April, the anniver-sary of the farmer-general's arrest."

"What an odd coincidence!" said Lupin. "And considering the period at which it took place, the arrest, no doubt, had serious consequences?"

"Oh, most serious!" said the notary, laughing. "Three months later, at the beginning of Thermidor, the farmer-general mounted the scaffold. His son Charles was forgotten in prison and their property was confiscated."

"The property was immense, I suppose?" said Lupin.

"Well, there you are! That's just where the thing becomes complicated. The property, which was, in fact, immense, could never be traced. It was discovered that the Faubourg Saint-Germain mansion had been sold, before the Revolution, to an Englishman, together with all the country-seats and estates and all the jewels, securities and collections belonging to the farmer-general. The Convention instituted minute inquiries, as did the Directory afterward. But the inquiries led to no result."

"There remained, at any rate, the Passy house," said Lupin.

"The house at Passy was bought, for a mere song, by a delegate of the Commune, the very man who had arrested d'Ernemont, one Citizen Broquet. Citizen Broquet shut himself up in the house, barricaded the doors, fortified the walls and, when Charles d'Ernemont was at last set free and appeared outside, received him by firing a musket at him. Charles instituted one law-suit after another, lost them all, and then proceeded to offer large sums of money. But Citizen Broquet proved intractable. He had bought the house and he stuck to the house; and he would have stuck to it until his death, if Charles had not obtained the support of Bonaparte. Citizen Broquet cleared out on the 12th of February, 1803; but Charles d'Ernemont's joy was so great and his brain, no doubt, had been so violently unhinged by all that he had gone through, that, on reaching the threshold of the house of which he had at last recovered the ownership, even before opening the door he began to dance and sing in the street. He had gone clean off his head."

"By Jove!" said Lupin. "And what became of him?"

"His mother and his sister Pauline, who had ended by marrying a cousin of the same name at Geneva, were both dead. The old servant-woman took care of him and they lived together in the Passy house. Years passed without any notable event; but, suddenly, in 1812, an unexpected incident happened. The old servant made a series of strange revelations on her death-bed, in the presence of two witnesses whom she sent for. She declared that the farmer-general had carried to his house at Passy a number of bags filled with gold and silver and that those bags had disappeared a few days before the arrest. According to earlier confidences made by Charles d'Ernemont, who had them from his father, the treasures were hidden in the garden, between the rotunda, the sun-dial, and the well. In proof of her statement, she produced three pictures, or rather, for they were not yet framed, three canvases, which the farmer-general had painted during his captivity and which he had succeeded in conveying to her, with instructions to hand them to his wife, his son, and his daughter. Tempted by the lure of wealth, Charles and the old servant had kept silence. Then came the law-suits, the recovery of the house, Charles's madness, the servant's own useless searches; and the treasures were still there."

"And they are there now," chuckled Lupin.

"And they will be there always," exclaimed Maître Valandier. "Unless . . . unless Citizen Broquet, who no doubt smelt a rat, succeeded in ferreting them out. But this is an unlikely supposition, for Citizen Broquet died in extreme poverty."

"So then . . . ?"

"So then everybody began to hunt. The children of Pauline, the sister, hastened from Geneva. It was discovered that Charles had been secretly married and that he had sons. All these heirs set to work."

"But Charles himself?"

"Charles lived in the most absolute retirement. He did not leave his room."

"Never?"

"Well, that is the most extraordinary, the most astounding part of the story. Once a year, Charles d'Ernemont, impelled by a sort of subconscious will-power, came downstairs, took the exact road which his father had taken, walked across the garden, and sat down either on the steps of the rotunda, which you see here, in the picture, or on the curb of the well. At twenty-seven minutes past five, he rose and went indoors again; and until his death, which occurred in 1820, he never once failed to perform this incomprehensible pilgrimage. Well, the day on which this happened was invariably the 15th of April, the anniversary of the arrest."

Maître Valandier was no longer smiling and himself seemed impressed by the amazing story which he was telling us.

"And, since Charles's death?" asked Lupin, after a moment's reflection.

"Since that time," replied the lawyer, with a certain solemnity of manner, "for nearly a hundred years, the heirs of Charles and Pauline d'Ernemont have kept up the pilgrimage of the 15th of April. During the first few years they made the most thorough excavations. Every inch of the garden was searched, every clod of ground dug up. All this is now over. They take hardly any pains. All they do is, from time to time, for no particular reason, to turn over a stone or explore the well. For the most part, they are content to sit down on the steps of the rotunda, like the poor madman; and, like him, they wait. And that, you see, is the sad part of their destiny. In those hundred years, all these people who have succeeded one another, from father to son, have lost—what shall I say?—the energy of life. They have no courage left, no initiative. They wait. They wait for the 15th of April; and, when the 15th of April comes, they wait for a miracle to take place. Poverty has ended by overtaking every one of them. My predecessors and I have sold first the house, in order to build another which yields a better rent, followed by bits of the garden and further bits. But, as to that corner over there," pointing to the picture, "they would rather die than sell it. On this they are all agreed: Louise d'Ernemont, who is the direct heiress of Pauline, as well as the beggars, the workman, the footman, the circus-rider, and so on, who represent the unfortunate Charles."

There was a fresh pause; and Lupin asked:

"What is your own opinion, Maître Valandier?"

"My private opinion is that there's nothing in it. What credit can we give to the statements of an old servant enfeebled by age? What importance can we attach to the crotchets of a madman? Besides, if the farmer-general had realized his fortune, don't you think that that fortune would have been found? One could manage to hide a paper, a document, in a confined space like that, but not treasures."

"Still, the pictures? . . ."

"Yes, of course. But, after all, are they a sufficient proof?"

Lupin bent over the copy which the solicitor had taken from the cupboard and, after examining it at length, said:

"You spoke of three pictures."

"Yes, the one which you see was handed to my predecessor by the heirs of Charles. Louise d'Ernemont possesses another. As for the third, no one knows what became of it."

Lupin looked at me and continued:

"And do they all bear the same date?"

"Yes, the date inscribed by Charles d'Ernemont when he had them framed, not long before his death. . . . The same date, that is to say the 15th of April, Year II, according to the revolutionary calendar, as the arrest took place in April, 1794."

"Oh, yes, of course," said Lupin. "The figure 2 means . . ."

He thought for a few moments and resumed:

"One more question, if I may. Did no one ever come forward to solve the problem?"

Maître Valandier threw up his arms:

"Goodness gracious me!" he cried. "Why, it was the plague of the office! One of my predecessors, Maître Turbon, was summoned to Passy no fewer than eighteen times, between 1820 and 1843, by the groups of heirs, whom fortune-tellers, clairvoyants, visionaries, impostors of all sorts had promised that they would discover the farmer-general's treasures. At last, we laid down a rule: any outsider applying to institute a search was to begin by depositing a certain sum."

"What sum?"

"A thousand francs."

"And did this have the effect of frightening them off?"

"No. Four years ago, an Hungarian hypnotist tried the experiment and made me waste a whole day. After that, we fixed the deposit at five thousand francs. In case of success, a third of the treasure goes to the finder. In case of failure, the deposit is forfeited to the heirs. Since then, I have been left in peace."

"Here are your five thousand francs."

The lawyer gave a start:

"Eh? What do you say?"

"I say," repeated Lupin, taking five bank-notes from his pocket and calmly spreading them on the table, "I say that here is the deposit of five thousand francs. Please give me a receipt and invite all the d'Ernemont heirs to meet me at Passy on the 15th of April next year."

The notary could not believe his senses. I myself, although Lupin had accustomed me to these surprises, was utterly taken back.

"Are you serious?" asked Maître Valandier.

"Perfectly serious."

"But, you know, I told you my opinion. All these improbable stories rest upon no evidence of any kind."

"I don't agree with you," said Lupin.

The notary gave him the look which we give to a person who is not quite right in his head. Then, accepting the situation, he took his pen and drew up a contract on stamped paper, acknowledging the payment of the deposit by Captain Jeanniot and promising him a third of such moneys as he should discover:

"If you change your mind," he added, "you might let me know a week before the time comes. I shall not inform the d'Ernemont family until the last moment, so as not to give those poor people too long a spell of hope."

"You can inform them this very day, Maître Valandier. It will make them spend a happier year."

We said good-bye. Outside, in the street, I cried:

"So you have hit upon something?"

"I?" replied Lupin. "Not a bit of it! And that's just what amuses me."

"But they have been searching for a hundred years!"

"It is not so much a matter of searching as of thinking. Now I have three hundred and sixty-five days to think in. It is a great deal more than I want; and I am afraid that I shall forget all about the business, interesting though it may be. Oblige me by reminding me, will you?"

⁜⁜⁜⁜⁜⁜⁜⁜⁜⁜⁜⁜⁜⁜⁜⁜

I reminded him of it several times during the following months, though he never seemed to attach much importance to the matter. Then came a long period during which I had no opportunity of seeing him. It was the period, as I afterward learnt, of his visit to Armenia and of the terrible struggle on which he embarked against Abdul the Damned, a struggle which ended in the tyrant's downfall.

I used to write to him, however, at the address which he gave me and I was thus able to send him certain particulars which I had succeeded in gathering, here and there, about my neighbor Louise d'Ernemont, such as the love which she had conceived, a few years earlier, for a very rich young man, who still loved her, but who had been compelled by his family to throw her over; the young widow's despair, and the plucky life which she led with her little daughter.

Lupin replied to none of my letters. I did not know whether they reached him; and, meantime, the date was drawing near and I could not help wondering whether his numerous undertakings would not prevent him from keeping the appointment which he himself had fixed.

As a matter of fact, the morning of the 15th of April arrived and Lupin was not with me by the time I had finished lunch. It was a quarter-past twelve. I left my flat and took a cab to Passy.

I had no sooner entered the lane than I saw the workman's four brats standing outside the door in the wall. Maître Valandier, informed by them of my arrival, hastened in my direction:

"Well?" he cried. "Where's Captain Jeanniot?"

"Hasn't he come?"

"No; and I can assure you that everybody is very impatient to see him."

The different groups began to crowd round the lawyer; and I noticed that all those faces which I recognized had thrown off the gloomy and despondent expression which they wore a year ago.

"They are full of hope," said Maître Valandier, "and it is my fault. But what could I do? Your friend made such an impression upon me that I spoke to these good people with a confidence . . . which I cannot say I feel. However, he seems a queer sort of fellow, this Captain Jeanniot of yours . . ."

He asked me many questions and I gave him a number of more or less fanciful details about the captain, to which the heirs listened, nodding their heads in appreciation of my remarks.

"Of course, the truth was bound to be discovered sooner or later," said the fat gentleman, in a tone of conviction.

The infantry corporal, dazzled by the captain's rank, did not entertain a doubt in his mind.

The lady with the little dog wanted to know if Captain Jeanniot was young.

But Louise d'Ernemont said:

"And suppose he does not come?"

"We shall still have the five thousand francs to divide," said the beggar-man.

For all that, Louise d'Ernemont's words had damped their enthusiasm. Their faces began to look sullen and I felt an atmosphere as of anguish weighing upon us.

At half-past one, the two lean sisters felt faint and sat down. Then the fat gentleman in the soiled suit suddenly rounded on the notary:

"It's you, Maître Valandier, who are to blame. . . . You ought to have brought the captain here by main force. . . . He's a humbug, that's quite clear."

He gave me a savage look, and the footman, in his turn, flung muttered curses at me.

I confess that their reproaches seemed to me well-founded and that Lupin's absence annoyed me greatly:

"He won't come now," I whispered to the lawyer.

And I was thinking of beating a retreat, when the eldest of the brats appeared at the door, yelling:

"There's someone coming! . . . A motor-cycle! . . ."

A motor was throbbing on the other side of the wall. A man on a motor-bicycle came tearing down the lane at the risk of breaking his neck. Suddenly, he put on his brakes, outside the door, and sprang from his machine.

Under the layer of dust which covered him from head to foot, we could see that his navy-blue reefer-suit, his carefully creased trousers, his black felt hat and patent-leather boots were not the clothes in which a man usually goes cycling.

"But that's not Captain Jeanniot!" shouted the notary, who failed to recognize him.

"Yes, it is," said Lupin, shaking hands with us. "I'm Captain Jeanniot right enough . . . only I've shaved off my moustache. . . . Besides, Maître Valandier, here's your receipt."

He caught one of the workman's children by the arm and said:

"Run to the cab-rank and fetch a taxi to the corner of the Rue Raynouard. Look sharp! I have an urgent appointment to keep at two o'clock, or a quarter-past at the latest."

There was a murmur of protest. Captain Jeanniot took out his watch:

"Well! It's only twelve minutes to two! I have a good quarter of an hour before me. But, by Jingo, how tired I feel! And how hungry into the bargain!"

The corporal thrust his ammunition-bread into Lupin's hand; and he munched away at it as he sat down and said:

"You must forgive me. I was in the Marseilles express, which left the rails between Dijon and Laroche. There were twelve people killed and any number injured, whom I had to help. Then I found this motor-cycle in the luggage-van. . . . Maître Valandier, you must be good enough to restore it to the owner. You will find the label fastened to the handle-bar. Ah, you're back, my boy! Is the taxi there? At the corner of the Rue Raynouard? Capital!"

He looked at his watch again:

"Hullo! No time to lose!"

I stared at him with eager curiosity. But how great must the excitement of the d'Ernemont heirs have been! True, they had not the same faith in Captain Jeanniot that I had in Lupin. Nevertheless, their faces were pale and drawn. Captain Jeanniot turned slowly to the left and walked up to the sun-dial. The pedestal represented the figure of a man with a powerful torso, who bore on his shoulders a marble slab the surface of which had been so much worn by time that we could hardly distinguish the engraved lines that marked the hours. Above the slab, a Cupid, with outspread wings, held an arrow that served as a gnomon.

The captain stood leaning forward for a minute, with attentive eyes.

Then he said:

"Somebody lend me a knife, please."

A clock in the neighborhood struck two. At that exact moment, the shadow of the arrow was thrown upon the sunlit dial along the line of a crack in the marble which divided the slab very nearly in half. The captain took the knife handed to him. And with the point, very gently, he began to scratch the mixture of earth and moss that filled the narrow cleft.

Almost immediately, at a couple of inches from the edge, he stopped, as though his knife had encountered an obstacle, inserted his thumb and forefinger, and withdrew a small object which he rubbed between the palms of his hands and gave to the lawyer:

"Here, Maître Valandier. Something to go on with."

It was an enormous diamond, the size of a hazelnut and beautifully cut.

The captain resumed his work. The next moment, a fresh stop. A second diamond, magnificent and brilliant as the first, appeared in sight.

And then came a third and a fourth.

In a minute's time, following the crack from one edge to the other and certainly without digging deeper than half an inch, the captain had taken out eighteen diamonds of the same size.

During this minute, there was not a cry, not a movement around the sun-dial. The heirs seemed paralyzed with a sort of stupor. Then the fat gentleman muttered:

"Geminy!"

And the corporal moaned:

"Oh, captain! . . . Oh, captain! . . ."

The two sisters fell in a dead faint. The lady with the little dog dropped on her knees and prayed, while the footman, staggering like a drunken man, held his head in his two hands, and Louise d'Ernemont wept.

When calm was restored and all became eager to thank Captain Jeanniot, they saw that he was gone.

Some years passed before I had an opportunity of talking to Lupin about this business. He was in a confidential vein and answered:

"The business of the eighteen diamonds? By Jove, when I think that three or four generations of my fellow-men had been hunting for the solution! And the eighteen diamonds were there all the time, under a little mud and dust!"

"But how did you guess? . . ."

"I did not guess. I reflected. I doubt if I need even have reflected. I was struck, from the beginning, by the fact that the whole circumstance was governed by one primary question: the question of time. When Charles d'Ernemont was still in possession of his wits, he wrote a date upon the three pictures. Later, in the gloom in which he was struggling, a faint glimmer of intelligence led him every year to the center of the old garden; and the same faint glimmer led him away from it every year at the same moment, that is to say, at twenty-seven minutes past five. Something must have acted on the disordered machinery of his brain in this way. What was the superior force that controlled the poor madman's movements? Obviously, the instinctive notion of time represented by the sun-dial in the farmer-general's pictures. It was the annual revolution of the earth around the sun that brought Charles d'Ernemont back to the garden at a fixed date. And it was the earth's daily revolution upon its own axis that took him from it at a fixed hour, that is to say, at the hour, most likely, when the sun, concealed by objects different from those of to-day, ceased to light the Passy garden. Now of all this the sun-dial was the symbol. And that is why I at once knew where to look."

"But how did you settle the hour at which to begin looking?"

"Simply by the pictures. A man living at that time, such as Charles d'Ernemont, would have written either 26 Germinal, Year II, or else 15 April, 1794, but not 15 April, Year II. I was astounded that no one had thought of that."

"Then the figure 2 stood for two o'clock?"

"Evidently. And what must have happened was this: the farmer-general began by turning his fortune into solid gold and silver money. Then, by way of additional precaution, with this gold and silver he bought eighteen wonderful diamonds. When he was surprised by the arrival of the patrol, he fled into his garden. Which was the best place to hide the diamonds? Chance caused his eyes to light upon the sun-dial. It was two o'clock. The shadow of the arrow was then falling along the crack in the marble. He obeyed this sign of the shadow, rammed his eighteen diamonds into the dust, and calmly went back and surrendered to the soldiers."

"But the shadow of the arrow coincides with the crack in the marble every day of the year and not only on the 15th of April."

"You forget, my dear chap, that we are dealing with a lunatic and that he remembered only this date of the 15th of April."

"Very well; but you, once you had solved the riddle, could easily have made your way into the enclosure and taken the diamonds."

"Quite true; and I should not have hesitated, if I had had to do with people of another description. But I really felt sorry for those poor wretches. And then you know the sort of idiot that Lupin is. The idea of appearing suddenly as a benevolent genius and amazing his kind would be enough to make him commit any sort of folly."

"Tah!" I cried. "The folly was not so great as all that. Six magnificent diamonds! How delighted the d'Ernemont heirs must have been to fulfill their part of the contract!"

Lupin looked at me and burst into uncontrollable laughter:

"So you haven't heard? Oh, what a joke! The delight of the d'Ernemont heirs! . . . Why, my dear fellow, on the next day, that worthy Captain Jeanniot had so many mortal enemies! On the very next day, the two lean sisters and the fat gentleman organized an opposition. A contract? Not worth the paper it was written on, because, as could easily be proved, there was no such person as Captain Jeanniot. Where did that adventurer spring from? Just let him sue them and they'd soon show him what was what!"

"Louise d'Ernemont too?"

"No, Louise d'Ernemont protested against that piece of rascality. But what could she do against so many? Besides, now that she was rich, she got back her young man. I haven't heard of her since."

"So . . . ?"

"So, my dear fellow, I was caught in a trap, with not a leg to stand on, and I had to compromise and accept one modest diamond as my share, the smallest and the least handsome of the lot. That comes of doing one's best to help people!"

And Lupin grumbled between his teeth:

"Oh, gratitude! . . . All humbug! . . . Where should we honest men be if we had not our conscience and the satisfaction of duty performed to reward us?"

THE RED SILK SCARF

On leaving his house one morning, at his usual early hour for going to the Law Courts, Chief-inspector Ganimard noticed the curious behavior of an individual who was walking along the Rue Pergolèse in front of him. Shabbily dressed and wearing a straw hat, though the day was the first of December, the man stooped at every thirty or forty yards to fasten his boot-lace, or pick up his stick, or for some other reason. And, each time, he took a little piece of orange-peel from his pocket and laid it stealthily on the curb of the pavement. It was probably a mere display of eccentricity, a childish amusement to which no one else would have paid attention; but Ganimard was one of those shrewd observers who are indifferent to nothing that strikes their eyes and who are never satisfied until they know the secret cause of things. He therefore began to follow the man.

Now, at the moment when the fellow was turning to the right, into the Avenue de la Grande-Armée, the inspector caught him exchanging signals with a boy of twelve or thirteen, who was walking along the houses on the left-hand side. Twenty yards farther, the man stooped and turned up the bottom of his trousers legs. A bit of orange-peel marked the place. At the same moment, the boy stopped and, with a piece of chalk, drew a white cross, surrounded by a circle, on the wall of the house next to him.

The two continued on their way. A minute later, a fresh halt. The strange individual picked up a pin and dropped a piece of orange-peel; and the boy at once made a second cross on the wall and again drew a white circle round it.

"By Jove!" thought the chief-inspector, with a grunt of satisfaction. "This is rather promising.... What on earth can those two merchants be plotting?"

The two "merchants" went down the Avenue Friedland and the Rue du Faubourg-Saint-Honoré, but nothing occurred that was worthy of special mention. The double performance was repeated at almost regular intervals and, so to speak, mechanically. Nevertheless, it was obvious, on the one hand, that the man with the orange-peel did not do his part of the business until after he had picked out with a glance the house that was to be marked and, on the other hand, that the boy did not mark that particular house until after he had observed his companion's signal. It was certain, therefore, that there was an agreement between the two; and the proceedings presented no small interest in the chief-inspector's eyes.

At the Place Beauveau the man hesitated. Then, apparently making up his mind, he twice turned up and twice turned down the bottom of his trousers legs. Hereupon, the boy sat down on the curb, opposite the sentry who was mounting guard outside the Ministry of the Interior, and marked the flagstone with two little crosses contained within two circles. The same ceremony was gone through a little further on, when they reached the Elysée. Only, on the pavement where the President's sentry was marching up and down, there were three signs instead of two.

"Hang it all!" muttered Ganimard, pale with excitement and thinking, in spite of himself, of his inveterate enemy, Lupin, whose name came to his mind whenever a mysterious circumstance presented itself. "Hang it all, what does it mean?"

He was nearly collaring and questioning the two "merchants." But he was too clever to commit so gross a blunder. The man with the orange-peel had now lit a cigarette; and the boy, also placing a cigarette-end between his lips, had gone up to him, apparently with the object of asking for a light.

They exchanged a few words. Quick as thought, the boy handed his companion an object which looked—at least, so the inspector believed—like a revolver. They both bent over this object; and the man, standing with his face to the wall, put his hand six times in his pocket and made a movement as though he were loading a weapon.

As soon as this was done, they walked briskly to the Rue de Suréne; and the inspector, who followed them as closely as he was able to do without attracting their attention, saw them enter the gateway of an old house of which all the shutters were closed, with the exception of those on the third or top floor.

He hurried in after them. At the end of the carriage-entrance he saw a large courtyard, with a house-painter's sign at the back and a staircase on the left.

He went up the stairs and, as soon as he reached the first floor, ran still faster, because he heard, right up at the top, a din as of a free-fight.

When he came to the last landing he found the door open. He entered, listened for a second, caught the sound of a struggle, rushed to the room from which the sound appeared to proceed, and remained standing on the threshold, very much out of breath and greatly surprised to see the man of the orange-peel and the boy banging the floor with chairs.

At that moment a third person walked out of an adjoining room. It was a young man of twenty-eight or thirty, wearing a pair of short whiskers in addition to his moustache, spectacles, and a smoking-jacket with an astrakhan collar and looking like a foreigner, a Russian.

"Good morning, Ganimard," he said. And turning to the two companions, "Thank you, my friends, and all my congratulations on the successful result. Here's the reward I promised you."

He gave them a hundred-franc note, pushed them outside, and shut both doors.

"I am sorry, old chap," he said to Ganimard. "I wanted to talk to you . . . wanted to talk to you badly."

He offered him his hand and, seeing that the inspector remained flabbergasted and that his face was still distorted with anger, he exclaimed:

"Why, you don't seem to understand! . . . And yet it's clear enough. . . . I wanted to see you particularly. . . . So what could I do?" And, pretending to reply to an objection, "No, no, old chap," he continued. "You're quite wrong. If I had written or telephoned, you would not have come . . . or else you would have come with a regiment. Now I wanted to see you all alone; and I thought the best thing was to send those two decent fellows to meet you, with orders to scatter bits of orange-peel and draw crosses and circles, in short, to mark out your road to this place. . . . Why, you look quite bewildered! What is it? Perhaps you don't recognize me? Lupin. . . . Arsène Lupin. . . . Ransack your memory. . . . Doesn't the name remind you of anything?"

"You dirty scoundrel!" Ganimard snarled between his teeth.

Lupin seemed greatly distressed and, in an affectionate voice:

"Are you vexed? Yes, I can see it in your eyes. . . . The Dugrival business, I suppose? I ought to have waited for you to come and take me in charge? . . . There now, the thought never occurred to me! I promise you, next time . . ."

"You scum of the earth!" growled Ganimard.

"And I thinking I was giving you a treat! Upon my word, I did. I said to myself, 'That dear old Ganimard! We haven't met for an age. He'll simply rush at me when he sees me!'"

Ganimard, who had not yet stirred a limb, seemed to be waking from his stupor. He looked around him, looked at Lupin, visibly asked himself whether he would not do well to rush at him in reality and then, controlling himself, took hold of a chair and settled himself in it, as though he had suddenly made up his mind to listen to his enemy:

"Speak," he said. "And don't waste my time with any nonsense. I'm in a hurry."

"That's it," said Lupin, "let's talk. You can't imagine a quieter place than this. It's an old manor-house, which once stood in the open country, and it belongs to the Duc de Rochelaure. The duke, who has never lived in it, lets this floor to me and the outhouses to a painter and decorator. I always keep up a few establishments of this kind: it's a sound, practical plan. Here, in spite of my looking like a Russian nobleman, I am M. Daubreuil, an ex-cabinet-minister. . . . You understand, I had to select a rather overstocked profession, so as not to attract attention . . ."

"Do you think I care a hang about all this?" said Ganimard, interrupting him.

"Quite right, I'm wasting words and you're in a hurry. Forgive me. I sha'n't be long now. . . . Five minutes, that's all . . . I'll start at once . . . Have a cigar? No? Very well, no more will I."

He sat down also, drummed his fingers on the table, while thinking, and began in this fashion:

"On the 17th of October, 1599, on a warm and sunny autumn day . . . Do you follow me? . . . But, now that I come to think of it, is it really necessary to go back to the reign of Henry IV, and tell you all about the building of the Pont-Neuf? No, I don't suppose you are very well up in French history; and I should only end by muddling you. Suffice it, then, for you to know that, last night, at one o'clock in the morning, a boatman passing under the last arch of the Pont-Neuf aforesaid, along the left bank of the river, heard something drop into the front part of his barge. The thing had been flung from the bridge and its evident destination was the bottom of the Seine. The bargee's dog rushed forward, barking, and, when the man reached the end of his craft, he saw the animal worrying a piece of newspaper that had served to wrap up a number of objects. He took from the dog such of the contents as had not fallen into the water, went to his cabin and examined them carefully. The result struck him as interesting; and, as the man is connected with one of my friends, he sent to let me know. This morning I was woke up and placed in possession of the facts and of the objects which the man had collected. Here they are."

He pointed to them, spread out on a table. There were, first of all, the torn pieces of a newspaper. Next came a large cut-glass inkstand, with a long piece of string fastened to the lid. There was a bit of broken glass and a sort of flexible cardboard, reduced to shreds. Lastly, there was a piece of bright scarlet silk, ending in a tassel of the same material and color.

"You see our exhibits, friend of my youth," said Lupin. "No doubt, the problem would be more easily solved if we had the other objects which went overboard owing to the stupidity of the dog. But it seems to me, all the same, that we ought to be able to manage, with a little reflection and intelligence. And those are just your great qualities. How does the business strike you?"

Ganimard did not move a muscle. He was willing to stand Lupin's chaff, but his dignity commanded him not to speak a single word in answer nor even to give a nod or shake of the head that might have been taken to express approval or criticism.

"I see that we are entirely of one mind," continued Lupin, without appearing to remark the chief-inspector's silence. "And I can sum up the matter briefly, as told us by these exhibits. Yesterday evening, between nine and twelve o'clock, a showily dressed young woman was wounded with a knife and then caught round the throat and choked to death by a well-dressed gentleman, wearing a single eyeglass and interested in racing, with whom the aforesaid showily dressed young lady had been eating three meringues and a coffee éclair."

Lupin lit a cigarette and, taking Ganimard by the sleeve:

"Aha, that's up against you, chief-inspector! You thought that, in the domain of police deductions, such feats as those were prohibited to outsiders! Wrong, sir! Lupin juggles with inferences and deductions for all the world like a detective in a novel. My proofs are dazzling and absolutely simple."

And, pointing to the objects one by one, as he demonstrated his statement, he resumed:

"I said, after nine o'clock yesterday evening. This scrap of newspaper bears yesterday's date, with the words, 'Evening edition.' Also, you will see here, pasted to the paper, a bit of one of those yellow wrappers in which the subscribers' copies are sent out. These copies are always delivered by the nine o'clock post. Therefore, it was after nine o'clock. I said, a well-dressed man. Please observe that this tiny piece of glass has the round hole of a single eyeglass at one of the edges and that the single eyeglass is an essentially aristocratic article of wear. This well-dressed man walked into a pastry-cook's shop. Here is the very thin cardboard, shaped like a box, and still showing a little of the cream of the meringues and éclairs which were packed in it in the usual way. Having got his parcel, the gentleman with the eyeglass joined a young person whose eccentricity in the matter of dress is pretty clearly indicated by this bright-red silk scarf. Having joined her, for some reason as yet unknown he first stabbed her with a knife and then strangled her with the help of this same scarf. Take your magnifying glass, chief-inspector, and you will see, on the silk, stains of a darker red which are, here, the marks of a knife wiped on the scarf and, there, the marks of a hand, covered with blood, clutching the material. Having committed the murder, his next business is to leave no trace behind him. So he takes from his pocket, first, the newspaper to which he subscribes—a racing-paper, as you will see by glancing at the contents of this scrap; and you will have no difficulty in discovering the title—and, secondly, a cord, which, on inspection, turns out to be a length of whip-cord. These two details prove—do they not?—that our man is interested in racing and that he himself rides. Next, he picks up the fragments of his eyeglass, the cord of which has been broken in the struggle. He takes a pair of scissors— observe the hacking of the scissors—and cuts off the stained part of the scarf, leaving the other end, no doubt, in his victim's clenched hands. He makes a ball of the confectioner's cardboard box. He also puts in certain things that would have betrayed him, such as the knife, which must have slipped into the Seine. He wraps everything in the newspaper, ties it with the cord, and fastens this cut-glass inkstand to it, as a make-weight. Then he makes himself scarce. A little later, the parcel falls into the waterman's barge. And there you are. Oof, it's hot work! . . . What do you say to the story?"

He looked at Ganimard to see what impression his speech had produced on the inspector. Ganimard did not depart from his attitude of silence.

Lupin began to laugh:

"As a matter of fact, you're annoyed and surprised. But you're suspicious as well: 'Why should that confounded Lupin hand the business over to me,' say you, 'instead of keeping it for himself, hunting down the murderer and rifling his pockets, if there was a robbery?' The question is quite logical, of course. But—there is a 'but'—I have no time, you see. I am full up with work at the present moment: a burglary in London, another at Lausanne, an exchange of children at Marseilles, to say nothing of having to save a young girl who is at this moment shadowed by death. That's always the way: it never rains but it pours. So I said to myself, 'Suppose I handed the business over to my dear old Ganimard? Now that it is half-solved for him, he is quite capable of succeeding. And what a service I shall be doing him! How magnificently he will be able to distinguish himself!' No sooner said than done. At eight o'clock in the morning, I sent the joker with the orange-peel to meet you. You swallowed the bait; and you were here by nine, all on edge and eager for the fray."

Lupin rose from his chair. He went over to the inspector and, with his eyes in Ganimard's, said:

"That's all. You now know the whole story. Presently, you will know the victim: some ballet-dancer, probably, some singer at a music-hall. On the other hand, the chances are that the criminal lives near the Pont-Neuf, most likely on the left bank. Lastly, here are all the exhibits. I make you a present of them. Set to work. I shall only keep this end of the scarf. If ever you want to piece the scarf together, bring me the other end, the one which the police will find round the victim's neck. Bring it to me in four weeks from now to the day, that is to say, on the 29th of December, at ten o'clock in the morning. You can be sure of finding me here. And don't be afraid: this is all perfectly serious, friend of my youth; I swear it is. No humbug, honor bright. You can go straight ahead. Oh, by the way, when you arrest the fellow with the eyeglass, be a bit careful: he is left-handed! Good-bye, old dear, and good luck to you!"

Lupin spun round on his heel, went to the door, opened it, and disappeared before Ganimard had even thought of taking a decision. The inspector rushed after him, but at once found that the handle of the door, by some trick of mechanism which he did not know, refused to turn. It took him ten minutes to unscrew the lock and ten minutes more to unscrew the lock of the hall-door. By the time that he had scrambled down the three flights of stairs, Ganimard had given up all hope of catching Arsène Lupin.

Besides, he was not thinking of it. Lupin inspired him with a queer, complex feeling, made up of fear, hatred, involuntary admiration and also the vague instinct that he, Ganimard, in spite of all his efforts, in spite of the persistency of his endeavors, would never get the better of this particular adversary. He pursued him from a sense of duty and pride, but with the continual dread of being taken in by that formidable hoaxer and scouted and fooled in the face of a public that was always only too willing to laugh at the chief-inspector's mishaps.

This business of the red scarf, in particular, struck him as most suspicious. It was interesting, certainly, in more ways than one, but so very improbable! And Lupin's explanation, apparently so logical, would never stand the test of a severe examination!

"No," said Ganimard, "this is all swank: a parcel of suppositions and guesswork based upon nothing at all. I'm not to be caught with chaff."

|||||||||||||||||||||||||||||

When he reached the headquarters of police, at 36 Quai des Orfèvres, he had quite made up his mind to treat the incident as though it had never happened.

He went up to the Criminal Investigation Department. Here, one of his fellow-inspectors said:

"Seen the chief?"

"No."

"He was asking for you just now."

"Oh, was he?"

"Yes, you had better go after him."

"Where?"

"To the Rue de Berne . . . there was a murder there last night."

"Oh! Who's the victim?"

"I don't know exactly . . . a music-hall singer, I believe."

Ganimard simply muttered:

"By Jove!"

Twenty minutes later he stepped out of the underground railway-station and made for the Rue de Berne.

The victim, who was known in the theatrical world by her stage-name of Jenny Saphir, occupied a small flat on the second floor of one of the houses. A policeman took the chief-inspector upstairs and showed him the way, through two sitting-rooms, to a bedroom, where he found the magistrates in charge of the inquiry, together with the divisional surgeon and M. Dudouis, the head of the detective-service.

Ganimard started at the first glance which he gave into the room. He saw, lying on a sofa, the corpse of a young woman whose hands clutched a strip of red silk! One of the shoulders, which appeared above the low-cut bodice, bore the marks of two wounds surrounded with clotted blood. The distorted and almost blackened features still bore an expression of frenzied terror.

The divisional surgeon, who had just finished his examination, said:

"My first conclusions are very clear. The victim was twice stabbed with a dagger and afterward strangled. The immediate cause of death was asphyxia."

"By Jove!" thought Ganimard again, remembering Lupin's words and the picture which he had drawn of the crime.

The examining-magistrate objected:

"But the neck shows no discoloration."

"She may have been strangled with a napkin or a handkerchief," said the doctor.

"Most probably," said the chief detective, "with this silk scarf, which the victim was wearing and a piece of which remains, as though she had clung to it with her two hands to protect herself."

"But why does only that piece remain?" asked the magistrate. "What has become of the other?"

"The other may have been stained with blood and carried off by the murderer. You can plainly distinguish the hurried slashing of the scissors."

"By Jove!" said Ganimard, between his teeth, for the third time. "That brute of a Lupin saw everything without seeing a thing!"

"And what about the motive of the murder?" asked the magistrate. "The locks have been forced, the cupboards turned upside down. Have you anything to tell me, M. Dudouis?"

The chief of the detective-service replied:

"I can at least suggest a supposition, derived from the statements made by the servant. The victim, who enjoyed a greater reputation on account of her looks than through her talent as a singer, went to Russia, two years ago, and brought back with her a magnificent sapphire, which she appears to have received from some person of importance at the court. Since then, she went by the name of Jenny Saphir and seems generally to have been very proud of that present, although, for prudence sake, she never wore it. I daresay that we shall not be far out if we presume the theft of the sapphire to have been the cause of the crime."

"But did the maid know where the stone was?"

"No, nobody did. And the disorder of the room would tend to prove that the murderer did not know either."

"We will question the maid," said the examining-magistrate.

M. Dudouis took the chief-inspector aside and said:

"You're looking very old-fashioned, Ganimard. What's the matter? Do you suspect anything?"

"Nothing at all, chief."

"That's a pity. We could do with a bit of showy work in the department. This is one of a number of crimes, all of the same class, of which we have failed to discover the perpetrator. This time we want the criminal . . . and quickly!"

"A difficult job, chief."

"It's got to be done. Listen to me, Ganimard. According to what the maid says, Jenny Saphir led a very regular life. For a month past she was in the habit of frequently receiving visits, on her return from the music-hall, that is to say, at about half-past ten, from a man who would stay until midnight or so. 'He's a society man,' Jenny Saphir used to say, 'and he wants to marry me.' This society man took every precaution to avoid being seen, such as turning up his coat-collar and lowering the brim of his hat when he passed the porter's box. And Jenny Saphir always made a point of sending away her maid, even before he came. This is the man whom we have to find."

"Has he left no traces?"

"None at all. It is obvious that we have to deal with a very clever scoundrel, who prepared his crime beforehand and committed it with every possible chance of escaping unpunished. His arrest would be a great feather in our cap. I rely on you, Ganimard."

"Ah, you rely on me, chief?" replied the inspector. "Well, we shall see . . . we shall see. . . . I don't say no. . . . Only . . ."

He seemed in a very nervous condition, and his agitation struck M. Dudouis.

"Only," continued Ganimard, "only I swear . . . do you hear, chief? I swear . . ."

"What do you swear?"

"Nothing. . . . We shall see, chief . . . we shall see . . ."

Ganimard did not finish his sentence until he was outside, alone.

And he finished it aloud, stamping his foot, in a tone of the most violent anger:

"Only, I swear to Heaven that the arrest shall be effected by my own means, without my employing a single one of the clues with which that villain has supplied me. Ah, no! Ah, no! . . ."

Railing against Lupin, furious at being mixed up in this business and resolved, nevertheless, to get to the bottom of it, he wandered aimlessly about the streets. His brain was seething with irritation; and he tried to adjust his ideas a little and to discover, among the chaotic facts, some trifling detail, unperceived by all, unsuspected by Lupin himself, that might lead him to success.

He lunched hurriedly at a bar, resumed his stroll, and suddenly stopped, petrified, astounded, and confused. He was walking under the gateway of the very house in the Rue de Surène to which Lupin had enticed him a few hours earlier! A force stronger than his own will was drawing him there once more. The solution of the problem lay there. There and there alone were all the elements of the truth. Do and say what he would, Lupin's assertions were so precise, his calculations so accurate, that, worried to the innermost recesses of his being by so prodigious a display of perspicacity, he could not do other than take up the work at the point where his enemy had left it

Abandoning all further resistance, he climbed the three flights of stairs. The door of the flat was open. No one had touched the exhibits. He put them in his pocket and walked away.

From that moment, he reasoned and acted, so to speak, mechanically, under the influence of the master whom he could not choose but obey.

Admitting that the unknown person whom he was seeking lived in the neighborhood of the Pont-Neuf, it became necessary to discover, somewhere between that bridge and the Rue de Berne, the first-class confectioner's shop, open in the evenings, at which the cakes were bought. This did not take long to find. A pastry-cook near the Gare Saint-Lazare showed him some little cardboard boxes, identical in material and shape with the one in Ganimard's possession. Moreover, one of the shopgirls remembered having served, on the previous evening, a gentleman whose face was almost concealed in the collar of his fur coat, but whose eyeglass she had happened to notice.

"That's one clue checked," thought the inspector. "Our man wears an eyeglass."

He next collected the pieces of the racing-paper and showed them to a newsvendor, who easily recognized the *Turf Illustré*. Ganimard at once went to the offices of the *Turf* and asked to see the list of subscribers. Going through the list, he jotted down the names and addresses of all those who lived anywhere near the Pont-Neuf and principally—because Lupin had said so—those on the left bank of the river.

He then went back to the Criminal Investigation Department, took half a dozen men and packed them off with the necessary instructions.

At seven o'clock in the evening, the last of these men returned and brought good news with him. A certain M. Prévailles, a subscriber to the *Turf*, occupied an entresol flat on the Quai des Augustins. On the previous evening, he left his place, wearing a fur coat, took his letters and his paper, the *Turf Illustré*, from the porter's wife, walked away and returned home at midnight. This M. Prévailles wore a single eyeglass. He was a regular race-goer and himself owned several hacks which he either rode himself or jobbed out.

The inquiry had taken so short a time and the results obtained were so exactly in accordance with Lupin's predictions that Ganimard felt quite overcome on hearing the detective's report. Once more he was measuring the prodigious extent of the resources at Lupin's disposal. Never in the course of his life—and Ganimard was already well-advanced in years—had he come across such perspicacity, such a quick and far-seeing mind.

He went in search of M. Dudouis.

"Everything's ready, chief. Have you a warrant?"

"Eh?"

"I said, everything is ready for the arrest, chief."

"You know the name of Jenny Saphir's murderer?"

"Yes."

"But how? Explain yourself."

Ganimard had a sort of scruple of conscience, blushed a little and nevertheless replied:

"An accident, chief. The murderer threw everything that was likely to compromise him into the Seine. Part of the parcel was picked up and handed to me."

"By whom?"

"A boatman who refused to give his name, for fear of getting into trouble. But I had all the clues I wanted. It was not so difficult as I expected."

And the inspector described how he had gone to work.

"And you call that an accident!" cried M. Dudouis. "And you say that it was not difficult! Why, it's one of your finest performances! Finish it yourself, Ganimard, and be prudent."

Ganimard was eager to get the business done. He went to the Quai des Augustins with his men and distributed them around the house. He questioned the portress, who said that her tenant took his meals out of doors, but made a point of looking in after dinner.

A little before nine o'clock, in fact, leaning out of her window, she warned Ganimard, who at once gave a low whistle. A gentleman in a tall hat and a fur coat was coming along the pavement beside the Seine. He crossed the road and walked up to the house.

Ganimard stepped forward:

"M. Prévailles, I believe?"

"Yes, but who are you?"

"I have a commission to . . ."

He had not time to finish his sentence. At the sight of the men appearing out of the shadow, Prévailles quickly retreated to the wall and faced his adversaries, with his back to the door of a shop on the ground-floor, the shutters of which were closed.

"Stand back!" he cried. "I don't know you!"

His right hand brandished a heavy stick, while his left was slipped behind him and seemed to be trying to open the door.

Ganimard had an impression that the man might escape through this way and through some secret outlet:

"None of this nonsense," he said, moving closer to him. "You're caught. . . . You had better come quietly."

But, just as he was laying hold of Prévailles's stick, Ganimard remembered the warning which Lupin gave him: Prévailles was left-handed; and it was his revolver for which he was feeling behind his back.

The inspector ducked his head. He had noticed the man's sudden movement. Two reports rang out. No one was hit.

A second later, Prévailles received a blow under the chin from the butt-end of a revolver, which brought him down where he stood. He was entered at the Dépôt soon after nine o'clock.

Ganimard enjoyed a great reputation even at that time. But this capture, so quickly effected, by such very simple means, and at once made public by the police, won him a sudden celebrity. Prévailles was forthwith saddled with all the murders that had remained unpunished; and the newspapers vied with one another in extolling Ganimard's prowess.

The case was conducted briskly at the start. It was first of all ascertained that Prévailles, whose real name was Thomas Derocq, had already been in trouble. Moreover, the search instituted in his rooms, while not supplying any fresh proofs, at least led to the discovery of a ball of whip-cord similar to the cord used for doing up the parcel and also to the discovery of daggers which would have produced a wound similar to the wounds on the victim.

But, on the eighth day, everything was changed. Until then Prévailles had refused to reply to the questions put to him; but now, assisted by his counsel, he pleaded a circumstantial alibi and maintained that he was at the Folies Bergère on the night of the murder.

As a matter of fact, the pockets of his dinner-jacket contained the counterfoil of a stall-ticket and a program of the performance, both bearing the date of that evening.

"An alibi prepared in advance," objected the examining-magistrate.

"Prove it," said Prévailles.

The prisoner was confronted with the witnesses for the prosecution. The young lady from the confectioner's "thought she knew" the gentleman with the eyeglass. The hall-porter in the Rue de Berne "thought he knew" the gentleman who used to come to see Jenny Saphir. But nobody dared to make a more definite statement.

The examination, therefore, led to nothing of a precise character, provided no solid basis whereon to found a serious accusation.

The judge sent for Ganimard and told him of his difficulty.

"I can't possibly persist, at this rate. There is no evidence to support the charge."

"But surely you are convinced in your own mind, monsieur le juge d'instruction! Prévailles would never have resisted his arrest unless he was guilty."

"He says that he thought he was being assaulted. He also says that he never set eyes on Jenny Saphir; and, as a matter of fact, we can find no one to contradict his assertion. Then again, admitting that the sapphire has been stolen, we have not been able to find it at his flat."

"Nor anywhere else," suggested Ganimard.

"Quite true, but that is no evidence against him. I'll tell you what we shall want, M. Ganimard, and that very soon: the other end of this red scarf."

"The other end?"

"Yes, for it is obvious that, if the murderer took it away with him, the reason was that the stuff is stained with the marks of the blood on his fingers."

Ganimard made no reply. For several days he had felt that the whole business was tending to this conclusion. There was no other proof possible. Given the silk scarf—and in no other circumstances—Prévailles's guilt was certain. Now Ganimard's position required that Prévailles's guilt should be established. He was responsible for the arrest, it had cast a glamour around him, he had been praised to the skies as the most formidable adversary of criminals; and he would look absolutely ridiculous if Prévailles were released.

Unfortunately, the one and only indispensable proof was in Lupin's pocket. How was he to get hold of it?

Ganimard cast about, exhausted himself with fresh investigations, went over the inquiry from start to finish, spent sleepless nights in turning over the mystery of the Rue de Berne, studied the records of Prévailles's life, sent ten men hunting after the invisible sapphire. Everything was useless.

On the 28th of December, the examining-magistrate stopped him in one of the passages of the Law Courts:

"Well, M. Ganimard, any news?"

"No, monsieur le juge d'instruction."

"Then I shall dismiss the case."

"Wait one day longer."

"What's the use? We want the other end of the scarf; have you got it?"

"I shall have it to-morrow."

"To-morrow!"

"Yes, but please lend me the piece in your possession."

"What if I do?"

"If you do, I promise to let you have the whole scarf complete."

"Very well, that's understood."

Ganimard followed the examining-magistrate to his room and came out with the piece of silk:

"Hang it all!" he growled. "Yes, I will go and fetch the proof and I shall have it too . . . always presuming that Master Lupin has the courage to keep the appointment."

In point of fact, he did not doubt for a moment that Master Lupin would have this courage, and that was just what exasperated him. Why had Lupin insisted on this meeting? What was his object, in the circumstances?

Anxious, furious, and full of hatred, he resolved to take every precaution necessary not only to prevent his falling into a trap himself, but to make his enemy fall into one, now that the opportunity offered. And, on the next day, which was the 29th of December, the date fixed by Lupin, after spending the night in studying the old manor-house in the Rue de Surène and convincing himself that there was no other outlet than the front door, he warned his men that he was going on a dangerous expedition and arrived with them on the field of battle.

He posted them in a café and gave them formal instructions: if he showed himself at one of the third-floor windows, or if he failed to return within an hour, the detectives were to enter the house and arrest anyone who tried to leave it.

The chief-inspector made sure that his revolver was in working order and that he could take it from his pocket easily. Then he went upstairs.

He was surprised to find things as he had left them, the doors open and the locks broken. After ascertaining that the windows of the principal room looked out on the street, he visited the three other rooms that made up the flat. There was no one there.

"Master Lupin was afraid," he muttered, not without a certain satisfaction.

"Don't be silly," said a voice behind him.

Turning round, he saw an old workman, wearing a house-painter's long smock, standing in the doorway.

"You needn't bother your head," said the man. "It's I, Lupin. I have been working in the painter's shop since early morning. This is when we knock off for breakfast. So I came upstairs."

He looked at Ganimard with a quizzing smile and cried:

"'Pon my word, this is a gorgeous moment I owe you, old chap! I wouldn't sell it for ten years of your life; and yet you know how I love you! What do you think of it, artist? Wasn't it well thought out and well foreseen? Foreseen from alpha to omega? Did I understand the business? Did I penetrate the mystery of the scarf? I'm not saying that there were no holes in my argument, no links missing in the chain . . . But what a masterpiece of intelligence! Ganimard, what a reconstruction of events! What an intuition of everything that had taken place and of everything that was going to take place, from the discovery of the crime to your arrival here in search of a proof! What really marvelous divination! Have you the scarf?"

"Yes, half of it. Have you the other?"

"Here it is. Let's compare."

They spread the two pieces of silk on the table. The cuts made by the scissors corresponded exactly. Moreover, the colors were identical.

"But I presume," said Lupin, "that this was not the only thing you came for. What you are interested in seeing is the marks of the blood. Come with me, Ganimard: it's rather dark in here."

They moved into the next room, which, though it overlooked the courtyard, was lighter; and Lupin held his piece of silk against the window-pane:

"Look," he said, making room for Ganimard.

The inspector gave a start of delight. The marks of the five fingers and the print of the palm were distinctly visible. The evidence was undeniable. The murderer had seized the stuff in his bloodstained hand, in the same hand that had stabbed Jenny Saphir, and tied the scarf round her neck.

"And it is the print of a left hand," observed Lupin. "Hence my warning, which had nothing miraculous about it, you see. For, though I admit, friend of my youth, that you may look upon me as a superior intelligence, I won't have you treat me as a wizard."

Ganimard had quickly pocketed the piece of silk. Lupin nodded his head in approval:

"Quite right, old boy, it's for you. I'm so glad you're glad! And, you see, there was no trap about all this . . . only the wish to oblige . . . a service between friends, between pals. . . . And also, I confess, a little curiosity. . . . Yes, I wanted to examine this other piece of silk, the one the police had. . . . Don't be afraid: I'll give it back to you. . . . Just a second . . ."

Lupin, with a careless movement, played with the tassel at the end of this half of the scarf, while Ganimard listened to him in spite of himself:

"How ingenious these little bits of women's work are! Did you notice one detail in the maid's evidence? Jenny Saphir was very handy with her needle and used to make all her own hats and frocks. It is obvious that she made this scarf herself. . . . Besides, I noticed that from the first. I am naturally curious, as I have already told you, and I made a thorough examination of the piece of silk which you have just put in your pocket. Inside the tassel, I found a little sacred medal, which the poor girl had stitched into it to bring her luck. Touching, isn't it, Ganimard? A little medal of Our Lady of Good Succor."

The inspector felt greatly puzzled and did not take his eyes off the other. And Lupin continued:

"Then I said to myself, 'How interesting it would be to explore the other half of the scarf, the one which the police will find round the victim's neck!' For this other half, which I hold in my hands at last, is finished off in the same way . . . so I shall be able to see if it has a hiding-place too and what's inside it. . . . But look, my friend, isn't it cleverly made? And so simple! All you have to do is to take a skein of red cord and braid it round a wooden cup, leaving a little recess, a little empty space in the middle, very small, of course, but large enough to hold a medal of a saint . . . or anything. . . . A precious stone, for instance. . . . Such as a sapphire . . ."

At that moment he finished pushing back the silk cord and, from the hollow of a cup he took between his thumb and forefinger a wonderful blue stone, perfect in respect of size and purity.

"Ha! What did I tell you, friend of my youth?"

He raised his head. The inspector had turned livid and was staring wild-eyed, as though fascinated by the stone that sparkled before him. He at last realized the whole plot:

"You dirty scoundrel!" he muttered, repeating the insults which he had used at the first interview. "You scum of the earth!"

The two men were standing one against the other.

"Give me back that," said the inspector.

Lupin held out the piece of silk.

"And the sapphire," said Ganimard, in a peremptory tone.

"Don't be silly."

"Give it back, or . . ."

"Or what, you idiot!" cried Lupin. "Look here, do you think I put you on to this soft thing for nothing?"

"Give it back!"

"You haven't noticed what I've been about, that's plain! What! For four weeks I've kept you on the move like a deer; and you want to . . . ! Come, Ganimard, old chap, pull yourself together! . . . Don't you see that you've been playing the good dog for four weeks on end? . . . Fetch it, Rover! . . . There's a nice blue pebble over there, which master can't get at. Hunt it, Ganimard, fetch it . . . bring it to master. . . . Ah, he's his master's own good little dog! . . . Sit up! Beg! . . . Does'ms want a bit of sugar, then? . . ."

Ganimard, containing the anger that seethed within him, thought only of one thing, summoning his detectives. And, as the room in which he now was looked out on the courtyard, he tried gradually to work his way round to the communicating door. He would then run to the window and break one of the panes.

"All the same," continued Lupin, "what a pack of dunderheads you and the rest must be! You've had the silk all this time and not one of you ever thought of feeling it, not one of you ever asked himself the reason why the poor girl hung on to her scarf. Not one of you!

You just acted at haphazard, without reflecting, without foreseeing anything..."

The inspector had attained his object. Taking advantage of a second when Lupin had turned away from him, he suddenly wheeled round and grasped the door-handle. But an oath escaped him: the handle did not budge.

Lupin burst into a fit of laughing:

"Not even that! You did not even foresee that! You lay a trap for me and you won't admit that I may perhaps smell the thing out beforehand. . . . And you allow yourself to be brought into this room without asking whether I am not bringing you here for a particular reason and without remembering that the locks are fitted with a special mechanism. Come now, speaking frankly, what do you think of it yourself?"

"What do I think of it?" roared Ganimard, beside himself with rage.

He had drawn his revolver and was pointing it straight at Lupin's face.

"Hands up!" he cried. "That's what I think of it!"

Lupin placed himself in front of him and shrugged his shoulders:

"Sold again!" he said.

"Hands up, I say, once more!"

"And sold again, say I. Your deadly weapon won't go off."

"What?"

"Old Catherine, your housekeeper, is in my service. She damped the charges this morning while you were having your breakfast coffee."

Ganimard made a furious gesture, pocketed the revolver, and rushed at Lupin.

"Well?" said Lupin, stopping him short with a well-aimed kick on the shin.

Their clothes were almost touching. They exchanged defiant glances, the glances of two adversaries who mean to come to blows. Nevertheless, there was no fight. The recollection of the earlier struggles made any present struggle useless. And Ganimard, who remembered all his past failures, his vain attacks, Lupin's crushing reprisals, did not lift a limb. There was nothing to be done. He felt it. Lupin had forces at his command against which any individual force simply broke to pieces. So what was the good?

"I agree," said Lupin, in a friendly voice, as though answering Ganimard's unspoken thought, "you would do better to let things be as they are. Besides, friend of my youth, think of all that this incident has brought you: fame, the certainty of quick promotion, and, thanks to that, the prospect of a happy and comfortable old age! Surely, you don't want the discovery of the sapphire and the head of poor Arsène Lupin in addition! It wouldn't be fair. To say nothing of the fact that poor Arsène Lupin saved your life. . . . Yes, sir! Who warned you, at this very spot, that Prévailles was left-handed? . . . And is this the way you thank me? It's not pretty of you, Ganimard. Upon my word, you make me blush for you!"

While chattering, Lupin had gone through the same performance as Ganimard and was now near the door. Ganimard saw that his foe was about to escape him. Forgetting all prudence, he tried to block his way and received a tremendous butt in the stomach, which sent him rolling to the opposite wall.

Lupin dexterously touched a spring, turned the handle, opened the door, and slipped away, roaring with laughter as he went.

Twenty minutes later, when Ganimard at last succeeded in joining his men, one of them said to him:

"A house-painter left the house, as his mates were coming back from breakfast, and put a letter in my hand. 'Give that to your governor,' he said. 'Which governor?' I asked; but he was gone. I suppose it's meant for you."

"Let's have it."

Ganimard opened the letter. It was hurriedly scribbled in pencil and contained these words:

> "This is to warn you, friend of my youth, against excessive credulity. When a fellow tells you that the cartridges in your revolver are damp, however great your confidence in that fellow may be, even though his name be Arsène Lupin, never allow yourself to be taken in. Fire first; and, if the fellow hops the twig, you will have acquired the proof (1) that the cartridges are not damp; and (2) that old Catherine is the most honest and respectable of housekeepers.

"*One of these days, I hope to have the pleasure of making her acquaintance.*

"*Meanwhile, friend of my youth, believe me always affectionately and sincerely yours,*

                                        "*Arsène Lupin.*"

LUPIN'S MARRIAGE

"Monsieur Arsène Lupin has the honor to inform you of his approaching marriage with Mademoiselle Angélique de Sarzeau-Vendôme, Princesse de Bourbon-Condé, and to request the pleasure of your company at the wedding, which will take place at the church of Sainte-Clotilde . . ."

"The Duc de Sarzeau-Vendôme has the honor to inform you of the approaching marriage of his daughter Angélique, Princesse de Bourbon-Condé, with Monsieur Arsène Lupin, and to request . . ."

Jean Duc de Sarzeau-Vendôme could not finish reading the invitations which he held in his trembling hand. Pale with anger, his long, lean body shaking with tremors:

"There!" he gasped, handing the two communications to his daughter. "This is what our friends have received! This has been the talk of Paris since yesterday! What do you say to that dastardly insult, Angélique? What would your poor mother say to it, if she were alive?"

Angélique was tall and thin like her father, skinny and angular like him. She was thirty-three years of age, always dressed in black stuff, shy and retiring in manner, with a head too small in proportion to her height and narrowed on either side until the nose seemed to jut forth in protest against such parsimony. And yet it would be impossible to say that she was ugly, for her eyes were extremely beautiful, soft and grave, proud and a little sad: pathetic eyes which to see once was to remember.

She flushed with shame at hearing her father's words, which told her the scandal of which she was the victim. But, as she loved him, notwithstanding his harshness to her, his injustice and despotism, she said:

"Oh, I think it must be meant for a joke, father, to which we need pay no attention!"

"A joke? Why, everyone is gossiping about it! A dozen papers have printed the confounded notice this morning, with satirical comments. They quote our pedigree, our ancestors, our illustrious dead. They pretend to take the thing seriously . . ."

"Still, no one could believe . . ."

"Of course not. But that doesn't prevent us from being the by-word of Paris."

"It will all be forgotten by to-morrow."

"To-morrow, my girl, people will remember that the name of Angélique de Sarzeau-Vendôme has been bandied about as it should not be. Oh, if I could find out the name of the scoundrel who has dared . . ."

At that moment, Hyacinthe, the duke's valet, came in and said that monsieur le duc was wanted on the telephone. Still fuming, he took down the receiver and growled:

"Well? Who is it? Yes, it's the Duc de Sarzeau-Vendôme speaking."

A voice replied:

"I want to apologize to you, monsieur le duc, and to Mlle. Angélique. It's my secretary's fault."

"Your secretary?"

"Yes, the invitations were only a rough draft which I meant to submit to you. Unfortunately my secretary thought . . ."

"But, tell me, monsieur, who are you?"

"What, monsieur le duc, don't you know my voice? The voice of your future son-in-law?"

"What!"

"Arsène Lupin."

The duke dropped into a chair. His face was livid.

"Arsène Lupin . . . it's he . . . Arsène Lupin . . ."

Angélique gave a smile:

"You see, father, it's only a joke, a hoax."

But the duke's rage broke out afresh and he began to walk up and down, moving his arms:

"I shall go to the police! . . . The fellow can't be allowed to make a fool of me in this way! . . . If there's any law left in the land, it must be stopped!"

Hyacinthe entered the room again. He brought two visiting-cards.

"Chotois? Lepetit? Don't know them."

"They are both journalists, monsieur le duc."

"What do they want?"

"They would like to speak to monsieur le duc with regard to . . . the marriage . . ."

"Turn them out!" exclaimed the duke. "Kick them out! And tell the porter not to admit scum of that sort to my house in future."

"Please, father . . ." Angélique ventured to say.

"As for you, shut up! If you had consented to marry one of your cousins when I wanted you to this wouldn't have happened."

The same evening, one of the two reporters printed, on the front page of his paper, a somewhat fanciful story of his expedition to the family mansion of the Sarzeau-Vendômes, in the Rue de Varennes, and expatiated pleasantly upon the old nobleman's wrathful protests.

The next morning, another newspaper published an interview with Arsène Lupin which was supposed to have taken place in a lobby at the Opera. Arsène Lupin retorted in a letter to the editor:

> "I share my prospective father-in-law's indignation to the full. The sending out of the invitations was a gross breach of etiquette for which I am not responsible, but for which I wish to make a public apology. Why, sir, the date of the marriage is not yet fixed. My bride's father suggests early in May. She and I think that six weeks is really too long to wait! . . ."

That which gave a special piquancy to the affair and added immensely to the enjoyment of the friends of the family was the duke's well-known character: his pride and the uncompromising nature of his ideas and principles. Duc Jean was the last descendant of the Barons de Sarzeau, the most ancient family in Brittany; he was the lineal descendant of that Sarzeau who, upon marrying a Vendôme, refused to bear the new title which Louis XV forced upon him until after he had been imprisoned for ten years in the Bastille; and he had abandoned none of the prejudices of the old régime. In his youth, he followed the Comte de Chambord into exile. In his old age, he refused a seat in the Chamber on the pretext that a Sarzeau could only sit with his peers.

The incident stung him to the quick. Nothing could pacify him. He cursed Lupin in good round terms, threatened him with every sort of punishment and rounded on his daughter:

"There, if you had only married! . . . After all you had plenty of chances. Your three cousins, Mussy, d'Emboise, and Caorches, are noblemen of good descent, allied to the best families, fairly well-off; and they are still anxious to marry you. Why do you refuse them? Ah, because miss is a dreamer, a sentimentalist; and because her cousins are too fat, or too thin, or too coarse for her . . ."

She was, in fact, a dreamer. Left to her own devices from childhood, she had read all the books of chivalry, all the colorless romances of olden-time that littered the ancestral presses; and she looked upon life as a fairy-tale in which the beauteous maidens are always happy, while the others wait till death for the bridegroom who does not come. Why should she marry one of her cousins when they were only after her money, the millions which she had inherited from her mother? She might as well remain an old maid and go on dreaming . . .

She answered, gently:

"You will end by making yourself ill, father. Forget this silly business."

But how could he forget it? Every morning, some pin-prick renewed his wound. Three days running, Angélique received a wonderful sheaf of flowers, with Arsène Lupin's card peeping from it. The duke could not go to his club but a friend accosted him:

"That was a good one to-day!"

"What was?"

"Why, your son-in-law's latest! Haven't you seen it? Here, read it for yourself: 'M. Arsène Lupin is petitioning the Council of State for permission to add his wife's name to his own and to be known henceforth as Lupin de Sarzeau-Vendôme.'"

And, the next day, he read:

> "As the young bride, by virtue of an unrepealed decree of Charles X, bears the title and arms of the Bourbon-Condés, of whom she is the heiress-of-line, the eldest son of the Lupins de Sarzeau-Vendôme will be styled Prince de Bourbon-Condé."

And, the day after, an advertisement.

> "Exhibition of Mlle. de Sarzeau-Vendôme's trousseau at Messrs. ————'s Great Linen Warehouse. Each article marked with initials L. S. V."

Then an illustrated paper published a photographic scene: the duke, his daughter and his son-in-law sitting at a table playing three-handed auction-bridge.

And the date also was announced with a great flourish of trumpets: the 4th of May.

And particulars were given of the marriage-settlement. Lupin showed himself wonderfully disinterested. He was prepared to sign, the newspapers said, with his eyes closed, without knowing the figure of the dowry.

All these things drove the old duke crazy. His hatred of Lupin assumed morbid proportions. Much as it went against the grain, he called on the prefect of police, who advised him to be on his guard:

"We know the gentleman's ways; he is employing one of his favorite dodges. Forgive the expression, monsieur le duc, but he is 'nursing' you. Don't fall into the trap."

"What dodge? What trap?" asked the duke, anxiously.

"He is trying to make you lose your head and to lead you, by intimidation, to do something which you would refuse to do in cold blood."

"Still, M. Arsène Lupin can hardly hope that I will offer him my daughter's hand!"

"No, but he hopes that you will commit, to put it mildly, a blunder."

"What blunder?"

"Exactly that blunder which he wants you to commit."

"Then you think, monsieur le préfet . . . ?"

"I think the best thing you can do, monsieur le duc, is to go home, or, if all this excitement worries you, to run down to the country and stay there quietly, without upsetting yourself."

This conversation only increased the old duke's fears. Lupin appeared to him in the light of a terrible person, who employed diabolical methods and kept accomplices in every sphere of society. Prudence was the watchword.

And life, from that moment, became intolerable. The duke grew more crabbed and silent than ever and denied his door to all his old friends and even to Angélique's three suitors, her Cousins de Mussy, d'Emboise, and de Caorches, who were none of them on speaking terms with the others, in consequence of their rivalry, and who were in the habit of calling, turn and turn about, every week.

For no earthly reason, he dismissed his butler and his coachman. But he dared not fill their places, for fear of engaging creatures of Arsène Lupin's; and his own man, Hyacinthe, in whom he had every confidence, having had him in his service for over forty years, had to take upon himself the laborious duties of the stables and the pantry.

"Come, father," said Angélique, trying to make him listen to common-sense. "I really can't see what you are afraid of. No one can force me into this ridiculous marriage."

"Well, of course, that's not what I'm afraid of."

"What then, father?"

"How can I tell? An abduction! A burglary! An act of violence! There is no doubt that the villain is scheming something; and there is also no doubt that we are surrounded by spies."

One afternoon, he received a newspaper in which the following paragraph was marked in red pencil:

"The signing of the marriage-contract is fixed for this evening, at the Sarzeau-Vendôme town-house. It will be quite a private ceremony and only a few privileged friends will be present to congratulate the happy pair. The witnesses to the contract on behalf of Mlle. de Sarzeau-Vendôm, the Prince de la Rochefoucauld-Limours and the Comte de Chartres, will be introduced by M. Arsène Lupin to the two gentlemen who have claimed the honor of acting as his groomsmen, namely, the prefect of police and the governor of the Santé Prison."

Ten minutes later, the duke sent his servant Hyacinthe to the post with three express messages. At four o'clock, in Angélique's presence, he saw the three cousins: Mussy, fat, heavy, pasty-faced; d'Emboise, slender, fresh-colored, and shy; Caorches short, thin, and unhealthy-looking: all three, old bachelors by this time, lacking distinction in dress or appearance.

The meeting was a short one. The duke had worked out his whole plan of campaign, a defensive campaign, of which he set forth the first stage in explicit terms:

"Angélique and I will leave Paris to-night for our place in Brittany. I rely on you, my three nephews, to help us get away. You, d'Emboise, will come and fetch us in your car, with the hood up. You, Mussy, will bring your big motor and kindly see to the luggage with Hyacinthe, my man. You, Caorches, will go to the Gare d'Orléans and book our berths in the sleeping-car for Vannes by the 10:40 train. Is that settled?"

The rest of the day passed without incident. The duke, to avoid any accidental indiscretion, waited until after dinner to tell Hyacinthe to pack a trunk and a portmanteau. Hyacinthe was to accompany them, as well as Angélique's maid.

At nine o'clock, all the other servants went to bed, by their master's order. At ten minutes to ten, the duke, who was completing his preparations, heard the sound of a motor-horn. The porter opened the gates of the courtyard. The duke, standing at the window, recognized d'Emboise's landaulette:

"Tell him I shall be down presently," he said to Hyacinthe, "and let mademoiselle know."

In a few minutes, as Hyacinthe did not return, he left his room. But he was attacked on the landing by two masked men, who gagged and bound him before he could utter a cry. And one of the men said to him, in a low voice:

"Take this as a first warning, monsieur le duc. If you persist in leaving Paris and refusing your consent, it will be a more serious matter."

And the same man said to his companion:

"Keep an eye on him. I will see to the young lady."

By that time, two other confederates had secured the lady's maid; and Angélique, herself gagged, lay fainting on a couch in her boudoir.

She came to almost immediately, under the stimulus of a bottle of salts held to her nostrils; and, when she opened her eyes, she saw bending over her a young man, in evening-clothes, with a smiling and friendly face, who said:

"I implore your forgiveness, mademoiselle. All these happenings are a trifle sudden and this behavior rather out of the way. But circumstances often compel us to deeds of which our conscience does not approve. Pray pardon me."

He took her hand very gently and slipped a broad gold ring on the girl's finger, saying:

"There, now we are engaged. Never forget the man who gave you this ring. He entreats you not to run away from him . . . and to stay in Paris and await the proofs of his devotion. Have faith in him."

He said all this in so serious and respectful a voice, with so much authority and deference, that she had not the strength to resist. Their eyes met. He whispered:

"The exquisite purity of your eyes! It would be heavenly to live with those eyes upon one. Now close them . . ."

He withdrew. His accomplices followed suit. The car drove off, and the house in the Rue de Varennes remained still and silent until the moment when Angélique, regaining complete consciousness, called out for the servants.

They found the duke, Hyacinthe, the lady's maid, and the porter and his wife all tightly bound. A few priceless ornaments had disappeared, as well as the duke's pocket-book and all his jewelry; tie pins, pearl studs, watch, and so on.

The police were advised without delay. In the morning it appeared that, on the evening before, d'Emboise, when leaving his house in the motor-car, was stabbed by his own chauffeur and thrown, half-dead, into a deserted street. Mussy and Caorches had each received a telephone-message, purporting to come from the duke, countermanding their attendance.

Next week, without troubling further about the police investigation, without obeying the summons of the examining-magistrate, without even reading Arsène Lupin's letters to the papers on "the Varennes Flight," the duke, his daughter, and his valet stealthily took a slow train for Vannes and arrived one evening, at the old feudal castle that towers over the headland of Sarzeau. The duke at once organized a defense with the aid of the Breton peasants, true mediæval vassals to a man. On the fourth day, Mussy arrived; on the fifth, Caorches; and, on the seventh, d'Emboise, whose wound was not as severe as had been feared.

The duke waited two days longer before communicating to those about him what, now that his escape had succeeded in spite of Lupin, he called the second part of his plan. He did so, in the presence of the three cousins, by a dictatorial order to Angélique, expressed in these peremptory terms:

"All this bother is upsetting me terribly. I have entered on a struggle with this man whose daring you have seen for yourself; and the struggle is killing me. I want to end it at all costs. There is only one way of doing so, Angélique, and that is for you to release me from all responsibility by accepting the hand of one of your cousins. Before a month is out, you must be the wife of Mussy, Caorches, or d'Emboise. You have a free choice. Make your decision."

For four whole days Angélique wept and entreated her father, but in vain. She felt that he would be inflexible and that she must end by submitting to his wishes. She accepted:

"Whichever you please, father. I love none of them. So I may as well be unhappy with one as with the other."

Thereupon a fresh discussion ensued, as the duke wanted to compel her to make her own choice. She stood firm. Reluctantly and for financial considerations, he named d'Emboise.

The banns were published without delay.

From that moment, the watch in and around the castle was increased twofold, all the more inasmuch as Lupin's silence and the sudden cessation of the campaign which he had been conducting in the press could not but alarm the Duc de Sarzeau-Vendôme. It was obvious that the enemy was getting ready to strike and would endeavor to oppose the marriage by one of his characteristic moves.

Nevertheless, nothing happened: nothing two days before the ceremony, nothing on the day before, nothing on the morning itself. The marriage took place in the mayor's office, followed by the religious celebration in church; and the thing was done.

Then and not till then, the duke breathed freely. Notwithstanding his daughter's sadness, notwithstanding the embarrassed silence of his son-in-law, who found the situation a little trying, he rubbed his hands with an air of pleasure, as though he had achieved a brilliant victory:

"Tell them to lower the drawbridge," he said to Hyacinthe, "and to admit everybody. We have nothing more to fear from that scoundrel."

After the wedding-breakfast, he had wine served out to the peasants and clinked glasses with them. They danced and sang.

At three o'clock, he returned to the ground-floor rooms. It was the hour for his afternoon nap. He walked to the guard-room at the end of the suite. But he had no sooner placed his foot on the threshold than he stopped suddenly and exclaimed:

"What are you doing here, d'Emboise? Is this a joke?"

D'Emboise was standing before him, dressed as a Breton fisherman, in a dirty jacket and breeches, torn, patched, and many sizes too large for him.

The duke seemed dumbfounded. He stared with eyes of amazement at that face which he knew and which, at the same time, roused memories of a very distant past within his brain. Then he strode abruptly to one of the windows overlooking the castle-terrace and called:

"Angélique!"

"What is it, father?" she asked, coming forward.

"Where's your husband?"

"Over there, father," said Angélique, pointing to d'Emboise, who was smoking a cigarette and reading, some way off.

The duke stumbled and fell into a chair, with a great shudder of fright:

"Oh, I shall go mad!"

But the man in the fisherman's garb knelt down before him and said:

"Look at me, uncle. You know me, don't you? I'm your nephew, the one who used to play here in the old days, the one whom you called Jacquot.... Just think a minute ... Here, look at this scar ..."

"Yes, yes," stammered the duke, "I recognize you. It's Jacques. But the other one ..."

He put his hands to his head:

"And yet, no, it can't be ... Explain yourself ... I don't understand ... I don't want to understand ..."

There was a pause, during which the newcomer shut the window and closed the door leading to the next room. Then he came up to the old duke, touched him gently on the shoulder, to wake him from his torpor, and without further preface, as though to cut short any explanation that was not absolutely necessary, spoke as follows:

"Four years ago, that is to say, in the eleventh year of my voluntary exile, when I settled in the extreme south of Algeria, I made the acquaintance, in the course of a hunting-expedition arranged by a big Arab chief, of a man whose geniality, whose charm of manner, whose consummate prowess, whose indomitable pluck, whose combined humor and depth of mind fascinated me in the highest degree. The Comte d'Andrésy spent six weeks as my guest. After he left, we kept up a correspondence at regular intervals. I also often saw his name in the papers, in the society and sporting columns. He was to come back and I was preparing to receive him, three months ago, when, one evening as I was out riding, my two Arab attendants flung themselves upon me, bound me, blindfolded me and took me, traveling day and night, for a week, along deserted roads, to a bay on the coast, where five men awaited them. I was at once carried on board a small steam-yacht, which weighed anchor without delay. There was nothing to tell me who the men were nor what their object was in kidnapping me. They had locked me into a narrow cabin, secured by a massive door and lighted by a port-hole protected by two iron cross-bars. Every morning, a hand was inserted through a hatch between the next cabin and my own and placed on my bunk two or three pounds of bread, a good helping of food, and a flagon of wine and removed the remains of yesterday's meals, which I put there for the purpose. From time to time, at night, the yacht stopped and I heard the sound of the boat rowing to some harbor and then returning, doubtless with provisions. Then we set out once more, without hurrying, as though on a cruise of people of our class, who travel for pleasure and are not pressed for time. Sometimes, standing on a chair, I would see the coastline, through my port-hole, too indistinctly, however, to locate it. And this lasted for weeks. One morning, in the ninth week, I perceived that the hatch had been left unfastened and I pushed it open. The cabin was empty at the time. With an effort, I was able to take a nail-file from a dressing-table. Two weeks after that, by dint of patient perseverance, I had succeeded in filing through the bars of my port-hole and I could have escaped that way, only, though I am a good swimmer, I soon grow tired. I had therefore to choose a moment when the yacht was not too far from the land. It was not until yesterday that, perched on my chair, I caught sight of the coast; and, in the evening, at sunset, I recognized, to my astonishment, the outlines of the Château de Sarzeau, with its pointed turrets and its square keep. I wondered if this was the goal of my mysterious voyage. All night long, we cruised in the offing. The same all day yesterday. At last, this morning, we put in at a distance which I considered favorable, all the more so as we were steaming through rocks under cover of which I could swim unobserved. But, just as I was about to make my escape, I noticed that the shutter of the hatch, which they thought they had closed, had once more opened of itself and was flapping against the partition. I again pushed it ajar from curiosity. Within arm's length was a little cupboard which I managed to open and in which my hand, groping at random, laid hold of a bundle of papers. This consisted of letters, letters containing instructions addressed to the pirates who held me prisoner. An hour later, when I wriggled through the port-hole and slipped into the sea, I knew all: the reasons for my abduction, the means employed, the object in view, and the infamous scheme plotted during the last three months against the Duc de Sarzeau-Vendôme and his daughter. Unfortunately, it was too late. I was obliged, in order not to be seen from the yacht, to crouch in the cleft of a rock and did not reach land until mid-day. By the time that I had been to a fisherman's cabin, exchanged my clothes for his, and come on here, it was three o'clock. On my arrival, I learnt that Angélique's marriage was celebrated this morning."

The old duke had not spoken a word. With his eyes riveted on the stranger's, he was listening in ever-increasing dismay. At times, the thought of the warnings given him by the prefect of police returned to his mind:

"They're nursing you, monsieur le duc, they are nursing you."

He said, in a hollow voice:

"Speak on . . . finish your story . . . All this is ghastly . . . I don't understand it yet . . . and I feel nervous . . ."

The stranger resumed:

"I am sorry to say, the story is easily pieced together and is summed up in a few sentences. It is like this: the Comte d'Andrésy remembered several things from his stay with me and from the confidences which I was foolish enough to make to him. First of all, I was your nephew and yet you had seen comparatively little of me, because I left Sarzeau when I was quite a child, and since then our intercourse was limited to the few weeks which I spent here, fifteen years ago, when I proposed for the hand of my Cousin Angélique; secondly, having broken with the past, I received no letters; lastly, there was a certain physical resemblance between d'Andrésy and myself which could be accentuated to such an extent as to become striking. His scheme was built up on those three points. He bribed my Arab servants to give him warning in case I left Algeria. Then he went back to Paris, bearing my name and made up to look exactly like me, came to see you, was invited to your house once a fortnight, and lived under my name, which thus became one of the many aliases beneath which he conceals his real identity. Three months ago, when 'the apple was ripe,' as he says in his letters, he began the attack by a series of communications to the press; and, at the same time, fearing no doubt that some newspaper would tell me in Algeria the part that was being played under my name in Paris, he had me assaulted by my servants and kidnapped by his confederates. I need not explain any more in so far as you are concerned, uncle."

The Duc de Sarzeau-Vendôme was shaken with a fit of nervous trembling. The awful truth to which he refused to open his eyes appeared to him in its nakedness and assumed the hateful countenance of the enemy. He clutched his nephew's hands and said to him, fiercely, despairingly:

"It's Lupin, is it not?"

"Yes, uncle."

"And it's to him . . . it's to him that I have given my daughter!"

"Yes, uncle, to him, who has stolen my name of Jacques d'Emboise from me and stolen your daughter from you. Angélique is the wedded wife of Arsène Lupin; and that in accordance with your orders. This letter in his handwriting bears witness to it. He has upset your whole life, thrown you off your balance, besieging your hours of waking and your nights of dreaming, rifling your town-house, until the moment when, seized with terror, you took refuge here, where, thinking that you would escape his artifices and his rapacity, you told your daughter to choose one of her three cousins, Mussy, d'Emboise, or Caorches, as her husband."

"But why did she select that one rather than the others?"

"It was you who selected him, uncle."

"At random . . . because he had the biggest income . . ."

"No, not at random, but on the insidious, persistent, and very clever advice of your servant Hyacinthe."

The duke gave a start:

"What! Is Hyacinthe an accomplice?"

"No, not of Arsène Lupin, but of the man whom he believes to be d'Emboise and who promised to give him a hundred thousand francs within a week after the marriage."

"Oh, the villain! . . . He planned everything, foresaw everything . . ."

"Foresaw everything, uncle, down to shamming an attempt upon his life so as to avert suspicion, down to shamming a wound received in your service."

"But with what object? Why all these dastardly tricks?"

"Angélique has a fortune of eleven million francs. Your solicitor in Paris was to hand the securities next week to the counterfeit d'Emboise, who had only to realize them forthwith and disappear. But, this very morning, you yourself were to hand your son-in-law, as a personal wedding-present, five hundred thousand francs' worth of bearer-stock, which he has arranged to deliver to one of his accomplices at nine o'clock this evening, outside the castle, near the Great Oak, so that they may be negotiated to-morrow morning in Brussels."

The Duc de Sarzeau-Vendôme had risen from his seat and was stamping furiously up and down the room:

"At nine o'clock this evening?" he said. "We'll see about that . . . We'll see about that . . . I'll have the gendarmes here before then . . ."

"Arsène Lupin laughs at gendarmes."

"Let's telegraph to Paris."

"Yes, but how about the five hundred thousand francs? . . . And, still worse, uncle, the scandal? . . . Think of this: your daughter, Angélique de Sarzeau-Vendôme, married to that swindler, that thief. . . . No, no, it would never do. . . ."

"What then?"

"What? . . ."

The nephew now rose and, stepping to a gun-rack, took down a rifle, and laid it on the table, in front of the duke:

"Away in Algeria, uncle, on the verge of the desert, when we find ourselves face to face with a wild beast, we do not send for the gendarmes. We take our rifle and we shoot the wild beast. Otherwise, the beast would tear us to pieces with its claws."

"What do you mean?"

"I mean that, over there, I acquired the habit of dispensing with the gendarmes. It is a rather summary way of doing justice, but it is the best way, believe me, and to-day, in the present case, it is the only way. Once the beast is killed, you and I will bury it in some corner, unseen and unknown."

"And Angélique?"

"We will tell her later."

"What will become of her?"

"She will be my wife, the wife of the real d'Emboise. I desert her to-morrow and return to Algeria. The divorce will be granted in two months' time."

The duke listened, pale and staring, with set jaws. He whispered:

"Are you sure that his accomplices on the yacht will not inform him of your escape?"

"Not before to-morrow."

"So that . . . ?"

"So that inevitably, at nine o'clock this evening, Arsène Lupin, on his way to the Great Oak, will take the patrol-path that follows the old ramparts and skirts the ruins of the chapel. I shall be there, in the ruins."

"I shall be there too," said the Duc de Sarzeau-Vendôme, quietly, taking down a gun.

It was now five o'clock. The duke talked some time longer to his nephew, examined the weapons, loaded them with fresh cartridges. Then, when night came, he took d'Emboise through the dark passages to his bedroom and hid him in an adjoining closet.

Nothing further happened until dinner. The duke forced himself to keep calm during the meal. From time to time, he stole a glance at his son-in-law and was surprised at the likeness between him and the real d'Emboise. It was the same complexion, the same cast of features, the same cut of hair. Nevertheless, the look of the eye was different, keener in this case and brighter; and gradually the duke discovered minor details which had passed unperceived till then and which proved the fellow's imposture.

The party broke up after dinner. It was eight o'clock. The duke went to his room and released his nephew. Ten minutes later, under cover of the darkness, they slipped into the ruins, gun in hand.

Meanwhile, Angélique, accompanied by her husband, had gone to the suite of rooms which she occupied on the ground-floor of a tower that flanked the left wing. Her husband stopped at the entrance to the rooms and said:

"I am going for a short stroll, Angélique. May I come to you here, when I return?"

"Yes," she replied.

He left her and went up to the first floor, which had been assigned to him as his quarters. The moment he was alone, he locked the door, noiselessly opened a window that looked over the landscape, and leant out. He saw a shadow at the foot of the tower, some hundred feet or more below him. He whistled and received a faint whistle in reply.

He then took from a cupboard a thick leather satchel, crammed with papers, wrapped it in a piece of black cloth, and tied it up. Then he sat down at the table and wrote:

> *"Glad you got my message, for I think it unsafe to walk out of the castle with that large bundle of securities. Here they are. You will be in Paris, on your motor-cycle, in time to catch the morning train to Brussels, where you will hand over the bonds to Z; and he will negotiate them at once.*
>
> *"A. L.*
>
> *"P. S.—As you pass by the Great Oak, tell our chaps that I'm coming. I have some instructions to give them. But everything is going well. No one here has the least suspicion."*

He fastened the letter to the parcel and lowered both through the window with a length of string:

"Good," he said. "That's all right. It's a weight off my mind."

He waited a few minutes longer, stalking up and down the room and smiling at the portraits of two gallant gentlemen hanging on the wall:

"Horace de Sarzeau-Vendôme, marshal of France. . . . And you, the Great Condé . . . I salute you, my ancestors both. Lupin de Sarzeau-Vendôme will show himself worthy of you."

At last, when the time came, he took his hat and went down. But, when he reached the ground-floor, Angélique burst from her rooms and exclaimed, with a distraught air:

"I say . . . if you don't mind . . . I think you had better . . ."

And then, without saying more, she went in again, leaving a vision of irresponsible terror in her husband's mind.

"She's out of sorts," he said to himself. "Marriage doesn't suit her."

He lit a cigarette and went out, without attaching importance to an incident that ought to have impressed him:

"Poor Angélique! This will all end in a divorce . . ."

The night outside was dark, with a cloudy sky.

The servants were closing the shutters of the castle. There was no light in the windows, it being the duke's habit to go to bed soon after dinner.

Lupin passed the gate-keeper's lodge and, as he put his foot on the drawbridge, said:

"Leave the gate open. I am going for a breath of air; I shall be back soon."

The patrol-path was on the right and ran along one of the old ramparts, which used to surround the castle with a second and much larger enclosure, until it ended at an almost demolished postern-gate. The park, which skirted a hillock and afterward followed the side of a deep valley, was bordered on the left by thick coppices.

"What a wonderful place for an ambush!" he said. "A regular cut-throat spot!"

He stopped, thinking that he heard a noise. But no, it was a rustling of the leaves. And yet a stone went rattling down the slopes, bounding against the rugged projections of the rock. But, strange to say, nothing seemed to disquiet him. The crisp sea-breeze came blowing over the plains of the headland; and he eagerly filled his lungs with it:

"What a thing it is to be alive!" he thought. "Still young, a member of the old nobility, a multimillionaire: what could a man want more?"

At a short distance, he saw against the darkness the yet darker outline of the chapel, the ruins of which towered above the path. A few drops of rain began to fall; and he heard a clock strike nine. He quickened his pace. There was a short descent; then the path rose again. And suddenly, he stopped once more.

A hand had seized his.

He drew back, tried to release himself.

But someone stepped from the clump of trees against which he was brushing; and a voice said; "Ssh! . . . Not a word! . . ."

He recognized his wife, Angélique:

"What's the matter?" he asked.

She whispered, so low that he could hardly catch the words:

"They are lying in wait for you . . . they are in there, in the ruins, with their guns . . ."

"Who?"

"Keep quiet.... Listen ..."

They stood for a moment without stirring; then she said:

"They are not moving ... Perhaps they never heard me ... Let's go back ..."

"But ..."

"Come with me."

Her accent was so imperious that he obeyed without further question. But suddenly she took fright:

"Run! ... They are coming! ... I am sure of it! ..."

True enough, they heard a sound of footsteps.

Then, swiftly, still holding him by the hand, she dragged him, with irresistible energy, along a shortcut, following its turns without hesitation in spite of the darkness and the brambles. And they very soon arrived at the drawbridge.

She put her arm in his. The gate-keeper touched his cap. They crossed the courtyard and entered the castle; and she led him to the corner tower in which both of them had their apartments:

"Come in here," she said.

"To your rooms?"

"Yes."

Two maids were sitting up for her. Their mistress ordered them to retire to their bedrooms, on the third floor.

Almost immediately after, there was a knock at the door of the outer room; and a voice called:

"Angélique!"

"Is that you, father?" she asked, suppressing her agitation.

"Yes. Is your husband here?"

"We have just come in."

"Tell him I want to speak to him. Ask him to come to my room. It's important."

"Very well, father, I'll send him to you."

She listened for a few seconds, then returned to the boudoir where her husband was and said:

"I am sure my father is still there."

He moved as though to go out:

"In that case, if he wants to speak to me ..."

"My father is not alone," she said, quickly, blocking his way.

"Who is with him?"

"His nephew, Jacques d'Emboise."

There was a moment's silence. He looked at her with a certain astonishment, failing quite to understand his wife's attitude. But, without pausing to go into the matter:

"Ah, so that dear old d'Emboise is there?" he chuckled. "Then the fat's in the fire? Unless, indeed . . ."

"My father knows everything," she said. "I overheard a conversation between them just now. His nephew has read certain letters . . . I hesitated at first about telling you . . . Then I thought that my duty . . ."

He studied her afresh. But, at once conquered by the queerness of the situation, he burst out laughing:

"What? Don't my friends on board ship burn my letters? And they have let their prisoner escape? The idiots! Oh, when you don't see to everything yourself! . . . No matter, it's distinctly humorous. . . . D'Emboise versus d'Emboise . . . Oh, but suppose I were no longer recognized? Suppose d'Emboise himself were to confuse me with himself?"

He turned to a wash-hand-stand, took a towel, dipped it in the basin and soaped it and, in the twinkling of an eye, wiped the make-up from his face and altered the set of his hair:

"That's it," he said, showing himself to Angélique under the aspect in which she had seen him on the night of the burglary in Paris. "I feel more comfortable like this for a discussion with my father-in-law."

"Where are you going?" she cried, flinging herself in front of the door.

"Why, to join the gentlemen."

"You shall not pass!"

"Why not?"

"Suppose they lull you?"

"Kill me?"

"That's what they mean to do, to kill you . . . to hide your body somewhere. . . . Who would know of it?"

"Very well," he said, "from their point of view, they are quite right. But, if I don't go to them, they will come here. That door won't stop them. . . . Nor you, I'm thinking. Therefore, it's better to have done with it."

"Follow me," commanded Angélique.

She took up the lamp that lit the room, went into her bedroom, pushed aside the wardrobe, which slid easily on hidden castors, pulled back an old tapestry-hanging, and said:

"Here is a door that has not been used for years. My father believes the key to be lost. I have it here. Unlock the door with it. A staircase in the wall will take you to the bottom of the tower. You need only draw the bolts of another door and you will be free."

He could hardly believe his ears. Suddenly, he grasped the meaning of Angélique's whole behavior. In front of that sad, plain, but wonderfully gentle face, he stood for a moment discountenanced, almost abashed. He no longer thought of laughing. A feeling of respect, mingled with remorse and kindness, overcame him.

"Why are you saving me?" he whispered.

"You are my husband."

He protested:

"No, no . . . I have stolen that title. The law will never recognize my marriage."

"My father does not want a scandal," she said.

"Just so," he replied, sharply, "just so. I foresaw that; and that was why I had your cousin d'Emboise near at hand. Once I disappear, he becomes your husband. He is the man you have married in the eyes of men."

"You are the man I have married in the eyes of the Church."

"The Church! The Church! There are means of arranging matters with the Church. . . . Your marriage can be annulled."

"On what pretext that we can admit?"

He remained silent, thinking over all those points which he had not considered, all those points which were trivial and absurd for him, but which were serious for her, and he repeated several times:

"This is terrible . . . this is terrible . . . I should have anticipated . . ."

And, suddenly, seized with an idea, he clapped his hands and cried:

"There, I have it! I'm hand in glove with one of the chief figures at the Vatican. The Pope never refuses me anything. I shall obtain an audience and I have no doubt that the Holy Father, moved by my entreaties . . ."

His plan was so humorous and his delight so artless that Angélique could not help smiling; and she said:

"I am your wife in the eyes of God."

She gave him a look that showed neither scorn nor animosity, nor even anger; and he realized that she omitted to see in him the outlaw and the evil-doer and remembered only the man who was her husband and to whom the priest had bound her until the hour of death.

He took a step toward her and observed her more attentively. She did not lower her eyes at first. But she blushed. And never had he seen so pathetic a face, marked with such modesty and such dignity. He said to her, as on that first evening in Paris:

"Oh, your eyes . . . the calm and sadness of your eyes . . . the beauty of your eyes!"

She dropped her head and stammered:

"Go away . . . go . . ."

In the presence of her confusion, he received a quick intuition of the deeper feelings that stirred her, unknown to herself. To that spinster soul, of which he recognized the romantic power of imagination, the unsatisfied yearnings, the poring over old-world books, he suddenly represented, in that exceptional moment and in consequence of the unconventional circumstances of their meetings, somebody special, a Byronic hero, a chivalrous brigand of romance. One evening, in spite of all obstacles, he, the world-famed adventurer, already ennobled in song and story and exalted by his own audacity, had come to her and slipped the magic ring upon her finger: a mystic and passionate betrothal, as in the days of the *Corsair* and *Hernani*. . . . Greatly moved and touched, he was on the verge of giving way to an enthusiastic impulse and exclaiming:

"Let us go away together! . . . Let us fly! . . . You are my bride . . . my wife. . . . Share my dangers, my sorrows and my joys. . . . It will be a strange and vigorous, a proud and magnificent life . . ."

But Angélique's eyes were raised to his again; and they were so pure and so noble that he blushed in his turn. This was not the woman to whom such words could be addressed.

He whispered:

"Forgive me. . . . I am a contemptible wretch. . . . I have wrecked your life . . ."

"No," she replied, softly. "On the contrary, you have shown me where my real life lies."

He was about to ask her to explain. But she had opened the door and was pointing the way to him. Nothing more could be spoken between them. He went out without a word, bowing very low as he passed.

||||||||||||||||||||||||

A month later, Angélique de Sarzeau-Vendôme, Princesse de Bourbon-Condé, lawful wife of Arsène Lupin, took the veil and, under the name of Sister Marie-Auguste, buried herself within the walls of the Visitation Convent.

On the day of the ceremony, the mother superior of the convent received a heavy sealed envelope containing a letter with the following words:

"For Sister Marie-Auguste's poor."

Enclosed with the letter were five hundred bank-notes of a thousand francs each.

EDITH SWAN-NECK

A rsène Lupin, what's your real opinion of Inspector Ganimard?"

"A very high one, my dear fellow."

"A very high one? Then why do you never miss a chance of turning him into ridicule?"

"It's a bad habit; and I'm sorry for it. But what can I say? It's the way of the world. Here's a decent detective-chap, here's a whole pack of decent men, who stand for law and order, who protect us against the apaches, who risk their lives, for honest people like you and me; and we have nothing to give them in return but flouts and gibes. It's preposterous!"

"Bravo, Lupin! you're talking like a respectable ratepayer!"

"What else am I? I may have peculiar views about other people's property; but I assure you that it's very different when my own's at stake. By Jove, it doesn't do to lay hands on what belongs to me! Then I'm out for blood! Aha! It's *my* pocket, *my* money, *my* watch . . . hands off! I have the soul of a conservative, my dear fellow, the instincts of a retired tradesman and a due respect for every sort of tradition and authority. And that is why Ganimard inspires me with no little gratitude and esteem."

"But not much admiration?"

"Plenty of admiration too. Over and above the dauntless courage which comes natural to all those gentry at the Criminal Investigation Department, Ganimard possesses very sterling qualities: decision, insight, and judgment. I have watched him at work. He's somebody, when all's said. Do you know the Edith Swan-neck story, as it was called?"

"I know as much as everybody knows."

"That means that you don't know it at all. Well, that job was, I daresay, the one which I thought out most cleverly, with the utmost care and the utmost precaution, the one which I shrouded in the greatest darkness and mystery, the one which it took the biggest generalship to carry through. It was a regular game of chess, played according to strict scientific and mathematical rules. And yet Ganimard ended by unraveling the knot. Thanks to him, they know the truth to-day on the Quai des Orfèvres. And it is a truth quite out of the common, I assure you."

"May I hope to hear it?"

"Certainly . . . one of these days . . . when I have time . . . But the Brunelli is dancing at the Opera to-night; and, if she were not to see me in my stall . . . !"

I do not meet Lupin often. He confesses with difficulty, when it suits him. It was only gradually, by snatches, by odds and ends of confidences, that I was able to obtain the different incidents and to piece the story together in all its details.

The main features are well known and I will merely mention the facts.

Three years ago, when the train from Brest arrived at Rennes, the door of one of the luggage vans was found smashed in. This van had been booked by Colonel Sparmiento, a rich Brazilian, who was traveling with his wife in the same train. It contained a complete set of tapestry-hangings. The case in which one of these was packed had been broken open and the tapestry had disappeared.

Colonel Sparmiento started proceedings against the railway-company, claiming heavy damages, not only for the stolen tapestry, but also for the loss in value which the whole collection suffered in consequence of the theft.

The police instituted inquiries. The company offered a large reward. A fortnight later, a letter which had come undone in the post was opened by the authorities and revealed the fact that the theft had been carried out under the direction of Arsène Lupin and that a package was to leave next day for the United States. That same evening, the tapestry was discovered in a trunk deposited in the cloak-room at the Gare Saint-Lazare.

The scheme, therefore, had miscarried. Lupin felt the disappointment so much that he vented his ill-humor in a communication to Colonel Sparmiento, ending with the following words, which were clear enough for anybody:

> "It was very considerate of me to take only one. Next time, I shall take the twelve. Verbum sap.
>
> "A. L."

Colonel Sparmiento had been living for some months in a house standing at the end of a small garden at the corner of the Rue de la Faisanderie and the Rue Dufresnoy. He was a rather thick-set, broad-shouldered man, with black hair and a swarthy skin, always well and quietly dressed. He was married to an extremely pretty but delicate Englishwoman, who was much upset by the business of the tapestries. From the first she implored her husband to sell them for what they would fetch. The Colonel had much too forcible and dogged a nature to yield to what he had every right to describe as a woman's fancies. He sold nothing, but he redoubled his precautions and adopted every measure that was likely to make an attempt at burglary impossible.

To begin with, so that he might confine his watch to the garden-front, he walled up all the windows on the ground-floor and the first floor overlooking the Rue Dufresnoy. Next, he enlisted the services of a firm which made a speciality of protecting private houses against robberies. Every window of the gallery in which the tapestries were hung was fitted with invisible burglar alarms, the position of which was known to none but himself. These, at the least touch, switched on all the electric lights and set a whole system of bells and gongs ringing.

In addition to this, the insurance companies to which he applied refused to grant policies to any considerable amount unless he consented to let three men, supplied by the companies and paid by himself, occupy the ground-floor of his house every night. They selected for the purpose three ex-detectives, tried and trustworthy men, all of whom hated Lupin like poison. As for the servants, the colonel had known them for years and was ready to vouch for them.

After taking these steps and organizing the defense of the house as though it were a fortress, the colonel gave a great house-warming, a sort of private view, to which he invited the members of both his clubs, as well as a certain number of ladies, journalists, art-patrons, and critics.

They felt, as they passed through the garden-gate, much as if they were walking into a prison. The three private detectives, posted at the foot of the stairs, asked for each visitor's invitation card and eyed him up and down suspiciously, making him feel as though they were going to search his pockets or take his finger-prints.

The colonel, who received his guests on the first floor, made laughing apologies and seemed delighted at the opportunity of explaining the arrangements which he had invented to secure the safety of his hangings. His wife stood by him, lookingly charmingly young and pretty, fair-haired, pale and sinuous, with a sad and gentle expression, the expression of resignation often worn by those who are threatened by fate.

When all the guests had come, the garden-gates and the hall-doors were closed. Then everybody filed into the middle gallery, which was reached through two steel doors, while its windows, with their huge shutters, were protected by iron bars. This was where the twelve tapestries were kept.

They were matchless works of art and, taking their inspiration from the famous Bayeux Tapestry, attributed to Queen Matilda, they represented the story of the Norman Conquest. They had been ordered in the fourteenth century by the descendant of a man-at-arms in William the Conqueror's train; were executed by Jehan Gosset, a famous Arras weaver; and were discovered, five hundred years later, in an old Breton manor-house. On hearing of this, the colonel had struck a bargain for fifty thousand francs. They were worth ten times the money.

But the finest of the twelve hangings composing the set, the most uncommon because the subject had not been treated by Queen Matilda, was the one which Arsène Lupin had stolen and which had been so fortunately recovered. It portrayed Edith Swan-neck on the battlefield of Hastings, seeking among the dead for the body of her sweetheart Harold, last of the Saxon kings.

The guests were lost in enthusiasm over this tapestry, over the unsophisticated beauty of the design, over the faded colors, over the life-like grouping of the figures and the pitiful sadness of the scene. Poor Edith Swan-neck stood drooping like an overweighted lily. Her white gown revealed the lines of her languid figure. Her long, tapering hands were outstretched in a gesture of terror and entreaty. And nothing could be more mournful than her profile, over which flickered the most dejected and despairing of smiles.

"A harrowing smile," remarked one of the critics, to whom the others listened with deference. "A very charming smile, besides; and it reminds me, Colonel, of the smile of Mme. Sparmiento."

And seeing that the observation seemed to meet with approval, he enlarged upon his idea:

"There are other points of resemblance that struck me at once, such as the very graceful curve of the neck and the delicacy of the hands . . . and also something about the figure about the general attitude . . ."

"What you say is so true," said the colonel, "that I confess that it was this likeness that decided me to buy the hangings. And there was another reason, which was that, by a really curious chance, my wife's name happens to be Edith. I have called her Edith Swan-neck ever since." And the colonel added, with a laugh, "I hope that the coincidence will stop at this and that my dear Edith will never have to go in search of her true-love's body, like her prototype."

He laughed as he uttered these words, but his laugh met with no echo; and we find the same impression of awkward silence in all the accounts of the evening that appeared during the next few days. The

people standing near him did not know what to say. One of them
tried to jest:

"Your name isn't Harold, Colonel?"

"No, thank you," he declared, with continued merriment. "No,
that's not my name; nor am I in the least like the Saxon king."

All have since agreed in stating that, at that moment, as the colonel
finished speaking, the first alarm rang from the windows—the right
or the middle window: opinions differ on this point—rang short and
shrill on a single note. The peal of the alarm-bell was followed by an
exclamation of terror uttered by Mme. Sparmiento, who caught hold
of her husband's arm. He cried:

"What's the matter? What does this mean?"

The guests stood motionless, with their eyes staring at the windows. The colonel repeated:

"What does it mean? I don't understand. No one but myself knows
where that bell is fixed . . ."

And, at that moment—here again the evidence is unanimous—at
that moment came sudden, absolute darkness, followed immediately
by the maddening din of all the bells and all the gongs, from top to
bottom of the house, in every room and at every window.

For a few seconds, a stupid disorder, an insane terror, reigned. The
women screamed. The men banged with their fists on the closed doors.
They hustled and fought. People fell to the floor and were trampled
under foot. It was like a panic-stricken crowd, scared by threatening
flames or by a bursting shell. And, above the uproar, rose the colonel's
voice, shouting:

"Silence! . . . Don't move! . . . It's all right! . . . The switch is over
there, in the corner. . . . Wait a bit. . . . Here!"

He had pushed his way through his guests and reached a corner
of the gallery; and, all at once, the electric light blazed up again, while
the pandemonium of bells stopped.

Then, in the sudden light, a strange sight met the eyes. Two ladies
had fainted. Mme. Sparmiento, hanging to her husband's arm, with
her knees dragging on the floor, and livid in the face, appeared half
dead. The men, pale, with their neckties awry, looked as if they had
all been in the wars.

"The tapestries are there!" cried someone.

There was a great surprise, as though the disappearance of those hangings ought to have been the natural result and the only plausible explanation of the incident. But nothing had been moved. A few valuable pictures, hanging on the walls, were there still. And, though the same din had reverberated all over the house, though all the rooms had been thrown into darkness, the detectives had seen no one entering or trying to enter.

"Besides," said the colonel, "it's only the windows of the gallery that have alarms. Nobody but myself understands how they work; and I had not set them yet."

People laughed loudly at the way in which they had been frightened, but they laughed without conviction and in a more or less shamefaced fashion, for each of them was keenly alive to the absurdity of his conduct. And they had but one thought—to get out of that house where, say what you would, the atmosphere was one of agonizing anxiety.

Two journalists stayed behind, however; and the colonel joined them, after attending to Edith and handing her over to her maids. The three of them, together with the detectives, made a search that did not lead to the discovery of anything of the least interest. Then the colonel sent for some champagne; and the result was that it was not until a late hour—to be exact, a quarter to three in the morning—that the journalists took their leave, the colonel retired to his quarters, and the detectives withdrew to the room which had been set aside for them on the ground-floor.

They took the watch by turns, a watch consisting, in the first place, in keeping awake and, next, in looking round the garden and visiting the gallery at intervals.

These orders were scrupulously carried out, except between five and seven in the morning, when sleep gained the mastery and the men ceased to go their rounds. But it was broad daylight out of doors. Besides, if there had been the least sound of bells, would they not have woke up?

Nevertheless, when one of them, at twenty minutes past seven, opened the door of the gallery and flung back the shutters, he saw that the twelve tapestries were gone.

This man and the others were blamed afterward for not giving the alarm at once and for starting their own investigations before informing the colonel and telephoning to the local commissary. Yet this very excusable delay can hardly be said to have hampered the action of the police. In any case, the colonel was not told until half-past eight. He was dressed and ready to go out. The news did not seem to upset him beyond measure, or, at least, he managed to control his emotion. But the effort must have been too much for him, for he suddenly dropped into a chair and, for some moments, gave way to a regular fit of despair and anguish, most painful to behold in a man of his resolute appearance.

Recovering and mastering himself, he went to the gallery, stared at the bare walls, and then sat down at a table and hastily scribbled a letter, which he put into an envelope and sealed:

"There," he said. "I'm in a hurry. . . . I have an important engagement. . . . Here is a letter for the commissary of police." And, seeing the detectives' eyes upon him, he added, "I am giving the commissary my views . . . telling him of a suspicion that occurs to me. . . . He must follow it up. . . . I will do what I can . . ."

He left the house at a run, with excited gestures which the detectives were subsequently to remember.

A few minutes later, the commissary of police arrived. He was handed the letter, which contained the following words:

> "I am at the end of my tether. The theft of those tapestries completes the crash which I have been trying to conceal for the past year. I bought them as a speculation and was hoping to get a million francs for them, thanks to the fuss that was made about them. As it was, an American offered me six hundred thousand. It meant my salvation. This means utter destruction.
>
> "I hope that my dear wife will forgive the sorrow which I am bringing upon her. Her name will be on my lips at the last moment."

Mme. Sparmiento was informed. She remained aghast with horror, while inquiries were instituted and attempts made to trace the colonel's movements.

Late in the afternoon, a telephone-message came from Ville d'Avray. A gang of railway-men had found a man's body lying at the entrance to a tunnel after a train had passed. The body was hideously mutilated; the face had lost all resemblance to anything human. There were no papers in the pockets. But the description answered to that of the colonel.

Mme. Sparmiento arrived at Ville d'Avray, by motor-car, at seven o'clock in the evening. She was taken to a room at the railway-station. When the sheet that covered it was removed, Edith, Edith Swan-neck, recognized her husband's body.

<hr />

In these circumstances, Lupin did not receive his usual good notices in the press:

> "Let him look to himself," jeered one leader-writer, sum-ming up the general opinion. "It would not take many exploits of this kind for him to forfeit the popularity which has not been grudged him hitherto. We have no use for Lupin, except when his rogueries are perpetrated at the expense of shady company-promoters, foreign adventurers, German barons, banks, and financial compa-nies. And, above all, no murders! A burglar we can put up with; but a murderer, no! If he is not directly guilty, he is at least responsible for this death. There is blood upon his hands; the arms on his escutcheon are stained gules . . ."

The public anger and disgust were increased by the pity which Edith's pale face aroused. The guests of the night before gave their version of what had happened, omitting none of the impressive details; and a legend formed straightway around the fair-haired Englishwoman, a legend that assumed a really tragic character, owing to the popular story of the swan-necked heroine.

And yet the public could not withhold its admiration of the

extraordinary skill with which the theft had been effected. The police explained it, after a fashion. The detectives had noticed from the first and subsequently stated that one of the three windows of the gallery was wide open. There could be no doubt that Lupin and his confederates had entered through this window. It seemed a very plausible suggestion. Still, in that case, how were they able, first, to climb the garden railings, in coming and going, without being seen; secondly, to cross the garden and put up a ladder on the flower-border, without leaving the least trace behind; thirdly, to open the shutters and the window, without starting the bells and switching on the lights in the house?

The police accused the three detectives of complicity. The magistrate in charge of the case examined them at length, made minute inquiries into their private lives, and stated formally that they were above all suspicion. As for the tapestries, there seemed to be no hope that they would be recovered.

It was at this moment that Chief-inspector Ganimard returned from India, where he had been hunting for Lupin on the strength of a number of most convincing proofs supplied by former confederates of Lupin himself. Feeling that he had once more been tricked by his everlasting adversary, fully believing that Lupin had dispatched him on this wild-goose chase so as to be rid of him during the business of the tapestries, he asked for a fortnight's leave of absence, called on Mme. Sparmiento and promised to avenge her husband.

Edith had reached the point at which not even the thought of vengeance relieves the sufferer's pain. She had dismissed the three detectives on the day of the funeral and engaged just one man and an old cook-housekeeper to take the place of the large staff of servants the sight of whom reminded her too cruelly of the past. Not caring what happened, she kept her room and left Ganimard free to act as he pleased.

He took up his quarters on the ground-floor and at once instituted a series of the most minute investigations. He started the inquiry afresh, questioned the people in the neighborhood, studied the distribution of the rooms, and set each of the burglar-alarms going thirty and forty times over.

At the end of the fortnight, he asked for an extension of leave. The chief of the detective-service, who was at that time M. Dudouis, came to see him and found him perched on the top of a ladder, in the gallery. That day, the chief-inspector admitted that all his searches had proved useless.

Two days later, however, M. Dudouis called again and discovered Ganimard in a very thoughtful frame of mind. A bundle of newspapers lay spread in front of him. At last, in reply to his superior's urgent questions, the chief-inspector muttered:

"I know nothing, chief, absolutely nothing; but there's a confounded notion worrying me. . . . Only it seems so absurd. . . . And then it doesn't explain things. . . . On the contrary, it confuses them rather . . ."

"Then . . . ?"

"Then I implore you, chief, to have a little patience . . . to let me go my own way. But if I telephone to you, some day or other, suddenly, you must jump into a taxi, without losing a minute. It will mean that I have discovered the secret."

Forty-eight hours passed. Then, one morning, M. Dudouis received a telegram:

"Going to Lille.

"GANIMARD."

"What the dickens can he want to go to Lille for?" wondered the chief-detective.

The day passed without news, followed by another day. But M. Dudouis had every confidence in Ganimard. He knew his man, knew that the old detective was not one of those people who excite themselves for nothing. When Ganimard "got a move on him," it meant that he had sound reasons for doing so.

As a matter of fact, on the evening of that second day, M. Dudouis was called to the telephone.

"Is that you, chief?"

"Is it Ganimard speaking?"

Cautious men both, they began by making sure of each other's identity. As soon as his mind was eased on this point, Ganimard continued, hurriedly:

"Ten men, chief, at once. And please come yourself."

"Where are you?"

"In the house, on the ground-floor. But I will wait for you just inside the garden-gate."

"I'll come at once. In a taxi, of course?"

"Yes, chief. Stop the taxi fifty yards from the house. I'll let you in when you whistle."

Things took place as Ganimard had arranged. Shortly after midnight, when all the lights were out on the upper floors, he slipped into the street and went to meet M. Dudouis. There was a hurried consultation. The officers distributed themselves as Ganimard ordered. Then the chief and the chief-inspector walked back together, noiselessly crossed the garden, and closeted themselves with every precaution:

"Well, what's it all about?" asked M. Dudouis. "What does all this mean? Upon my word, we look like a pair of conspirators!"

But Ganimard was not laughing. His chief had never seen him in such a state of perturbation, nor heard him speak in a voice denoting such excitement:

"Any news, Ganimard?"

"Yes, chief, and . . . this time . . . ! But I can hardly believe it myself. . . . And yet I'm not mistaken: I know the real truth. . . . It may be as unlikely as you please, but it is the truth, the whole truth and nothing but the truth."

He wiped away the drops of perspiration that trickled down his forehead and, after a further question from M. Dudouis, pulled himself together, swallowed a glass of water, and began:

"Lupin has often got the better of me . . ."

"Look here, Ganimard," said M. Dudouis, interrupting him. "Why can't you come straight to the point? Tell me, in two words, what's happened."

"No, chief," retorted the chief-inspector, "it is essential that you should know the different stages which I have passed through. Excuse me, but I consider it indispensable." And he repeated: "I was saying, chief, that Lupin has often got the better of me and led me many a dance. But, in this contest in which I have always come out worst . . . so far . . . I have at least gained experience of his manner of play and learnt to know his tactics. Now, in the matter of the tapestries, it occurred to me almost from the start to set myself two problems. In the first place, Lupin, who never makes a move without knowing what he is after, was obviously aware that Colonel Sparmiento had come to the end of his money and that the loss of the tapestries might drive him to suicide. Nevertheless, Lupin, who hates the very thought of bloodshed, stole the tapestries."

"There was the inducement," said M. Dudouis, "of the five or six hundred thousand francs which they are worth."

"No, chief, I tell you once more, whatever the occasion might be, Lupin would not take life, nor be the cause of another person's death, for anything in this world, for millions and millions. That's the first point. In the second place, what was the object of all that disturbance, in the evening, during the house-warming party? Obviously, don't you think, to surround the business with an atmosphere of anxiety and terror, in the shortest possible time, and also to divert suspicion from the truth, which, otherwise, might easily have been suspected? . . . You seem not to understand, chief?"

"Upon my word, I do not!"

"As a matter of fact," said Ganimard, "as a matter of fact, it is not particularly plain. And I myself, when I put the problem before my mind in those same words, did not understand it very clearly . . . And yet I felt that I was on the right track . . . Yes, there was no doubt about it that Lupin wanted to divert suspicions . . . to divert them to himself, Lupin, mark you . . . so that the real person who was working the business might remain unknown . . ."

"A confederate," suggested M. Dudouis. "A confederate, moving among the visitors, who set the alarms going . . . and who managed to hide in the house after the party had broken up."

"You're getting warm, chief, you're getting warm! It is certain that the tapestries, as they cannot have been stolen by anyone making his way surreptitiously into the house, were stolen by somebody who remained in the house; and it is equally certain that, by taking the list of the people invited and inquiring into the antecedents of each of them, one might . . ."

"Well?"

"Well, chief, there's a 'but,' namely, that the three detectives had this list in their hands when the guests arrived and that they still had it when the guests left. Now sixty-three came in and sixty-three went away. So you see . . ."

"Then do you suppose a servant? . . ."

"No."

"The detectives?"

"No."

"But, still . . . but, still," said the chief, impatiently, "if the robbery was committed from the inside . . ."

"That is beyond dispute," declared the inspector, whose excitement seemed to be nearing fever-point. "There is no question about it. All my investigations led to the same certainty. And my conviction gradually became so positive that I ended, one day, by drawing up this startling axiom: in theory and in fact, the robbery can only have been committed with the assistance of an accomplice staying in the house. Whereas there was no accomplice!"

"That's absurd," said Dudouis.

"Quite absurd," said Ganimard. "But, at the very moment when I uttered that absurd sentence, the truth flashed upon me."

"Eh?"

"Oh, a very dim, very incomplete, but still sufficient truth! With that clue to guide me, I was bound to find the way. Do you follow me, chief?"

M. Dudouis sat silent. The same phenomenon that had taken place in Ganimard was evidently taking place in him. He muttered:

"If it's not one of the guests, nor the servants, nor the private detectives, then there's no one left . . ."

"Yes, chief, there's one left . . ."

M. Dudouis started as though he had received a shock; and, in a voice that betrayed his excitement:

"But, look here, that's preposterous."

"Why?"

"Come, think for yourself!"

"Go on, chief: say what's in your mind."

"Nonsense! What do you mean?"

"Go on, chief."

"It's impossible! How can Sparmiento have been Lupin's accomplice?"

Ganimard gave a little chuckle.

"Exactly, Arsène Lupin's accomplice! ... That explains everything. During the night, while the three detectives were downstairs watching, or sleeping rather, for Colonel Sparmiento had given them champagne to drink and perhaps doctored it beforehand, the said colonel took down the hangings and passed them out through the window of his bedroom. The room is on the second floor and looks out on another street, which was not watched, because the lower windows are walled up."

M. Dudouis reflected and then shrugged his shoulders:

"It's preposterous!" he repeated.

"Why?"

"Why? Because, if the colonel had been Arsène Lupin's accomplice, he would not have committed suicide after achieving his success."

"Who says that he committed suicide?"

"Why, he was found dead on the line!"

"I told you, there is no such thing as death with Lupin."

"Still, this was genuine enough. Besides, Mme. Sparmiento identified the body."

"I thought you would say that, chief. The argument worried me too. There was I, all of a sudden, with three people in front of me instead of one: first, Arsène Lupin, cracksman; secondly, Colonel Sparmiento, his accomplice; thirdly, a dead man. Spare us! It was too much of a good thing!"

Ganimard took a bundle of newspapers, untied it, and handed one of them to Mr. Dudouis:

"You remember, chief, last time you were here, I was looking through the papers. ... I wanted to see if something had not happened, at that period, that might bear upon the case and confirm my supposition. Please read this paragraph."

M. Dudouis took the paper and read aloud:

"Our Lille correspondent informs us that a curious incident has occurred in that town. A corpse has disappeared from the local morgue, the corpse of a man unknown who threw himself under the wheels of a steam tramcar on the day before. No one is able to suggest a reason for this disappearance."

M. Dudouis sat thinking and then asked:

"So . . . you believe . . . ?"

"I have just come from Lille," replied Ganimard, "and my inquiries leave not a doubt in my mind. The corpse was removed on the same night on which Colonel Sparmiento gave his house-warming. It was taken straight to Ville d'Avray by motor-car; and the car remained near the railway-line until the evening."

"Near the tunnel, therefore," said M. Dudouis.

"Next to it, chief."

"So that the body which was found is merely that body, dressed in Colonel Sparmiento's clothes."

"Precisely, chief."

"Then Colonel Sparmiento is not dead?"

"No more dead than you or I, chief."

"But then why all these complications? Why the theft of one tap-estry, followed by its recovery, followed by the theft of the twelve? Why that house-warming? Why that disturbance? Why everything? Your story won't hold water, Ganimard."

"Only because you, chief, like myself, have stopped half-way; because, strange as this story already sounds, we must go still far-ther, very much farther, in the direction of the improbable and the astounding. And why not, after all? Remember that we are dealing with Arsène Lupin. With him, is it not always just the improbable and the astounding that we must look for? Must we not always go straight for the maddest suppositions? And, when I say the mad-dest, I am using the wrong word. On the contrary, the whole thing is wonderfully logical and so simple that a child could understand it. Confederates only betray you. Why employ confederates, when it is so easy and so natural to act for yourself, by yourself, with your own hands and by the means within your own reach?"

"What are you saying? . . . What are you saying? . . . What are you saying?" cried M. Dudouis, in a sort of sing-song voice and a tone of bewilderment that increased with each separate exclamation.

Ganimard gave a fresh chuckle.

"Takes your breath away, chief, doesn't it? So it did mine, on the day when you came to see me here and when the notion was beginning to grow upon me. I was flabbergasted with astonishment. And yet I've had experience of my customer. I know what he's capable of. . . . But this, no, this was really a bit too stiff!"

"It's impossible! It's impossible!" said M. Dudouis, in a low voice.

"On the contrary, chief, it's quite possible and quite logical and quite normal. It's the threefold incarnation of one and the same individual. A schoolboy would solve the problem in a minute, by a simple process of elimination. Take away the dead man: there remains Sparmiento and Lupin. Take away Sparmiento . . ."

"There remains Lupin," muttered the chief-detective.

"Yes, chief, Lupin simply, Lupin in five letters and two syllables, Lupin taken out of his Brazilian skin, Lupin revived from the dead, Lupin translated, for the past six months, into Colonel Sparmiento, traveling in Brittany, hearing of the discovery of the twelve tapestries, buying them, planning the theft of the best of them, so as to draw attention to himself, Lupin, and divert it from himself, Sparmiento. Next, he brings about, in full view of the gaping public, a noisy contest between Lupin and Sparmiento or Sparmiento and Lupin, plots and gives the house-warming party, terrifies his guests, and, when everything is ready, arranges for Lupin to steal Sparmiento's tapestries and for Sparmiento, Lupin's victim, to disappear from sight and die unsuspected, unsuspectable, regretted by his friends, pitied by the public, and leaving behind him, to pocket the profits of the swindle . . ."

Ganimard stopped, looked the chief in the eyes, and, in a voice that emphasized the importance of his words, concluded:

"Leaving behind him a disconsolate widow."

"Mme. Sparmiento! You really believe . . . ?"

"Hang it all!" said the chief-inspector. "People don't work up a whole business of this sort, without seeing something ahead of them . . . solid profits."

"But the profits, it seems to me, lie in the sale of the tapestries which Lupin will effect in America or elsewhere."

"First of all, yes. But Colonel Sparmiento could effect that sale just as well. And even better. So there's something more."

"Something more?"

"Come, chief, you're forgetting that Colonel Sparmiento has been the victim of an important robbery and that, though he may be dead, at least his widow remains. So it's his widow who will get the money."

"What money?"

"What money? Why, the money due to her! The insurance-money, of course!"

M. Dudouis was staggered. The whole business suddenly became clear to him, with its real meaning. He muttered:

"That's true! . . . That's true! . . . The colonel had insured his tapestries . . ."

"Rather! And for no trifle either."

"For how much?"

"Eight hundred thousand francs."

"Eight hundred thousand?"

"Just so. In five different companies."

"And has Mme. Sparmiento had the money?"

"She got a hundred and fifty thousand francs yesterday and two hundred thousand to-day, while I was away. The remaining payments are to be made in the course of this week."

"But this is terrible! You ought to have . . ."

"What, chief? To begin with, they took advantage of my absence to settle up accounts with the companies. I only heard about it on my return when I ran up against an insurance-manager whom I happen to know and took the opportunity of drawing him out."

The chief-detective was silent for some time, not knowing what to say. Then he mumbled:

"What a fellow, though!"

Ganimard nodded his head:

"Yes, chief, a blackguard, but, I can't help saying, a devil of a clever fellow. For his plan to succeed, he must have managed in such a way that, for four or five weeks, no one could express or even conceive the least suspicion of the part played by Colonel Sparmiento. All the indignation and all the inquiries had to be concentrated upon Lupin alone. In the last resort, people had to find themselves faced simply with a mournful, pitiful, penniless widow, poor Edith Swan-neck, a beautiful and legendary vision, a creature so pathetic that the gentlemen of the insurance-companies were almost glad to place something in her hands to relieve her poverty and her grief. That's what was wanted and that's what happened."

The two men were close together and did not take their eyes from each other's faces.

The chief asked:

"Who is that woman?"

"Sonia Kritchnoff."

"Sonia Kritchnoff?"

"Yes, the Russian girl whom I arrested last year at the time of the theft of the coronet, and whom Lupin helped to escape."

"Are you sure?"

"Absolutely. I was put off the scent, like everybody else, by Lupin's machinations, and had paid no particular attention to her. But, when I knew the part which she was playing, I remembered. She is certainly Sonia, metamorphosed into an Englishwoman; Sonia, the most innocent-looking and the trickiest of actresses; Sonia, who would not hesitate to face death for love of Lupin."

"A good capture, Ganimard," said M. Dudouis, approvingly.

"I've something better still for you, chief!"

"Really? What?"

"Lupin's old foster-mother."

"Victoire?"

"She has been here since Mme. Sparmiento began playing the widow; she's the cook."

"Oho!" said M. Dudouis. "My congratulations, Ganimard!"

"I've something for you, chief, that's even better than that!"

M. Dudouis gave a start. The inspector's hand clutched his and was shaking with excitement.

"What do you mean, Ganimard?"

"Do you think, chief, that I would have brought you here, at this late hour, if I had had nothing more attractive to offer you than Sonia and Victoire? Pah! They'd have kept!"

"You mean to say . . . ?" whispered M. Dudouis, at last, understanding the chief-inspector's agitation.

"You've guessed it, chief!"

"Is he here?"

"He's here."

"In hiding?"

"Not a bit of it. Simply in disguise. He's the man-servant."

This time, M. Dudouis did not utter a word nor make a gesture. Lupin's audacity confounded him.

Ganimard chuckled.

"It's no longer a threefold, but a fourfold incarnation. Edith Swan-neck might have blundered. The master's presence was necessary; and he had the cheek to return. For three weeks, he has been beside me during my inquiry, calmly following the progress made."

"Did you recognize him?"

"One doesn't recognize him. He has a knack of making-up his face and altering the proportions of his body so as to prevent anyone from knowing him. Besides, I was miles from suspecting. . . . But, this evening, as I was watching Sonia in the shadow of the stairs, I heard Victoire speak to the man-servant and call him, 'Dearie.' A light flashed in upon me. 'Dearie'! That was what she always used to call him. And I knew where I was."

M. Dudouis seemed flustered, in his turn, by the presence of the enemy, so often pursued and always so intangible:

"We've got him, this time," he said, between his teeth. "We've got him; and he can't escape us."

"No, chief, he can't: neither he nor the two women."

"Where are they?"

"Sonia and Victoire are on the second floor; Lupin is on the third."

M. Dudouis suddenly became anxious:

"Why, it was through the windows of one of those floors that the tapestries were passed when they disappeared!"

"That's so, chief."

"In that case, Lupin can get away too. The windows look out on the Rue Dufresnoy."

"Of course they do, chief; but I have taken my precautions. The moment you arrived, I sent four of our men to keep watch under the windows in the Rue Dufresnoy. They have strict instructions to shoot, if anyone appears at the windows and looks like coming down. Blank cartridges for the first shot, ball-cartridges for the next."

"Good, Ganimard! You have thought of everything. We'll wait here; and, immediately after sunrise . . ."

"Wait, chief? Stand on ceremony with that rascal? Bother about rules and regulations, legal hours and all that rot? And suppose he's not quite so polite to us and gives us the slip meanwhile? Suppose he plays us one of his Lupin tricks? No, no, we must have no nonsense! We've got him: let's collar him; and that without delay!"

And Ganimard, all a-quiver with indignant impatience, went out, walked across the garden and presently returned with half-a-dozen men:

"It's all right, chief. I've told them, in the Rue Dufresnoy, to get their revolvers out and aim at the windows. Come along."

These alarums and excursions had not been effected without a certain amount of noise, which was bound to be heard by the inhabitants of the house. M. Dudouis felt that his hand was forced. He made up his mind to act:

"Come on, then," he said.

The thing did not take long. The eight of them, Browning pistols in hand, went up the stairs without overmuch precaution, eager to surprise Lupin before he had time to organize his defenses.

"Open the door!" roared Ganimard, rushing at the door of Mme. Sparmiento's bedroom.

A policeman smashed it in with his shoulder.

There was no one in the room; and no one in Victoire's bedroom either.

"They're all upstairs!" shouted Ganimard. "They've gone up to Lupin in his attic. Be careful now!"

All the eight ran up the third flight of stairs. To his great astonishment, Ganimard found the door of the attic open and the attic empty. And the other rooms were empty too.

"Blast them!" he cursed. "What's become of them?"

But the chief called him. M. Dudouis, who had gone down again to the second floor, noticed that one of the windows was not latched, but just pushed to:

"There," he said, to Ganimard, "that's the road they took, the road of the tapestries. I told you as much: the Rue Dufresnoy . . ."

"But our men would have fired on them," protested Ganimard, grinding his teeth with rage. "The street's guarded."

"They must have gone before the street was guarded."

"They were all three of them in their rooms when I rang you up, chief!"

"They must have gone while you were waiting for me in the garden."

"But why? Why? There was no reason why they should go to-day rather than to-morrow, or the next day, or next week, for that matter, when they had pocketed all the insurance-money!"

Yes, there was a reason; and Ganimard knew it when he saw, on the table, a letter addressed to himself and opened it and read it. The letter was worded in the style of the testimonials which we hand to people in our service who have given satisfaction:

"I, the undersigned, Arsène Lupin, gentleman-burglar, ex-colonel, ex-man-of-all-work, ex-corpse, hereby certify that the person of the name of Ganimard gave proof of the most remarkable qualities during his stay in this house. He was exemplary in his behavior, thoroughly devoted and attentive; and, unaided by the least clue, he foiled a part of my plans and saved the insurance-companies four hundred and fifty thousand francs. I congratulate him; and I am quite willing to overlook his blunder in not anticipating that the downstair telephone communicates with the telephone in Sonia Kritchnoff's bedroom and that, when telephoning to Mr. Chief-detective, he was at the same time telephoning to me to clear out as fast as I could. It was a pardonable slip, which must not be allowed to dim the glamour of his services nor to detract from the merits of his victory.

"Having said this, I beg him to accept the homage of my admiration and of my sincere friendship.

"ARSÈNE LUPIN"

* Throughout this collection, Lupin disguises himself as Prince Serge Rénine.

ON THE TOP OF THE TOWER

Hortense Daniel pushed her window ajar and whispered:
"Are you there, Rossigny?"

"I am here," replied a voice from the shrubbery at the front of the house.

Leaning forward, she saw a rather fat man looking up at her out of a gross red face with its cheeks and chin set in unpleasantly fair whiskers.

"Well?" he asked.

"Well, I had a great argument with my uncle and aunt last night. They absolutely refuse to sign the document of which my lawyer sent them the draft, or to restore the dowry squandered by my husband."

"But your uncle is responsible by the terms of the marriage-settlement."

"No matter. He refuses."

"Well, what do you propose to do?"

"Are you still determined to run away with me?" she asked, with a laugh.

"More so than ever."

"Your intentions are strictly honorable, remember!"

"Just as you please. You know that I am madly in love with you."

"Unfortunately I am not madly in love with you!"

"Then what made you choose me?"

"Chance. I was bored. I was growing tired of my humdrum existence. So I'm ready to run risks . . . Here's my luggage: catch!"

She let down from the window a couple of large leather kit-bags. Rossigny caught them in his arms.

"The die is cast," she whispered. "Go and wait for me with your car at the If cross-roads. I shall come on horseback."

"Hang it, I can't run off with your horse!"

"He will go home by himself."

"Capital! . . . Oh, by the way . . ."

"What is it?"

"Who is this Prince Rénine,* who's been here the last three days and whom nobody seems to know?"

"I don't know much about him. My uncle met him at a friend's shoot and asked him here to stay."

"You seem to have made a great impression on him. You went for a long ride with him yesterday. He's a man I don't care for."

"In two hours I shall have left the house in your company. The scandal will cool him off . . . Well, we've talked long enough. We have no time to lose."

For a few minutes she stood watching the fat man bending under the weight of her traps as he moved away in the shelter of an empty avenue. Then she closed the window.

Outside, in the park, the huntsmen's horns were sounding the reveille. The hounds burst into frantic baying. It was the opening day of the hunt that morning at the Château de la Marèze, where, every year, in the first week in September, the Comte d'Aigleroche, a mighty

---

* These adventures were told to me in the old days by Arsène Lupin, as though they had happened to a friend of his, named Prince Rénine. As for me, considering the way in which they were conducted, the actions, the behavior, and the very character of the hero, I find it very difficult not to identify the two friends as one and the same person. Arsène Lupin is gifted with a powerful imagination and is quite capable of attributing to himself adventures which are not his at all and of disowning those which are really his. The reader will judge for himself.
—M. L.

hunter before the Lord, and his countess were accustomed to invite a few personal friends and the neighboring landowners.

Hortense slowly finished dressing, put on a riding-habit, which revealed the lines of her supple figure, and a wide-brimmed felt hat, which encircled her lovely face and auburn hair, and sat down to her writing-desk, at which she wrote to her uncle, M. d'Aigleroche, a farewell letter to be delivered to him that evening. It was a difficult letter to word; and, after beginning it several times, she ended by giving up the idea.

"I will write to him later," she said to herself, "when his anger has cooled down."

And she went downstairs to the dining-room.

Enormous logs were blazing in the hearth of the lofty room. The walls were hung with trophies of rifles and shotguns. The guests were flocking in from every side, shaking hands with the Comte d'Aigleroche, one of those typical country squires, heavily and powerfully built, who lives only for hunting and shooting. He was standing before the fire, with a large glass of old brandy in his hand, drinking the health of each new arrival.

Hortense kissed him absently:

"What, uncle! You who are usually so sober!"

"Pooh!" he said. "A man may surely indulge himself a little once a year! . . ."

"Aunt will give you a scolding!"

"Your aunt has one of her sick headaches and is not coming down. Besides," he added, gruffly, "it is not her business . . . and still less is it yours, my dear child."

Prince Rénine came up to Hortense. He was a young man, very smartly dressed, with a narrow and rather pale face, whose eyes held by turns the gentlest and the harshest, the most friendly and the most satirical expression. He bowed to her, kissed her hand and said:

"May I remind you of your kind promise, dear madame?"

"My promise?"

"Yes, we agreed that we should repeat our delightful excursion of yesterday and try to go over that old boarded-up place the look of which made us so curious. It seems to be known as the Domaine de Halingre."

She answered a little curtly:

"I'm extremely sorry, monsieur, but it would be rather far and I'm feeling a little done up. I shall go for a canter in the park and come indoors again."

There was a pause. Then Serge Rénine said, smiling, with his eyes fixed on hers and in a voice which she alone could hear:

"I am sure that you'll keep your promise and that you'll let me come with you. It would be better."

"For whom? For you, you mean?"

"For you, too, I assure you."

She colored slightly, but did not reply, shook hands with a few people around her, and left the room.

A groom was holding the horse at the foot of the steps. She mounted and set off toward the woods beyond the park.

It was a cool, still morning. Through the leaves, which barely quivered, the sky showed crystalline blue. Hortense rode at a walk down winding avenues which in half an hour brought her to a countryside of ravines and bluffs intersected by the high-road.

She stopped. There was not a sound. Rossigny must have stopped his engine and concealed the car in the thickets around the If crossroads.

She was five hundred yards at most from that circular space. After hesitating for a few seconds, she dismounted, tied her horse carelessly, so that he could release himself by the least effort and return to the house, shrouded her face in the long brown veil that hung over her shoulders and walked on.

As she expected, she saw Rossigny directly she reached the first turn in the road. He ran up to her and drew her into the coppice!

"Quick, quick! Oh, I was so afraid that you would be late . . . or even change your mind! And here you are! It seems too good to be true!"

She smiled:

"You appear to be quite happy to do an idiotic thing!"

"I should think I *am* happy! And so will you be, I swear you will! Your life will be one long fairy-tale. You shall have every luxury, and all the money you can wish for."

"I want neither money nor luxuries."

"What then?"

"Happiness."

"You can safely leave your happiness to me."

She replied, jestingly:

"I rather doubt the quality of the happiness which you would give me."

"Wait! You'll see! You'll see!"

They had reached the motor. Rossigny, still stammering expressions of delight, started the engine. Hortense stepped in and wrapped herself in a wide cloak. The car followed the narrow, grassy path which led back to the cross-roads and Rossigny was accelerating the speed, when he was suddenly forced to pull up. A shot had rung out from the neighboring wood, on the right. The car was swerving from side to side.

"A front tire burst," shouted Rossigny, leaping to the ground.

"Not a bit of it!" cried Hortense. "Somebody fired!"

"Impossible, my dear! Don't be so absurd!"

At that moment, two slight shocks were felt and two more reports were heard, one after the other, some way off and still in the wood.

Rossigny snarled:

"The back tires burst now . . . both of them . . . But who, in the devil's name, can the ruffian be? . . . Just let me get hold of him, that's all! . . ."

He clambered up the road-side slope. There was no one there. Moreover, the leaves of the coppice blocked the view.

"Damn it! Damn it!" he swore. "You were right: somebody was firing at the car! Oh, this is a bit thick! We shall be held up for hours! Three tires to mend! . . . But what are you doing, dear girl?"

Hortense herself had alighted from the car. She ran to him, greatly excited:

"I'm going."

"But why?"

"I want to know. Someone fired. I want to know who it was."

"Don't let us separate, please!"

"Do you think I'm going to wait here for you for hours?"

"What about your running away? . . . All our plans . . . ?"

"We'll discuss that to-morrow. Go back to the house. Take back my things with you . . . And good-bye for the present."

She hurried, left him, had the good luck to find her horse and set off at a gallop in a direction leading away from La Marèze.

There was not the least doubt in her mind that the three shots had been fired by Prince Rénine.

"It was he," she muttered, angrily, "it was he. No one else would be capable of such behavior."

Besides, he had warned her, in his smiling, masterful way, that he would expect her.

She was weeping with rage and humiliation. At that moment, had she found herself face to face with Prince Rénine, she could have struck him with her riding-whip.

Before her was the rugged and picturesque stretch of country which lies between the Orne and the Sarthe, above Alençon, and which is known as Little Switzerland. Steep hills compelled her frequently to moderate her pace, the more so as she had to cover some six miles before reaching her destination. But, though the speed at which she rode became less headlong, though her physical effort gradually slackened, she nevertheless persisted in her indignation against Prince Rénine. She bore him a grudge not only for the unspeakable action of which he had been guilty, but also for his behavior to her during the last three days, his persistent attentions, his assurance, his air of excessive politeness.

She was nearly there. In the bottom of a valley, an old park-wall, full of cracks and covered with moss and weeds, revealed the ball-turret of a château and a few windows with closed shutters. This was the Domaine de Halingre.

She followed the wall and turned a corner. In the middle of the crescent-shaped space before which lay the entrance-gates, Serge Rénine stood waiting beside his horse.

She sprang to the ground, and, as he stepped forward, hat in hand, thanking her for coming, she cried:

"One word, monsieur, to begin with. Something quite inexplicable happened just now. Three shots were fired at a motor-car in which I was sitting. Did you fire those shots?"

"Yes."

She seemed dumbfounded:

"Then you confess it?"

"You have asked a question, madame, and I have answered it."

"But how dared you? What gave you the right?"

"I was not exercising a right, madame; I was performing a duty!"

"Indeed! And what duty, pray?"

"The duty of protecting you against a man who is trying to profit by your troubles."

"I forbid you to speak like that. I am responsible for my own actions, and I decided upon them in perfect liberty."

"Madame, I overheard your conversation with M. Rossigny this morning and it did not appear to me that you were accompanying him with a light heart. I admit the ruthlessness and bad taste of my interference and I apologize for it humbly; but I risked being taken for a ruffian in order to give you a few hours for reflection."

"I have reflected fully, monsieur. When I have once made up my mind to a thing, I do not change it."

"Yes, madame, you do, sometimes. If not, why are you here instead of there?"

Hortense was confused for a moment. All her anger had subsided. She looked at Rénine with the surprise which one experiences when confronted with certain persons who are unlike their fellows, more capable of performing unusual actions, more generous and disinterested. She realized perfectly that he was acting without any ulterior motive or calculation, that he was, as he had said, merely fulfilling his duty as a gentleman to a woman who has taken the wrong turning.

Speaking very gently, he said:

"I know very little about you, madame, but enough to make me wish to be of use to you. You are twenty-six years old and have lost both your parents. Seven years ago, you became the wife of the Comte d'Aigleroche's nephew by marriage, who proved to be of unsound mind, half insane indeed, and had to be confined. This made it impossible for you to obtain a divorce and compelled you, since your dowry had been squandered, to live with your uncle and at his expense. It's a depressing environment. The count and countess do not agree. Years ago, the count was deserted by his first wife, who ran away with the countess's first husband. The abandoned husband and wife decided out of spite to unite their fortunes, but found nothing but disappointment and ill-will in this second marriage. And you suffer the consequences. They lead a monotonous, narrow, lonely life for eleven months or more out of the year. One day, you met M. Rossigny, who fell in love with you and suggested an elopement. You did not care for him. But you were bored, your youth was being wasted, you longed for the unexpected, for adventure . . . in a word, you accepted with the very definite intention of keeping your admirer at arm's length, but also with the rather ingenuous hope that the scandal would force your uncle's hand and make him account for his trusteeship and assure you of an independent existence. That is how you stand. At present you have to choose between placing yourself in M. Rossigny's hands . . . or trusting yourself to me."

She raised her eyes to his. What did he mean? What was the purport of this offer which he made so seriously, like a friend who asks nothing but to prove his devotion?

After a moment's silence, he took the two horses by the bridle and tied them up. Then he examined the heavy gates, each of which was strengthened by two planks nailed cross-wise. An electoral poster, dated twenty years earlier, showed that no one had entered the domain since that time.

Rénine tore up one of the iron posts which supported a railing that ran round the crescent and used it as a lever. The rotten planks gave way. One of them uncovered the lock, which he attacked with a big knife, containing a number of blades and implements. A minute later, the gate opened on a waste of bracken which led up to a long, dilapidated building, with a turret at each corner and a sort of a belvedere, built on a taller tower, in the middle.

The prince turned to Hortense:

"You are in no hurry," he said. "You will form your decision this evening; and, if M. Rossigny succeeds in persuading you for the second time, I give you my word of honor that I shall not cross your path. Until then, grant me the privilege of your company. We made up our minds yesterday to inspect the château. Let us do so. Will you? It is as good a way as any of passing the time and I have a notion that it will not be uninteresting."

He had a way of talking which compelled obedience. He seemed to be commanding and entreating at the same time. Hortense did not even seek to shake off the enervation into which her will was slowly sinking. She followed him to a half-demolished flight of steps at the top of which was a door likewise strengthened by planks nailed in the form of a cross.

Rénine went to work in the same way as before. They entered a spacious hall paved with white and black flagstones, furnished with old sideboards and choir-stalls and adorned with a carved escutcheon which displayed the remains of armorial bearings, representing an eagle standing on a block of stone, all half-hidden behind a veil of cobwebs which hung down over a pair of folding-doors.

"The door of the drawing-room, evidently," said Rénine.

He found this more difficult to open; and it was only by repeatedly charging it with his shoulder that he was able to move one of the doors.

Hortense had not spoken a word. She watched not without surprise this series of forcible entries, which were accomplished with a really masterly skill. He guessed her thoughts and, turning round, said in a serious voice:

"It's child's-play to me. I was a locksmith once."

She seized his arm and whispered:

"Listen!"

"To what?" he asked.

She increased the pressure of her hand, to demand silence. The next moment, he murmured:

"It's really very strange."

"Listen, listen!" Hortense repeated, in bewilderment. "Can it be possible?"

They heard, not far from where they were standing, a sharp sound, the sound of a light tap recurring at regular intervals; and they had only to listen attentively to recognize the ticking of a clock. Yes, it was this and nothing else that broke the profound silence of the dark room; it was indeed the deliberate ticking, rhythmical as the beat of a metronome, produced by a heavy brass pendulum. That was it! And nothing could be more impressive than the measured pulsation of this trivial mechanism, which by some miracle, some inexplicable phenomenon, had continued to live in the heart of the dead château.

"And yet," stammered Hortense, without daring to raise her voice, "no one has entered the house?"

"No one."

"And it is quite impossible for that clock to have kept going for twenty years without being wound up?"

"Quite impossible."

"Then . . . ?"

Serge Rénine opened the three windows and threw back the shutters.

He and Hortense were in a drawing-room, as he had thought; and the room showed not the least sign of disorder. The chairs were in their places. Not a piece of furniture was missing. The people who had lived there and who had made it the most individual room in their house had gone away leaving everything just as it was, the books which they used to read, the knick-knacks on the tables and consoles.

Rénine examined the old grandfather's clock, contained in its tall carved case which showed the disk of the pendulum through an oval pane of glass. He opened the door of the clock. The weights hanging from the cords were at their lowest point.

At that moment there was a click. The clock struck eight with a serious note which Hortense was never to forget.

"How extraordinary!" she said.

"Extraordinary indeed," said he, "for the works are exceedingly simple and would hardly keep going for a week."

"And do you see nothing out of the common?"

"No, nothing . . . or, at least . . ."

He stooped and, from the back of the case, drew a metal tube which was concealed by the weights. Holding it up to the light:

"A telescope," he said, thoughtfully. "Why did they hide it? . . . And they left it drawn out to its full length . . . That's odd . . . What does it mean?"

The clock, as is sometimes usual, began to strike a second time, sounding eight strokes. Rénine closed the case and continued his inspection without putting his telescope down. A wide arch led from the drawing-room to a smaller apartment, a sort of smoking-room. This also was furnished, but contained a glass case for guns of which the rack was empty. Hanging on a panel near by was a calendar with the date of the 5th of September.

"Oh," cried Hortense, in astonishment, "the same date as to-day! . . . They tore off the leaves until the 5th of September . . . And this is the anniversary! What an astonishing coincidence!"

"Astonishing," he echoed. "It's the anniversary of their departure . . . twenty years ago to-day."

"You must admit," she said, "that all this is incomprehensible."

"Yes, of course . . . but, all the same . . . perhaps not."

"Have you any idea?"

He waited a few seconds before replying:

"What puzzles me is this telescope hidden, dropped in that corner, at the last moment. I wonder what it was used for . . . From the ground-floor windows you see nothing but the trees in the garden . . . and the same, I expect, from all the windows . . . We are in a valley, without the least open horizon . . . To use the telescope, one would have to go up to the top of the house . . . Shall we go up?"

She did not hesitate. The mystery surrounding the whole adventure excited her curiosity so keenly that she could think of nothing but accompanying Rénine and assisting him in his investigations.

They went upstairs accordingly, and, on the second floor, came to a landing where they found the spiral staircase leading to the belvedere.

At the top of this was a platform in the open air, but surrounded by a parapet over six feet high.

"There must have been battlements which have been filled in since," observed Prince Rénine. "Look here, there were loop-holes at one time. They may have been blocked."

"In any case," she said, "the telescope was of no use up here either and we may as well go down again."

"I don't agree," he said. "Logic tells us that there must have been some gap through which the country could be seen and this was the spot where the telescope was used."

He hoisted himself by his wrists to the top of the parapet and then saw that this point of vantage commanded the whole of the valley, including the park, with its tall trees marking the horizon; and, beyond, a depression in a wood surmounting a hill, at a distance of some seven or eight hundred yards, stood another tower, squat and in ruins, covered with ivy from top to bottom.

Rénine resumed his inspection. He seemed to consider that the key to the problem lay in the use to which the telescope was put and that the problem would be solved if only they could discover this use.

He studied the loop-holes one after the other. One of them, or rather the place which it had occupied, attracted his attention above the rest. In the middle of the layer of plaster, which had served to block it, there was a hollow filled with earth in which plants had grown. He pulled out the plants and removed the earth, thus clearing the mouth of a hole some five inches in diameter, which completely penetrated the wall. On bending forward, Rénine perceived that this deep and narrow opening inevitably carried the eye, above the dense tops of the trees and through the depression in the hill, to the ivy-clad tower.

At the bottom of this channel, in a sort of groove which ran through it like a gutter, the telescope fitted so exactly that it was quite impossible to shift it, however little, either to the right or to the left.

Rénine, after wiping the outside of the lenses, while taking care not to disturb the lie of the instrument by a hair's breadth, put his eye to the small end.

He remained for thirty or forty seconds, gazing attentively and silently. Then he drew himself up and said, in a husky voice:

"It's terrible . . . it's really terrible."

"What is?" she asked, anxiously.

"Look."

She bent down but the image was not clear to her and the telescope had to be focused to suit her sight. The next moment she shuddered and said:

"It's two scarecrows, isn't it, both stuck up on the top? But why?"

"Look again," he said. "Look more carefully under the hats . . . the faces . . ."

"Oh!" she cried, turning faint with horror, "how awful!"

The field of the telescope, like the circular picture shown by a magic lantern, presented this spectacle: the platform of a broken tower, the walls of which were higher in the more distant part and formed as it were a back-drop, over which surged waves of ivy. In front, amid a cluster of bushes, were two human beings, a man and a woman, leaning back against a heap of fallen stones.

But the words man and woman could hardly be applied to these two forms, these two sinister puppets, which, it is true, wore clothes and hats—or rather shreds of clothes and remnants of hats—but had lost their eyes, their cheeks, their chins, every particle of flesh, until they were actually and positively nothing more than two skeletons.

"Two skeletons," stammered Hortense. "Two skeletons with clothes on. Who carried them up there?"

"Nobody."

"But still . . ."

"That man and that woman must have died at the top of the tower, years and years ago . . . and their flesh rotted under their clothes and the ravens ate them."

"But it's hideous, hideous!" cried Hortense, pale as death, her face drawn with horror.

Half an hour later, Hortense Daniel and Rénine left the Château de Halingre. Before their departure, they had gone as far as the ivy-grown tower, the remains of an old donjon-keep more than half demolished. The inside was empty. There seemed to have been a way of climbing to the top, at a comparatively recent period, by means of wooden stairs and ladders which now lay broken and scattered over the ground. The tower backed against the wall which marked the end of the park.

A curious fact, which surprised Hortense, was that Prince Rénine had neglected to pursue a more minute enquiry, as though the matter had lost all interest for him. He did not even speak of it any longer; and, in the inn at which they stopped and took a light meal in the nearest village, it was she who asked the landlord about the abandoned château. But she learnt nothing from him, for the man was new to the district and could give her no particulars. He did not even know the name of the owner.

They turned their horses' heads toward La Marèze. Again and again Hortense recalled the squalid sight which had met their eyes. But Rénine, who was in a lively mood and full of attentions to his companion, seemed utterly indifferent to those questions.

"But, after all," she exclaimed, impatiently, "we can't leave the matter there! It calls for a solution."

"As you say," he replied, "a solution is called for. M. Rossigny has to know where he stands and you have to decide what to do about him."

She shrugged her shoulders: "He's of no importance for the moment. The thing to-day . . ."

"Is what?"

"Is to know what those two dead bodies are."

"Still, Rossigny . . ."

"Rossigny can wait. But I can't. You have shown me a mystery which is now the only thing that matters. What do you intend to do?"

"To do?"

"Yes. There are two bodies . . . You'll inform the police, I suppose."

"Gracious goodness!" he exclaimed, laughing. "What for?"

"Well, there's a riddle that has to be cleared up at all costs, a terrible tragedy."

"We don't need anyone to do that."

"What! Do you mean to say that you understand it?"

"Almost as plainly as though I had read it in a book, told in full detail, with explanatory illustrations. It's all so simple!"

She looked at him askance, wondering if he was making fun of her. But he seemed quite serious.

"Well?" she asked, quivering with curiosity.

The light was beginning to wane. They had trotted at a good pace; and the hunt was returning as they neared La Marèze.

"Well," he said, "we shall get the rest of our information from people living round about . . . from your uncle, for instance; and you will see how logically all the facts fit in. When you hold the first link of a chain, you are bound, whether you like it or not, to reach the last. It's the greatest fun in the world."

Once in the house, they separated. On going to her room, Hortense found her luggage and a furious letter from Rossigny in which he bade her good-bye and announced his departure.

Then Rénine knocked at her door:

"Your uncle is in the library," he said. "Will you go down with me? I've sent word that I am coming."

She went with him. He added:

"One word more. This morning, when I thwarted your plans and begged you to trust me, I naturally undertook an obligation toward you which I mean to fulfill without delay. I want to give you a positive proof of this."

She laughed:

"The only obligation which you took upon yourself was to satisfy my curiosity."

"It shall be satisfied," he assured her, gravely, "and more fully than you can possibly imagine."

M. d'Aigleroche was alone. He was smoking his pipe and drinking sherry. He offered a glass to Rénine, who refused.

"Well, Hortense!" he said, in a rather thick voice. "You know that it's pretty dull here, except in these September days. You must make the most of them. Have you had a pleasant ride with Rénine?"

"That's just what I wanted to talk about, my dear sir," interrupted the prince.

"You must excuse me, but I have to go to the station in ten minutes, to meet a friend of my wife's."

"Oh, ten minutes will be ample!"

"Just the time to smoke a cigarette?"

"No longer."

He took a cigarette from the case which M. d'Aigleroche handed to him, lit it, and said:

"I must tell you that our ride happened to take us to an old domain which you are sure to know, the Domaine de Halingre."

"Certainly I know it. But it has been closed, boarded up for twenty-five years or so. You weren't able to get in, I suppose?"

"Yes, we were."

"Really? Was it interesting?"

"Extremely. We discovered the strangest things."

"What things?" asked the count, looking at his watch.

Rénine described what they had seen:

"On a tower some way from the house there were two dead bodies, two skeletons rather . . . a man and a woman still wearing the clothes which they had on when they were murdered."

"Come, come, now! Murdered?"

"Yes; and that is what we have come to trouble you about. The tragedy must date back to some twenty years ago. Was nothing known of it at the time?"

"Certainly not," declared the count. "I never heard of any such crime or disappearance."

"Oh, really!" said Rénine, looking a little disappointed. "I hoped to obtain a few particulars."

"I'm sorry."

"In that case, I apologize."

He consulted Hortense with a glance and moved toward the door. But on second thought:

"Could you not at least, my dear sir, bring me into touch with some persons in the neighborhood, some members of your family, who might know more about it?"

"Of my family? And why?"

"Because the Domaine de Halingre used to belong and no doubt still belongs to the d'Aigleroches. The arms are an eagle on a heap of stones, on a rock. This at once suggested the connection."

This time the count appeared surprised. He pushed back his decanter and his glass of sherry and said:

"What's this you're telling me? I had no idea that we had any such neighbors."

Rénine shook his head and smiled:

"I should be more inclined to believe, sir, that you were not very eager to admit any relationship between yourself... and the unknown owner of the property."

"Then he's not a respectable man?"

"The man, to put it plainly, is a murderer."

"What do you mean?"

The count had risen from his chair. Hortense, greatly excited, said:

"Are you really sure that there has been a murder and that the murder was done by someone belonging to the house?"

"Quite sure."

"But why are you so certain?"

"Because I know who the two victims were and what caused them to be killed."

Prince Rénine was making none but positive statements and his method suggested the belief that he supported by the strongest proofs.

M. d'Aigleroche strode up and down the room, with his hands behind his back. He ended by saying:

"I always had an instinctive feeling that something had happened, but I never tried to find out... Now, as a matter of fact, twenty years ago, a relation of mine, a distant cousin, used to live at the Domaine de Halingre. I hoped, because of the name I bear, that this story, which, as I say, I never knew but suspected, would remain hidden for ever."

"So this cousin killed somebody?"

"Yes, he was obliged to."

Rénine shook his head:

"I am sorry to have to amend that phrase, my dear sir. The truth, on the contrary, is that your cousin took his victims' lives in cold blood and in a cowardly manner. I never heard of a crime more deliberately and craftily planned."

"What is it that you know?"

"The moment had come for Rénine to explain himself, a solemn and anguish-stricken moment, the full gravity of which Hortense understood, though she had not yet divined any part of the tragedy which the prince unfolded step by step."

"It's a very simple story," he said. "There is every reason to believe that M. d'Aigleroche was married and that there was another couple living in the neighborhood with whom the owner of the Domaine de Halingre were on friendly terms. What happened one day, which of these four persons first disturbed the relations between the two households, I am unable to say. But a likely version, which at once occurs to the mind, is that your cousin's wife, Madame d'Aigleroche, was in the habit of meeting the other husband in the ivy-covered tower, which had a door opening outside the estate. On discovering the intrigue, your cousin d'Aigleroche resolved to be revenged, but in such a manner that there should be no scandal and that no one even should ever know that the guilty pair had been killed. Now he had ascertained—as I did just now—that there was a part of the house, the belvedere, from which you can see, over the trees and the undulations of the park, the tower standing eight hundred yards away, and that this was the only place that overlooked the top of the tower. He therefore pierced a hole in the parapet, through one of the former loopholes, and from there, by using a telescope which fitted exactly in the grove which he had hollowed out, he watched the meetings of the two lovers. And it was from there, also, that, after carefully taking all his measurements, and calculating all his distances, on a Sunday, the 5th of September, when the house was empty, he killed them with two shots."

The truth was becoming apparent. The light of day was breaking. The count muttered:

"Yes, that's what must have happened. I expect that my cousin d'Aigleroche . . ."

"The murderer," Rénine continued, "stopped up the loophole neatly with a clod of earth. No one would ever know that two dead bodies were decaying on the top of that tower which was never visited and of which he took the precaution to demolish the wooden stairs. Nothing therefore remained for him to do but to explain the disappearance of his wife and his friend. This presented no difficulty. He accused them of having eloped together."

Hortense gave a start. Suddenly, as though the last sentence were a complete and to her an absolutely unexpected revelation, she understood what Rénine was trying to convey:

"What do you mean?" she asked.

"I mean that M. d'Aigleroche accused his wife and his friend of eloping together."

"No, no!" she cried. "I can't allow that! . . . You are speaking of a cousin of my uncle's? Why mix up the two stories?"

"Why mix up this story with another which took place at that time?" said the prince. "But I am not mixing them up, my dear madame; there is only one story and I am telling it as it happened."

Hortense turned to her uncle. He sat silent, with his arms folded; and his head remained in the shadow cast by the lamp-shade. Why had he not protested?

Rénine repeated in a firm tone:

"There is only one story. On the evening of that very day, the 5th of September at eight o'clock, M. d'Aigleroche, doubtless alleging as his reason that he was going in pursuit of the runaway couple, left his house after boarding up the entrance. He went away, leaving all the rooms as they were and removing only the firearms from their glass case. At the last minute, he had a presentiment, which has been justified to-day, that the discovery of the telescope which had played so great a part in the preparation of his crime might serve as a clue to an enquiry; and he threw it into the clock-case, where, as luck would have it, it interrupted the swing of the pendulum. This unreflecting action, one of those which every criminal inevitably commits, was to betray him twenty years later. Just now, the blows which I struck to force the door of the drawing-room released the pendulum. The clock was set going, struck eight o'clock . . . and I possessed the clue of thread which was to lead me through the labyrinth."

"Proofs!" stammered Hortense. "Proofs!"

"Proofs?" replied Rénine, in a loud voice. "Why, there are any number of proofs; and you know them as well as I do. Who could have killed at that distance of eight hundred yards, except an expert shot, an ardent sportsman? You agree, M. d'Aigleroche, do you not? . . . Proofs? Why was nothing removed from the house, nothing except the guns, those guns which an ardent sportsman cannot afford to leave behind—you agree, M. d'Aigleroche—those guns which we find here, hanging in trophies on the walls! . . . Proofs? What about that date, the 5th of September, which was the date of the crime and which has left such a horrible memory in the criminal's mind that every year at this time—at this time alone—he surrounds himself with distractions and that every year, on this same 5th of September, he forgets his habits of temperance? Well, to-day, is the 5th of September . . . Proofs? Why, if there weren't any others, would that not be enough for you?"

And Rénine, flinging out his arm, pointed to the Comte d'Aigleroche, who, terrified by this evocation of the past, had sunk huddled into a chair and was hiding his head in his hands.

Hortense did not attempt to argue with him. She had never liked her uncle, or rather her husband's uncle. She now accepted the accusation laid against him.

Sixty seconds passed. Then M. d'Aigleroche walked up to them and said:

"Whether the story be true or not, you can't call a husband a criminal for avenging his honor and killing his faithless wife."

"No," replied Rénine, "but I have told only the first version of the story. There is another which is infinitely more serious . . . and more probable, one to which a more thorough investigation would be sure to lead."

"What do you mean?"

"I mean this. It may not be a matter of a husband taking the law into his own hands, as I charitably supposed. It may be a matter of a ruined man who covets his friend's money and his friend's wife and who, with this object in view, to secure his freedom, to get rid of his friend and of his own wife, draws them into a trap, suggests to them that they should visit that lonely tower and kills them by shooting them from a distance safely under cover."

"No, no," the count protested. "No, all that is untrue."

"I don't say it isn't. I am basing my accusation on proofs, but also on intuitions and arguments which up to now have been extremely accurate. All the same, I admit that the second version may be incorrect. But, if so, why feel any remorse? One does not feel remorse for punishing guilty people."

"One does for taking life. It is a crushing burden to bear."

"Was it to give himself greater strength to bear this burden that M. d'Aigleroche afterward married his victim's widow? For that, sir, is the crux of the question. What was the motive of that marriage? Was M. d'Aigleroche penniless? Was the woman he was taking as his second wife rich? Or were they both in love with each other and did M. d'Aigleroche plan with her to kill his first wife and the husband of his second wife? These are problems to which I do not know the answer. They have no interest for the moment; but the police, with all the means at their disposal, would have no great difficulty in elucidating them."

M. d'Aigleroche staggered and had to steady himself against the back of a chair. Livid in the face, he spluttered:

"Are you going to inform the police?"

"No, no," said Rénine. "To begin with, there is the statute of limitations. Then there are twenty years of remorse and dread, a memory which will pursue the criminal to his dying hour, accompanied no doubt by domestic discord, hatred, a daily hell . . . and, in the end, the necessity of returning to the tower and removing the traces of the two murders, the frightful punishment of climbing that tower, of touching those skeletons, of undressing them and burying them. That will be enough. We will not ask for more. We will not give it to the public to batten on and create a scandal which would recoil upon M. d'Aigleroche's niece. No, let us leave this disgraceful business alone."

The count resumed his seat at the table, with his hands clutching his forehead, and asked:

"Then why . . . ?"

"Why do I interfere?" said Rénine. "What you mean is that I must have had some object in speaking. That is so. There must indeed be a penalty, however slight, and our interview must lead to some practical result. But have no fear: M. d'Aigleroche will be let off lightly."

The contest was ended. The count felt that he had only a small formality to fulfill, a sacrifice to accept; and, recovering some of his self-assurance, he said, in an almost sarcastic tone:

"What's your price?"

Rénine burst out laughing:

"Splendid! You see the position. Only, you make a mistake in drawing me into the business. I'm working for the glory of the thing."

"In that case?"

"You will be called upon at most to make restitution."

"Restitution?"

Rénine leant over the table and said:

"In one of those drawers is a deed awaiting your signature. It is a draft agreement between you and your niece Hortense Daniel, relating to her private fortune, which fortune was squandered and for which you are responsible. Sign the deed."

M. d'Aigleroche gave a start:

"Do you know the amount?"

"I don't wish to know it."

"And if I refuse? . . ."

"I shall ask to see the Comtesse d'Aigleroche."

Without further hesitation, the count opened a drawer, produced a document on stamped paper, and quickly signed it:

"Here you are," he said, "and I hope . . ."

"You hope, as I do, that you and I may never have any future dealings? I'm convinced of it. I shall leave this evening, your niece, no doubt, to-morrow. Good-bye."

In the drawing-room, which was still empty, while the guests at the house were dressing for dinner, Rénine handed the deed to Hortense. She seemed dazed by all that she had heard; and the thing that bewildered her even more than the relentless light shed upon her uncle's past was the miraculous insight and amazing lucidity displayed by this man: the man who for some hours had controlled events and conjured up before her eyes the actual scenes of a tragedy which no one had beheld.

"Are you satisfied with me?" he asked.

She gave him both her hands:

"You have saved me from Rossigny. You have given me back my freedom and my independence. I thank you from the bottom of my heart."

"Oh, that's not what I am asking you to say!" he answered. "My first and main object was to amuse you. Your life seemed so humdrum and lacking in the unexpected. Has it been so to-day?"

"How can you ask such a question? I have had the strangest and most stirring experiences."

"That is life," he said. "When one knows how to use one's eyes. Adventure exists everywhere, in the meanest hovel, under the mask of the wisest of men. Everywhere, if you are only willing, you will find an excuse for excitement, for doing good, for saving a victim, for ending an injustice."

Impressed by his power and authority, she murmured:

"Who are you exactly?"

"An adventurer. Nothing more. A lover of adventures. Life is not worth living except in moments of adventure, the adventures of others or personal adventures. To-day's has upset you because it affected the innermost depths of your being. But those of others are no less stimulating. Would you like to make the experiment?"

"How?"

"Become the companion of my adventures. If anyone calls on me for help, help him with me. If chance or instinct puts me on the track of a crime or the trace of a sorrow, let us both set out together. Do you consent?"

"Yes," she said, "but . . ."

She hesitated, as though trying to guess Rénine's secret intentions.

"But," he said, expressing her thoughts for her, with a smile, "you are a trifle skeptical. What you are saying to yourself is, 'How far does that lover of adventures want to make me go? It is quite obvious that I attract him; and sooner or later he would not be sorry to receive payment for his services.' You are quite right. We must have a formal contract."

"Very formal," said Hortense, preferring to give a jesting tone to the conversation. "Let me hear your proposals."

He reflected for a moment and continued:

"Well, we'll say this. The clock at Halingre gave eight strokes this afternoon, the day of the first adventure. Will you accept its decree and agree to carry out seven more of these delightful enterprises with me, during a period, for instance, of three months? And shall we say that, at the eighth, you will be pledged to grant me . . ."

"What?"

He deferred his answer:

"Observe that you will always be at liberty to leave me on the road if I do not succeed in interesting you. But, if you accompany me to the end, if you allow me to begin and complete the eighth enterprise with you, in three months, on the 5th of December, at the very moment when the eighth stroke of that clock sounds—and it will sound, you may be sure of that, for the old brass pendulum will not stop swinging again—you will be pledged to grant me . . ."

"What?" she repeated, a little unnerved by waiting.

He was silent. He looked at the beautiful lips which he had meant to claim as his reward. He felt perfectly certain that Hortense had understood and he thought it unnecessary to speak more plainly:

"The mere delight of seeing you will be enough to satisfy me. It is not for me but for you to impose conditions. Name them: what do you demand?"

She was grateful for his respect and said, laughingly:

"What do I demand?"

"Yes."

"Can I demand anything I like, however difficult and impossible?"

"Everything is easy and everything is possible to the man who is bent on winning you."

Then she said:

"I demand that you shall restore to me a small, antique clasp, made of a cornelian set in a silver mount. It came to me from my mother and everyone knew that it used to bring her happiness and me too. Since the day when it vanished from my jewel-case, I have had nothing but unhappiness. Restore it to me, my good genius."

"When was the clasp stolen?"

She answered gaily:

"Seven years ago . . . or eight . . . or nine; I don't know exactly . . . I don't know where . . . I don't know how . . . I know nothing about it . . ."

"I will find it," Rénine declared, "and you shall be happy."

THE CASE OF JEAN LOUIS

Monsieur," continued the young girl, addressing Serge Rénine, "it was while I was spending the Easter holidays at Nice with my father that I made the acquaintance of Jean Louis d'Imbleval . . ."

Rénine interrupted her:

"Excuse me, mademoiselle, but just now you spoke of this young man as Jean Louis Vaurois."

"That's his name also," she said.

"Has he two names then?"

"I don't know . . . I don't know anything about it," she said, with some embarrassment, "and that is why, by Hortense's advice, I came to ask for your help."

This conversation was taking place in Rénine's flat on the Boulevard Haussmann, to which Hortense had brought her friend Geneviève Aymard, a slender, pretty little creature with a face over-shadowed by an expression of the greatest melancholy.

"Rénine will be successful, take my word for it, Geneviève. You will, Rénine, won't you?"

"Please tell me the rest of the story, mademoiselle," he said.

Geneviève continued:

"I was already engaged at the time to a man whom I loathe and detest. My father was trying to force me to marry him and is still trying to do so. Jean Louis and I felt the keenest sympathy for each other, a sympathy that soon developed into a profound and passionate affection which, I can assure you, was equally sincere on both sides. On my return to Paris, Jean Louis, who lives in the country with his mother and his aunt, took rooms in our part of the town; and, as I am allowed to go out by myself, we used to see each other daily. I need not tell you that we were engaged to be married. I told my father so. And this is what he said: 'I don't particularly like the fellow. But, whether it's he or another, what I want is that you should get married. So let him come and ask for your hand. If not, you must do as I say.' In the middle of June, Jean Louis went home to arrange matters with his mother and aunt. I received some passionate letters; and then just these few words:

> 'There are too many obstacles in the way of our happiness. I give up. I am mad with despair. I love you more than ever. Good-bye and forgive me.'

"Since then, I have received nothing: no reply to my letters and telegrams."

"Perhaps he has fallen in love with somebody else?" asked Rénine. "Or there may be some old connection which he is unable to shake off."

Geneviève shook her head:

"Monsieur, believe me, if our engagement had been broken off for an ordinary reason, I should not have allowed Hortense to trouble you. But it is something quite different, I am absolutely convinced. There's a mystery in Jean Louis's life, or rather an endless number of mysteries which hamper and pursue him. I never saw such distress in a human face; and, from the first moment of our meeting, I was conscious in him of a grief and melancholy which have always persisted, even at times when he was giving himself to our love with the greatest confidence."

"But your impression must have been confirmed by minor details, by things which happened to strike you as peculiar?"

"I don't quite know what to say."

"These two names, for instance?"

"Yes, there was certainly that."

"By what name did he introduce himself to you?"

"Jean Louis d'Imbleval."

"But Jean Louis Vaurois?"

"That's what my father calls him."

"Why?"

"Because that was how he was introduced to my father, at Nice, by a gentleman who knew him. Besides, he carries visiting-cards which describe him under either name."

"Have you never questioned him on this point?"

"Yes, I have, twice. The first time, he said that his aunt's name was Vaurois and his mother's d'Imbleval."

"And the second time?"

"He told me the contrary: he spoke of his mother as Vaurois and of his aunt as d'Imbleval. I pointed this out. He colored up and I thought it better not to question him any further."

"Does he live far from Paris?"

"Right down in Brittany: at the Manoir d'Elseven, five miles from Carhaix."

Rénine rose and asked the girl, seriously:

"Are you quite certain that he loves you, mademoiselle?"

"I am certain of it and I know too that he represents all my life and all my happiness. He alone can save me. If he can't, then I shall be married in a week's time to a man whom I hate. I have promised my father; and the banns have been published."

"We shall leave for Carhaix, Madame Daniel and I, this evening," said Rénine.

That evening he and Hortense took the train for Brittany. They reached Carhaix at ten o'clock in the morning; and, after lunch, at half past twelve o'clock they stepped into a car borrowed from a leading resident of the district.

"You're looking a little pale, my dear," said Rénine, with a laugh, as they alighted by the gate of the garden at Elseven.

"I'm very fond of Geneviève," she said. "She's the only friend I have. And I'm feeling frightened."

He called her attention to the fact that the central gate was flanked by two wickets bearing the names of Madame d'Imbleval and Madame Vaurois respectively. Each of these wickets opened on a narrow path which ran among the shrubberies of box and aucuba to the left and right of the main avenue. The avenue itself led to an old manor-house, long, low and picturesque, but provided with two clumsily-built, ugly wings, each in a different style of architecture and each forming the destination of one of the side-paths. Madame d'Imbleval evidently lived on the left and Madame Vaurois on the right.

Hortense and Rénine listened. Shrill, hasty voices were disputing inside the house. The sound came through one of the windows of the ground-floor, which was level with the garden and covered throughout its length with red creepers and white roses.

"We can't go any farther," said Hortense. "It would be indiscreet."

"All the more reason," whispered Rénine. "Look here: if we walk straight ahead, we shan't be seen by the people who are quarrelling."

The sounds of conflict were by no means abating; and, when they reached the window next to the front-door, through the roses and creepers they could both see and hear two old ladies shrieking at the tops of their voices and shaking their fists at each other.

The women were standing in the foreground, in a large dining-room where the table was not yet cleared; and at the farther side of the table sat a young man, doubtless Jean Louis himself, smoking his pipe and reading a newspaper, without appearing to trouble about the two old harridans.

One of these, a thin, tall woman, was wearing a purple silk dress; and her hair was dressed in a mass of curls much too yellow for the ravaged face around which they tumbled. The other, who was still thinner, but quite short, was bustling round the room in a cotton dressing-gown and displayed a red, painted face blazing with anger:

"A baggage, that's what you are!" she yelped. "The wickedest woman in the world and a thief into the bargain!"

"I, a thief!" screamed the other.

"What about that business with the ducks at ten francs apiece: don't you call that thieving?"

"Hold your tongue, you low creature! Who stole the fifty-franc note from my dressing-table? Lord, that I should have to live with such a wretch!"

The other started with fury at the outrage and, addressing the young man, cried:

"Jean, are you going to sit there and let me be insulted by your hussy of a d'Imbleval?"

And the tall one retorted, furiously:

"Hussy! Do you hear that, Louis? Look at her, your Vaurois! She's got the airs of a superannuated barmaid! Make her stop, can't you?"

Suddenly Jean Louis banged his fist upon the table, making the plates and dishes jump, and shouted:

"Be quiet, both of you, you old lunatics!"

They turned upon him at once and loaded him with abuse:

"Coward! . . . Hypocrite! . . . Liar! . . . A pretty sort of son you are! . . . The son of a slut and not much better yourself! . . ."

The insults rained down upon him. He stopped his ears with his fingers and writhed as he sat at table like a man who has lost all patience and has need to restrain himself lest he should fall upon his enemy.

Rénine whispered:

"Now's the time to go in."

"In among all those infuriated people?" protested Hortense.

"Exactly. We shall see them better with their masks off."

And, with a determined step, he walked to the door, opened it, and entered the room, followed by Hortense.

His advent gave rise to a feeling of stupefaction. The two women stopped yelling, but were still scarlet in the face and trembling with rage. Jean Louis, who was very pale, stood up.

Profiting by the general confusion, Rénine said briskly:

"Allow me to introduce myself. I am Prince Rénine. This is Madame Daniel. We are friends of Mlle. Geneviève Aymard and we have come in her name. I have a letter from her addressed to you, monsieur."

Jean Louis, already disconcerted by the newcomers' arrival, lost countenance entirely on hearing the name of Geneviève. Without quite knowing what he was saying and with the intention of responding to Rénine's courteous behavior, he tried in his turn to introduce the two ladies and let fall the astounding words:

"My mother, Madame d'Imbleval; my mother, Madame Vaurois."

For some time no one spoke. Rénine bowed. Hortense did not know with whom she should shake hands, with Madame d'Imbleval, the mother, or with Madame Vaurois, the mother. But what happened was that Madame d'Imbleval and Madame Vaurois both at the same time attempted to snatch the letter which Rénine was holding out to Jean Louis, while both at the same time mumbled:

"Mlle. Aymard! . . . She has had the coolness . . . she has had the audacity . . . !"

Then Jean Louis, recovering his self-possession, laid hold of his mother d'Imbleval and pushed her out of the room by a door on the left and next of his mother Vaurois and pushed her out of the room by a door on the right. Then, returning to his two visitors, he opened the envelope and read, in an undertone:

> *I am to be married in a week, Jean Louis. Come to my*
> *rescue, I beseech you. My friend Hortense and Prince*
> *Rénine will help you to overcome the obstacles that baffle*
> *you. Trust them. I love you.*
>
> *GENEVIÈVE*

He was a rather dull-looking young man, whose very swarthy, lean, and bony face certainly bore the expression of melancholy and distress described by Geneviève. Indeed, the marks of suffering were visible in all his harassed features, as well as in his sad and anxious eyes.

He repeated Geneviève's name over and over again, while looking about him with a distracted air. He seemed to be seeking a course of conduct.

He seemed on the point of offering an explanation but could find nothing to say. The sudden intervention had taken him at a disadvantage, like an unforeseen attack which he did not know how to meet.

Rénine felt that the adversary would capitulate at the first summons. The man had been fighting so desperately during the last few months and had suffered so severely in the retirement and obstinate silence in which he had taken refuge that he was not thinking of defending himself. Moreover, how could he do so, now that they had forced their way into the privacy of his odious existence?

"Take my word for it, monsieur," declared Rénine, "that it is in your best interests to confide in us. We are Geneviève Aymard's friends. Do not hesitate to speak."

"I can hardly hesitate," he said, "after what you have just heard. This is the life I lead, monsieur. I will tell you the whole secret, so that you may tell it to Geneviève. She will then understand why I have not gone back to her ... and why I have not the right to do so."

He pushed a chair forward for Hortense. The two men sat down, and, without any need of further persuasion, rather as though he himself felt a certain relief in unburdening himself, he said:

"You must not be surprised, monsieur, if I tell my story with a certain flippancy, for, as a matter of fact, it is a frankly comical story and cannot fail to make you laugh. Fate often amuses itself by playing these imbecile tricks, these monstrous farces which seem as though they must have been invented by the brain of a madman or a drunkard. Judge for yourself. Twenty-seven years ago, the Manoir d'Elseven, which at that time consisted only of the main building, was occupied by an old doctor who, to increase his modest means, used to receive one or two paying guests. In this way, Madame d'Imbleval spent the summer here one year and Madame Vaurois the following summer. Now these two ladies did not know each other. One of them was married to a Breton of a merchant-vessel and the other to a commercial traveler from the Vendée.

"It so happened that they lost their husbands at the same time, at a period when each of them was expecting a baby. And, as they both lived in the country, at places some distance from any town, they wrote to the old doctor that they intended to come to his house for their confinement ... He agreed. They arrived almost on the same day, in the autumn. Two small bedrooms were prepared for them, behind the room in which we are sitting. The doctor had engaged a nurse, who slept in this very room. Everything was perfectly satisfactory. The ladies were putting the finishing touches to their baby-clothes and were getting on together splendidly. They were determined that their children should be boys and had chosen the names of Jean and Louis respectively ... One evening the doctor was called out to a case and drove off in his gig with the man-servant, saying that he would not be back till next day. In her master's absence, a little girl who served as maid-of-all-work ran out to keep company with her sweetheart. These accidents destiny turned to account with diabolical malignity. At about midnight, Madame d'Imbleval was seized with the first pains. The nurse, Mlle. Boussignol, had had some training as a midwife and did not lose her head. But, an hour later, Madame Vaurois's turn came; and the tragedy, or I might rather say the tragi-comedy, was enacted amid the screams and moans of the two patients and the bewildered agitation of the nurse running from one to the other, bewailing her fate, opening the window to call out for the doctor or falling on her knees to implore the aid of Providence . . . Madame Vaurois was the first to bring a son into the world. Mlle. Boussignol hurriedly carried him in here, washed and tended him, and laid him in the cradle prepared for him . . . But Madame d'Imbleval was screaming with pain; and the nurse had to attend to her while the newborn child was yelling like a stuck pig and the terrified mother, unable to stir from her bed, fainted . . . Add to this all the wretchedness of darkness and disorder, the only lamp, without any oil, for the servant had neglected to fill it, the candles burning out, the moaning of the wind, the screeching of the owls, and you will understand that Mlle. Boussignol was scared out of her wits. However, at five o'clock in the morning, after many tragic incidents, she came in here with the d'Imbleval baby, likewise a boy, washed and tended him, laid him in his cradle, and went off to help Madame Vaurois, who had come to herself and was crying out, while Madame d'Imbleval had fainted in her turn. And, when Mlle. Boussignol, having settled the two mothers, but half-crazed with fatigue, her brain in a whirl, returned to the new-born children, she realized with horror that she had wrapped them in similar binders, thrust their feet into similar woolen socks, and laid them both, side by side, *in the same cradle*, so that it was impossible to tell Louis d'Imbleval from Jean Vaurois! . . . To make matters worse, when she lifted one of them out of the cradle, she found that his hands were cold as ice and that he had ceased to breathe. He was dead. What was his name and what the survivor's? . . . Three hours later, the doctor found the two women in a condition of frenzied delirium, while the nurse was dragging herself from one bed to the other, entreating the two mothers to forgive her. She held me out first to one, then to the other, to receive their caresses—for I was the surviving child—and they first kissed me and then pushed me away; for, after all, who was I? The son of the widowed Madame d'Imbleval and the late merchant-captain or the son of the widowed Madame Vaurois and the late commercial traveler? There was not a clue by which they could tell . . . The doctor begged each of the two mothers to sacrifice her rights, at least from the legal point of view, so that I might be called either Louis d'Imbleval or Jean Vaurois. They refused absolutely. 'Why Jean Vaurois, if he's a d'Imbleval?' protested the one. 'Why Louis d'Imbleval, if he's a Vaurois?' retorted the other. And I was registered under the name of Jean Louis, the son of an unknown father and mother."

Prince Rénine had listened in silence. But Hortense, as the story approached its conclusion, had given way to a hilarity which she could no longer restrain and suddenly, in spite of all her efforts, she burst into a fit of the wildest laughter:

"Forgive me," she said, her eyes filled with tears, "do forgive me; it's too much for my nerves . . ."

"Don't apologize, madame," said the young man, gently, in a voice free from resentment. "I warned you that my story was laughable; I, better than anyone, know how absurd, how nonsensical it is. Yes, the whole thing is perfectly grotesque. But believe me when I tell you that it was no fun in reality. It seems a humorous situation and it remains humorous by the force of circumstances; but it is also horrible. You can see that for yourself, can't you? The two mothers, neither of whom was certain of being a mother, but neither of whom was certain that she was not one, both clung to Jean Louis. He might be a stranger; on the other hand, he might be their own flesh and blood. They loved him to excess and fought for him furiously. And, above all, they both came to hate each other with a deadly hatred. Differing completely in character and education and obliged to live together because neither was willing to forego the advantage of her possible maternity, they lived the life of irreconcilable enemies who can never lay their weapons aside . . . I grew up in the midst of this hatred and had it instilled into me by both of them. When my childish heart, hungering for affection, inclined me to one of them, the other would seek to inspire me with loathing and contempt for her. In this manorhouse, which they bought on the old doctor's death and to which they added the two wings, I was the involuntary torturer and their daily victim. Tormented as a child, and, as a young man, leading the most hideous of lives, I doubt if anyone on earth ever suffered more than I did."

"You ought to have left them!" exclaimed Hortense, who had stopped laughing.

"One can't leave one's mother; and one of those two women was my mother. And a woman can't abandon her son; and each of them was entitled to believe that I was her son. We were all three chained together like convicts, with chains of sorrow, compassion, doubt and also of hope that the truth might one day become apparent. And here we still are, all three, insulting one another and blaming one another for our wasted lives. Oh, what a hell! And there was no escaping it. I tried often enough . . . but in vain. The broken bonds became tied again. Only this summer, under the stimulus of my love for Geneviève, I tried to free myself and did my utmost to persuade the two women whom I call mother. And then . . . and then! I was up against their complaints, their immediate hatred of the wife, of the stranger, whom I was proposing to force upon them . . . I gave way. What sort of a life would Geneviève have had here, between Madame d'Imbleval and Madame Vaurois? I had no right to victimize her."

Jean Louis, who had been gradually becoming excited, uttered these last words in a firm voice, as though he would have wished his conduct to be ascribed to conscientious motives and a sense of duty. In reality, as Rénine and Hortense clearly saw, his was an unusually weak nature, incapable of reacting against a ridiculous position from which he had suffered ever since he was a child and which he had come to look upon as final and irremediable. He endured it as a man bears a cross which he has no right to cast aside; and at the same time he was ashamed of it. He had never spoken of it to Geneviève, from dread of ridicule; and afterward, on returning to his prison, he had remained there out of habit and weakness.

He sat down to a writing-table and quickly wrote a letter which he handed to Rénine:

"Would you be kind enough to give this note to Mlle. Aymard and beg her once more to forgive me?"

Rénine did not move and, when the other pressed the letter upon him, he took it and tore it up.

"What does this mean?" asked the young man.

"It means that I will not charge myself with any message."

"Why?"

"Because you are coming with us."

"I?"

"Yes. You will see Mlle. Aymard to-morrow and ask for her hand in marriage."

Jean Louis looked at Rénine with a rather disdainful air, as though he were thinking:

"Here's a man who has not understood a word of what I've been explaining to him."

But Hortense went up to Rénine:

"Why do you say that?"

"Because it will be as I say."

"But you must have your reasons?"

"One only; but it will be enough, provided this gentleman is so kind as to help me in my enquiries."

"Enquiries? With what object?" asked the young man.

"With the object of proving that your story is not quite accurate."

Jean Louis took umbrage at this:

"I must ask you to believe, monsieur, that I have not said a word which is not the exact truth."

"I expressed myself badly," said Rénine, with great kindliness. "Certainly you have not said a word that does not agree with what you believe to be the exact truth. But the truth is not, cannot be what you believe it to be."

The young man folded his arms:

"In any case, monsieur, it seems likely that I should know the truth better than you do."

"Why better? What happened on that tragic night can obviously be known to you only at secondhand. You have no proofs. Neither have Madame d'Imbleval and Madame Vaurois."

"No proofs of what?" exclaimed Jean Louis, losing patience.

"No proofs of the confusion that took place."

"What! Why, it's an absolute certainty! The two children were laid in the same cradle, with no marks to distinguish one from the other; and the nurse was unable to tell . . ."

"At least, that's her version of it," interrupted Rénine.

"What's that? Her version? But you're accusing the woman."

"I'm accusing her of nothing."

"Yes, you are: you're accusing her of lying. And why should she lie? She had no interest in doing so; and her tears and despair are so much evidence of her good faith. For, after all, the two mothers were there... they saw the woman weeping... they questioned her... And then, I repeat, what interest had she...?"

Jean Louis was greatly excited. Close beside him, Madame d'Imbleval and Madame Vaurois, who had no doubt been listening behind the doors and who had stealthily entered the room, stood stammering, in amazement:

"No, no... it's impossible... We've questioned her over and over again. Why should she tell a lie?..."

"Speak, monsieur, speak," Jean Louis enjoined. "Explain yourself. Give your reasons for trying to cast doubt upon an absolute truth!"

"Because that truth is inadmissible," declared Rénine, raising his voice and growing excited in turn to the point of punctuating his remarks by thumping the table. "No, things don't happen like that. No, fate does not display those refinements of cruelty and chance is not added to chance with such reckless extravagance! It was already an unprecedented chance that, on the very night on which the doctor, his man-servant, and his maid were out of the house, the two ladies should be seized with labor-pains at the same hour and should bring two sons into the world at the same time. Don't let us add a still more exceptional event! Enough of the uncanny! Enough of lamps that go out and candles that refuse to burn! No and again no, it is not admissible that a midwife should become confused in the essential details of her trade. However bewildered she may be by the unforeseen nature of the circumstances, a remnant of instinct is still on the alert, so that there is a place prepared for each child and each is kept distinct from the other. The first child is here, the second is there. Even if they are lying side by side, one is on the left and the other on the right. Even if they are wrapped in the same kind of binders, some little detail differs, a trifle which is recorded by the memory and which is inevitably recalled to the mind without any need of reflection. Confusion? I refuse to believe in it. Impossible to tell one from the other? It isn't true. In the world of fiction, yes, one can imagine all sorts of fantastic accidents and heap contradiction on contradiction. But, in the world of reality, at the very heart of reality, there is always a fixed point, a solid nucleus, about which the facts group themselves in accordance with a logical order. I therefore declare most positively that Nurse Boussignol could not have mixed up the two children."

All this he said decisively, as though he had been present during the night in question; and so great was his power of persuasion that from the very first he shook the certainty of those who for more than a quarter of a century had never doubted.

The two women and their son pressed round him and questioned him with breathless anxiety:

"Then you think that she may know . . . that she may be able to tell us . . . ?"

He corrected himself:

"I don't say yes and I don't say no. All I say is that there was something in her behavior during those hours that does not tally with her statements and with reality. All the vast and intolerable mystery that has weighed down upon you three arises not from a momentary lack of attention but from something of which we do not know, but of which she does. That is what I maintain; and that is what happened."

Jean Louis said, in a husky voice:

"She is alive . . . She lives at Carhaix . . . We can send for her . . ."

Hortense at once proposed:

"Would you like me to go for her? I will take the motor and bring her back with me. Where does she live?"

"In the middle of the town, at a little draper's shop. The chauffeur will show you. Mlle. Boussignol: everybody knows her . . ."

"And, whatever you do," added Rénine, "don't warn her in any way. If she's uneasy, so much the better. But don't let her know what we want with her."

Twenty minutes passed in absolute silence. Rénine paced the room, in which the fine old furniture, the handsome tapestries, the well-bound books and pretty knick-knacks denoted a love of art and a seeking after style in Jean Louis. This room was really his. In the adjoining apartments on either side, through the open doors, Rénine was able to note the bad taste of the two mothers.

He went up to Jean Louis and, in a low voice, asked:

"Are they well off?"

"Yes."

"And you?"

"They settled the manor-house upon me, with all the land around it, which makes me quite independent."

"Have they any relations?"

"Sisters, both of them."

"With whom they could go to live?"

"Yes; and they have sometimes thought of doing so. But there can't be any question of that. Once more, I assure you . . ."

Meantime the car had returned. The two women jumped up hurriedly, ready to speak.

"Leave it to me," said Rénine, "and don't be surprised by anything that I say. It's not a matter of asking her questions but of frightening her, of flurrying her . . . The sudden attack," he added between his teeth.

The car drove round the lawn and drew up outside the windows. Hortense sprang out and helped an old woman to alight, dressed in a fluted linen cap, a black velvet bodice, and a heavy gathered skirt.

The old woman entered in a great state of alarm. She had a pointed face, like a weasel's, with a prominent mouth full of protruding teeth.

"What's the matter, Madame d'Imbleval?" she asked, timidly stepping into the room from which the doctor had once driven her. "Good day to you, Madame Vaurois."

The ladies did not reply. Rénine came forward and said, sternly:

"Mlle. Boussignol, I have been sent by the Paris police to throw light upon a tragedy which took place here twenty-seven years ago. I have just secured evidence that you have distorted the truth and that, as the result of your false declarations, the birth-certificate of one of the children born in the course of that night is inaccurate. Now false declarations in matters of birth-certificates are misdemeanors punishable by law. I shall therefore be obliged to take you to Paris to be interrogated . . . unless you are prepared here and now to confess everything that might repair the consequences of your offense."

The old maid was shaking in every limb. Her teeth were chattering. She was evidently incapable of opposing the least resistance to Rénine.

"Are you ready to confess everything?" he asked.

"Yes," she panted.

"Without delay? I have to catch a train. The business must be settled immediately. If you show the least hesitation, I take you with me. Have you made up your mind to speak?"

"Yes."

He pointed to Jean Louis:

"Whose son is this gentleman? Madame d'Imbleval's?"

"No."

"Madame Vaurois's, therefore?"

"No."

A stupefied silence welcomed the two replies.

"Explain yourself," Rénine commanded, looking at his watch.

Then Madame Boussignol fell on her knees and said, in so low and dull a voice that they had to bend over her in order to catch the sense of what she was mumbling:

"Someone came in the evening . . . a gentleman with a new-born baby wrapped in blankets, which he wanted the doctor to look after. As the doctor wasn't there, he waited all night and it was he who did it all."

"Did what?" asked Rénine. "What did he do? What happened?"

"Well, what happened was that it was not one child but the two of them that died: Madame d'Imbleval's and Madame Vaurois's too, both in convulsions. Then the gentleman, seeing this, said, 'This shows me where my duty lies. I must seize this opportunity of making sure that my own boy shall be happy and well cared for. Put him in the place of one of the dead children.' He offered me a big sum of money, saying that this one payment would save him the expense of providing for his child every month; and I accepted. Only, I did not know in whose place to put him and whether to say that the boy was Louis d'Imbleval or Jean Vaurois. The gentleman thought a moment and said neither. Then he explained to me what I was to do and what I was to say after he had gone. And, while I was dressing his boy in vest and binders the same as one of the dead children, he wrapped the other in the blankets he had brought with him and went out into the night."

Mlle. Boussignol bent her head and wept. After a moment, Rénine said:

"Your deposition agrees with the result of my investigations."

"Can I go?"

"Yes."

"And is it over, as far as I'm concerned? They won't be talking about this all over the district?"

"No. Oh, just one more question: do you know the man's name?"

"No. He didn't tell me his name."

"Have you ever seen him since?"

"Never."

"Have you anything more to say?"

"No."

"Are you prepared to sign the written text of your confession?"

"Yes."

"Very well. I shall send for you in a week or two. Till then, not a word to anybody."

He saw her to the door and closed it after her. When he returned, Jean Louis was between the two old ladies and all three were holding hands. The bond of hatred and wretchedness which had bound them had suddenly snapped; and this rupture, without requiring them to reflect upon the matter, filled them with a gentle tranquility of which they were hardly conscious, but which made them serious and thoughtful.

"Let's rush things," said Rénine to Hortense. "This is the decisive moment of the battle. We must get Jean Louis on board."

Hortense seemed preoccupied. She whispered:

"Why did you let the woman go? Were you satisfied with her statement?"

"I don't need to be satisfied. She told us what happened. What more do you want?"

"Nothing ... I don't know ..."

"We'll talk about it later, my dear. For the moment, I repeat, we must get Jean Louis on board. And immediately ... Otherwise ..."

He turned to the young man:

"You agree with me, don't you, that, things being as they are, it is best for you and Madame Vaurois and Madame d'Imbleval to separate for a time? That will enable you all to see matters more clearly and to decide in perfect freedom what is to be done. Come with us, monsieur. The most pressing thing is to save Geneviève Aymard, your *fiancée*."

Jean Louis stood perplexed and undecided. Rénine turned to the two women:

"That is your opinion too, I am sure, ladies?"

They nodded.

"You see, monsieur," he said to Jean Louis, "we are all agreed. In great crises, there is nothing like separation . . . a few days' respite. Quickly now, monsieur."

And, without giving him time to hesitate, he drove him towards his bedroom to pack up.

Half an hour later, Jean Louis left the manor-house with his new friends.

"And he won't go back until he's married," said Rénine to Hortense, as they were waiting at Carhaix station, to which the car had taken them, while Jean Louis was attending to his luggage. "Everything's for the best. Are you satisfied?"

"Yes, Geneviève will be glad," she replied, absently.

When they had taken their seats in the train, Rénine and she repaired to the dining-car. Rénine, who had asked Hortense several questions to which she had replied only in monosyllables, protested:

"What's the matter with you, my child? You look worried!"

"I? Not at all!"

"Yes, yes, I know you. Now, no secrets, no mysteries!"

She smiled:

"Well, since you insist on knowing if I am satisfied, I am bound to admit that of course I am . . . as regards my friend Geneviève, but that, in another respect—from the point of view of the adventure—I have an uncomfortable sort of feeling . . ."

"To speak frankly, I haven't 'staggered' you this time?"

"Not very much."

"I seem to you to have played a secondary part. For, after all, what have I done? We arrived. We listened to Jean Louis's tale of woe. I had a midwife fetched. And that was all."

"Exactly. I want to know if that *was* all; and I'm not quite sure. To tell you the truth, our other adventures left behind them an impression which was—how shall I put it?—more definite, clearer."

"And this one strikes you as obscure?"

"Obscure, yes, and incomplete."

"But in what way?"

"I don't know. Perhaps it has something to do with that woman's confession. Yes, very likely that is it. It was all so unexpected and so short."

"Well, of course, I cut it short, as you can readily imagine!" said Rénine, laughing. "We didn't want too many explanations."

"What do you mean?"

"Why, if she had given her explanations with too much detail, we should have ended by doubting what she was telling us."

"By doubting it?"

"Well, hang it all, the story is a trifle far-fetched! That fellow arriving at night, with a live baby in his pocket, and going away with a dead one: the thing hardly holds water. But you see, my dear, I hadn't much time to coach the unfortunate woman in her part."

Hortense stared at him in amazement:

"What on earth do you mean?"

"Well, you know how dull-witted these countrywomen are. And she and I had no time to spare. So we worked out a little scene in a hurry... and she really didn't act it so badly. It was all in the right key: terror, *tremolo*, tears..."

"Is it possible?" murmured Hortense. "Is it possible? You had seen her beforehand?"

"I had to, of course."

"But when?"

"This morning, when we arrived. While you were titivating yourself at the hotel at Carhaix, I was running round to see what information I could pick up. As you may imagine, everybody in the district knows the d'Imbleval-Vaurois story. I was at once directed to the former midwife, Mlle. Boussignol. With Mlle. Boussignol it did not take long. Three minutes to settle a new version of what had happened and ten thousand francs to induce her to repeat that... more or less credible... version to the people at the manor-house."

"A quite incredible version!"

"Not so bad as all that, my child, seeing that you believed it... and the others too. And that was the essential thing. What I had to do was to demolish at one blow a truth which had been twenty-seven years in existence and which was all the more firmly established because it was founded on actual facts. That was why I went for it with all my might and attacked it by sheer force of eloquence. Impossible to identify the children? I deny it. Inevitable confusion? It's not true. 'You're all three,' I say, 'the victims of something which I don't know but which it is your duty to clear up!' 'That's easily done,' says Jean Louis, whose conviction is at once shaken. 'Let's send for Mlle. Boussignol.' 'Right! Let's send for her.' Whereupon Mlle. Boussignol arrives and mumbles out the little speech which I have taught her. Sensation! General stupefaction . . . of which I take advantage to carry off our young man!"

Hortense shook her head:

"But they'll get over it, all three of them, on thinking!"

"Never! Never! They will have their doubts, perhaps. But they will never consent to feel certain! They will never agree to think! Use your imagination! Here are three people whom I have rescued from the hell in which they have been floundering for a quarter of a century. Do you think they're going back to it? Here are three people who, from weakness or a false sense of duty, had not the courage to escape. Do you think that they won't cling like grim death to the liberty which I'm giving them? Nonsense! Why, they would have swallowed a hoax twice as difficult to digest as that which Mlle. Boussignol dished up for them! After all, my version was no more absurd than the truth. On the contrary. And they swallowed it whole! Look at this: before we left, I heard Madame d'Imbleval and Madame Vaurois speak of an immediate removal. They were already becoming quite affectionate at the thought of seeing the last of each other."

"But what about Jean Louis?"

"Jean Louis? Why, he was fed up with his two mothers! By Jingo, one can't do with two mothers in a life-time! What a situation! And when one has the luck to be able to choose between having two mothers or none at all, why, bless me, one doesn't hesitate! And, besides, Jean Louis is in love with Geneviève." He laughed. "And he loves her well enough, I hope and trust, not to inflict two mothers-in-law upon her! Come, you may be easy in your mind. Your friend's happiness is assured; and that is all you asked for. All that matters is the object which we achieve and not the more or less peculiar nature of the methods which we employ. And, if some adventures are wound up and some mysteries elucidated by looking for and finding cigarette-ends, or incendiary water-bottles and blazing hat-boxes as on our last expedition, others call for psychology and for purely psychological solutions. I have spoken. And I charge you to be silent."

"Silent?"

"Yes, there's a man and woman sitting behind us who seem to be saying something uncommonly interesting."

"But they're talking in whispers."

"Just so. When people talk in whispers, it's always about something shady."

He lit a cigarette and sat back in his chair. Hortense listened, but in vain. As for him, he was emitting little slow puffs of smoke.

Fifteen minutes later, the train stopped and the man and woman got out.

"Pity," said Rénine, "that I don't know their names or where they're going. But I know where to find them. My dear, we have a new adventure before us."

Hortense protested:

"Oh, no, please, not yet! . . . Give me a little rest! . . . And oughtn't we to think of Geneviève?"

He seemed greatly surprised:

"Why, all that's over and done with! Do you mean to say you want to waste any more time over that old story? Well, I for my part confess that I've lost all interest in the man with the two mammas."

And this was said in such a comical tone and with such diverting sincerity that Hortense was once more seized with a fit of giggling. Laughter alone was able to relax her exasperated nerves and to distract her from so many contradictory emotions.

THÉRÈSE AND GERMAINE

The weather was so mild that autumn that, on the 12th of October, in the morning, several families still lingering in their villas at Étretat had gone down to the beach. The sea, lying between the cliffs and the clouds on the horizon, might have suggested a mountain-lake slumbering in the hollow of the enclosing rocks, were it not for that crispness in the air and those pale, soft and indefinite colors in the sky which give a special charm to certain days in Normandy.

"It's delicious," murmured Hortense. But the next moment she added: "All the same, we did not come here to enjoy the spectacle of nature or to wonder whether that huge stone Needle on our left was really at one time the home of Arsène Lupin."

"We came here," said Prince Rénine, "because of the conversation which I overheard, a fortnight ago, in a dining-car, between a man and a woman."

"A conversation of which I was unable to catch a single word."

"If those two people could have guessed for an instant that it was possible to hear a single word of what they were saying, they would not have spoken, for their conversation was one of extraordinary gravity and importance. But I have very sharp ears; and though I could not follow every sentence, I insist that we may be certain of two things. First, that man and woman, who are brother and sister, have an appointment at a quarter to twelve this morning, the 12th of October, at the spot known as the Trois Mathildes, with a third person, who is married and who wishes at all costs to recover his or her liberty. Secondly, this appointment, at which they will come to a final agreement, is to be followed this evening by a walk along the cliffs, when the third person will bring with him or her the man or woman, I can't definitely say which, whom they want to get rid of. That is the gist of the whole thing. Now, as I know a spot called the Trois Mathildes some way above Étretat and as this is not an everyday name, we came down yesterday to thwart the plan of these objectionable persons."

"What plan?" asked Hortense. "For, after all, it's only your assumption that there's to be a victim and that the victim is to be flung off the top of the cliffs. You yourself told me that you heard no allusion to a possible murder."

"That is so. But I heard some very plain words relating to the marriage of the brother or the sister with the wife or the husband of the third person, which implies the need for a crime."

They were sitting on the terrace of the casino, facing the stairs which run down to the beach. They therefore overlooked the few privately-owned cabins on the shingle, where a party of four men were playing bridge, while a group of ladies sat talking and knitting.

A short distance away and nearer to the sea was another cabin, standing by itself and closed.

Half-a-dozen bare-legged children were paddling in the water.

"No," said Hortense, "all this autumnal sweetness and charm fails to attract me. I have so much faith in all your theories that I can't help thinking, in spite of everything, of this dreadful problem. Which of those people yonder is threatened? Death has already selected its victim. Who is it? Is it that young, fair haired woman, rocking herself and laughing? Is it that tall man over there, smoking his cigar? And which of them has the thought of murder hidden in his heart? All the people we see are quietly enjoying themselves. Yet death is prowling among them."

"Capital!" said Rénine. "You too are becoming enthusiastic. What did I tell you? The whole of life's an adventure; and nothing but adventure is worth while. At the first breath of coming events, there you are, quivering in every nerve. You share in all the tragedies stirring around you; and the feeling of mystery awakens in the depths of your being. See, how closely you are observing that couple who have just arrived. You never can tell: that may be the gentleman who proposes to do away with his wife? Or perhaps the lady contemplates making away with her husband?"

"The d'Ormevals? Never! A perfectly happy couple! Yesterday, at the hotel, I had a long talk with the wife. And you yourself . . ."

"Oh, I played a round of golf with Jacques d'Ormeval, who rather fancies himself as an athlete, and I played at dolls with their two charming little girls!"

The d'Ormevals came up and exchanged a few words with them. Madame d'Ormeval said that her two daughters had gone back to Paris that morning with their governess. Her husband, a great tall fellow with a yellow beard, carrying his blazer over his arm and puffing out his chest under a cellular shirt, complained of the heat:

"Have you the key of the cabin, Thérèse?" he asked his wife, when they had left Rénine and Hortense and stopped at the top of the stairs, a few yards away.

"Here it is," said the wife. "Are you going to read your papers?"

"Yes. Unless we go for a stroll? . . ."

"I had rather wait till the afternoon: do you mind? I have a lot of letters to write this morning."

"Very well. We'll go on the cliff."

Hortense and Rénine exchanged a glance of surprise. Was this suggestion accidental? Or had they before them, contrary to their expectations, the very couple of whom they were in search?

Hortense tried to laugh:

"My heart is thumping," she said. "Nevertheless, I absolutely refuse to believe in anything so improbable. 'My husband and I have never had the slightest quarrel,' she said to me. No, it's quite clear that those two get on admirably."

"We shall see presently, at the Trois Mathildes, if one of them comes to meet the brother and sister."

M. d'Ormeval had gone down the stairs, while his wife stood

leaning on the balustrade of the terrace. She had a beautiful, slender, supple figure. Her clear-cut profile was emphasized by a rather too prominent chin when at rest; and, when it was not smiling, the face gave an expression of sadness and suffering.

"Have you lost something, Jacques?" she called out to her husband, who was stooping over the shingle.

"Yes, the key," he said. "It slipped out of my hand."

She went down to him and began to look also. For two or three minutes, as they sheered off to the right and remained close to the bottom of the under-cliff, they were invisible to Hortense and Rénine. Their voices were covered by the noise of a dispute which had arisen among the bridge-players.

They reappeared almost simultaneously. Madame d'Ormeval slowly climbed a few steps of the stairs and then stopped and turned her face towards the sea. Her husband had thrown his blazer over his shoulders and was making for the isolated cabin. As he passed the bridge-players, they asked him for a decision, pointing to their cards spread out upon the table. But, with a wave of the hand, he refused to give an opinion and walked on, covered the thirty yards which divided them from the cabin, opened the door and went in.

Thérèse d'Ormeval came back to the terrace and remained for ten minutes sitting on a bench. Then she came out through the casino. Hortense, on leaning forward, saw her entering one of the chalets annexed to the Hôtel Hauville and, a moment later, caught sight of her again on the balcony.

"Eleven o'clock," said Rénine. "Whoever it is, he or she, or one of the card-players, or one of their wives, it won't be long before someone goes to the appointed place."

Nevertheless, twenty minutes passed and twenty-five; and no one stirred.

"Perhaps Madame d'Ormeval has gone." Hortense suggested, anxiously. "She is no longer on her balcony."

"If she is at the Trois Mathildes," said Rénine, "we will go and catch her there."

He was rising to his feet, when a fresh discussion broke out among the bridge-players and one of them exclaimed:

"Let's put it to d'Ormeval."

"Very well," said his adversary. "I'll accept his decision . . . if he consents to act as umpire. He was rather huffy just now."

They called out:

"D'Ormeval! D'Ormeval!"

They then saw that d'Ormeval must have shut the door behind him, which kept him in the half dark, the cabin being one of the sort that has no window.

"He's asleep," cried one. "Let's wake him up."

All four went to the cabin, began by calling to him and, on receiving no answer, thumped on the door:

"Hi! D'Ormeval! Are you asleep?"

On the terrace Serge Rénine suddenly leapt to his feet with so uneasy an air that Hortense was astonished. He muttered:

"If only it's not too late!"

And, when Hortense asked him what he meant, he tore down the steps and started running to the cabin. He reached it just as the bridge-players were trying to break in the door:

"Stop!" he ordered. "Things must be done in the regular fashion."

"What things?" they asked.

He examined the Venetian shutters at the top of each of the folding-doors and, on finding that one of the upper slats was partly broken, hung on as best he could to the roof of the cabin and cast a glance inside. Then he said to the four men:

"I was right in thinking that, if M. d'Ormeval did not reply, he must have been prevented by some serious cause. There is every reason to believe that M. d'Ormeval is wounded . . . or dead."

"Dead!" they cried. "What do you mean? He has only just left us."

Rénine took out his knife, prized open the lock and pulled back the two doors.

There were shouts of dismay. M. d'Ormeval was lying flat on his face, clutching his jacket and his newspaper in his hands. Blood was flowing from his back and staining his shirt.

"Oh!" said someone. "He has killed himself!"

"How can he have killed himself?" said Rénine. "The wound is right in the middle of the back, at a place which the hand can't reach. And, besides, there's not a knife in the cabin."

The others protested:

"If so, he has been murdered. But that's impossible! There has been nobody here. We should have seen, if there had been. Nobody could have passed us without our seeing..."

The other men, all the ladies and the children paddling in the sea had come running up. Rénine allowed no one to enter the cabin, except a doctor who was present. But the doctor could only say that M. d'Ormeval was dead, stabbed with a dagger.

At that moment, the mayor and the policeman arrived, together with some people of the village. After the usual enquiries, they carried away the body.

A few persons went on ahead to break the news to Thérèse d'Ormeval, who was once more to be seen on her balcony.

||||||||||||||||||||||||||||

And so the tragedy had taken place without any clue to explain how a man, protected by a closed door with an uninjured lock, could have been murdered in the space of a few minutes and in front of twenty witnesses, one might almost say, twenty spectators. No one had entered the cabin. No one had come out of it. As for the dagger with which M. d'Ormeval had been stabbed between the shoulders, it could not be traced. And all this would have suggested the idea of a trick of sleight-of-hand performed by a clever conjuror, had it not concerned a terrible murder, committed under the most mysterious conditions.

Hortense was unable to follow, as Rénine would have liked, the small party who were making for Madame d'Ormeval; she was paralyzed with excitement and incapable of moving. It was the first time that her adventures with Rénine had taken her into the very heart of the action and that, instead of noting the consequences of a murder, or assisting in the pursuit of the criminals, she found herself confronted with the murder itself.

It left her trembling all over; and she stammered: "How horrible!... The poor fellow!... Ah, Rénine, you couldn't save him this time!... And that's what upsets me more than anything, that we could and should have saved him, since we knew of the plot..."

Rénine made her sniff at a bottle of salts; and when she had quite recovered her composure, he said, while observing her attentively:

"So you think that there is some connection between the murder and the plot which we were trying to frustrate?"

"Certainly," said she, astonished at the question.

"Then, as that plot was hatched by a husband against his wife or by a wife against her husband, you admit that Madame d'Ormeval . . . ?"

"Oh, no, impossible!" she said. "To begin with, Madame d'Ormeval did not leave her rooms . . . and then I shall never believe that pretty woman capable . . . No, no, of course there was something else . . ."

"What else?"

"I don't know . . . You may have misunderstood what the brother and sister were saying to each other . . . You see, the murder has been committed under quite different conditions . . . at another hour and another place . . ."

"And therefore," concluded Rénine, "the two cases are not in any way related?"

"Oh," she said, "there's no making it out! It's all so strange!"

Rénine became a little satirical:

"My pupil is doing me no credit to-day," he said. "Why, here is a perfectly simple story, unfolded before your eyes. You have seen it reeled off like a scene in the cinema; and it all remains as obscure to you as though you were hearing of an affair that happened in a cave a hundred miles away!"

Hortense was confounded:

"What are you saying? Do you mean that you have understood it? What clues have you to go by?"

Rénine looked at his watch:

"I have not understood everything," he said. "The murder itself, the mere brutal murder, yes. But the essential thing, that is to say, the psychology of the crime: I've no clue to that. Only, it is twelve o'clock. The brother and sister, seeing no one come to the appointment at the Trois Mathildes, will go down to the beach. Don't you think that we shall learn something then of the accomplice whom I accuse them of having and of the connection between the two cases?"

They reached the esplanade in front of the Hauville chalets, with the capstans by which the fishermen haul up their boats to the beach. A number of inquisitive persons were standing outside the door of one of the chalets. Two coastguards, posted at the door, prevented them from entering.

The mayor shouldered his way eagerly through the crowd. He was back from the post-office, where he had been telephoning to Le Havre, to the office of the procurator-general, and had been told that the public prosecutor and an examining-magistrate would come on to Étretat in the course of the afternoon.

"That leaves us plenty of time for lunch," said Rénine. "The tragedy will not be enacted before two or three o'clock. And I have an idea that it will be sensational."

They hurried nevertheless. Hortense, overwrought by fatigue and her desire to know what was happening, continually questioned Rénine, who replied evasively, with his eyes turned to the esplanade, which they could see through the windows of the coffee-room.

"Are you watching for those two?" asked Hortense.

"Yes, the brother and sister."

"Are you sure that they will venture? . . ."

"Look out! Here they come!"

He went out quickly.

Where the main street opened on the sea-front, a lady and gentleman were advancing with hesitating steps, as though unfamiliar with the place. The brother was a puny little man, with a sallow complexion. He was wearing a motoring-cap. The sister too was short, but rather stout, and was wrapped in a large cloak. She struck them as a woman of a certain age, but still good-looking under the thin veil that covered her face.

They saw the groups of bystanders and drew nearer. Their gait betrayed uneasiness and hesitation.

The sister asked a question of a seaman. At the first words of his answer, which no doubt conveyed the news of d'Ormeval's death, she uttered a cry and tried to force her way through the crowd. The brother, learning in his turn what had happened, made great play with his elbows and shouted to the coast-guards:

"I'm a friend of d'Ormeval's! . . . Here's my card! Frédéric Astaing . . . My sister, Germaine Astaing, knows Madame d'Ormeval intimately! . . . They were expecting us . . . We had an appointment! . . ."

They were allowed to pass. Rénine, who had slipped behind them, followed them in without a word, accompanied by Hortense.

The d'Ormevals had four bedrooms and a sitting-room on the second floor. The sister rushed into one of the rooms and threw herself on her knees beside the bed on which the corpse lay stretched. Thérèse d'Ormeval was in the sitting-room and was sobbing in the midst of a small company of silent persons. The brother sat down beside her, eagerly seized her hands, and said, in a trembling voice:

"My poor friend! . . . My poor friend! . . ."

Rénine and Hortense gazed at the pair of them: and Hortense whispered:

"And she's supposed to have killed him for that? Impossible!"

"Nevertheless," observed Rénine, "they are acquaintances; and we know that Astaing and his sister were also acquainted with a third person who was their accomplice. So that . . ."

"It's impossible!" Hortense repeated.

And, in spite of all presumption, she felt so much attracted by Thérèse that, when Frédéric Astaing stood up, she proceeded straightway to sit down beside her and consoled her in a gentle voice. The unhappy woman's tears distressed her profoundly.

Rénine, on the other hand, applied himself from the outset to watching the brother and sister, as though this were the only thing that mattered, and did not take his eyes off Frédéric Astaing, who, with an air of indifference, began to make a minute inspection of the premises, examining the sitting-room, going into all the bedrooms, mingling with the various groups of persons present and asking questions about the manner in which the murder had been committed. Twice his sister came up and spoke to him. Then he went back to Madame d'Ormeval and again sat down beside her, full of earnest sympathy. Lastly, in the lobby, he had a long conversation with his sister, after which they parted, like people who have come to a perfect understanding. Frédéric then left. These maneuvers had lasted quite thirty or forty minutes.

It was at this moment that the motor-car containing the examining-magistrate and the public prosecutor pulled up outside the chalets. Rénine, who did not expect them until later, said to Hortense:

"We must be quick. On no account leave Madame d'Ormeval."

Word was sent up to the persons whose evidence might be of any service that they were to go to the beach, where the magistrate was beginning a preliminary investigation. He would call on Madame

d'Ormeval afterward. Accordingly, all who were present left the chalet. No one remained behind except the two guards and Germaine
Astaing.

Germaine knelt down for the last time beside the dead man and,
bending low, with her face in her hands, prayed for a long time. Then
she rose and was opening the door on the landing, when Rénine came
forward:

"I should like a few words with you, madame."

She seemed surprised and replied:

"What is it, monsieur? I am listening."

"Not here."

"Where then, monsieur?"

"Next door, in the sitting-room."

"No," she said, sharply.

"Why not? Though you did not even shake hands with her, I presume that Madame d'Ormeval is your friend?"

He gave her no time to reflect, drew her into the next room, closed
the door and, at once pouncing upon Madame d'Ormeval, who was
trying to go out and return to her own room, said:

"No, madame, listen, I implore you. Madame Astaing's presence
need not drive you away. We have very serious matters to discuss,
without losing a minute."

The two women, standing face to face, were looking at each other
with the same expression of implacable hatred, in which might be
read the same confusion of spirit and the same restrained anger.
Hortense, who believed them to be friends and who might, up to a
certain point, have believed them to be accomplices, foresaw with
terror the hostile encounter which she felt to be inevitable. She compelled Madame d'Ormeval to resume her seat, while Rénine took up
his position in the middle of the room and spoke in resolute tones:

"Chance, which has placed me in possession of part of the truth,
will enable me to save you both, if you are willing to assist me with a
frank explanation that will give me the particulars which I still need.
Each of you knows the danger in which she stands, because each of
you is conscious in her heart of the evil for which she is responsible.
But you are carried away by hatred; and it is for me to see clearly and
to act. The examining-magistrate will be here in half an hour. By that
time, you must have come to an agreement."

They both started, as though offended by such a word.

"Yes, an agreement," he repeated, in a more imperious tone. "Whether you like it or not, you will come to an agreement. You are not the only ones to be considered. There are your two little daughters, Madame d'Ormeval. Since circumstances have set me in their path, I am intervening in their defense and for their safety. A blunder, a word too much; and they are ruined. That must not happen."

At the mention of her children, Madame d'Ormeval broke down and sobbed. Germaine Astaing shrugged her shoulders and made a movement towards the door. Rénine once more blocked the way:

"Where are you going?"

"I have been summoned by the examining-magistrate."

"No, you have not."

"Yes, I have. Just as all those have been who have any evidence to give."

"You were not on the spot. You know nothing of what happened. Nobody knows anything of the murder."

"I know who committed it."

"That's impossible."

"It was Thérèse d'Ormeval."

The accusation was hurled forth in an outburst of rage and with a fiercely threatening gesture.

"You wretched creature!" exclaimed Madame d'Ormeval, rushing at her. "Go! Leave the room! Oh, what a wretch the woman is!"

Hortense was trying to restrain her, but Rénine whispered:

"Let them be. It's what I wanted . . . to pitch them one against the other and so to let in the day-light."

Madame Astaing had made a convulsive effort to ward off the insult with a jest; and she sniggered:

"A wretched creature? Why? Because I have accused you?"

"Why? For every reason! You're a wretched creature! You hear what I say, Germaine: you're a wretch!"

Thérèse d'Ormeval was repeating the insult as though it afforded her some relief. Her anger was abating. Very likely also she no longer had the strength to keep up the struggle; and it was Madame Astaing who returned to the attack, with her fists clenched and her face distorted and suddenly aged by fully twenty years:

"You! You dare to insult me, you! You after the murder you have committed! You dare to lift up your head when the man whom you killed is lying in there on his death-bed! Ah, if one of us is a wretched creature, it's you, Thérèse, and you know it! You have killed your husband! You have killed your husband!"

She leapt forward, in the excitement of the terrible words which she was uttering; and her finger-nails were almost touching her friend's face.

"Oh, don't tell me you didn't kill him!" she cried. "Don't say that: I won't let you. Don't say it. The dagger is there, in your bag. My brother felt it, while he was talking to you; and his hand came out with stains of blood upon it: your husband's blood, Thérèse. And then, even if I had not discovered anything, do you think that I should not have guessed, in the first few minutes? Why, I knew the truth at once, Thérèse! When a sailor down there answered, 'M. d'Ormeval? He has been murdered,' I said to myself then and there, 'It's she, it's Thérèse, she killed him.'"

Thérèse did not reply. She had abandoned her attitude of protest. Hortense, who was watching her with anguish, thought that she could perceive in her the despondency of those who know themselves to be lost. Her cheeks had fallen in and she wore such an expression of despair that Hortense, moved to compassion, implored her to defend herself:

"Please, please, explain things. When the murder was committed, you were here, on the balcony . . . But then the dagger . . . how did you come to have it . . . ? How do you explain it? . . ."

"Explanations!" sneered Germaine Astaing. "How could she possibly explain? What do outward appearances matter? What does it matter what anyone saw or did not see? The proof is the thing that tells . . . The dagger is there, in your bag, Thérèse: that's a fact . . . Yes, yes, it was you who did it! You killed him! You killed him in the end! . . . Ah, how often I've told my brother, 'She will kill him yet!' Frédéric used to try to defend you. He always had a weakness for you. But in his innermost heart he foresaw what would happen . . . And now the horrible thing has been done. A stab in the back! Coward! Coward! . . . And you would have me say nothing? Why, I didn't hesitate a moment! Nor did Frédéric. We looked for proofs at once . . . And I've denounced you of my own free will, perfectly well aware of what I was doing . . . And it's over, Thérèse. You're done for. Nothing can save you now. The dagger is in that bag which you are clutching in your hand. The magistrate is coming; and the dagger will be found, stained with the blood of your husband. So will your pocket-book They're both there. And they will be found . . ."

Her rage had incensed her so vehemently that she was unable to continue and stood with her hand outstretched and her chin twitching with nervous tremors.

Rénine gently took hold of Madame d'Ormeval's bag. She clung to it, but he insisted and said:

"Please allow me, madame. Your friend Germaine is right. The examining-magistrate will be here presently; and the fact that the dagger and the pocket-book are in your possession will lead to your immediate arrest. This must not happen. Please allow me."

His insinuating voice diminished Thérèse d'Ormeval's resistance. She released her fingers, one by one. He took the bag, opened it, produced a little dagger with an ebony handle and a grey leather pocket-book and quietly slipped the two into the inside pocket of his jacket.

Germaine Astaing gazed at him in amazement: "You're mad, monsieur! What right have you . . . ?"

"These things must not be left lying about. I sha'n't worry now. The magistrate will never look for them in my pocket."

"But I shall denounce you to the police," she exclaimed, indignantly. "They shall be told!"

"No, no," he said, laughing, "you won't say anything! The police have nothing to do with this. The quarrel between you must be settled in private. What an idea, to go dragging the police into every incident of one's life!"

Madame Astaing was choking with fury:

"But you have no right to talk like this, monsieur! Who are you, after all? A friend of that woman's?"

"Since you have been attacking her, yes."

"But I'm only attacking her because she's guilty. For you can't deny it: she has killed her husband."

"I don't deny it," said Rénine, calmly. "We are all agreed on that point. Jacques d'Ormeval was killed by his wife. But, I repeat, the police must not know the truth."

"They shall know it through me, monsieur, I swear they shall. That woman must be punished: she has committed murder."

Rénine went up to her and, touching her on the shoulder:

"You asked me just now by what right I was interfering. And you yourself, madame?"

"I was a friend of Jacques d'Ormeval."

"Only a friend?"

She was a little taken aback, but at once pulled herself together and replied:

"I was his friend and it is my duty to avenge his death."

"Nevertheless, you will remain silent, as he did."

"He did not know, when he died."

"That's where you are wrong. He could have accused his wife, if he had wished. He had ample time to accuse her; and he said nothing."

"Why?"

"Because of his children."

Madame Astaing was not appeased; and her attitude displayed the same longing for revenge and the same detestation. But she was influenced by Rénine in spite of herself. In the small, closed room, where there was such a clash of hatred, he was gradually becoming the master; and Germaine Astaing understood that it was against him that she had to struggle, while Madame d'Ormeval felt all the comfort of that unexpected support which was offering itself on the brink of the abyss:

"Thank you, monsieur," she said. "As you have seen all this so clearly, you also know that it was for my children's sake that I did not give myself up. But for that . . . I am so tired . . . !"

And so the scene was changing and things assuming a different aspect. Thanks to a few words let fall in the midst of the dispute, the culprit was lifting her head and taking heart, whereas her accuser was hesitating and seemed to be uneasy. And it also came about that the accuser dared not say anything further and that the culprit was nearing the moment at which the need is felt of breaking silence and of speaking, quite naturally, words that are at once a confession and a relief.

"The time, I think, has come," said Rénine to Thérèse, with the same unvarying gentleness, "when you can and ought to explain yourself."

She was again weeping, lying huddled in a chair. She too revealed a face aged and ravaged by sorrow; and, in a very low voice, with no display of anger, she spoke, in short, broken sentences:

"She has been his mistress for the last four years . . . I can't tell you how I suffered . . . She herself told me of it . . . out of sheer wickedness . . . Her loathing for me was even greater than her love for Jacques . . . and every day I had some fresh injury to bear . . . She would ring me up to tell me of her appointments with my husband . . . she hoped to make me suffer so much I should end by killing myself . . . I did think of it sometimes, but I held out, for the children's sake . . . Jacques was weakening. She wanted him to get a divorce . . . and little by little he began to consent . . . dominated by her and by her brother, who is slyer than she is, but quite as dangerous . . . I felt all this . . . Jacques was becoming harsh to me . . . He had not the courage to leave me, but I was the obstacle and he bore me a grudge . . . Heavens, the tortures I suffered! . . ."

"You should have given him his liberty," cried Germaine Astaing. "A woman doesn't kill her husband for wanting a divorce."

Thérèse shook her head and answered:

"I did not kill him because he wanted a divorce. If he had really wanted it, he would have left me; and what could I have done? But your plans had changed, Germaine; divorce was not enough for you; and it was something else that you would have obtained from him, another, much more serious thing which you and your brother had insisted on . . . and to which he had consented . . . out of cowardice . . . in spite of himself . . ."

"What do you mean?" spluttered Germaine. "What other thing?"

"My death."

"You lie!" cried Madame Astaing.

Thérèse did not raise her voice. She made not a movement of aversion or indignation and simply repeated:

"My death, Germaine. I have read your latest letters, six letters from you which he was foolish enough to leave about in his pocket-book and which I read last night, six letters in which the terrible word is not set down, but in which it appears between every line. I trembled as I read it! That Jacques should come to this! . . . Nevertheless the idea of stabbing him did not occur to me for a second. A woman like myself, Germaine, does not readily commit murder . . . If I lost my head, it was after that . . . and it was your fault . . ."

She turned her eyes to Rénine as if to ask him if there was no danger in her speaking and revealing the truth.

"Don't be afraid," he said. "I will be answerable for everything."

She drew her hand across her forehead. The horrible scene was being reenacted within her and was torturing her. Germaine Astaing did not move, but stood with folded arms and anxious eyes, while Hortense Daniel sat distractedly awaiting the confession of the crime and the explanation of the unfathomable mystery.

"It was after that and it was through your fault Germaine . . . I had put back the pocket-book in the drawer where it was hidden; and I said nothing to Jacques this morning . . . I did not want to tell him what I knew . . . It was too horrible . . . All the same, I had to act quickly; your letters announced your secret arrival to-day . . . I thought at first of running away, of taking the train . . . I had mechanically picked up that dagger, to defend myself . . . But when Jacques and I went down to the beach, I was resigned . . . Yes, I had accepted death: 'I will die,' I thought, 'and put an end to all this nightmare!' . . . Only, for the children's sake, I was anxious that my death should look like an accident and that Jacques should have no part in it. That was why your plan of a walk on the cliff suited me . . . A fall from the top of a cliff seems quite natural . . . Jacques therefore left me to go to his cabin, from which he was to join you later at the Trois Mathildes. On the way, below the terrace, he dropped the key of the cabin. I went down and began to look for it with him . . . And it happened then . . . through your fault . . . yes, Germaine, through your fault . . . Jacques's pocket-book had slipped from his jacket, without his noticing it, and, together with the pocket-book, a photograph which I recognized at once: a photograph, taken this year, of myself and my two children. I picked it up . . . and I saw . . . You know what I saw, Germaine. Instead of my face, the face in the photograph was *yours*! . . . You had put in your likeness, Germaine, and blotted me out! It was your face! One of your arms was round my elder daughter's neck; and the younger was sitting on your knees . . . It was you, Germaine, the wife of my husband, the future mother of my children, you, who were going to bring them up . . . you, you! . . . Then I lost my head. I had the dagger . . . Jacques was stooping . . . I stabbed him . . ."

Every word of her confession was strictly true. Those who listened to her felt this profoundly; and nothing could have given Hortense and Rénine a keener impression of tragedy.

She had fallen back into her chair, utterly exhausted. Nevertheless, she went on speaking unintelligible words; and it was only gradually by leaning over her, that they were able to make out:

"I thought that there would be an outcry and that I should be arrested. But no. It happened in such a way and under such conditions that no one had seen anything. Further, Jacques had drawn himself up at the same time as myself; and he actually did not fall. No, he did not fall! I had stabbed him; and he remained standing! I saw him from the terrace, to which I had returned. He had hung his jacket over his shoulders, evidently to hide his wound, and he moved away without staggering . . . or staggering so little that I alone was able to perceive it. He even spoke to some friends who were playing cards. Then he went to his cabin and disappeared . . . In a few moments, I came back indoors. I was persuaded that all of this was only a bad dream . . . that I had not killed him . . . or that at the worst the wound was a slight one. Jacques would come out again. I was certain of it . . . I watched from my balcony . . . If I had thought for a moment that he needed assistance, I should have flown to him . . . But truly I didn't know . . . I didn't guess . . . People speak of presentiments: there are no such things. I was perfectly calm, just as one is after a nightmare of which the memory is fading away . . . No, I swear to you, I knew nothing . . . until the moment . . ."

She interrupted herself, stifled by sobs.

Rénine finished her sentence for her,

"Until the moment when they came and told you, I suppose?"

Thérèse stammered:

"Yes. It was not till then that I was conscious of what I had done . . . and I felt that I was going mad and that I should cry out to all those people, 'Why, it was I who did it! Don't search! Here is the dagger . . . I am the culprit!' Yes, I was going to say that, when suddenly I caught sight of my poor Jacques . . . They were carrying him along . . . His face was very peaceful, very gentle . . . And, in his presence, I understood my duty, as he had understood his . . . He had kept silent, for the sake of the children. I would be silent too. We were both guilty of the murder of which he was the victim; and we must both do all we could to prevent the crime from recoiling upon them . . . He had seen this clearly in his dying agony. He had had the amazing courage to keep his feet, to answer the people who spoke to him, and to lock himself up to die. He had done this, wiping out all his faults with a single action, and in so doing had granted me his forgiveness, because he was not accusing me . . . and was ordering me to hold my peace . . . and to defend myself . . . against everybody . . . especially against you, Germaine."

She uttered these last words more firmly. At first wholly overwhelmed by the unconscious act which she had committed in killing her husband, she had recovered her strength a little in thinking of what she had done and in defending herself with such energy. Faced by the intriguing woman whose hatred had driven both of them to death and crime, she clenched her fists, ready for the struggle, all quivering with resolution.

Germaine Astaing did not flinch. She had listened without a word, with a relentless expression which grew harder and harder as Thérèse's confessions became precise. No emotion seemed to soften her and no remorse to penetrate her being. At most, toward the end, her thin lips shaped themselves into a faint smile. She was holding her prey in her clutches.

Slowly, with her eyes raised to a mirror, she adjusted her hat and powdered her face. Then she walked to the door.

Thérèse darted forward:

"Where are you going?"

"Where I choose."

"To see the examining-magistrate?"

"Very likely."

"You sha'n't pass!"

"As you please. I'll wait for him here."

"And you'll tell him what?"

"Why, all that you've said, of course, all that you've been silly enough to say. How could he doubt the story? You have explained it all to me so fully."

Thérèse took her by the shoulders:

"Yes, but I'll explain other things to him at the same time, Germaine, things that concern you. If I'm ruined, so shall you be."

"You can't touch me."

"I can expose you, show your letters."

"What letters?"

"Those in which my death was decided on."

"Lies, Thérèse! You know that famous plot exists only in your imagination. Neither Jacques nor I wished for your death."

"You did, at any rate. Your letters condemn you."

"Lies! They were the letters of a friend to a friend."

"Letters of a mistress to her paramour."

"Prove it."

"They are there, in Jacques's pocket-book."

"No, they're not."

"What's that you say?"

"I say that those letters belonged to me. I've taken them back, or rather my brother has."

"You've stolen them, you wretch! And you shall give them back again," cried Thérèse, shaking her.

"I haven't them. My brother kept them. He has gone."

Thérèse staggered and stretched out her hands to Rénine with an expression of despair. Rénine said:

"What she says is true. I watched the brother's proceedings while he was feeling in your bag. He took out the pocket-book, looked through it with his sister, came and put it back again, and went off with the letters."

Rénine paused and added,

"Or, at least, with five of them."

The two women moved closer to him. What did he intend to convey? If Frédéric Astaing had taken away only five letters, what had become of the sixth?

"I suppose," said Rénine, "that, when the pocket-book fell on the shingle, that sixth letter slipped out at the same time as the photograph and that M. d'Ormeval must have picked it up, for I found it in the pocket of his blazer, which had been hung up near the bed. Here it is. It's signed Germaine Astaing and it is quite enough to prove the writer's intentions and the murderous counsels which she was pressing upon her lover."

Madame Astaing had turned grey in the face and was so much disconcerted that she did not try to defend herself. Rénine continued, addressing his remarks to her:

"To my mind, madame, you are responsible for all that happened. Penniless, no doubt, and at the end of your resources, you tried to profit by the passion with which you inspired M. d'Ormeval in order to make him marry you, in spite of all the obstacles, and to lay your hands upon his fortune. I have proofs of this greed for money and these abominable calculations and can supply them if need be. A few minutes after I had felt in the pocket of that jacket, you did the same. I had removed the sixth letter, but had left a slip of paper which you looked for eagerly and which also must have dropped out of the pocket-book. It was an uncrossed cheque for a hundred thousand francs, drawn by M. d'Ormeval in your brother's name . . . just a little wedding-present . . . what we might call pin-money. Acting on your instructions, your brother dashed off by motor to Le Havre to reach the bank before four o'clock. I may as well tell you that he will not have cashed the cheque, for I had a telephone-message sent to the bank to announce the murder of M. d'Ormeval, which stops all payments. The upshot of all this is that the police, if you persist in your schemes of revenge, will have in their hands all the proofs that are wanted against you and your brother. I might add, as an edifying piece of evidence, the story of the conversation which I overheard between your brother and yourself in a dining-car on the railway between Brest and Paris, a fortnight ago. But I feel sure that you will not drive me to adopt these extreme measures and that we understand each other. Isn't that so?"

Natures like Madame Astaing's, which are violent and headstrong so long as a fight is possible and while a gleam of hope remains, are easily swayed in defeat. Germaine was too intelligent not to grasp the fact that the least attempt at resistance would be shattered by such an adversary as this. She was in his hands. She could but yield.

She therefore did not indulge in any play-acting, nor in any demonstration such as threats, outbursts of fury, or hysterics. She bowed:

"We are agreed," she said. "What are your terms?"

"Go away. If ever you are called upon for your evidence, say that you know nothing."

She walked away. At the door, she hesitated and then, between her teeth, said:

"The cheque."

Rénine looked at Madame d'Ormeval, who declared:

"Let her keep it. I would not touch that money."

⸻

When Rénine had given Thérèse d'Ormeval precise instructions as to how she was to behave at the enquiry and to answer the questions put to her, he left the chalet, accompanied by Hortense Daniel.

On the beach below, the magistrate and the public prosecutor were continuing their investigations, taking measurements, examining the witnesses and generally laying their heads together.

"When I think," said Hortense, "that you have the dagger and M. d'Ormeval's pocket-book on you!"

"And it strikes you as awfully dangerous, I suppose?" he said, laughing. "It strikes *me* as awfully comic."

"Aren't you afraid?"

"Of what?"

"That they may suspect something?"

"Lord, they won't suspect a thing! We shall tell those good people what we saw and our evidence will only increase their perplexity, for we saw nothing at all. For prudence sake we will stay a day or two, to see which way the wind is blowing. But it's quite settled: they will never be able to make head or tail of the matter."

"Nevertheless, *you* guessed the secret and from the first. Why?"

"Because, instead of seeking difficulties where none exist, as people generally do, I always put the question as it should be put; and the solution comes quite naturally. A man goes to his cabin and locks himself in. Half an hour later, he is found inside, dead. No one has gone in. What has happened? To my mind there is only one answer. There is no need to think about it. As the murder was not committed in the cabin, it must have been committed beforehand and the man was already mortally wounded when he entered his cabin. And forthwith the truth in this particular case appeared to me. Madame d'Ormeval, who was to have been killed this evening, forestalled her murderers and while her husband was stooping to the ground, in a moment of frenzy stabbed him in the back. There was nothing left to do but look for the reasons that prompted her action. When I knew them, I took her part unreservedly. That's the whole story."

The day was beginning to wane. The blue of the sky was becoming darker and the sea, even more peaceful than before.

"What are you thinking of?" asked Rénine, after a moment.

"I am thinking," she said, "that if I too were the victim of some machination, I should trust you whatever happened, trust you through and against all. I know, as certainly as I know that I exist, that you would save me, whatever the obstacles might be. There is no limit to the power of your will."

He said, very softly:

"There is no limit to my wish to please you."

FOOTPRINTS IN THE SNOW

To Prince Serge Rénine,
Boulevard Haussmann,
Paris
LA RONCIÈRE
NEAR BASSICOURT,

14 NOVEMBER.

MY DEAR FRIEND—

  "You must be thinking me very ungrateful. I have been here three weeks; and you have had not one letter from me! Not a word of thanks! And yet I ended by realizing from what terrible death you saved me and understanding the secret of that terrible business! But indeed, indeed I couldn't help it! I was in such a state of prostration after it all! I needed rest and solitude so badly! Was I to stay in Paris? Was I to continue my expeditions with you? No, no,

no! I had had enough adventures! Other people's are very interesting, I admit. But when one is one's self the victim and barely escapes with one's life? . . . Oh, my dear friend, how horrible it was! Shall I ever forget it? . . .

"Here, at la Roncière, I enjoy the greatest peace. My old spinster cousin Ermelin pets and coddles me like an invalid. I am getting back my color and am very well, physically . . . so much so, in fact, that I no longer ever think of interesting myself in other people's business. Never again! For instance (I am only telling you this because you are incorrigible, as inquisitive as any old charwoman, and always ready to busy yourself with things that don't concern you), yesterday I was present at a rather curious meeting. Antoinette had taken me to the inn at Bassicourt, where we were having tea in the public room, among the peasants (it was market-day), when the arrival of three people, two men and a woman, caused a sudden pause in the conversation.

"One of the men was a fat farmer in a long blouse, with a jovial, red face, framed in white whiskers. The other was younger, was dressed in corduroy and had lean, yellow, cross-grained features. Each of them carried a gun slung over his shoulder. Between them was a short, slender young woman, in a brown cloak and a fur cap, whose rather thin and extremely pale face was surprisingly delicate and distinguished-looking.

"'Father, son, and daughter-in-law,' whispered my cousin.

"'What! Can that charming creature be the wife of that clod-hopper?'

"'And the daughter-in-law of Baron de Gorne.'

"'Is the old fellow over there a baron?'

"'Yes, descended from a very ancient, noble family which used to own the château in the old days. He has always lived like a peasant: a great hunter, a great drinker, a great litigant, always at law with somebody, now very nearly ruined. His son Mathias was more ambitious and

*less attached to the soil and studied for the bar. Then he
went to America. Next, the lack of money brought him
back to the village, whereupon he fell in love with a young
girl in the nearest town. The poor girl consented, no one
knows why, to marry him; and for five years past she has
been leading the life of a hermit, or rather of a prisoner,
in a little manor-house close by, the Manoir-au-Puits, the
Well Manor.'*

"'With the father and the son?' I asked.

*"'No, the father lives at the far end of the village, on a
lonely farm.'*

"'And is Master Mathias jealous?'

"'A perfect tiger!'

"'Without reason?'

*"'Without reason, for Natalie de Gorne is the straightest
woman in the world and it is not her fault if a handsome
young man has been hanging around the manor-house
for the past few months. However, the de Gornes can't get
over it.'*

"'What, the father neither?'

*"'The handsome young man is the last descendant of the
people who bought the château long ago. This explains old
de Gorne's hatred. Jérôme Vignal—I know him and am
very fond of him—is a good-looking fellow and very well
off; and he has sworn to run off with Natalie de Gorne. It's
the old man who says so, whenever he has had a drop too
much. There, listen!'*

*"The old chap was sitting among a group of men who
were amusing themselves by making him drink and plying
him with questions. He was already a little bit 'on' and was
holding forth with a tone of indignation and a mocking
smile which formed the most comic contrast:*

*"'He's wasting his time, I tell you, the coxcomb! It's no
manner of use his poaching round our way and making
sheep's-eyes at the wench . . . The coverts are watched! If he
comes too near, it means a bullet, eh, Mathias?'*

"He gripped his daughter-in-law's hand:

"'And then the little wench knows how to defend herself too,' he chuckled. 'Eh, you don't want any admirers, do you, Natalie?'

"The young wife blushed, in her confusion at being addressed in these terms, while her husband growled:

"'You'd do better to hold your tongue, father. There are things one doesn't talk about in public.'

"'Things that affect one's honor are best settled in public,' retorted the old one. 'Where I'm concerned, the honor of the de Gornes comes before everything; and that fine spark, with his Paris airs, sha'n't . . .'"

"He stopped short. Before him stood a man who had just come in and who seemed to be waiting for him to finish his sentence. The newcomer was a tall, powerfully-built young fellow, in riding-kit, with a hunting-crop in his hand. His strong and rather stern face was lighted up by a pair of fine eyes in which shone an ironical smile.

"'Jérôme Vignal,' whispered my cousin.

"The young man seemed not at all embarrassed. On seeing Natalie, he made a low bow; and, when Mathias de Gorne took a step forward, he eyed him from head to foot, as though to say:

"'Well, what about it?'

"And his attitude was so haughty and contemptuous that the de Gornes unslung their guns and took them in both hands, like sportsmen about to shoot. The son's expression was very fierce.

"Jérôme was quite unmoved by the threat. After a few seconds, turning to the inn-keeper, he remarked:

"'Oh, I say! I came to see old Vasseur. But his shop is shut. Would you mind giving him the holster of my revolver? It wants a stitch or two.'

"He handed the holster to the inn-keeper and added, laughing:

"'I'm keeping the revolver, in case I need it. You never can tell!'

"Then, still very calmly, he took a cigarette from a silver case, lit it, and walked out. We saw him through the

*window vaulting on his horse and riding off at a slow
trot.*

*"Old de Gorne tossed off a glass of brandy, swearing
most horribly.*

*"His son clapped his hand to the old man's mouth and
forced him to sit down. Natalie de Gorne was weeping
beside them . . .*

*"That's my story, dear friend. As you see, it's not
tremendously interesting and does not deserve your
attention. There's no mystery in it and no part for you to
play. Indeed, I particularly insist that you should not seek
a pretext for any untimely interference. Of course, I should
be glad to see the poor thing protected: she appears to be
a perfect martyr. But, as I said before, let us leave other
people to get out of their own troubles and go no farther
with our little experiments . . ."*

Rénine finished reading the letter, read it over again, and ended by
saying:

"That's it. Everything's right as right can be. She doesn't want to
continue our little experiments, because this would make the seventh
and because she's afraid of the eighth, which under the terms of our
agreement has a very particular significance. She doesn't want to . . .
and she does want to . . . without seeming to want to."

|||||||||||||||||||||||||

He rubbed his hands. The letter was an invaluable witness to the
influence which he had gradually, gently and patiently gained over
Hortense Daniel. It betrayed a rather complex feeling, composed of
admiration, unbounded confidence, uneasiness at times, fear, and
almost terror, but also love: he was convinced of that. His companion
in adventures which she shared with a good fellowship that excluded
any awkwardness between them, she had suddenly taken fright; and a
sort of modesty, mingled with a certain coquetry, was impelling her
to hold back.

That very evening, Sunday, Rénine took the train.

And, at break of day, after covering by diligence, on a road white with snow, the five miles between the little town of Pompignat, where he alighted, and the village of Bassicourt, he learnt that his journey might prove of some use: three shots had been heard during the night in the direction of the Manoir-au-Puits.

"Three shots, sergeant. I heard them as plainly as I see you standing before me," said a peasant whom the gendarmes were questioning in the parlor of the inn which Rénine had entered.

"So did I," said the waiter. "Three shots. It may have been twelve o'clock at night. The snow, which had been falling since nine, had stopped . . . and the shots sounded across the fields, one after the other: bang, bang, bang."

Five more peasants gave their evidence. The sergeant and his men had heard nothing, because the police-station backed on the fields. But a farm-laborer and a woman arrived, who said that they were in Mathias de Gorne's service, that they had been away for two days because of the intervening Sunday and that they had come straight from the manor-house, where they were unable to obtain admission:

"The gate of the grounds is locked, sergeant," said the man. "It's the first time I've known this to happen. M. Mathias comes out to open it himself, every morning at the stroke of six, winter and summer. Well, it's past eight now. I called and shouted. Nobody answered. So we came on here."

"You might have enquired at old M. de Gorne's," said the sergeant. "He lives on the high-road."

"On my word, so I might! I never thought of that."

"We'd better go there now," the sergeant decided. Two of his men went with him, as well as the peasants and a locksmith whose services were called into requisition. Rénine joined the party.

Soon, at the end of the village, they reached old de Gorne's farmyard, which Rénine recognized by Hortense's description of its position.

The old fellow was harnessing his horse and trap. When they told him what had happened, he burst out laughing:

"Three shots? Bang, bang, bang? Why, my dear sergeant, there are only two barrels to Mathias's gun!"

"What about the locked gate?"

"It means that the lad's asleep, that's all. Last night, he came and cracked a bottle with me . . . perhaps two . . . or even three; and he'll be sleeping it off, I expect . . . he and Natalie."

He climbed on to the box of his trap—an old cart with a patched tilt—and cracked his whip:

"Good-bye, gentlemen all. Those three shots of yours won't stop me from going to market at Pompignat, as I do every Monday. I've a couple of calves under the tilt; and they're just fit for the butcher. Good-day to you!"

The others walked on. Rénine went up to the sergeant and gave him his name:

"I'm a friend of Mlle. Ermelin, of La Roncière; and, as it's too early to call on her yet, I shall be glad if you'll allow me to go round by the manor with you. Mlle. Ermelin knows Madame de Gorne; and it will be a satisfaction to me to relieve her mind, for there's nothing wrong at the manor-house, I hope?"

"If there is," replied the sergeant, "we shall read all about it as plainly as on a map, because of the snow."

He was a likable young man and seemed smart and intelligent. From the very first he had shown great acuteness in observing the tracks which Mathias had left behind him, the evening before, on returning home, tracks which soon became confused with the footprints made in going and coming by the farm-laborer and the woman. Meanwhile they came to the walls of a property of which the locksmith readily opened the gate.

From here onward, a single trail appeared upon the spotless snow, that of Mathias; and it was easy to perceive that the son must have shared largely in the father's libations, as the line of footprints described sudden curves which made it swerve right up to the trees of the avenue.

Two hundred yards farther stood the dilapidated two-storied building of the Manoir-au-Puits. The principal door was open.

"Let's go in," said the sergeant.

And, the moment he had crossed the threshold, he muttered:

"Oho! Old de Gorne made a mistake in not coming. They've been fighting in here."

The big room was in disorder. Two shattered chairs, the overturned table, and much broken glass and china bore witness to the violence of the struggle. The tall clock, lying on the ground, had stopped at twenty past eleven.

With the farm-girl showing them the way, they ran up to the first floor. Neither Mathias nor his wife was there. But the door of their bedroom had been broken down with a hammer which they discovered under the bed.

Rénine and the sergeant went downstairs again. The living-room had a passage communicating with the kitchen, which lay at the back of the house and opened on a small yard fenced off from the orchard. At the end of this enclosure was a well near which one was bound to pass.

Now, from the door of the kitchen to the well, the snow, which was not very thick, had been pressed down to this side and that, as though a body had been dragged over it. And all around the well were tangled traces of trampling feet, showing that the struggle must have been resumed at this spot. The sergeant again discovered Mathias's footprints, together with others which were shapelier and lighter.

These latter went straight into the orchard, by themselves. And, thirty yards on, near the footprints, a revolver was picked up and recognized by one of the peasants as resembling that which Jérôme Vignal had produced in the inn two days before.

The sergeant examined the cylinder. Three of the seven bullets had been fired.

And so the tragedy was little by little reconstructed in its main outlines; and the sergeant, who had ordered everybody to stand aside and not to step on the site of the footprints, came back to the well, leant over, put a few questions to the farm-girl, and, going up to Rénine, whispered:

"It all seems fairly clear to me."

Rénine took his arm:

"Let's speak out plainly, sergeant. I understand the business pretty well, for, as I told you, I know Mlle. Ermelin, who is a friend of Jérôme Vignal's and also knows Madame de Gorne. Do you suppose . . . ?"

"I don't want to suppose anything. I simply declare that someone came there last night . . ."

"By which way? The only tracks of a person coming toward the manor are those of M. de Gorne."

"That's because the other person arrived before the snowfall, that is to say, before nine o'clock."

"Then he must have hidden in a corner of the living-room and waited for the return of M. de Gorne, who came after the snow?"

"Just so. As soon as Mathias came in, the man went for him. There was a fight. Mathias made his escape through the kitchen. The man ran after him to the well and fired three revolver-shots."

"And where's the body?"

"Down the well."

Rénine protested:

"Oh, I say! Aren't you taking a lot for granted?"

"Why, sir, the snow's there, to tell the story; and the snow plainly says that, after the struggle, after the three shots, one man alone walked away and left the farm, one man only, and his footprints are not those of Mathias de Gorne. Then where can Mathias de Gorne be?"

"But the well . . . can be dragged?"

"No. The well is practically bottomless. It is known all over the district and gives its name to the manor."

"So you really believe . . . ?"

"I repeat what I said. Before the snowfall, a single arrival, Mathias, and a single departure, the stranger."

"And Madame de Gorne? Was she too killed and thrown down the well like her husband?"

"No, carried off."

"Carried off?"

"Remember that her bedroom was broken down with a hammer."

"Come, come, sergeant! You yourself declare that there was only one departure, the stranger's."

"Stoop down. Look at the man's footprints. See how they sink into the snow, until they actually touch the ground. Those are the footprints of a man, laden with a heavy burden. The stranger was carrying Madame de Gorne on his shoulder."

"Then there's an outlet this way?"

"Yes, a little door of which Mathias de Gorne always had the key on him. The man must have taken it from him."

"A way out into the open fields?"

"Yes, a road which joins the departmental highway three quarters of a mile from here . . . And do you know where?"

"Where?"

"At the corner of the château."

"Jérôme Vignal's château?"

"By Jove, this is beginning to look serious! If the trail leads to the château and stops there, we shall know where we stand."

The trail did continue to the château, as they were able to perceive after following it across the undulating fields, on which the snow lay heaped in places. The approach to the main gates had been swept, but they saw that another trail, formed by the two wheels of a vehicle, was running in the opposite direction to the village.

The sergeant rang the bell. The porter, who had also been sweeping the drive, came to the gates, with a broom in his hand. In answer to a question, the man said that M. Vignal had gone away that morning before anyone else was up and that he himself had harnessed the horse to the trap.

"In that case," said Rénine, when they had moved away, "all we have to do is to follow the tracks of the wheels."

"That will be no use," said the sergeant. "They have taken the railway."

"At Pompignat station, where I came from? But they would have passed through the village."

"They have gone just the other way, because it leads to the town, where the express trains stop. The procurator-general has an office in the town. I'll telephone; and, as there's no train before eleven o'clock, all that they need do is to keep a watch at the station."

"I think you're doing the right thing, sergeant," said Rénine, "and I congratulate you on the way in which you have carried out your investigation."

They parted. Rénine went back to the inn in the village and sent a note to Hortense Daniel by hand:

MY VERY DEAR FRIEND,

  "I seemed to gather from your letter that, touched as always by anything that concerns the heart, you were anxious to protect the love-affair of Jérôme and Natalie. Now there is every reason to suppose that these two, without

consulting their fair protectress, have run away, after
throwing Mathias de Gorne down a well.

"Forgive me for not coming to see you. The whole thing
is extremely obscure; and, if I were with you, I should not
have the detachment of mind which is needed to think the
case over."

It was then half-past ten. Rénine went for a walk into the country, with his hands clasped behind his back and without vouchsafing a glance at the exquisite spectacle of the white meadows. He came back for lunch, still absorbed in his thoughts and indifferent to the talk of the customers of the inn, who on all sides were discussing recent events.

He went up to his room and had been asleep some time when he was awakened by a tapping at the door. He got up and opened it:

"Is it you? . . . Is it you?" he whispered.

Hortense and he stood gazing at each other for some seconds in silence, holding each other's hands, as though nothing, no irrelevant thought and no utterance, must be allowed to interfere with the joy of their meeting. Then he asked:

"Was I right in coming?"

"Yes," she said, gently, "I expected you."

"Perhaps it would have been better if you had sent for me sooner, instead of waiting . . . Events did not wait, you see, and I don't quite know what's to become of Jérôme Vignal and Natalie de Gorne."

"What, haven't you heard?" she said, quickly. "They've been arrested. They were going to travel by the express."

"Arrested? No." Rénine objected. "People are not arrested like that. They have to be questioned first."

"That's what's being done now. The authorities are making a search."

"Where?"

"At the château. And, as they are innocent . . . For they are innocent, aren't they? You don't admit that they are guilty, any more than I do?"

He replied:

"I admit nothing, I can admit nothing, my dear. Nevertheless, I am bound to say that everything is against them . . . except one fact, which is that everything is too much against them. It is not normal for so many proofs to be heaped up one on top of the other and for the man who commits a murder to tell his story so frankly. Apart from this, there's nothing but mystery and discrepancy."

"Well?"

"Well, I am greatly puzzled."

"But you have a plan?"

"None at all, so far. Ah, if I could see him, Jérôme Vignal, and her, Natalie de Gorne, and hear them and know what they are saying in their own defense! But you can understand that I sha'n't be permitted either to ask them any questions or to be present at their examination. Besides, it must be finished by this time."

"It's finished at the château," she said, "but it's going to be continued at the manor-house."

"Are they taking them to the manor-house?" he asked eagerly.

"Yes . . . at least, judging by what was said to the chauffeur of one of the procurator's two cars."

"Oh, in that case," exclaimed Rénine, "the thing's done! The manor-house! Why, we shall be in the front row of the stalls! We shall see and hear everything; and, as a word, a tone of the voice, a quiver of the eyelids will be enough to give me the tiny clue I need, we may entertain some hope. Come along."

He took her by the direct route which he had followed that morning, leading to the gate which the locksmith had opened. The gendarmes on duty at the manor-house had made a passage through the snow, beside the line of footprints and around the house. Chance enabled Rénine and Hortense to approach unseen and through a side-window to enter a corridor near a back-staircase. A few steps up was a little chamber which received its only light through a sort of bull's-eye, from the large room on the ground-floor. Rénine, during the morning visit, had noticed the bull's-eye, which was covered on the inside with a piece of cloth. He removed the cloth and cut out one of the panes.

A few minutes later, a sound of voices rose from the other side of the house, no doubt near the well. The sound grew more distinct. A number of people flocked into the house. Some of them went up stairs to the first floor, while the sergeant arrived with a young man of whom Rénine and Hortense were able to distinguish only the tall figure:

"Jérôme Vignal," said she.

"Yes," said Rénine. "They are examining Madame de Gorne first, upstairs, in her bedroom."

A quarter of an hour passed. Then the persons on the first floor came downstairs and went in. They were the procurator's deputy, his clerk, a commissary of police and two detectives.

Madame de Gorne was shown in and the deputy asked Jérôme Vignal to step forward.

Jérôme Vignal's face was certainly that of the strong man whom Hortense had depicted in her letter. He displayed no uneasiness, but rather decision and a resolute will. Natalie, who was short and very slight, with a feverish light in her eyes, nevertheless produced the same impression of quiet confidence.

The deputy, who was examining the disordered furniture and the traces of the struggle, invited her to sit down and said to Jérôme:

"Monsieur, I have not asked you many questions so far. This is a summary enquiry which I am conducting in your presence and which will be continued later by the examining-magistrate; and I wished above all to explain to you the very serious reasons for which I asked you to interrupt your journey and to come back here with Madame de Gorne. You are now in a position to refute the truly distressing charges that are hanging over you. I therefore ask you to tell me the exact truth."

"Mr. Deputy," replied Jérôme, "the charges in question trouble me very little. The truth for which you are asking will defeat all the lies which chance has accumulated against me. It is this."

He reflected for an instant and then, in clear, frank tones, said:

"I love Madame de Gorne. The first time I met her, I conceived the greatest sympathy and admiration for her. But my affection has always been directed by the sole thought of her happiness. I love her, but I respect her even more. Madame de Gorne must have told you and I tell you again that she and I exchanged our first few words last night."

He continued, in a lower voice:

"I respect her the more inasmuch as she is exceedingly unhappy. All the world knows that every minute of her life was a martyrdom. Her husband persecuted her with ferocious hatred and frantic jealousy. Ask the servants. They will tell you of the long suffering of Natalie de Gorne, of the blows which she received and the insults which she had to endure. I tried to stop this torture by restoring to the rights of appeal which the merest stranger may claim when unhappiness and injustice pass a certain limit. I went three times to old de Gorne and begged him to interfere; but I found in him an almost equal hatred toward his daughter-in-law, the hatred which many people feel for anything beautiful and noble. At last I resolved on direct action and last night I took a step with regard to Mathias de Gorne which was . . . a little unusual, I admit, but which seemed likely to succeed, considering the man's character. I swear, Mr. Deputy, that I had no other intention than to talk to Mathias de Gorne. Knowing certain particulars of his life which enabled me to bring effective pressure to bear upon him, I wished to make use of this advantage in order to achieve my purpose. If things turned out differently, I am not wholly to blame . . . So I went there a little before nine o'clock. The servants, I knew, were out. He opened the door himself. He was alone."

"Monsieur," said the deputy, interrupting him, "you are saying something—as Madame de Gorne, for that matter, did just now—which is manifestly opposed to the truth. Mathias de Gorne did not come home last night until eleven o'clock. We have two definite proofs of this: his father's evidence and the prints of his feet in the snow, which fell from a quarter past nine o'clock to eleven."

"Mr. Deputy," Jérôme Vignal declared, without heeding the bad effect which his obstinacy was producing, "I am relating things as they were and not as they may be interpreted. But to continue. That clock marked ten minutes to nine when I entered this room. M. de Gorne, believing that he was about to be attacked, had taken down his gun. I placed my revolver on the table, out of reach of my hand, and sat down: 'I want to speak to you, monsieur,' I said. 'Please listen to me.' He did not stir and did not utter a single syllable. So I spoke. And straightway, crudely, without any previous explanations which might have softened the bluntness of my proposal, I spoke the few words which I had prepared beforehand: 'I have spent some months, monsieur,' I said, 'in making careful enquiries into your financial position. You have mortgaged every foot of your land. You have signed bills which will shortly be falling due and which it will be absolutely impossible for you to honor. You have nothing to hope for from your father, whose own affairs are in a very bad condition. So you are ruined. I have come to save you.' . . . He watched me, still without speaking, and sat down, which I took to mean that my suggestion was not entirely displeasing. Then I took a sheaf of bank-notes from my pocket, placed it before him, and continued: 'Here is sixty thousand francs, monsieur. I will buy the Manoir-au-Puits, its lands and dependencies and take over the mortgages. The sum named is exactly twice what they are worth.' . . . I saw his eyes glittering. He asked my conditions. 'Only one,' I said, 'that you go to America.' . . . Mr. Deputy, we sat discussing for two hours. It was not that my offer roused his indignation—I should not have risked it if I had not known with whom I was dealing—but he wanted more and haggled greedily, though he refrained from mentioning the name of Madame de Gorne, to whom I myself had not once alluded. We might have been two men engaged in a dispute and seeking an agreement on common ground, whereas it was the happiness and the whole destiny of a woman that were at stake. At last, weary of the discussion, I accepted a compromise and we came to terms, which I resolved to make definite then and there. Two letters were exchanged between us: one in which he made the Manoir-au-Puits over to me for the sum which I had paid him; and one, which he pocketed immediately, by which I was to send him as much more in America on the day on which the decree of divorce was pronounced . . . So the affair was settled. I am sure that at that moment he was accepting in good faith. He looked upon me less as an enemy and a rival than as a man who was doing him a service. He even went so far as to give me the key of the little door which opens on the fields, so that I might go home by the short cut. Unfortunately, while I was picking up my cap and greatcoat, I made the mistake of leaving on the table the letter of sale which he had signed. In a moment, Mathias de Gorne had seen the advantage which he could take of my slip: he could keep his property, keep his wife . . . and keep the money. Quick as lightning, he tucked away the paper, hit me over the head with the butt-end of his gun, threw the gun on the floor, and seized me by the throat with both hands. He had reckoned without his host. I was the stronger of the two; and after a sharp but short struggle, I mastered him and tied him up with a cord which I found lying in a corner . . . Mr. Deputy, if my enemy's resolve was sudden, mine was no less so. Since, when all was said, he had accepted the bargain, I would force him to keep it, at least in so far as I was interested. A very few steps brought me to the first floor . . . I had not a doubt that Madame de Gorne was there and had heard the sound of our discussion. Switching on the light of my pocket-torch, I looked into three bedrooms. The fourth was locked. I knocked at the door. There was no reply. But this was one of the moments in which a man allows no obstacle to stand in his way. I had seen a hammer in one of the rooms. I picked it up and smashed in the door . . . Yes, Natalie was lying there, on the floor, in a dead faint. I took her in my arms, carried her downstairs and went through the kitchen. On seeing the snow outside, I at once realized that my footprints would be easily traced. But what did it matter? Was there any reason why I should put Mathias de Gorne off the scent? Not at all. With the sixty thousand francs in his possession, as well as the paper in which I undertook to pay him a like sum on the day of his divorce, to say nothing of his house and land, he would go away, leaving Natalie de Gorne to me. Nothing was changed between us, except one thing: instead of awaiting his good pleasure, I had at once seized the precious pledge which I coveted. What I feared, therefore, was not so much any subsequent attack on the part of Mathias de Gorne, but rather the indignant reproaches of his wife. What would she say when she realized that she was a prisoner in my hands? . . . The reasons why I escaped reproach Madame de Gorne has, I believe, had the frankness to tell you. Love calls forth love. That night, in my house, broken by emotion, she confessed her feeling for me. She loved me as I loved her. Our destinies were henceforth mingled. She and I set out at five o'clock this morning . . . not foreseeing for an instant that we were amenable to the law."

Jérôme Vignal's story was finished. He had told it straight off the reel, like a story learnt by heart and incapable of revision in any detail.

There was a brief pause, during which Hortense whispered:

"It all sounds quite possible and, in any case, very logical."

"There are the objections to come," said Rénine. "Wait till you hear them. They are very serious. There's one in particular . . ."

The deputy-procurator stated it at once:

"And what became of M. de Gorne in all this?"

"Mathias de Gorne?" asked Jérôme.

"Yes. You have related, with an accent of great sincerity, a series of facts which I am quite willing to admit. Unfortunately, you have forgotten a point of the first importance: what became of Mathias de Gorne? You tied him up here, in this room. Well, this morning he was gone."

"Of course, Mr. Deputy, Mathias de Gorne accepted the bargain in the end and went away."

"By what road?"

"No doubt by the road that leads to his father's house."

"Where are his footprints? The expanse of snow is an impartial witness. After your fight with him, we see you, on the snow, moving away. Why don't we see him? He came and did not go away again. Where is he? There is not a trace of him . . . or rather . . ."

The deputy lowered his voice:

"Or rather, yes, there are some traces on the way to the well and around the well . . . traces which prove that the last struggle of all took place there . . . And after that there is nothing . . . not a thing . . ."

Jérôme shrugged his shoulders:

"You have already mentioned this, Mr. Deputy, and it implies a charge of homicide against me. I have nothing to say to it."

"Have you anything to say to the fact that your revolver was picked up within fifteen yards of the well?"

"No."

"Or to the strange coincidence between the three shots heard in the night and the three cartridges missing from your revolver?"

"No, Mr. Deputy, there was not, as you believe, a last struggle by the well, because I left M. de Gorne tied up, in this room, and because I also left my revolver here. On the other hand, if shots were heard, they were not fired by me."

"A casual coincidence, therefore?"

"That's a matter for the police to explain. My only duty is to tell the truth and you are not entitled to ask more of me."

"And if that truth conflicts with the facts observed?"

"It means that the facts are wrong, Mr. Deputy."

"As you please. But, until the day when the police are able to make them agree with your statements, you will understand that I am obliged to keep you under arrest."

"And Madame de Gorne?" asked Jérôme, greatly distressed.

The deputy did not reply. He exchanged a few words with the commissary of police and then, beckoning to a detective, ordered him to bring up one of the two motor-cars. Then he turned to Natalie:

"Madame, you have heard M. Vignal's evidence. It agrees word for word with your own. M. Vignal declares in particular that you had fainted when he carried you away. But did you remain unconscious all the way?"

It seemed as though Jérôme's composure had increased Madame de Gorne's assurance. She replied:

"I did not come to, monsieur, until I was at the château."

"It's most extraordinary. Didn't you hear the three shots which were heard by almost every one in the village?"

"I did not."

"And did you see nothing of what happened beside the well?"

"Nothing did happen. M. Vignal has told you so."

"Then what has become of your husband?"

"I don't know."

"Come, madame, you really must assist the officers of the law and at least tell us what you think. Do you believe that there may have been an accident and that possibly M. de Gorne, who had been to see his father and had more to drink than usual, lost his balance and fell into the well?"

"When my husband came back from seeing his father, he was not in the least intoxicated."

"His father, however, has stated that he was. His father and he had drunk two or three bottles of wine."

"His father is not telling the truth."

"But the snow tells the truth, madame," said the deputy, irritably. "And the line of his footprints wavers from side to side."

"My husband came in at half-past-eight, monsieur, before the snow had begun to fall."

The deputy struck the table with his fist:

"But, really, madame, you're going right against the evidence! . . . That sheet of snow cannot speak false! . . . I may accept your denial of matters that cannot be verified. But these footprints in the snow . . . in the snow . . ."

He controlled himself.

The motor-car drew up outside the windows. Forming a sudden resolve, he said to Natalie:

"You will be good enough to hold yourself at the disposal of the authorities, madame, and to remain here, in the manor-house . . ."

And he made a sign to the sergeant to remove Jérôme Vignal in the car.

The game was lost for the two lovers. Barely united, they had to separate and to fight, far away from each other, against the most grievous accusations.

Jérôme took a step toward Natalie. They exchanged a long, sorrowful look. Then he bowed to her and walked to the door, in the wake of the sergeant of gendarmes.

"Halt!" cried a voice. "Sergeant, right about . . . turn! . . . Jérôme Vignal, stay where you are!"

The ruffled deputy raised his head, as did the other people present. The voice came from the ceiling. The bull's-eye window had opened and Rénine, leaning through it, was waving his arms:

"I wish to be heard! . . . I have several remarks to make . . . especially in respect of the zigzag footprints! . . . It all lies in that! . . . Mathias had not been drinking! . . ."

He had turned round and put his two legs through the opening, saying to Hortense, who tried to prevent him:

"Don't move . . . No one will disturb you."

And, releasing his hold, he dropped into the room.

The deputy appeared dumfounded:

"But, really, monsieur, who are you? Where do you come from?"

Rénine brushed the dust from his clothes and replied:

"Excuse me, Mr. Deputy. I ought to have come the same way as everybody else. But I was in a hurry. Besides, if I had come in by the door instead of falling from the ceiling, my words would not have made the same impression."

The infuriated deputy advanced to meet him:

"Who are you?"

"Prince Rénine. I was with the sergeant this morning when he was pursuing his investigations, wasn't I, sergeant? Since then I have been hunting about for information. That's why, wishing to be present at the hearing, I found a corner in a little private room . . ."

"You were there? You had the audacity? . . ."

"One must needs be audacious, when the truth's at stake. If I had not been there, I should not have discovered just the one little clue which I missed. I should not have known that Mathias de Gorne was not the least bit drunk. Now that's the key to the riddle. When we know that, we know the solution."

The deputy found himself in a rather ridiculous position. Since he had failed to take the necessary precautions to ensure the secrecy of his enquiry, it was difficult for him to take any steps against this interloper. He growled:

"Let's have done with this. What are you asking?"

"A few minutes of your kind attention."

"And with what object?"

"To establish the innocence of M. Vignal and Madame de Gorne."

He was wearing that calm air, that sort of indifferent look which was peculiar to him in moments of actions when the crisis of the drama depended solely upon himself. Hortense felt a thrill pass through her and at once became full of confidence:

"They're saved," she thought, with sudden emotion. "I asked him to protect that young creature; and he is saving her from prison and despair."

Jérôme and Natalie must have experienced the same impression of sudden hope, for they had drawn nearer to each other, as though this stranger, descended from the clouds, had already given them the right to clasp hands.

The deputy shrugged his shoulders:

"The prosecution will have every means, when the time comes, of establishing their innocence for itself. You will be called."

"It would be better to establish it here and now. Any delay might lead to grievous consequences."

"I happen to be in a hurry."

"Two or three minutes will do."

"Two or three minutes to explain a case like this!"

"No longer, I assure you."

"Are you as certain of it as all that?"

"I am now. I have been thinking hard since this morning."

The deputy realized that this was one of those gentry who stick to you like a leech and that there was nothing for it but to submit. In a rather bantering tone, he asked:

"Does your thinking enable you to tell us the exact spot where M. Mathias de Gorne is at this moment?"

Rénine took out his watch and answered:

"In Paris, Mr. Deputy."

"In Paris? Alive then?"

"Alive and, what is more, in the pink of health."

"I am delighted to hear it. But then what's the meaning of the footprints around the well and the presence of that revolver and those three shots?"

"Simply camouflage."

"Oh, really? Camouflage contrived by whom?"

"By Mathias de Gorne himself."

"That's curious! And with what object?"

"With the object of passing himself off for dead and of arranging subsequent matters in such a way that M. Vignal was bound to be accused of the death, the murder."

"An ingenious theory," the deputy agreed, still in a satirical tone. "What do you think of it, M. Vignal?"

"It is a theory which flashed through my own mind. Mr. Deputy," replied Jérôme. "It is quite likely that, after our struggle and after I had gone, Mathias de Gorne conceived a new plan by which, this time, his hatred would be fully gratified. He both loved and detested his wife. He held me in the greatest loathing. This must be his revenge."

"His revenge would cost him dear, considering that, according to your statement, Mathias de Gorne was to receive a second sum of sixty thousand francs from you."

"He would receive that sum in another quarter, Mr. Deputy. My examination of the financial position of the de Gorne family revealed to me the fact that the father and son had taken out a life-insurance policy in each other's favor. With the son dead, or passing for dead, the father would receive the insurance-money and indemnify his son."

"You mean to say," asked the deputy, with a smile, "that in all this camouflage, as you call it, M. de Gorne the elder would act as his son's accomplice?"

Rénine took up the challenge:

"Just so, Mr. Deputy. The father and son are accomplices."

"Then we shall find the son at the father's?"

"You would have found him there last night."

"What became of him?"

"He took the train at Pompignat."

"That's a mere supposition."

"No, a certainty."

"A moral certainty, perhaps, but you'll admit there's not the slightest proof."

The deputy did not wait for a reply. He considered that he had displayed an excessive goodwill and that patience has its limits and he put an end to the interview:

"Not the slightest proof," he repeated, taking up his hat. "And, above all, . . . above all, there's nothing in what you've said that can contradict in the very least the evidence of that relentless witness, the snow. To go to his father, Mathias de Gorne must have left this house. Which way did he go?"

"Hang it all, M. Vignal told you: by the road which leads from here to his father's!"

"There are no tracks in the snow."

"Yes, there are."

"But they show him coming here and not going away from here."

"It's the same thing."

"What?"

"Of course it is. There's more than one way of walking. One doesn't always go ahead by following one's nose."

"In what other way can one go ahead?"

"By walking backwards, Mr. Deputy."

These few words, spoken very simply, but in a clear tone which gave full value to every syllable, produced a profound silence. Those present at once grasped their extreme significance and, by adapting it to the actual happenings, perceived in a flash the impenetrable truth, which suddenly appeared to be the most natural thing in the world.

Rénine continued his argument. Stepping backwards in the direction of the window, he said:

"If I want to get to that window, I can of course walk straight up to it; but I can just as easily turn my back to it and walk that way. In either case I reach my goal."

And he at once proceeded in a vigorous tone:

"Here's the gist of it all. At half-past eight, before the snow fell, M. de Gorne comes home from his father's house. M. Vignal arrives twenty minutes later. There is a long discussion and a struggle, taking up three hours in all. It is then, after M. Vignal has carried off Madame de Gorne and made his escape, that Mathias de Gorne, foaming at the mouth, wild with rage, but suddenly seeing his chance of taking the most terrible revenge, hits upon the ingenious idea of using against his enemy the very snowfall upon whose evidence you are now relying. He therefore plans his own murder, or rather the appearance of his murder and of his fall to the bottom of the well and makes off backwards, step by step, thus recording his arrival instead of his departure on the white page."

The deputy sneered no longer. This eccentric intruder suddenly appeared to him in the light of a person worthy of attention, whom it would not do to make fun of. He asked:

"And how could he have left his father's house?"

"In a trap, quite simply."

"Who drove it?"

"The father. This morning the sergeant and I saw the trap and spoke to the father, who was going to market as usual. The son was hidden under the tilt. He took the train at Pompignat and is in Paris by now."

Rénine's explanation, as promised, had taken hardly five minutes. He had based it solely on logic and the probabilities of the case. And yet not a jot was left of the distressing mystery in which they were floundering. The darkness was dispelled. The whole truth appeared.

Madame de Gorne wept for joy and Jérôme Vignal thanked the good genius who was changing the course of events with a stroke of his magic wand.

"Shall we examine those footprints together, Mr. Deputy?" asked

Rénine. "Do you mind? The mistake which the sergeant and I made this morning was to investigate only the footprints left by the alleged murderer and to neglect Mathias de Gorne's. Why indeed should they have attracted our attention? Yet it was precisely there that the crux of the whole affair was to be found."

They stepped into the orchard and went to the well. It did not need a long examination to observe that many of the footprints were awkward, hesitating, too deeply sunk at the heel and toe and differing from one another in the angle at which the feet were turned.

"This clumsiness was unavoidable," said Rénine. "Mathias de Gorne would have needed a regular apprenticeship before his backward progress could have equaled his ordinary gait; and both his father and he must have been aware of this, at least as regards the zigzags which you see here since old de Gorne went out of his way to tell the sergeant that his son had had too much drink." And he added "Indeed it was the detection of this falsehood that suddenly enlightened me. When Madame de Gorne stated that her husband was not drunk, I thought of the footprints and guessed the truth."

The deputy frankly accepted his part in the matter and began to laugh:

"There's nothing left for it but to send detectives after the bogus corpse."

"On what grounds, Mr. Deputy?" asked Rénine. "Mathias de Gorne has committed no offense against the law. There's nothing criminal in trampling the soil around a well, in shifting the position of a revolver that doesn't belong to you, in firing three shots or in walking backwards to one's father's house. What can we ask of him? The sixty thousand francs? I presume that this is not M. Vignal's intention and that he does not mean to bring a charge against him?"

"Certainly not," said Jérôme.

"Well, what then? The insurance-policy in favor of the survivor? But there would be no misdemeanor unless the father claimed payment. And I should be greatly surprised if he did . . . Hullo, here the old chap is! You'll soon know all about it."

Old de Gorne was coming along, gesticulating as he walked. His easy-going features were screwed up to express sorrow and anger.

"Where's my son?" he cried. "It seems the brute's killed him! . . . My poor Mathias dead! Oh, that scoundrel of a Vignal!"

And he shook his fist at Jérôme.

The deputy said, bluntly:

"A word with you, M. de Gorne. Do you intend to claim your rights under a certain insurance-policy?"

"Well, what do *you* think?" said the old man, off his guard.

"The fact is . . . your son's not dead. People are even saying that you were a partner in his little schemes and that you stuffed him under the tilt of your trap and drove him to the station."

The old fellow spat on the ground, stretched out his hand as though he were going to take a solemn oath, stood for an instant without moving, and then, suddenly, changing his mind and his tactics with ingenuous cynicism, he relaxed his features, assumed a conciliatory attitude and burst out laughing:

"That blackguard Mathias! So he tried to pass himself off as dead? What a rascal! And he reckoned on me to collect the insurance-money and send it to him? As if I should be capable of such a low, dirty trick! . . . You don't know me, my boy!"

And, without waiting for more, shaking with merriment like a jolly old fellow amused by a funny story, he took his departure, not forgetting, however, to set his great hob-nail boots on each of the compromising footprints which his son had left behind him.

|||||||||||||||||||||||||

Later, when Rénine went back to the manor to let Hortense out, he found that she had disappeared.

He called and asked for her at her cousin Ermelin's. Hortense sent down word asking him to excuse her: she was feeling a little tired and was lying down.

"Capital!" thought Rénine. "Capital! She avoids me, therefore she loves me. The end is not far off."

---

[*] In this collection, Lupin disguises himself as a detective named Jim Barnett.

THE ROYAL LOVE LETTER

There was a knock at the door of the modest office in the Rue Laborde.

It roused Jim Barnett of the Barnett Agency from his doze in the comfortable armchair, where he sat awaiting clients.

"Come in!" he cried, and, as the door opened to admit his visitor, "why, Inspector Béchoux, how nice of you to look me up! How are you?"

In both manner and appearance, Inspector Béchoux was a striking contrast to the usual type of detective. He aimed at sartorial elegance, exaggerated the crease in his trousers, had a pretty taste in ties, and was very particular about the starching of his collars. He had a curious waxen pallor. In build, he was small, lean, and seemingly weedy. Oddly enough, he had the muscular arms of a heavyweight champion—arms which gave the impression of having been tacked haphazard on to his limp frame. He was intensely proud of those arms. Though quite a young man, his bearing was most self-assured. His eyes gleamed alert and intelligent.

"I happened to be passing," he announced, "and, knowing your clock-like habits, I thought: 'This being old Barnett's consultation hour, he's sure to be there. Why not drop in . . .'"

"And ask his advice," finished Jim Barnett.

"Perhaps," admitted the Inspector, to whom Barnett's perspicacity was a never-failing source of surprise.

Seeing his hesitation, Barnett spoke again: "What's up, old son? Finding it a bit difficult to consult the oracle to-day?"

Béchoux smote the table with his clenched fist; no mean blow, with his great arm to back it.

"Fact is, I'm a bit stumped. We've worked together on three cases now, Barnett—you as a private detective and I as a police inspector—and each time I haven't been able to help feeling that your clients—Baronne Assermann, for instance—ended by regarding you with a very jaundiced eye."

"As if I'd taken advantage of my opportunity to blackmail them," Barnett interrupted, fiddling with his eternal monocle, and smiling sardonically.

"No, I don't mean . . ." Béchoux forgot his resolve to find out just what *had* happened in the case of Baronne Assermann.

Barnett clapped him on the shoulder.

"Inspector Béchoux, you're forgetting the slogan of this firm: 'Information Free.' I give you my word of honor that I never ask my clients for a penny and I never accept a penny from them."

Béchoux breathed more freely.

"Thanks," he said. "I'm glad to have that assurance. My professional conscience will only allow me to avail myself of your cooperation on certain conditions. You understand, don't you? But if you don't mind my asking the question, there's one thing I feel I must know. Just what financial backing have you in the Barnett Agency?"

"I have a sleeping partner—a philanthropist." Barnett's tone was remote and casual.

"Is he anybody I know?"

"I rather think so. In fact, I'm almost certain. For even a police inspector must at some time have heard the name of—Arsène Lupin!"

Béchoux jumped.

"That's no name to jest about, Barnett."

Inspector Béchoux's existence was dominated by two emotions—his admiration for Barnett's detective ability and his fierce hatred of Arsène Lupin. Béchoux was one of Gaminard's little band and fully shared that great man's bitterness, especially as he had himself suffered humiliating defeats at the enemy's hands. He still smarted with resentment at the memory of these, and never forgot that Arsène Lupin had added insult to injury by robbing him more than once of the lady of his choice.

"We won't discuss the fellow," he said gruffly, "unless there's a chance of my laying hands on him."

"Or I," and Barnett blandly extended his own hands—oddly enough, at the level of his nose! "But let's get to work. Whereabouts is your new job?"

"Near Marly. It's the business of the murder of old Vaucherel. You've heard about it?"

"Only vaguely."

Barnett's attitude was one of acute detachment from anything so mundane as murder.

"I'm not surprised. The newspapers aren't giving it much space yet, though it's infernally baffling . . ."

"He was done in with a knife, wasn't he?" After all, Barnett's detachment was only assumed.

"Yes. Stabbed between the shoulder-blades."

"Any finger-marks on the knife?"

"None. We found a piece of paper in ashes; it was probably wrapped round the handle by the murderer."

"Any clews?"

Inspector Béchoux shook his head. "Vaucherel's room was a bit disordered. Some of the furniture had been knocked over and the drawer of a table had been broken open, but we don't know why that was done or what's missing."

"Where have they got to on the inquest?"

"They're confronting a retired official called Leboc with the Gaudu cousins—three ne'er-do-well blackguards of poachers. Without any real evidence, each side is accusing the other of the murder. Want me to run you over there in my car? Nothing like a good, stiff cross-examination, you know!"

"Right you are." Barnett rose, albeit reluctantly.

"Just one thing, Barnett. Formerie, who's conducting the inquiry, hopes to attract attention and get a Paris appointment. He's a touchy sort of chap and he won't stand for your usual bright bedside manner with the law, so cut out the flippancy." Béchoux's tone was eloquent with painful memories of Barnett's past exploits.

"I promise to treat him *most* respectfully," replied Barnett, "and I *never* break my word!"

Half-way between the village of Fontines and Marly Forest, in a copse separated from the forest by a strip of ground, stands a one-storied house with a small kitchen garden, surrounded by a low wall. Eight days before Béchoux's conversation with Jim Barnett, the cottage was still inhabited by a retired bookseller, old Vaucherel, who never left his little domain of flowers and vegetables except to browse in the bookstalls along the Paris quays. He was very miserly and reputed a rich man, although frugal in his habits. He had no visitors except his friend, Leboc, who lived at Fontines.

The reconstruction of the crime and the examination of Leboc were over, and the inspection of the garden had begun, when Jim Barnett and Inspector Béchoux alighted from their car. Béchoux made himself known to the gendarmes guarding the cottage gate and, followed by Barnett, he joined the examining magistrate and the deputy just as the latter had halted before an angle of the wall. The three Gaudu cousins were there to give their evidence. They were all three farmhands of just about the same age; they bore no facial resemblance to one another save for a similar sly stubbornness of expression. The eldest Gaudu was speaking:

"Yes, your worship, that's where we jumped over when we ran to the rescue, as you might say."

"You were coming from Fontines?"

"Yes, your worship, from Fontines. We were on our way back to work, about two o'clock it must have been. It was like this: we were chatting with Mère Denise close by at the edge of the copse, when we heard screams. 'Somebody's crying for help,' I says. 'It's from the cottage.' Old Vaucherel, that we knew as well as anything, your worship. So we ran like mad. We climbed over this here wall—a nasty bit of work, with all them broken bottles on top—and we were across the garden in no time, as you might say."

"Where exactly were you when the front door flew open"

"Right here," said the eldest Gaudu, leading the way to a flower-bed.

"That means about twenty yards from the porch," said the magistrate, pointing to the two steps leading up to the hall. "And from where you stood you saw——" He paused expectantly.

"Monsieur Leboc himself. . . . I saw him as clear as I see you, your worship . . . he was rushing out, as if the devil was at his heels—or the police, for that matter, which they soon may be—and when he saw us he bolted straight back again."

"You're quite sure it was he?"

"I swear to God it was!"

The other two men took a similar oath.

"You can't have been mistaken?"

"Why, he's been living near our place for five years now, down the end of the village," the eldest Gaudu stated. "I've even delivered milk at his house!"

The magistrate gave an order. The door of the hall opened and a man came out. He was about sixty, and wore a brown drill suit and a straw hat. His face was pink and smiling.

The three Gaudus spoke simultaneously.

"Monsieur Leboc!"

Their choral affirmation made Leboc's entrance grotesquely like something in musical comedy.

The deputy whispered, "It's obvious there can't be any mistake at such close range and the Gaudu cousins can't have gone wrong on the identity of the fugitive—which means, of the murderer."

"Quite so," said the magistrate. "But are they speaking the truth? Was it Monsieur Leboc they saw? Now we'll go on."

The party went into the house and entered a big room whose walls were literally lined with books. There were just a few sticks of furniture; a large table—the one whose drawer had been broken into; and an unframed full-length portrait of old Vaucherel—a life-size daub by some unskilled artist who had yet managed to invest his subject with a certain verisimilitude.

A dummy lay stretched on the floor to represent the victim of the tragedy.

The magistrate resumed his examination.

"When you came on the scene, Gaudu, you did not see Monsieur Leboc again?"

"No, your worship. We heard groans from this room and rushed in at once."

"That means that Monsieur Vaucherel was still alive?"

"Hardly that, as you might say. He was lying face down with a knife stuck right in the middle of his back . . . we knelt down by him . . . the poor gentleman was trying to speak."

"Could you catch what he said?"

"No, your worship. We could only make out the name of Leboc— he said it over several times—'Monsieur Leboc, Monsieur Leboc . . .' like that. Then a kind of shudder passed over him and he was gone. After that we searched everywhere, but Monsieur Leboc had vanished. He must have jumped out of the kitchen window, which was open, and made off down the little gravel path. It goes straight to his house and the trees hide it all the way. . . . Then we all went together to the gendarmes . . . and we told them all about it . . .'"

The magistrate asked a few more questions, made the three cousins formulate even more definitely their charge against Monsieur Leboc, and then turned his attention to the latter.

Monsieur Leboc had listened without attempting to interrupt. His perfect calm was unruffled by any display of indignation. He gave the impression of finding the Gaudus' story so utterly absurd that he did not for a moment doubt that the magistrate would take a precisely similar view of it. Why bother to refute such a tale?

"Have you anything to add, Monsieur Leboc?"

"Nothing further."

"Then you still maintain——"

"I maintain what you, monsieur, know as well as I to be the truth. All the villagers you have examined have testified that I never go out during the daytime. At midday I have my lunch sent in from the inn. From one to four I sit at my window reading and smoking my pipe. The day in question was fine. My window was open, and five people—no less than five—saw me, as on any other day, from the garden gate."

"I have summoned them to appear later on."

"I'm glad to hear it. They will repeat their evidence. Since I am not ubiquitous and cannot at one and the same moment be here and in my own house you must admit that I could not have been seen leaving the cottage, that my poor friend Vaucherel could not have spoken my name in his agony, and therefore that these three Gaudus are unmitigated scoundrels."

"And you turn the murder charge against them, don't you?"

"Oh! Merely a matter of surmise . . ."

"On the other hand, an old woman, Mère Denise, who was out gathering firewood, states that she was talking with the men when they first heard the screams."

"She was talking with *two* of them. Where was the third?"

"A little way behind."

"Did she *see* him?"

"She thinks so . . . she isn't positive . . ."

"In that case, what proof have you that the third Gaudu wasn't right here, committing the murder? What proof have you that the other two, posted near, didn't climb the wall, not to rush to the victim's help but to smother his cries and finish him off?"

"If that were so, why should they accuse you personally?"

"I have a small shoot and the Gaudus are incorrigible poachers. It was thanks to me that they were twice caught in the act and sentenced. Now, as they've got to accuse someone to shift suspicion from themselves, they're getting their own back."

"Merely surmise, as you said yourself. Why should they want to kill Vaucherel?"

"How should I know?" Leboc shrugged his shoulders.

"You have no idea what it was that may have been stolen from the drawer in the table?"

"None, your lordship. My friend Vaucherel was not rich, whatever people may have said. I happen to know that he had entrusted his savings to a broker and kept no money in the house."

"Nor anything valuable?"

"Nothing whatever."

"What about his books?"

"They aren't worth anything, as you can see for yourself. He always wanted to collect first editions and old bindings, but he could never afford it."

"Did he ever mention the Gaudu cousins to you?"

"Never. Much as I long to avenge my poor friend's death, I have no wish to speak anything but the strict truth."

The examination went on. The magistrate questioned the cousins closely, but at the finish the confrontation showed no results. Having cleared up a few minor points, the magistrates adjourned to Fontines.

Monsieur Leboc's property, at the end of the village, was no bigger than the cottage. The garden was enclosed by a very high, neatly clipped hedge. The white-painted brick house faced on to a tiny, perfectly circular lawn. As at the cottage the distance from gate to porch was between fifteen and twenty yards.

The magistrate asked Monsieur Leboc to take up his position as on the fatal afternoon. Monsieur Leboc thereupon seated himself at the window, a book on his knees, and his pipe in his mouth.

Here again no mistake was possible. Anyone passing the gate and glancing towards the house could not fail to see Monsieur Leboc distinctly. The five witnesses who had been summoned—laborers and shopkeepers of Fontines—repeated their evidence in such a way that it was quite impossible to doubt Monsieur Leboc's whereabouts between midday and four o'clock on the day of the crime.

The magistrates did not attempt to hide their bewilderment from the inspector, and Formerie, to whom Béchoux had introduced Barnett as a detective of exceptional ability, could not help saying:

"A complicated case, monsieur. What do you make of it?"

"Yes, what do you make of it?" echoed Béchoux, sighing pointedly to remind Barnett of the need for tact.

Jim Barnett had followed the whole investigation at the cottage in silence. Béchoux had kept asking him questions, to which he had only replied with nods and muttered monosyllables. Now he answered pleasantly:

"A *most* complicated case, monsieur."

"Ah, you think so too. All things considered, the allegations of the two parties balance each other. On the one hand, we have Monsieur Leboc's alibi. It is incontestable that he could not have left his house that afternoon. On the other hand, the story of the three cousins impresses me favorably."

"That's so. One side or the other is acting an abject farce. But which side? Can the three Gaudus, bad characters of brutal aspect, be innocent? Or may the smiling Monsieur Leboc, all candor and calm, be guilty? Or are we to take it that the appearance of the actors in this drama is an indication of their respective roles, Monsieur Leboc being innocent and the Gaudus guilty?"

"After all," Monsieur Formerie concluded with some satisfaction, "you're no nearer seeing daylight than we are."

"Oh, yes, I am!" Jim Barnett declared, a twinkle in his eye.

Monsieur Formerie bit his lip.

"That being so," he observed icily, "perhaps you will be so good as to tell us what more you have been able to discover."

"I will certainly do so at the proper moment. To-day, monsieur, all I can do is to beg you to call a new witness."

"A new witness? But—what's his name?"

"I really don't know."

"What's that? *You don't know?*"

Monsieur Formerie was wondering whether this super-detective was ragging him. Béchoux showed signs of anxiety. Was Barnett going to pull a hornet's nest about his ears at the start?

At last Jim Barnett leaned over to Monsieur Formerie and pointing to Monsieur Leboc, who was still puffing conscientiously at his pipe by the window, he whispered:

"In the inner compartment of Monsieur Leboc's pocket-book there is a visiting card pierced with four small holes in lozenge formation. That card will give us the name and address of our new witness."

This ridiculous oracular pronouncement was hardly calculated to restore Formerie's equilibrium, but Inspector Béchoux did not hesitate to act. Without giving any reason, he ordered Monsieur Leboc to hand over his pocket-book. He opened it and took out a visiting card pierced with four holes arranged in a lozenge and bearing the name: *Miss Elizabeth Lovendale*, with an address in blue pencil: *Grand Hotel Vendôme, Paris.*

The two magistrates looked at one another in amazement. Béchoux fairly beamed, while Monsieur Leboc, utterly unembarrassed, exclaimed:

"Good gracious! What a search I had for that card! And so did poor Vaucherel!"

"Why should he have been looking for it?"

"Really, your lordship, you can't expect me to know that. I expect he wanted the address."

"Then what are the four holes doing?"

"Oh, I made those to mark the four points I scored in a game of *écarté*. We often played *écarté* together, and I must have picked this visiting card up without thinking and put it in my pocket-book."

Leboc gave this plausible explanation in a perfectly natural manner and it seemed to satisfy Formerie. What remained unexplained was how on earth Jim Barnett could have guessed that such a card was hidden in the pocket-book of a man he had never seen before in his life.

And Barnett himself furnished no elucidation. He merely smiled and insisted that they should call Elizabeth Lovendale as a witness. This they agreed to do.

|||||||||||||||||||||||||

Miss Lovendale was out of town and did not put in an appearance for a week. The inquiry was at a standstill for that time, although Formerie zealously pursued his investigations, the memory of Jim Barnett egging him on.

"You've riled him," Béchoux told Barnett on the afternoon when they were all assembled again at the cottage. "So much so that he's determined to decline your assistance."

"Ought I to clear out?" Barnett asked. "I don't want to cloud anyone's sky—not even Formerie's!"

"No, you can stay," Béchoux told him. "Anyway, I fancy he's come to a definite decision."

"All the better. It's sure to be the wrong one. There's a good time coming!"

"Don't be so disrespectful, Barnett!"

"Oh, all right, I'll be respectful and, of course, absolutely disinterested. Nothing in hand or pocket. But, I must say, a little more Formerie will about finish me!"

Monsieur Leboc had been waiting half an hour when a car drew up and Miss Lovendale got out. Monsieur Formerie came up briskly.

"How do you do, Mr. Barnett," he said. "Any more bright ideas?"

"Perhaps, monsieur," was Barnett's cautious reply.

"Well, wait till you've heard mine. But first we must get through with your witness. Absolutely irrelevant and a sheer waste of time, you'll be glad to hear. Still, it can't be helped."

Elizabeth Lovendale was a dowdily dressed, middle-aged English-woman, her slight eccentricity of manner heightened by her disheveled hair. She spoke French fluently, but so volubly that she was hard to understand.

At once, before any question could be put to her, she launched forth:

"That poor Monsieur Vaucherel! Murdered! Such a nice man, if he was a bit queer. And you want to know whether I knew him? Oh, not well. I only came here once—on business. I wanted to buy something from him. We disagreed about the price. I was going to have another appointment with him after seeing my brothers. My brothers are well known in London—Lovendale and Lovendale, Limited, the big pro-vision merchants."

Monsieur Formerie strove to stem this flow of eloquence.

"What was it you wanted to buy, mademoiselle?"

"A little scrap of paper—nothing but a scrap of paper. Sentimental value only, as people say. But it was worth a lot to me and I made the mistake of telling him so. It all goes back to my great-grandmother, Dorothy Lovendale. She was a beauty and much admired by King George the Fourth. She kept eighteen love-letters that he wrote her and hid them, one in each volume of an eighteen-volume calfbound edition of Richardson's works. When she died, the family found every volume except the fourteenth, which was missing, together with the letter inside of it—the fourteenth letter and the most interesting, for it was known to prove that the lovely Dorothy had stepped aside from virtue's path,"—Miss Lovendale lowered her eyes discreetly so as not to meet Barnett's look of amusement—"just nine months before the birth of her eldest son. You can understand what it would mean to us to get that letter back! Why, it would prove our royal descent!"

Formerie was growing more and more impatient.

Elizabeth Lovendale took a deep breath and went on with her story.

"After searching and advertising for nearly thirty years, I learned one day that among a number of books sold at auction was the fourteenth volume of the set of Richardson. I flew to the purchaser, a secondhand bookseller on the Quai Voltaire, who referred me to Monsieur Vaucherel who had just bought the book. Monsieur Vaucherel produced the precious volume, and, like a fool, I told him that the letter I was after must be in the back of the binding. He examined it closely and changed color. Then, of course, I realized my stupidity. If I had kept quiet about the letter he would have sold me the book for fifty francs. I offered him a thousand. Monsieur Vaucherel, shaking with excitement, asked ten thousand. I agreed. We both lost our heads. It was like a nightmare auction. Twenty thousand—thirty—finally he demanded fifty thousand francs, yelling like a madman, with his eyes blazing. 'Fifty thousand,' he cried, 'not a sou less—that will buy me all the books I want—the rarest and finest—fifty thousand francs!' He wanted a deposit then and there—a check. I said I would come back. He let me go and I saw him lock the book into the drawer of this table."

Elizabeth Lovendale went on embellishing her statement with much unnecessary detail. Nobody paid any attention to her. All eyes were for the contorted countenance of the magistrate. He was obviously the prey of somewhat violent emotion and was quite overwhelmed with excessive jubilation. At last he managed to get out:

"In short, mademoiselle, you are asking for the return of the fourteenth volume of Richardson's collected works?"

"I am." She looked at him with sudden hope.

"Then here it is," he cried, and with a theatrical gesture he produced a small calf-bound book from his pocket.

"Not really!" cried Miss Lovendale.

"Here it is," he repeated. "But King George's love-letter isn't there. I should have noticed it. But I'll wager I can find it if I was able to discover the missing volume that people have been after for the past century. The man who stole the one indubitably stole the other."

Monsieur Formerie paced the room, his hands behind his back, enjoying his triumph. Suddenly he drummed on the table and spoke again.

"*Now* we know the motive for the murder. Someone overheard the conversation between Vaucherel and Miss Lovendale and saw where Vaucherel had put the book. A few days later that person murdered Vaucherel to rob him of the book so that he could later on dispose of the fourteenth letter. Who was it? Why, Gaudu, the farmhand, whose guilt I never doubted. I searched his house yesterday and noticed a large crack between the bricks of the fireplace. Hidden in a hole behind this crack I found a book, which obviously belonged to Monsieur Vaucherel's library. Miss Lovendale's story, coming as it does, proves the accuracy of my deductions. The Gaudu cousins will be placed under arrest, the scum, as the murderers of poor old Vaucherel and the criminal accusers of Monsieur Leboc."

Monsieur Formerie solemnly shook hands with Monsieur Leboc as a mark of his esteem and was effusively thanked by the latter. Then he gallantly escorted Elizabeth Lovendale to her car and returned, rubbing his hands together.

After this, everybody made for the Gaudus' house, whither the three cousins were being brought under escort. It was a brilliant day. Monsieur Formerie, walking between Barnett and Béchoux, with Leboc bringing up the rear, was full of satisfaction. The coveted Paris appointment loomed ever nearer on his horizon.

"Well, well, Barnett," he remarked, "very neatly done, eh? Not quite what you expected, though. After all, you *were* inclined to be hostile to Monsieur Leboc, weren't you?"

"I admit, monsieur," Barnett confessed, "that I allowed my line of reasoning to be influenced by that confounded visiting card. Would you believe it? That card was lying on the cottage floor during the confrontation, and I actually saw Leboc drawing stealthily nearer and nearer till he got his right foot on it. When we left the place, he had it stuck to the sole of his boot. Afterward he detached it and slipped it into his pocket-book. Well, the imprint of his right sole on the damp ground showed me that the said sole had four spikes arranged in a lozenge. That meant that our friend Leboc, knowing that he had forgotten the card lying on the floor, and anxious to keep Elizabeth Lovendale's name and address out of things, hit upon this neat little dodge. And really, it's thanks to the visiting card that——"

Monsieur Formerie burst out laughing.

"My dear Barnett, don't be childish! Why all these pointless complications? You shouldn't waste your energy ferreting out mares' nests. It's a thing I never do. For goodness sake let's stick to the facts as we find them and refrain from distorting them to fit impossible theories."

The party was by now near Monsieur Leboc's house which was on their way to the Gaudus'. Monsieur Formerie took Barnett's arm and went affably on with his curtain lecture.

"Where you went wrong, Barnett, was in refusing to admit the incontrovertible truth that, after all, one man cannot be in two places at the same moment. Everything turns on that—Monsieur Leboc, smoking at his window, couldn't be at the same time committing a murder at the cottage. Here we have Monsieur Leboc just behind us. There is the gate of his house, three yards away. I say it's impossible to conceive a miracle by which Monsieur Leboc could be at once behind us and at his window."

Suddenly Formerie stood still in his tracks, choking, helpless and amazed.

"What is it?" Béchoux asked.

Formerie pointed toward the house.

"There! . . . Look! . . ."

Through the bars of the gate, twenty yards away, beyond the lawn, they could see Monsieur Leboc smoking his pipe, framed in the open window—Monsieur Leboc who nevertheless was standing with the group in the road.

A nightmare vision—a hallucination! It was incredible. Who could be impersonating the real Leboc, whom Formerie had by the arm?

Béchoux had opened the gate and was running to the house. Formerie followed him, shouting threats at Leboc's extraordinary double. But the figure in the window never heeded nor stirred. How should it heed or stir, since, as they could see on drawing closer, it was merely a picture, a painted canvas fitting the window-frame exactly and presenting a tolerably lifelike profile of Monsieur Leboc smoking his pipe. It was daubed in the same style as the portrait of Vaucherel hanging in the cottage. Obviously the same artist had painted both.

Formerie wheeled round. The mask of smiling placidity had dropped from Monsieur Leboc's face; the man had collapsed utterly under this unforeseen blow. He began a maudlin confession.

"I lost my head—I never meant to stab him—I only wanted to share in with him, fifty-fifty. . . . He refused—I didn't know what I was doing. I never meant to stab him."

His whining trailed off and Jim Barnett's voice, now harsh and scathing, was raised in mocking inquiry.

"What do you say to that, Monsieur Formerie? Nice lad, Leboc, all ready with a perfect alibi! How were the unobservant passers-by to doubt the reality of the Monsieur Leboc they only saw at a distance? Personally, I suspected something like this when I saw the portrait of old Vaucherel. I wondered if the same artist could have painted Leboc. I didn't have to look hard—Leboc was too sure he'd fooled us all. The canvas was rolled up and hidden in the corner of a shed under a heap of rusty tools. I only had to nail it in place at the window a little while ago, after Leboc had gone to answer your summons. That's how a man can simultaneously murder abroad and smoke his pipe at home!"

Jim Barnett was ruthless. His grating voice flayed the hapless Formerie.

"Just look what a clean sheet Leboc had. What a ready answer about the visiting card—the four holes marking his score at *écarté*. And the book he hid the other day in the Gaudus' fireplace. *I* was shadowing him! And the anonymous letter he sent you—for that was what got you going. Leboc, you scoundrel, I've had some real amusement out of you. D'you hear, my bright lad?"

Formerie was pale but restrained. After a prolonged scrutiny of Leboc, he murmured:

"I'm not surprised . . . shifty eyes . . . a slippery way with him. . . . What a rogue!" His wrath overflowed. "You blackguard, I'll see you get yours! Now then, where's that letter?"

Leboc, stricken helpless, stammered:

"In the bowl of the pipe that's hanging on the wall in the room on your left. I haven't cleaned it. The letter's there."

They rushed into the room. Béchoux fell upon the pipe and shook out the ashes. But the bowl was quite empty. Leboc seemed utterly overcome and Formerie's temper broke out again.

"You liar—you confounded faker! But you're going to tell me where that letter is—*at once!*"

At that moment the inspector met Barnett's gaze. Barnett was smiling a happy, childlike smile. Béchoux's fists clenched convulsively. He began to understand that the Barnett Agency was gratuitous in a peculiar fashion all its own. Dimly he saw how Jim Barnett, while protesting truthfully that he never asked his clients for a penny, could afford to live in comfort as a private detective.

He drew close to him and muttered:

"You think you're pretty clever, don't you? The Arsène Lupin touch!"

"What?" Barnett was all wide-eyed innocence.

"The way you spirited that letter away!"

"So you guessed my weakness? I always had a passion for the autographs of royalty!"

|||||||||||||||||||||||||||

Three months later there called upon Elizabeth Lovendale, then in London, a highly distinguished gentleman, who assured her that he could lay hands on King George's love-letter to great-grandmother Dorothy. His price was a mere bagatelle of a hundred thousand francs.

There were lengthy negotiations. Elizabeth took counsel with her brothers, the renowned provision merchants. They haggled, refused to pay, and finally gave in.

The highly distinguished gentleman pocketed his hundred thousand francs and appropriated, into the bargain, an entire vanload of choice groceries which disappeared into the void!

DOUBLE ENTRY

A serious breach in the Béchoux-Barnett friendship seemed to have been caused by the affair of the Old Dungeon at Mazurech, and the fleecing of Georges Cazévon, so that when a taxi came to a halt in the Rue Laborde and Inspector Béchoux leapt from it and hurled himself into the office of his friend, Jim Barnett, no one was more surprised than the latter.

"This is indeed a pleasure," he said, advancing with alacrity. "Our last parting was rather in silence and tears, and I was afraid you were feeling sore. And is there anything I can do for you in a small way this merry morning?"

"There is."

Barnett shook the inspector warmly by the hand.

"Splendid! But what's up? You look positively apoplectic. Please don't burst in *my* office."

"Kindly be serious, Barnett," said poor Béchoux stiffly. "I'm working on a most complicated case from which I particularly want to emerge triumphant."

"What's it all about?"

"My wife," said Béchoux, and there was anguish in his tone.

Barnett's eyebrows shot up.

"Your wife?" he echoed. "Then you're married?"

"Been divorced six years," was the laconic answer.

"Incompatibility?"

"No. My wife found she had a vocation for the stage! The stage—I ask you! Married to an inspector of police and she wanted to go on——" Béchoux sneezed abruptly and violently, giving Barnett time to ask:

"Then she became an actress?"

"A singer."

"At the Opéra?"

"No. The Folies Bergère. She's Olga Vaubant."

"What, not the lady who does the Acrobatic Arias? But she's wonderful, Béchoux. Olga Vaubant is a superb artiste. She has created a new art form. Her latest number brings down the house. It's sheer genius—absolutely. You know, she stands on her head and sings:

> "'I'm in luck, I gotta boy
> Fills his momma's heart with joy—
> Yes, you otta see my Jim!'

And she's your wife!"

"Was," said Béchoux shortly. "Well, I'm glad you like the lady's performance. I've just been honored with a note from her."

He produced a sheet of rose-colored notepaper, with an embossed crimson O in one corner. Scrawled in pencil and dated that very morning was the following message:

> "My bedroom suite has been stolen. Mother in a state of collapse. Come at once.—Olga."

"The moment I got this," said Béchoux, "I telephoned the préfecture. They had already been called in on the case, and I obtained permission to collaborate with the men who are handling it."

"Then why are you all of a dither?" asked Barnett.

"It's—it's because this will mean meeting her again," said Béchoux, ashamed and furious.

"Are you still in love with her?"

"Whenever I see her—it's idiotic, but something comes over me—I can't help myself. I feel myself blushing like a schoolboy. My mouth goes dry and I begin stammering. You must see, Barnett, that I can't take charge of the case like that. I should make a perfect fool of myself."

"Whereas, what you *want* to do is to impress madame with the cool dignity, the daring and resource that go to make Inspector Béchoux the Pride of Paris Police?"

"Er—yes."

"And you look to me to help you. Béchoux, you can count on me. Now tell me, what sort of life does your ex-wife lead off the stage?"

Béchoux looked almost pained at the question.

"She is above suspicion and lives for her art alone. If it weren't for her profession, Olga would still be Madame Béchoux."

"Which would be a nation's loss," pronounced Barnett solemnly, gathering up hat and coat.

A few minutes later the two men came to one of the quietest, most deserted streets near the Luxembourg. Olga Vaubant lived on the top floor of an old-fashioned house whose bricks breathed respectability. The ground-floor windows were heavily barred.

"Before we go any further," said Béchoux, "I am going to suggest that in this instance you refrain from playing your own hand and making a dishonorable private profit out of the case, as you have unhappily been known to do in the past."

"My conscience . . ." began Barnett, but Béchoux waved away the objection.

"Never mind *your* conscience," he said. "Think of the way mine has pricked me whenever we've worked together!"

"You don't think I'd rob your own ex-wife? Oh, Béchoux, how you wrong me!"

"I don't want you to rob *anyone*," said Béchoux.

"Not even those who deserve it?"

"Leave Justice to take its course. Heaven has not appointed you as an avenging angel."

Barnett sighed.

"You are spoiling all my fun, Béchoux, but what you say goes."

||||||||||||||||||||||||||

One policeman was on guard at the door, and another was with the concierges—husband and wife—who were badly upset by what had happened.

Béchoux learned that the district superintendent and two head-quarters' men had just left after making a preliminary investigation.

"Now's our chance," said Béchoux to Barnett. "Let's get a move on while the coast is clear."

As they went up the staircase he explained to his friend that the house was run on old-fashioned lines, and the street door was kept shut.

"No one has a key, and everyone has to ring for admittance. A priest lives on the first floor and a magistrate on the second. The concierge acts as housekeeper to both of them. Olga has the top floor flat and leads a most conventional existence, complete with her mother and two old maidservants who have always been in the family."

They knocked at the door of Olga Vaubant's flat, and one of the maids let them into the hall. Béchoux rapidly explained the position of the rooms to Barnett—the passage on the right led to Olga's bedroom and boudoir, that on the left to her mother's room and the servants' quarters. Straight ahead was a studio fitted up as a gymnasium, with a horizontal bar, a trapeze, rings, ropes, and ribstalls. Strewn about the place were Indian clubs, dumb-bells, foils, and so forth.

As the two men entered this vast room, something seemed to drop in a heap at their feet from the skylight. The heap resolved itself into a slender, laughing boy, with a mop of untidy red hair framing the delicate features of a charming face. Wide green eyes, tip-tilted nose, slightly crooked mouth—all were unmistakable, and Barnett immediately recognized in the pajama-clad "boy" the one and only Olga Vaubant. She exclaimed at once in the Parisian drawl that has its parallel in the Londoner's cockney:

"*Maman's* all right, Béchoux. Sleeping like a top, bless her. Lucky, isn't it?"

She made a sudden dive floorward, stood on her hands and, with her feet waving in the air, began singing in a husky, thrilling contralto:

> "*I'm in luck, I gotta boy,*
> *Fills his momma's heart with joy—*

And believe me, Béchoux, you fill my heart with joy, too, old dear," she added, standing up. "You're a real sport to have got here so soon. Who's the boy-friend?"

"Jim Barnett. He's an old—acquaintance," said Béchoux, vainly attempting to control his twitching countenance.

"Fine," said Olga. "Well let's hope between the pair of you you'll solve the mystery and get back my bedroom suite. I leave it to you. Now it's my turn to do a bit of introducing," as a bulky form hove up from the far end of the studio. "May I present Del Prego, my gym instructor? He's masseur, make-up expert, and beauty doctor, and he's the darling of the chorus. Regular osteopath, he is, for dislocation and rejuvenation! Say pretty to the gentlemen, Del Prego!"

Del Prego bowed low. He was a broad-shouldered, copper-skinned fellow, genial of countenance and vaguely suggesting the clown in his appearance. He wore a grey suit, with white spats and gloves, and held a light-colored felt hat in his hands.

Inmediately, gesticulating violently and speaking with a marked foreign accent, he began to discourse on his method of "progressive dislocation," larding his outlandish French with phrases in Spanish, English, and Russian. Olga cut him short.

"We've no time to waste. What do you want me to tell you, Béchoux?"

"First," said Béchoux, "will you show us your bedroom?"

"Right! Half a mo'." She sprang up in the air, caught on to the trapeze, swung from that to the rings, and landed at a door in the wall on the right.

"Here you are," she told them, kicking it open.

The room was absolutely empty. Bed, chairs, curtains, mirrors, rugs, dressing-table, ornaments, pictures—all gone. Furniture removers could not have made a better job of it. The place was stripped.

Olga began to giggle helplessly.

"See that? Thorough, weren't they? They even pinched my ivory toilet set. Almost walked off with the floor-boards. Don't you think it's a shame, Mr. Barnett?" she went on, addressing Jim, her eyes wider than ever. "I'm a girl that's real fond of good furniture. All pure Louis Quinze it was, that I'd collected bit by bit—and they all had a history, including a genuine Pompadour bed! Why, furnishing this room cost me nearly everything I made on my American tour."

Abruptly she broke off to turn a somersault, then tossed the hair off her face and went on cheerfully:

"Oh, well, there's plenty of good fish in the sea and I can replace all that lot. I needn't worry so long as I have my india rubber muscles and my bee-yewtiful cracked voice. . . . What are you looking at me like that for, Béchoux? Going to faint at my feet? Give us a kiss, and let's get on with any questions you want to ask before we have the rest of the police force back on the scene."

"Tell me exactly what happened," said Béchoux.

"Oh, there isn't much to tell," answered Olga. "Let's see, last night, it had just gone half-past ten. . . . Oh, I should have told you, I left here at eight with Del Prego, who escorted me to the Folies Bergère in *maman*'s place. . . . Well, as I was saying, it had just gone the half-hour, and *maman* was in her room knitting, when suddenly she heard a faint sound like someone moving about in my room. She rushed along the passage, and found two men taking my bed apart by the light of a flash-lamp! The light was switched off at once, and one chap sprang at her and knocked her down while the other flung a tablecloth over her head. How's that for assault and battery? Poor old *maman*! Then, if you please, these two blighters calmly proceeded to remove the furniture bit by bit, one of them carrying it downstairs, while the other stayed in the room. *Maman* kept quiet and managed not to scream. After a while she heard a big car starting up in the street outside, and then she was so overcome with the strain that she fainted right off."

"So that when you got back from the show——?" prompted Béchoux.

"I found the street door open, the flat door open, and *maman* lying unconscious on the floor of my room. You could have knocked me down with a feather!"

"What had the concierges to say?"

"You know them, Béchoux. Two old dears who've been here for thirty years now. An earthquake wouldn't rouse 'em. The only sound they ever hear is the doorbell. Well, they swear by all their gods that no one rang between ten o'clock, when they went to bed, and next morning."

"Which means," said Béchoux, "that they had no cause at any time during the night to pull the string that opens the door."

"You've said it."

"Did the other tenants hear nothing?"

"Nothing at all."

"Then the conclusion is——"

"How do you mean, conclusion?"

"Well, what do you make of it?"

Olga's expression was one of wrath.

"Don't be an idiot! It's not my business to make anything of it. That's your job, Béchoux. In a moment you'll have me thinking you as big a fool as those policemen we've had all over the flat."

"But," faltered Béchoux, "we're only beginning."

"Can't you get action with what I've told you, you boob? If that pal of yours there isn't any brighter than you, I can bid my Pompadour bed a fond farewell!"

The "pal" at this point stepped forward and asked:

"On what particular day would you like your bed back, madame?"

"What's that?" said Olga, staring at this stranger to whom, up to now, she had paid but slight attention.

Barnett became glibly detailed.

"I should like to know the day and hour on which you desire to regain possession of your Pompadour bed and of your furniture, etcetera."

"Is this your idea of a joke?"

"Let's fix the day," said the imperturbable Barnett. "To-day is Tuesday. Will next Tuesday be satisfactory?"

Olga's eyes widened, and widened yet again. She could not make Barnett out a bit. Suddenly she began to rock with mirth.

"You *are* a one, I must say! Where did you pick it up, Béchoux? Out of the asylum? I must say your friend's got a nerve. In a week, he says, cool as you please. You might think the bed was in his pocket! You've got another think coming if you fancy I'm going to waste my time with two mutts like you." With a hand on the chest of each, she pushed them vigorously into the hall. "Out you go, my lads, and you can stay out! And don't think I'm going to let *myself* be fooled by a couple of rotten jokers!"

The studio door slammed violently on the two "rotten jokers," and Béchoux groaned aloud.

"And we've only been in the flat ten minutes!"

Barnett was calmly examining the hall. He then talked to one of the old servants. After that, he went downstairs to the concierges' quarters and questioned the pair of them. He then hailed a passing taxi, giving the driver his address in the Rue Laborde. Inspector Béchoux, deserted and aghast, stood forlornly on the pavement and watched the disappearing chariot of his friend.

|||||||||||||||||||||||||||||

However much Jim Barnett held Inspector Béchoux spellbound, the latter stood in even greater awe of the imperious Olga. He never dreamed of doubting her assertion that Barnett had turned the whole thing off by making a promise no one could take seriously.

This gloomy view of affairs was confirmed next day when he called at the office in the Rue Laborde and found Barnett lolling back in an armchair, his feet upon his desk, smoking peacefully.

"Really, Barnett," said Béchoux in exasperation, "if this is your idea of getting down to things, we may as well give up the case. Back at the house we're all hopelessly at sea. We none of us know what to make of it. We are agreed on certain points, of course. The main thing is, that it's a physical impossibility to enter the place, even using a skeleton key, unless the door is opened from the inside. Since none of the residents can be suspected of being concerned in the burglary, we are driven to two unavoidable conclusions: first, that one of the thieves had been in the house, concealed, since early in the evening, and this man let in a confederate; second, that he could not have got inside without being seen by one of the concierges, as the street door is never left open. But who can have been in the house ready to admit the other thief? That's what floors us, and I don't see how on earth we're going to find it out. Have you any theory, Barnett?"

But Barnett was silent, absorbed in blowing smoke-rings. Béchoux's words might have fallen on deaf ears, but he continued:

"We've made a list of people who called during that day—there weren't many—and the concierges are positive that every single one of them left the house again. So you see we're without a clue. We can easily reconstruct the *modus operandi* of the crime, but its authors elude us. What do you make of it all?"

Barnett gave a prodigious yawn, stretched his arms and legs till they cracked, and then drawled:

"A perfect peach!"

"Wh-what's that? Who're you calling a peach?"

"Your ex-wife," Barnett told the astonished Béchoux. "She's as much of a knock-out off the stage as she is on. So full of *joie de vivre*, so—so electric! A regular *gamine*. Wonderful taste, too. I just can't get over the idea of her investing her earnings in that Pompadour bed! Béchoux, you're a lucky dog!"

"I lost my luck pretty quickly—only kept it a month!"

"A whole month? Then what *are* you grumbling at?"

<hr>

Next Saturday saw Béchoux back at the Barnett Agency, trying to rouse his torpid ally, but Barnett was wreathed in smoke and silence, and Béchoux got no satisfaction.

On Monday he came in again, thoroughly depressed.

"It's a mug's game," he averred, "the men on the job are utter idiots, and all this time Olga's bedroom suite is probably on its way to some port or other for shipment abroad. It's maddening! And what do you suppose all this makes me look like to Olga—me, a police inspector, I ask you? Why, she thinks I'm the most colossal ass that ever stepped."

He glared at the imperturbable Barnett, absorbed in his eternal smoke-rings, and let loose the full force of his fury.

"Here are we, up against an entirely new type of criminal—fighting men who must be adepts in their own line—and there you sit, you—you lotus-eater, and don't lift a finger to help!"

"One quality in her," said Barnett, musing aloud, "pleases me more than all."

"What?" shouted Béchoux.

"Her naturalness—her superb spontaneity. She is absolutely devoid of anything theatrical, any pose. Olga says exactly what she means, follows her instincts and lives according to impulse. Béchoux, she's a marvel!"

Béchoux brought his fist down on the desk with a bang.

"Would you like to know what she thinks of *you*? She thinks you're a d-u-d, dud! She and Del Prego can't mention your name without hooting. They speak of you as 'That boob Barnett—that crazy bluffer' . . . "

Barnett heaved a sigh.

"Harsh words! How can I prove the cap doesn't fit?"

"By ceasing to wear it," suggested Béchoux grimly. "To-morrow is Tuesday, and you've promised to produce that Pompadour bed!"

"Good lord, so I have!" said Barnett, as if realizing it for the first time. "The trouble is, I haven't the faintest idea where to look for it! Be a sportsman, Béchoux, and ladle out a word of advice."

"If you can lay hold of the thieves, they'll know where to find the bed."

"It might be done," said Barnett. "Got a warrant?"

Béchoux nodded.

"Right. Then telephone the préfecture to send two of their beefiest men to-day to the Odéon Arcades, near the Luxembourg."

Béchoux looked both surprised and irresolute.

"No fooling?"

"Absolutely not. Do you think I relish being thought a boob by Olga Vaubant? And, anyway, don't I always keep my promises?"

Béchoux thought hard for a moment. Something told him that Barnett meant what he said, and that during the last week, while he had lolled in his armchair, his brain had been alert and busy with the problem. He remembered Barnett's dictum that there were times when meditation proved more profitable than investigation. Without further hesitation, Béchoux took up the telephone and called up one, Albert, who was the right-hand man of the chief. He arranged for two inspectors to be sent to the Odéon.

Barnett heaved himself out of his chair, and the clock struck three as the two men left the Agency.

"Are we going to Olga's flat?" Béchoux asked.

"To that of the concierges," Barnett told him.

When they arrived Barnett conversed in low tones with the concierges and asked them to say nothing of his and Béchoux's presence in the house. They then stationed themselves in the rear of the concierges' quarters, concealed behind a voluminous bed-curtain. By peering out at each side, they could see anyone leave the house, or enter it when the door was opened.

They saw the priest from the first floor pass. Then came one of Olga's old servants, carrying a market-basket.

"Who on earth are we waiting for?" whispered Béchoux. "What's your game?"

"To teach you your job! Now then, not another word!"

At half-past three Del Prego was admitted, resplendent in white gloves, white spats, grey suit and grey Stetson. He waved a greeting to the concierges and went up the stairs two at time. It was the hour for Olga's gym lesson.

Three-quarters of an hour later he left the house, returning shortly with a packet of cigarettes he had gone out to buy. His white gloves and spats flickered up the stairs.

Three other people came and went. Suddenly Béchoux hissed in Barnett's ear:

"Look, he's coming in again for the third time. How on earth did he got out?"

"By the door, I suppose."

"Oh, surely not," said Béchoux, albeit less authoritatively. "That is, unless he caught us napping. Eh, Barnett?"

Barnett pushed back the curtain and answered:

"The time has come for action. Béchoux, go and pick up your beefy friends."

"And bring them here?"

"That's the stuff."

"What about you?"

"I'm going up aloft. When you get back, I want all three of you to station yourselves on the landing of the second floor. You'll get word when to move."

"Then it's zero at last?"

"It is, and pretty stiff odds. Now, off you go, and make it snappy."

Béchoux was off like the wind, while Barnett mounted to the third floor and rang the flat bell. He was shown into the studio-gymnasium where Olga was finishing her exercises under Del Prego's supervision.

"Fancy that now, here's that bright boy Barnett!" called Olga from the top of a rope-ladder. "Our Mr. Barnett, the Man of Mystery!" She peered at him from between her shapely legs. "Well, Mr. Barnett, I hope you've got my Pompadour bed with you!"

"Almost, but not quite, madame. I hope I'm not in the way?"

"Not a bit."

The incredible Olga continued her evolutions at Del Prego's curt commands. Her instructor alternately praised and criticized, and occasionally gave a brief personal demonstration. He was himself a trained acrobat, but vigorous rather than supple. He seemed out to demonstrate his prodigious muscular strength.

The lesson came to an end, and, Del Prego put on his coat, fastened his snowy spats, and gathered up his white gloves and ash-colored hat.

"See you to-night at the theatre, Madame Olga," he said.

"Oh, aren't you going to wait for me to-day, Del Prego? You might have escorted me. You know *maman* is away."

"Impossible, madame, I fear. Much as I regret, I fear I have another appointment before dinner."

He made for the door, but before he got there he was brought up short by Jim Barnett, who stood in his way.

"A word with you, my friend," said Barnett, "since chance has obligingly brought us together."

"I'm sorry, but really . . ."

"Must I, then, introduce myself afresh? Jim Barnett, private detective, of the Barnett Agency—Inspector Béchoux's friend."

Del Prego took another step toward the door.

"A thousand apologies, Mr. Barnett, but I'm in rather a hurry."

"Oh, I won't keep you a moment. I only want to call to your remembrance——" He paused dramatically.

"What?" snapped Del Prego.

"A certain Turk."

"I don't understand what you mean."

"A Turk called Ben-Vali."

The professor's face wore an expression of stony blankness.

"The name means nothing to me."

"Then perhaps you may remember a certain Avernoff?"

"Never heard of him either. Who were they both, anyway?"

"Two—murderers."

There was a brief, pregnant pause. Then Del Prego laughed noisily and said:

"Scarcely a class among which I care to cultivate my friendships."

"And yet," pursued Barnett, "rumor persists in urging that you knew both men well."

Del Prego's glance traveled like lightning up and down Barnett's form. Then he snarled, with scarcely a trace of foreign accent:

"What are you getting at? Cut out the mystery stuff. I don't go in for riddles."

"Sit down, Signor Del Prego," suggested Barnett. "We can chat more comfortably sitting down!"

Del Prego was fuming with impatience. Olga had come up to them, full of curiosity, looking like a bewitching boy in her gym kit.

"Do sit down, Del Prego," she said, laying a hand on the professor's arm. "After all, it's about my Pompadour bed."

"Just so," said Barnett. "And I can assure Signor Del Prego that I am not asking a riddle. Only, on my very first visit here after the robbery, I was forcibly reminded of two cases that made rather a sensation some time ago. I should like his opinion on them. It'll only take a few minutes."

Barnett's attitude had subtly changed from one of deference to one of authority. His tone was unmistakable in its note of command. Olga Vaubant found herself feeling impressed by this strange man. Del Prego, overborne, merely growled:

"Hurry up, then!"

Barnett began his story:

"Once upon a time—three years ago, to be precise—there lived in Paris a jeweler called Saurois. He and his father shared a big top-floor flat. This jeweler formed a business connection with a man named Ben-Vali. The latter went about in a turban and full Turkish costumes, baggy trousers and all, and traded in second-grade precious stones, such as oriental topazes, irregular pearls, amethysts, and so forth. Well, one evening, on a day when Ben-Vali had called several times at his flat, Saurois came back from the theatre and found his father stabbed to death, and all his jewels gone. The inquiry revealed that the crime had been committed not by Ben-Vali himself—he produced an unshakable alibi—but by someone he must have brought round in the afternoon. But they never managed to lay hands on the assassin, nor on the Turk. The case was shelved. Do you remember, now?"

"I've only been in Paris two years," Del Prego parried swiftly. "And, anyway, I don't see the point . . ."

Jim Barnett went on:

"Nearly a year before that a similar crime took place. The victim in this case was a collector of medals called Davoul. It was established that the man who killed him was brought to his place and hidden by a Count Avernoff, a Russian, who wore an astrakhan cap and a long overcoat."

"Why, I remember that," exclaimed Olga Vaubant, who had turned suddenly pale.

"I saw at once," continued Barnett, "that between these two cases and the burglary of your bedroom there existed not, perhaps, a very close analogy, but a certain family resemblance. The robberies of Saurois the jeweler and of Davoul the medal collector were both the work of a pair of foreigners, and here again the method is identical. I mean, in each case there was the introduction of an accomplice who was responsible for the actual crime. The problem is—how were those accomplices introduced? I own that at first this completely baffled me. For the last few days I have been thrashing the solution out in silence and solitude. Working with the two given quantities, so to speak, of the Ben-Vali crime and the Avernoff crime, I set myself to reconstruct the general scheme—the 'constant'—of a crime-system that had probably been applied in many other cases unknown to me."

"And did you succeed?" asked Olga breathlessly.

"I did," Barnett told her. "Frankly, the idea is superb. It's the highest form of art—a manifestation of creative genius, wholly original in conception and execution. While the ordinary run of thieves and gunmen work with great secrecy, disguising themselves sometimes as plumbers or commercial travelers to gain entrance to a house, these people keep full in the limelight, and do the job without any attempt at concealment. The more observation they meet with, the better pleased they are. The method is for one of them quite openly to enter a house where he is already a frequent visitor, and his comings and goings are familiar to the residents. Then, on a chosen day, he goes out . . . and comes in again . . . and goes out once more . . . and comes in yet again . . . and then, while this man is in the house, *another* man comes in who is so like the first man in appearance that no one spots the difference! And there you have your accomplice introduced. The first man leaves the house again, quite openly, and his accomplice remains there concealed. Then, in the watches of the night, the first man returns to the house, and is admitted by the accomplice. Ingenious, isn't it?"

Then, with a peculiar intensity in his tone, Barnett went on, now directly to Del Prego:

"It's genius, Del Prego, absolute genius. Ordinary crooks, as I said, try to make themselves as inconspicuous as possible in their criminal pursuits. They wear nondescript, neutral clothing, and do their best to merge with their surroundings like creatures of the jungle. But the men I'm telling you about realized that the great thing in their scheme was to make a vivid and outstanding impression—to attract plenty of attention. A Russian wearing a fur cap, or a Turk in baggy trousers is a conspicuous and unusual figure. If such a man is habitually seen four times a day going up and downstairs in a house, no one will notice whether he comes in once oftener than he goes out. The point is, though, that the fifth time he comes in, it's the accomplice! And no one suspects it. That's how it's done, and I take my hat off to the inventor. It stands to reason that a man must be a master criminal to evolve and apply such a method—the kind of arch-crook who only occurs once in a generation. To me it is obvious that Ben-Vali and Count Avernoff are the same person. From this, isn't it only logical to conclude that this man has materialized a third time, in yet another guise, in the particular case which concerns us? He began by being a Russian, later on he appeared as a Turk, and this time—well, who comes here who, besides being a foreigner, dresses rather unusually?"

There was a dead silence. Olga put out a hand toward Barnett as if to stop him from she hardly knew what. She had only just tumbled to what he had been leading up to all this time, and the realization frightened her.

"No, no!" she cried. "I won't have you accusing people!"

Del Prego smiled blandly.

"Come, come, Madame Olga, don't get upset. Mr. Barnett will have his little joke."

"That's it, Del Prego," said Barnett, "I *will* have my little joke. You're perfectly right not to take my yarn of mystery and adventure seriously—that is, not until you know the finish. Of course, there's the obvious fact that you're a foreigner, and that your get-up is calculated to attract attention. White gloves . . . white spats. . . . And, of course, too, you've got one of those mobile, india rubber faces, which could pretty easily turn you from a Russian into a Turk, and from a Turk into a shady adventurer, nationality unspecified! *And*, of course, you're well known in this house, and business brings you here several times a day. But, after all, your reputation for honesty is unblemished, and you enjoy the patronage of no less a person than Olgo Vaubant. So no one would *dream* of accusing *you*.

"But what was I to think? You see my difficulty, don't you? You were the only possible suspect, and yet you were above suspicion. Isn't that so, madame?" He turned to Olga for confirmation.

"Oh, yes," she agreed, eyes feverishly bright. "Then who *are* we to suspect? How can we find out who did it?"

"Aha," said Barnett, "that's simple enough. I've set a trap for the mystery mouse!"

"A trap? How could you do that?"

"Tell me, madame," said Barnett, "Baron de Laureins telephoned you on Saturday? I thought so. And yesterday he came to see you here?"

Olga nodded, full of wonder.

"And he brought you a chest full of silver, engraved with the Pompadour crest?"

"That's it," said Olga, "on the table. But——"

Barnett cut her short. In the manner of a fortuneteller he continued:

"Baron de Laureins, who is very hard up, is trying to sell the silver which is a family heirloom that has come down to him from the d'Etoiles, and he has left it in your care until to-morrow."

"How . . . how do you know all this?" Olga was quite scared.

"I," said Barnett, "am the Baron—very new *noblesse!* Have you displayed the handsome silverware to your admiring friends?"

"Certainly."

"And, on the other hand, I take it your mother has had a telegram from the country, summoning her to the bedside of your ailing aunt?"

"How on earth do you know *that?*"

"I sent the telegram. Oh, believe me, I'm the whole works! So your mother went off this morning, and the chest stays in this room till to-morrow. What a temptation for the unknown friend who so cleverly burgled your bedroom to get up to his tricks again and snaffle the chest of silver. Much easier than a suite of furniture!"

Olga, now thoroughly alarmed, demanded:

"Will the attempt be made to-night?"

"Of course it will," Barnett assured her.

"Oh, how awful!" she wailed.

Del Prego, who had listened to all this in silence, now got up.

"What's so awful, madame?" he asked, with a faint sneer. "Forewarned is forearmed. You have only to ring up the police. With your permission, I will do so at once."

"Oh, dear me, no," protested Barnett. "I shall need you, Del Prego."

"I fail to see in what way you can require my services."

"Why, in helping to arrest the accomplice, of course!"

"Plenty of time for that, if the attempt is to be made to-night."

"Yes, but *do* bear in mind," urged Barnett gently but firmly, "that the accomplice was, in each case, introduced beforehand!"

"You mean he's already in the flat?" asked Del Prego.

"He's been here for the last half-hour," declared Barnett.

"Since I arrived, you mean?"

"Since you arrived the second time," said Barnett quietly. "I saw him as plainly as I see you now."

"Then he's hiding in the flat?"

Barnett pointed to the door.

"In the hall there's a clothes cupboard which hasn't been opened all the afternoon. He's in there."

"But he couldn't have got into the flat on his own!"

"Of course not."

"Then who opened the door to him?"

"You, Del Prego."

The brief statement was almost shockingly abrupt.

Even though from the beginning of the conversation Barnett's remarks had been obviously aimed at the gym instructor, becoming increasingly plain in their import, yet this downright attack took Del Prego by surprise. Rage, fear, and the determination to act swiftly were easily discernible in his changed expression. Divining his adversary's perplexity, Barnett took advantage of it to run out into the hall. He jerked a man out of the cupboard, and pushed him, struggling, before him into the studio.

"Oh," cried Olga, utterly taken aback, "then it's true!"

The man was the same height as Del Prego. Like Del Prego he wore a grey suit and white spats. He had much the same type of greasy, mobile countenance.

"Milord has forgotten his hat and gloves," said Barnett, and clapped an ash-colored hat on the man's head, at the same time handing him a pair of white gloves.

Struck dumb with amazement, Olga drew slowly from the scene of action, and, never shifting her gaze from the two men, proceeded to climb a rope-ladder backwards. It had now fully dawned on her what kind of man Del Prego was, and what frightful risks she had run during the time spent in his company.

"Funny, isn't it?" Barnett said, laughing. "Not as like as twins, of course, but they're the same height and have much the same sort of physiog., and what with that and their dressing in duplicate, they might be brothers!"

The two crooks were recovering from their confusion, and simultaneously began to realize that, after all, they were only up against one man, and that a poor-looking specimen, with apparently a wretched physique under his shabby frock-coat.

Del Prego spluttered some words in a foreign language which Barnett translated immediately.

"No use speaking Russian," he observed, "to ask your friend if he's got a gun handy!"

Del Prego shook with rage and spoke again in a different language.

"Unluckily for you," Barnett told him, "I know Turkish inside out. Berlitz has nothing on me. Also, I think it only fair to tell you that Béchoux—you know, Olga's policeman husband that was—is waiting on the stairs with two friends. If that gun goes off, they will break down the door!"

Del Prego and the other man exchanged glances. They saw they were cornered, but they were the sort that doesn't give in without putting up a stiff fight.

Without seeming to move, they drew imperceptibly closer to Barnett.

"Fine!" the latter told them genially. "You propose to set upon me and finish me off at close quarters, do you? And when I'm done for, you'll try to elude Béchoux. Now then, madame, keep your eyes open and you'll see something! Tom Thumb and the two Giants! David and the twin Goliaths! Get a move on, Del Prego. Brace up, now! Try springing at my throat for a start!"

The distance between them had lessened again. The two men stood tense, ready to hurl themselves on Barnett.

But Barnett most unexpectedly forestalled them. In a flash he had dived to the floor, seized a leg of each, and brought them crashing! Before they had time to counter, the head of each was being ground into the floor by an implacable, murderous hand. They gasped convulsively, choking in Barnett's vise-like grip. Their countenances took on a purple tinge.

"Olga!" called Barnett with perfect calm, "be a good girl and open the door and call Béchoux, will you?"

Olga dropped, monkey-like, from her ladder, and tottered rather than ran out of the room, calling "Béchoux! Béchoux!"

A moment later she returned with the inspector, babbling excitedly to him:

"*He* did it! Bowled them both over single-handed! I'd never have believed it of him!"

"Behold," said Barnett to Béchoux, "your two bright lads. Just slip the bracelets on them so that I can let 'em come up for breath! You needn't worry about fixing them too tightly. They'll come quietly, won't you, Del Prego? All lamb-like and pretty!"

He rose from the floor, gallantly kissed Olga's hand, while she regarded him in ever-growing wonder, and chortled gaily:

"How's that for a haul, Béchoux? Two of the most cunning criminals in Paris snared at last. Really, Del Prego, you must allow me to congratulate you on your methods!"

He dug the professor playfully in the ribs, while the latter was powerless, handcuffed to Béchoux, and continued jubilantly:

"My good man, you're a genius. Why, when Béchoux and I were on the watch downstairs, I, having tumbled to your trick, naturally saw that it was *not* you the third time, but Béchoux, who didn't know, soon swallowed the bait and really thought the gentleman in white gloves, white spats, grey hat and grey suit was the same Del Prego that he had already seen pass several times. So Del Prego the Second was able to go quietly upstairs, sneak through the door—which you had left ajar for him—and hide in the hall cupboard. Exactly the same tactics as you employed on the night when the bedroom suite disappeared into space. You can't deny it, Del Prego, you're a genius!"

Barnett was by now bubbling over with sheer exuberance. With a flying leap, he was astride the trapeze; in a moment he was twirling like a top round and round an upright pole; he swung on to a rope, then to the rings, then up the ladder he went, swaying like a sailor in the rigging. The tails of his ancient frock-coat flapped stiffly, disapprovingly behind him, the venerable garment seeming to protest against these unseemly gambols.

Olga gave a little gasp as he unexpectedly landed at her feet, bowing low.

"Feel my heart, madame; beating quite normally. And I'm not the least bit out of breath. Don't you wonder, Béchoux, how I keep in training?"

He snatched up the telephone and called a number.

"That the préfecture? ... Extension two, please.... That you, Albert? Béchoux speaking.... It doesn't sound like my voice? ... Well, I can't help that. Now then, listen. You can report that I have just arrested two murderers who are wanted for the Olga Vaubant robbery."

He hung up, and held out a hand to Béchoux.

"The laurels are all yours, old chap. Madame, it's time I took my leave. What's up, Del Prego? You are not regarding me with that warm affection I could desire!"

Del Prego was muttering furiously:

"There's only one man alive who could get the better of me ... only one ..."

"Who's that?"

"Arsène Lupin!"

Barnett laughed as though he would split.

"Bully for you, my boy. You ought to have been a Professor of Psychology. And then you would never have got yourself into this mix-up!"

He had another joyous spasm, bowed to Olga, and went off in a gale of merriment, humming that catchy little tune:

"Yes, you otta see my Jim!"

Next day Del Prego, overwhelmed by the case against him, revealed the whereabouts of the garage in the suburbs in which he had hidden Olga Vaubant's bedroom suite. This was on the Tuesday. Barnett had fulfilled his promise.

Béchoux was sent out of Paris on a fresh case, and was away some days. When he got back he found a note from Barnett.

"You must own that I have played strictly fair. There hasn't been a sou of profit for me in the whole business—none of the 'pickings' that have distressed your gentle soul in the past. It is satisfaction for me to know that I retain your friendship and respect!"

That afternoon Béchoux, who had made up his mind to part brass-rags once and for all with Barnett, went along to the office in the Rue Laborde. The office was closed, and there was a notice on the door which read:

"Closed on account of a sudden attachment.
Reopening after the honeymoon trip."

"And what the hell may that mean?" muttered Béchoux, smitten with sudden vague anxiety. He rushed off to Olga's flat. It was shut up. He rushed on to the Folies Bergère. There he was told that the star had paid a large forfeit to break her contract and had gone off on holiday.

"*Nom d'un Nom d'un Nom!*" spluttered Béchoux when he got out in the street. "Is it possible? . . . Instead of collaring some cash, can he have used his triumph to . . . can he have dared to . . ."

The cloud of suspicion grew bigger and blacker. Béchoux became frantic. How was he to learn the truth? Or rather, what course could he take that would keep the truth from him, and save him from appalling certainty in place of his suspicion?

⁓⁓⁓⁓⁓⁓⁓⁓⁓⁓⁓⁓⁓

But Barnett was not the man to leave his victim in peace. At intervals the unlucky Béchoux was the recipient of highly colored post-cards, scrawled with even more lurid legends:

"*Oh, Béchoux! One moonlight night in Rome!*"

"*Béchoux, next time you're in love, bring her to Sicily!*"

And from Venice: "*If you were here, Béchoux, I should have to stop you jumping in a canal!*"

"I will never forgive him this, never! He has outraged me past hope of pardon! Next time I will have my revenge!"

And, like a mocking echo, he seemed to hear Olga's husky tones:

> "*I'm in luck, I gotta boy*
> *Fills his momma's heart with joy.*
> *Yes, you otta see my Jim!*"

ARRESTING ARSÈNE LUPIN!

Suddenly, unexpectedly, the fight between Barnett and Béchoux, which had dragged on so long under cover, had reached the last round—in the open!

Inspector Béchoux sped through the arched gateway of the préfecture and across a couple of courtyards, took the stairs two at a time, and dashed, without pausing to knock, into the sanctum of his chief. Pale and breathless, he stammered:

"Arsène Lupin is mixed up in the Desroques case!"

The chief gave a startled exclamation.

"Surely not!"

"I saw him myself only a little while ago, outside Desroques's flat, and recognized him at once."

"Don't try and be funny, Béchoux. Nobody ever *recognizes* Arsène Lupin."

"I do!" declared Béchoux. "This time he's disguised as a private detective and calls himself Jim Barnett—you remember, the chap I told you about before, who left Paris a little while ago."

The chief gave a slight chuckle.

"Left with Olga Vaubant of the Folies Bergère, didn't he?"

"Yes," assented Béchoux wrathfully. "Olga Vaubant, the singing acrobat, and my ex-wife!"

"Well," said the chief, "what did you do when you—recognized Lupin?"

"I shadowed him."

"Without his knowing it?" The other was frankly incredulous.

Béchoux drew himself up stiffly. "When I shadow a man, chief, he never knows it," he declared. "All the same," he added thoughtfully, "although the beggar was pretending to be out for a stroll, he didn't take any chances. First he walked round the Place de l'Etoile. Then he went along the Avenue Kléber and stopped on the east side of the Rond Point du Trocadéro. Sitting on a bench there was a gypsy girl. She was a pretty piece of goods, with her black head bare in the sunshine, and her colored shawl wrapped about her. Well I watched Lupin, alias Barnett, sit down beside her, and a minute later they were talking away together, but hardly moving their lips—an old prison trick that, chief. More than once I noticed them looking up at a house on the corner of the Place du Trocadéro and the Avenue Kléber. After a while, Lupin got up and took the Metro."

"Did you keep on shadowing him?"

"Yes—or, rather, I tried to," said Béchoux. "But he jumped aboard a train that was just moving while I was held up in the crowd. When I got back to the bench, the gypsy girl was gone."

"And what about the house they were looking up at?"

"That's where I've just come from," said Béchoux. He took a deep breath, and launched forth: "On the fourth floor of that house is a furnished flat where for the last month old General Desroques, Jean Desroques's father, has been living. You remember that he came up from Limoges to defend his son when the latter was arrested and charged"—Béchoux swelled with the majesty of the law—"with abduction, illegal detention, and willful murder!"

This repetition of the roll of crimes seemingly impressed the chief, who nodded solemnly and asked his subordinate:

"Did you call on the general?"

"I did, and he opened the door to me himself. Then I described to him the little comedy that had just been played under his windows, leaving out all mention of Arsène Lupin, of course. He was not surprised, and told me that the day before a gypsy girl had come to see him. She offered to tell his fortune and reveal the outcome of the trial. She demanded three thousand francs and said she would await his answer next afternoon in the Place du Trocadéro between two and half-past two."

"But why should the general pay her all that money?"

"She assured him that she could get hold of the mystery photograph and let him have it."

"What?" the chief was genuinely surprised. "You mean that photograph we've all been searching for and can't find anywhere?"

"That's it," said Béchoux. "The photograph that would save the general's son—or finally establish his guilt!"

Both were silent for a while. At last the chief said:

"I expect you know, Béchoux, how anxious we are to get hold of that photograph ourselves?"

Béchoux nodded.

"It means even more than you realize, though. Listen, Béchoux, if you can lay hands on that photograph it must be turned over to me before the Parquet gets wind of it." He added in a whisper: "The Department comes first, see?..."

And, with equal seriousness and set purpose, Béchoux replied, "Chief, you shall have it. I will get it for you, and, at the same time, I will get Jim Barnett, or rather Arsène Lupin!"

<hr />

Just a month before this conversation at the préfecture, Jacques Veraldy had been kept waiting for his dinner. Jacques Veraldy, one of the foremost figures in Parisian society, a man of vast wealth, one of the unscrupulous spiders that spin political webs, had waited till long past the dinner hour for the return of his wife, Christiane. But she did not come home that night, and next morning the police were called in. They soon elicited the following facts:

On the afternoon of her disappearance, Christiane Veraldy had gone for a walk in the Bois de Boulogne, near her house. On this walk she had been stopped by a well-dressed man who, after a brief conversation, had led her to a closed car, with the blinds pulled down, which was waiting in a deserted alley. They both got into the car and drove off quickly in the direction of Saint-Cloud.

None of the witnesses who came forward to describe this meeting in the Bois had been able to see the man's face. He seemed young, they said, and they were all agreed that he wore a very smart dark-blue overcoat and a black beret.

Two days passed, and still there was no news of the missing Christiane Veraldy. Then, suddenly, the tragedy happened.

About sunset, some peasants working in the fields on the main road from Paris to Chartres noticed a car being driven at a reckless speed. Even as they watched its onrush, the car door was pushed open, and a woman fell out on the road. They rushed to her assistance. At the same time the car raced up the steep bank at the side of the road, crashed into a tree, and overturned. A man sprang from it, miraculously uninjured, and dashed to where the woman lay. She was dead. Her head had struck a heap of stones in her fall. They carried her body to the nearest village and told the gendarmes what had happened.

The man made no secret of his identity. He was Député Jean Desroques, a well-known political figure, and at that time leader of the Opposition.

The dead woman was Christiane Veraldy.

Immediately trouble began brewing. The bereaved husband, thirsting for revenge rather than overcome with grief, was determined to make his supplanter, as he considered Jean Desroques, pay the penalty of the law. The accused man, on the other hand, had powerful political supporters, who strenuously denied that the leader of their party could be guilty of such a crime. These in turn brought pressure to bear on the police.

Meanwhile, the peasants, one and all, swore that they had seen a man's arm push the woman out of the car. Nor did there seem any possible doubt that the man who had been observed talking with Madame Veraldy in the Bois was indeed Desroques. At the time of the accident Jean Desroques was wearing a dark-blue greatcoat and a black beret.

In any case, Desroques did not attempt to advance an alibi. He admitted having abducted Madame Veraldy, and acknowledged that he had detained her illegally. On the other hand, he swore that he had done all in his power to prevent her committing—suicide! For that was his explanation of the tragic occurrence.

Desroques's account of what had happened was that he had been struggling to hold Madame Veraldy down in her seat, that the door of the car had been forced open when she flung her weight against it, and she had fallen out.

But concerning what had led up to the struggle, where they had spent the days since their meeting in the Bois, what had happened during that time, or even when and how he had first made the acquaintance of Madame Veraldy, Jean Desroques was obstinately silent.

This last point—the question of the first meeting of Desroques and the banker's wife—remained one of the minor yet most baffling mysteries of the case, since Veraldy declared he had never, since his marriage, had anything to do with Desroques, whom he regarded as a dangerous Radical. He testified to having frequently spoken disparagingly about him to Christiane, who had invariably refrained from comment.

The examining magistrate tried in vain to get past the accused's enigmatic barrier of reserve. The only reply his efforts elicited was:

"I have nothing to say. You can do what you like with me. Whatever happens I shall not speak another word."

And when the police officials, one of whom was Béchoux, called at Desroques's flat, he opened the door to them in person, saying:

"I am quite ready to come with you, gentlemen."

Before leaving, a thorough search was made of the flat. There was a pile of ashes in the study fireplace, showing that Desroques had been burning papers. The police found nothing of any importance in the drawers of the desk or anywhere else. They took down every volume from the well-stocked bookshelves and shook them vigorously, but no telltale document fluttered out to reward their efforts. They took up the carpet and discovered nothing but dust!

While this routine search was going on, Béchoux, pursuing his own rather more intuitive methods, stood perfectly still near the door and darted a lightning glance over the room. Suddenly he swooped down on the waste-paper basket. To one side of it lay a screw of paper which might have been an advertisement leaflet.

Béchoux had it in his hands and was just smoothing it out, when Jean Desroques, who had been standing quietly by during the search of his study, sprang forward and snatched it from the detective's hands.

"You don't want that," he cried, "its only an old photograph. It came off its mount and I threw it away."

Béchoux, struck by Desroques's eagerness to retain possession of an apparently worthless bit of rubbish that he had self-avowedly thrown away, was on the point of using force to make him give it up.

But Desroques was too quick for him. Before the detective could bar the way, he had darted into the adjoining room and slammed the door behind him.

There was a policeman on guard in the anteroom into which he had fled. When Béchoux and the others got the door open, this man had Desroques pinned on the floor. Immediately Béchoux searched his prisoner. He turned out the man's pockets, made him take off his shoes and socks. But the unmounted photograph had disappeared!

The window was tightly shut and there was no fire in the room. The policeman stated that he had stopped Desroques when he rushed in in case he should be trying to escape, but had seen no sign of any photograph or paper.

Béchoux had a warrant for Desroques's arrest, and, without vouchsafing a word, he went quietly off to prison.

The foregoing are the bare facts of the case which, a little while before the Great War, caused such a stir in the press and among the public of Paris. There is no need to give in detail the inquiry conducted by the examining magistrate, as it shed no light on the mystery. But there should be considerable interest in the relation for the first time of an episode which led up to certain startling disclosures and put an entirely different complexion on the case, besides marking the last encounter in the long duel between Inspector Béchoux and his "friendly enemy," Jim Barnett, of the Barnett Agency.

<hr/>

The stage was set, and for once Béchoux felt happy in the possession of a little advance information as to the program. He knew what

Barnett was up to—had watched his little confabulation with the gypsy girl under the windows of General Desroques's flat. This time he intended to be first on the scene and to spoil Barnett's entrance!

On the day after the conversation with his chief at the préfecture, Béchoux again called at General Desroques's flat. The latter had been advised by headquarters of the inspector's visit.

A rather corpulent, clean-shaven man-servant opened the door to Béchoux. In silence, and exuding a kind of aura of intense respectability, he ushered the inspector into the drawing-room, then softly withdrew.

Béchoux took up his stand at a window from which he could survey the entire extent of the Place du Trocadéro without himself being seen from the street. For a long while he scrutinized the people passing to and fro in the busy square below.

There was no sign of the gypsy girl, nor of the wily "Barnett" in whom Béchoux declared he had recognized Arsène Lupin.

Neither of the suspects showed up all that day, nor the day after.

During his self-imposed vigil, Béchoux sometimes had the company of General Desroques. The latter was tall, lean, grey-haired—the typical retired cavalry officer who has spent much of his life outdoors, and is in the habit of giving orders and having them promptly obeyed. Ordinarily taciturn, the general was one of those men who, when deeply moved, will lay aside some of their customary reserve. The charge against his son had wounded him terribly. Not only was he firmly convinced of Jean's innocence, but he was certain that the young man was the victim of one of those mysterious political plots which occasionally blot the fair fame of every state.

Although undetermined as to whence the blow had come, the old man stood at bay—like a lion defending its cub.

"Jean would not, could not, do such a thing," he declared. "The boy's only fault is that he is over-scrupulous, absurdly quixotic. He is perfectly capable of sacrificing his own interests to some exaggerated idea of honor. He is the sort of person who would unhesitatingly shoulder a friend's guilt and let the culprit go free. I am so sure of what I say, that I'm not going to see Jean in his cell. I won't pay the slightest attention to what his lawyer says, or to what they print in the newspapers. Pack of lies, probably! The boy's innocent, whether he says so or not. And I'm going to prove it, whether he likes it or not! We all have our own idea of what's our duty. He thinks he ought to keep his mouth shut. Well and good. But I know *I* ought to clear his name, no matter who gets hurt in the process!"

One day, when the reporters were harrying him with questions, the general burst out:

"Do you really want to know what I think? Jean never kidnapped anyone. The woman followed him of her own free will. He won't admit it, because he is trying to shield her reputation. But if the facts come to light—and, believe me, they will—we shall find that my son and she knew each other and were probably on terms of intimacy. And I'm going to get to the bottom of things, whatever the result!"

Now, while Béchoux crouched, like Sister Anne, at his window, and kept watch on the square, the general would come in and sit near him. Then the old man would go over the case and review the dead-lock reached by himself and the police.

"You and I, my friend, are after the same thing," he would say, "but someone else is after it, too! I have friends who are in the know, and they tell me Veraldy has offered a fabulous reward to anyone who will solve the mystery of his wife's death. He and my son's political opponents are convinced that Jean is guilty. What we all want to find, though for very different reasons, is that photograph! Veraldy and his friends believe that if they can lay hands on it they will have proof of Jean's guilt. I *know* that it will prove him innocent!"

From Béchoux's point of view, what the photograph might or might not prove was the least of his worries. His task was limited to getting hold of it for his chief. Any possible sequel had almost ceased to interest him.

Meanwhile, day after day, he sat at his window watching for the gypsy girl who never came, filled with anguished speculation as to Barnett's activities, and listening inattentively to the general's eternal monologue about his hopes and plans and disappointments.

One day old Desroques seemed unusually thoughtful. He obviously imagined he had hit on a fresh clue, or, at any rate, a new factor in the tragic problem. After a prolonged silence he addressed Béchoux at his post:

"Inspector, my friends and I have come to the conclusion that the only human being who can possibly throw any light on how the photograph disappeared is the policeman who stopped my son in his flight the day he was arrested. It's rather curious that he has never been called to give evidence. His name has never appeared in the press. In fact, but for the energetic inquiries of my friends, I should not now be in possession of"—he paused significantly—"certain information!"

Inspector Béchoux looked distinctly uncomfortable, but did not speak. The general resumed:

"We now know that this policeman was added to the group of men sent here from headquarters quite accidentally, just as they were leaving the police-station of this district on their way here. They rather doubted whether their numbers were strong enough in case my son offered violent resistance, and this policeman apparently offered to join them with some alacrity. They gladly accepted his assistance.

"My friends have not been able to ascertain the identity of that policeman. For some reason or other none of your colleagues has been willing or able to tell us. Yet we are certain that the higher officials at the préfecture know who he is, and have been questioning him daily. We have reason to believe that he has been under strict surveillance ever since the arrest of my son. That he was taken to the police-station immediately after the disappearance of the photograph and searched; that he has not been allowed home; that he is, in fact, a prisoner. And we have more than an inkling of the reason for the strict reticence of the police on his account!" The general bent nearer to Béchoux, a certain triumph overspreading his hawklike features.

Outwardly calm and indifferent, Béchoux was quaking inwardly. But he said nothing, feeling it wisest to let the general put all his cards on the table.

"What do you say," said the general, "to the suggestion that the mysterious policeman was, to say the least of it, rather a peculiar character to have got into the police force at all? A nice story it would make for the newspapers—and not particularly creditable. Ho, ho!" He waggled a gouty finger under the inspector's nose.

Still Béchoux was silent.

"Well," said the general, "it isn't going to further my son's interests to make a laughing-stock of the police force. But what I do demand as a right is that I may be allowed to question this policeman myself.

Your people haven't been able to get anything out of him. I think I may be more successful."

"And if I say that you cannot have this interview?" Béchoux's voice was cold and level as chilled steel.

"In that case, inspector, I shall—regretfully, of course—communicate with the editor of a well-known daily in regard to this somewhat curious ornament of the police force!"

"No need for that, general." Béchoux forced a smile. "There is no objection at all to your interviewing Constable Rimbourg—er, the policeman in question. I shall have pleasure in arranging for him to come along!"

In truth, Béchoux was not particularly unwilling in the matter. His own plans had proved fruitless. He was absolutely without information about Barnett's movements, and quite in the dark as to his adversary's connection with the case. In the past, Barnett had always met him openly, albeit under the guise of lending his aid. Barnett had even been noticeably to the fore throughout the cases on which he had "cooperated" with the inspector. Béchoux had an uneasy feeling that this time, for some reason of his own, Barnett was working under cover, ready to burst out at any moment with a startling and probably unwelcome dénouement of the whole affair. And then it would be too late to circumvent him!

His superiors gave Béchoux carte blanche to go ahead. Two days later, Sylvestre, the general's rotund man-servant, gravely ushered Béchoux and Constable Rimbourg into the drawing-room.

The constable was a very ordinary looking man—not at all the sort of figure to suggest a mystery. His eyes and mouth betrayed his weariness. He had been put through something of a "third degree" over the missing photograph. He was in uniform, with the customary revolver in a black leather case, and the policeman's baton—that world-wide symbol of law and order.

The general came in, and the three men sat a long while in conference. But no fresh light was shed on the problem of the photograph. Rimbourg was respectful, stolidly sympathetic, ready with his answers. But he denied having seen anything of any photograph.

Then the general changed the trend of his interrogation. Abruptly he asked:

"When did you first meet my son?"

"We did our military service together, sir," was the surprising answer.

"You said nothing of this," cried Béchoux.

"I was not asked about it, inspector," replied the man.

"I must tell you, general," said Béchoux, "that one of the reasons for our very strict surveillance of Constable Rimbourg was that he obtained his appointment through your son's influence!"

"What?" cried the general. "But it has been freely hinted that this man, Rimbourg——" He broke off, suddenly thoughtful. Then he asked the constable: "What was your profession before you joined the police force?"

"I did various odd jobs, sir. I was carpenter and scene-shifter for a touring company. I traveled round with a circus. I was lift-man in a hotel."

"Why did you leave the hotel?"

"I tired of the job, sir." Rimbourg's voice was infinitely respectful, but there was a slight flicker in his eyes that belied his stolid calm.

"And you found the police force suited you?"

"Oh, perfectly, sir."

The general gave a disheartened shrug of dismissal.

"Thank you, thank you; that will do for the present, I think," he said. "I wish I could believe what you tell me, but frankly, I cannot help feeling you are keeping something back. Your previous acquaintance with my son is certainly an extraordinary coincidence, and I think, Inspector Béchoux, if I were you, I would investigate Constable Rimbourg's past a bit more closely. Find out why he left that job as lift-man. And remember what I said before about the suggestion that he is, perhaps, a curious kind of constable altogether. Look up some of the cases in which he has been concerned—it might prove illuminating!" He rang the bell. "Sylvestre, give Monsieur Rimbourg a drink before he goes." The door closed. "He'll be quite safe with my man," the general told Béchoux, as he poured out a glass of wine for the inspector. Then, raising his own glass:

"Here's to my son's speedy liberation," he said.

For a second Béchoux could have sworn he saw a gleam of triumphant merriment in the general's eye. A most uncalled-for emotion, surely, and yet . . .

He wheeled sharply round, for the general was grinning broadly now. The drawing-room door had swung silently open. On the threshold he beheld a strange manifestation. There was slowly approaching a creature that walked *on its hands!* The empurpled face almost touched the floor. Above it protruded a comfortable paunch, surmounted by a pair of oddly slim and wildly kicking legs that pointed ceiling-wards. For a moment Béchoux was forcibly reminded of the antics of his acrobat wife, Olga.

All at once the creature somersaulted, bringing its feet neatly together, and, right side up, began spinning round and round at terrific speed like a human top. And now Béchoux recognized—Sylvestre, the man-servant. Obviously the fellow was out of his mind. As he spun around, his stomach quivered like a jelly, and from his wide mouth issued a series of rousing guffaws.

But—was it really Sylvestre? As he watched the extraordinary performance, Béchoux felt his brow bathed in a clammy dew. *Could* this wild figure be the imperturbable, perfectly trained, intensely respectable man-servant?

The top ceased spinning. Sylvestre, if he it was, fixed the detective with a steady stare, relaxed his set expression of grotesque mirth, undid jacket and waistcoat, divested himself of *a rubber paunch*, and slipped gracefully into the coat which General Desroques handed him. Once more looking fixedly at the inspector he murmured solemnly:

"Sold again, Béchoux!"

And Béchoux, incapable of protest, sank weakly into a chair, breathing the one word—"Barnett . . ."

"Yes, Barnett," said the erstwhile man-servant, smiling.

And Barnett it was, but a resplendent Barnett. Gone was the air of shabby gentility, the seedy get-up. This new Barnett approximated more nearly to Inspector Béchoux's mental portrait of the redoubtable Arsène Lupin!

And the general was chuckling unrestrainedly!

Turning to him, Barnett bowed courteously.

"Forgive my antics, sir, but whenever something happens that especially delights me I am apt to cut a few capers out of sheer exuberance. I am sure you will understand."

"In this instance, my friend, you are surely entitled to behave like a whole circus of clowns. Your little plan has succeeded to perfection."

"What's all this?" asked Béchoux, recovering slightly from his first sense of shock and dismay. "Have you any special cause for joy, Barnett?"

"Why, yes, Béchoux; and the best of it is that it is all thanks to you, dear old chap. (He's the best of good fellows, general, I may tell you.) But I can see you are bursting to hear all about it. I will reserve my praises for another time, and start in on my little story."

He lit a cigarette, handing his case to the general, who also elected to smoke. Then, puffing appreciatively, he began:

"Well, Béchoux, a short while ago I was traveling in Spain with a lady, if you remember? Ah, I see you do. A friend of mine telegraphed, asking me to help in unraveling the Desroques case. As it happened, my little—or—idyll was by then distinctly on the wane—a total eclipse of the honeymoon, if I may use the expression. I seized the chance of regaining my freedom. And fortune smiled on me. New lamps for old, Béchoux!

"For, at Granada, I fell in with a gypsy girl—a wild, southern beauty, Béchoux—and we traveled up together.

"I was attracted to the Desroques case chiefly, I own, because you were working on it. The more I thought about it, the more convinced I became that if there existed any proof of the guilt or innocence of Jean Desroques, it must be in the hands of the policeman who stopped him in his flight when they were making the arrest. But when I came to make investigations, I found myself up against a blank wall. I was unable to ascertain the identity of this man. I only guessed that he was being kept virtually a prisoner. What was I to do? Time was passing. The general and his son were both suffering severely under the strain. There was only one person in Paris who could help me—yourself!"

Béchoux did not move. He longed for the ground to open and swallow him up with his shame. He had been tricked once again, more thoroughly than ever before. Barnett had shown him up as being the typical, slow-witted detective, the butt of every mystery novelist!

"You were the only person who could help me," Barnett repeated, "for the reason that you, and only you, were in possession of the truth. You had been given the job of putting Rimbourg through the 'third degree.' But how was I to get in touch with you without your suspecting anything? How was I to work it so that you trotted off to retrieve the bird my chance shot had brought down?"

"In the end I found an easy way. I deliberately let you shadow me.

I led you along, like Follow-my-Leader, to the Place du Trocadéro. There my bright-eyed gypsy lass was waiting for me. A whispered colloquy . . . a furtive glance or two up at this flat . . . and you took the bait! Fired with the idea of catching me or my accomplice, you took up your vigil here, in this very flat, under the same roof as General Desroques and his faithful servant—Sylvestre Barnett! So that I was able to keep you under close observation, hear just what you were doing, and, through General Desroques, suggest to your receptive mind exactly such thoughts as I wanted to implant there."

Turning to the general, Jim Barnett gave the latter a glance of genuine admiration.

"I must tell you, general, that I cannot sufficiently commend your acting. You led Béchoux blindfold, step by step, toward our goal—namely, to find out the unknown constable's name, and then get him into this flat for a few minutes. Just a few minutes, Béchoux—not more. For the thing I was after was the same thing that you, the police, the State, and everyone else were after—that photograph!

"Knowing your industry, your ingenuity, your excessive energy in the pursuit of your duty, I realized that it would be useless to waste time going over ground you had already covered. What I had to do was to imagine the unimaginable—think of some utterly extraordinary and unheard-of hiding-place. I had to visualize it in advance, so that I could, if possible, possess myself of this secret receptacle on the day the constable came to the flat with you. And I had to obtain possession of it without his knowledge, for there wouldn't be time to search him, explore the linings of his clothes and the soles of his shoes, and so forth. And yet I *knew* that somewhere about his person he would have that photograph. The question was, where?

"I don't want to digress, but as soon as I knew the name of this constable of yours, Béchoux, I was considerably enlightened. The general's questions only confirmed what I already suspected—that this man, Rimbourg, was a clever fellow who, before he joined the police force, had had a distinctly varied experience and rather a checkered career! In short, I knew him to be just the man to hit upon some hiding-place so bold as to be unbelievable, so obvious as to seem fantastic! Something *he* could make use of, but which would never occur to anyone else as a possible place of concealment.

"Now, Béchoux, suppose we test the intelligence of the class. What is it that distinguishes a policeman on duty from a postman, a dustman, a railway porter, a fireman—in short, from every other kind of uniformed employee? Give it a moment's thought, while I count three. Your eagle intelligence will surely see it! One—two—three. Now, where was the hiding-place?"

Béchoux made no reply. Despite the disadvantage at which he found himself, he was trying desperately to snatch at this straw and guess the solution of the riddle, so apparent to the triumphant Barnett. But he could not for the life of him think what was the distinguishing characteristic of a policeman on duty.

"My poor friend," sympathized Barnett. "Out with the boys last night? Your brain seems a trifle dulled to-day. I don't usually have to enlighten you in words of one syllable only before you get your nose to the trail!"

But there was no role for Béchoux's nose to play in the incident which followed. Like a flash, Barnett darted out of the room, and returned a moment later gravely balancing on the tip of his own olfactory organ the shining baton—truncheon—nightstick—the same the wide world over, wielded by every police force, that bane of malefactors, that safeguard of life and property, that wooden club which has attained to the dignity of a symbol, and is able to break up the fiercest street-fight or halt the haughtiest limousine.

Barnett toyed with this particular baton like a music-hall juggler with a bottle. He let it slither down his nose, caught it, twirled it behind his leg, round his neck, and down his back. Before it could fall to the ground, he had grasped it again, and, holding it out between thumb and finger, he addressed it in accents of mock solemnity:

"O most honorable, most respectable, most admirable baton! Symbol of civic and municipal authority! A short while ago, you were hanging at Constable Rimbourg's belt. A little sleight of hand and, hey presto! another baton, your double hung in your place. You were left behind when the constable departed!" Béchoux started violently, but Barnett motioned him back to his seat. "He is unlikely to return to retrieve you. In fact, I doubt whether we shall ever hear from him again. His role in the drama is over; he filled it not unworthily. But you, O baton, will fulfill to the last *your* role of defender of those in distress, and from you we shall learn the secret of Jean Desroques and the beautiful Christiane Veraldy. Speak, little baton, I conjure you to speak!"

With his left hand Barnett seized firm hold of the handle, circled with narrow grooves. In his right, he held tightly the heavy body of the club, made of ash-wood, painted white, and attempted to twist it.

"I was right!" he exclaimed joyously. "But it's a miracle of workmanship. Not for nothing was Constable Rimbourg at one time a carpenter—the man must have been a master of his craft! See, he has hollowed out the heart of this club without ever breaking the outside, fixed this almost invisible channel for the screw, so that the two pieces of wood fit together so perfectly that there is no danger of the head of the club working loose."

Barnett gave the baton another twist. The handle came unscrewed, revealing a metal ring. The stick of the baton was now in two bits. In the longer section they could see a copper tube running the length of the club.

The faces of all three men wore expressions of rapt attention. They held their breath, so that the silence of the room was intensified. Despite himself, even Barnett was obviously impressed with the solemnity of the moment. He turned over the copper tubing, tapping it several times hard on the table. Out fell a roll of paper!

"That's it—the photograph!" murmured Béchoux.

"You recognize it, do you? It fits the official description all right. About six inches long, detached from its mount and rather crumpled. Will you kindly unroll it yourself, General Desroques?"

With trembling eagerness the general picked up the paper. His usually steady hand shook as he began unrolling the fateful scroll. There were four sheets of notepaper and a telegram pinned to the photograph. For a moment, the general stared in silence at the latter, then he showed it to the other two. In a voice vibrant with emotion he began speaking on a note of joy, which quickly gave place to one of grief.

"You see, it is the portrait of a woman. A young woman with a child on her lap. The face is that of Madame Veraldy—it tallies with the pictures in the press, except that here she is younger. This photograph must have been taken nine or ten years ago by the look of it.

Yes; here's the date, in the bottom, left-hand corner. I was right. This picture is eleven years old. And it is signed 'Christiane'—Madame Veraldy's name!"

The general paused, then added thoughtfully:

"This establishes the fact that Jean must have known this woman in the past, possibly before her marriage to Veraldy."

"Read the letters, monsieur," suggested Barnett, handing over the first sheet, closely covered with fine, feminine handwriting.

General Desroques began reading. He had hardly read the first few lines, when he gave a kind of groan, as of a man who stumbles suddenly on a terrible and painful secret. Hurriedly he scanned the first letter, then, with increasing anxiety, turned to the others which, with the telegram, Barnett passed to him one by one.

"Can you tell us what you have found out, general?"

The general did not answer at once. His eyes were filled with tears when at last he muttered huskily:

"It is I who am to blame! I alone who am guilty. . . . About twelve years ago Jean fell in love with a little shop-girl. They had a baby, a boy. Jean wanted to marry his *amie*, but my heart was hardened by pride and snobbishness. I forbade the marriage and refused to see the girl. Jean was meaning to disobey me—for the first time—and marry her out of hand. But she would not let him. She sacrificed her own happiness so that my son should not quarrel with me. Here is her letter—the first one. She says: *'It's good-bye, Jean. Your father won't let us get married. You must give in to him. If you don't it might mean bad luck for our darling baby. I send you a picture of us both. Keep it always, and don't forget about us too soon . . .'"*

The general paused, overcome with emotion. He continued, more calmly:

"But it was she who forgot. Some time later she got engaged to Veraldy, then at the beginning of his career. Jean learned of their marriage, and had his little son brought up by a retired schoolmaster near Chartres. There the mother would sometimes visit him secretly."

Béchoux and Barnett were listening intently so as not to lose a word. It was not easy to follow the general's speech, as he dropped his voice until it was little more than a whisper. The hand that had held the letters trembled uncontrollably.

"The last letter," he continued, "is dated five months ago. It is very short. Christiane tells of her remorse and unhappiness. She is passionately fond of her child, and it is agony to her not to have him with her. Then comes the telegram, sent to Jean by the old schoolmaster: '*Child dangerously ill, come at once.*' At the bottom of the telegraph form are just these few words, scrawled by my son after the tragedy: '*Our child is dead. Christiane has killed herself.*'"

Again the general paused. No further explanations were needed. It was easy to guess what had happened. On receipt of the telegram, Jean had immediately sought out Christiane and taken her to the bedside of the dying child. On the way back to Paris, Christiane overcome with grief, had committed suicide.

"What shall we do about it?" Barnett wanted to know.

"We must reveal the truth," was the general's reply.

"Jean's reasons for keeping silence are obvious. He was shielding the dead woman, but he also wanted to shield me, since I was really responsible for the terrible tragedy. Also, though he felt certain neither the schoolmaster at Chartres, nor Constable Rimbourg, who owed him a debt of gratitude, would betray him, he definitely did *not* want this conclusive piece of evidence to be destroyed. He wanted Fate to bring the truth to light. Now that you, Monsieur Barnett, have succeeded in effecting this revelation . . ."

"If I succeeded, general," said Barnett quickly, "it was solely due to the help of my friend, Béchoux. We mustn't lose sight of that. If Béchoux had not led us to Constable Rimbourg and his baton, I should have failed. It is Béchoux who deserves your thanks, general."

"My thanks are due to both of you," said the old soldier. "You have saved my son, and I shall not hesitate to do my duty."

Béchoux approved the general's decision. He was so deeply moved by what had just happened that he was even prepared to waive making any attempt to take possession of the documents the police were so urgently wanting. He was ready to take this course, although it meant sacrificing his personal prestige. His humanity triumphed over his professional conscience—not for the first time.

But as the general made to withdraw to his own room Béchoux stepped up to Barnett and tapped him on the shoulder with the curt words: "I arrest you, Jim Barnett!"

He spoke in the accents of sincerity. He was quite obviously going through what was a futile formality which he felt himself obliged to perform. He had instructions to arrest Barnett, and would do so, no matter what the circumstances.

Barnett held out his hand to the inspector.

"You win, Béchoux," he said, "you've arrested me, and carried out orders. Old Kaspar's work is done. And now, if you've no objection, I will make my escape. In that way our friendship will be saved and honor satisfied! You know I should do it anyway."

Béchoux shook the outstretched hand of his strange friend with heartfelt warmth. Between these two alternately allies and enemies, a truce was called—perhaps even a permanent amnesty. Both men recalled with genuine emotion their former encounters, the adventures they had experienced in company.

Béchoux expressed his feelings with that characteristic blunt simplicity that made him so popular with his colleagues and the world at large.

"You're the greatest of all of them, Barnett. You stand absolutely alone. Your feat to-day is nothing short of miraculous. No one but you could have solved the puzzle!"

"I don't know," said Barnett reflectively. "After all, I had that inkling of Rimbourg's past to help me. Do you know the man had actually worked for an illusionist and conjurer at one time. And his little idea in joining the police force was probably mainly the advantage of being in close proximity to the pickings on every possible occasion. Although he demonstrated unwavering loyalty to his benefactor, Jean Desroques, we must not lose sight of Rimbourg's real character. He was a policeman, much as you suspect me of being a detective——"

Béchoux cut him short.

"None of that now," he cried. "Oh, but you're a wonder. Who on earth but you would ever have discovered such an improbable hiding-place as the inside of a police baton?"

Barnett cocked his head on one side and simpered unbecomingly in imitation of a blushing schoolgirl.

"Anyone's wits are sharper when there is a prize at stake."

"A prize? How do you mean? Surely you're not thinking of any reward General Desroques may offer you? You must know he's not at all well off."

"And if he did offer me anything, I should have to refuse it. You mustn't forget the proud motto of the Barnett Agency. No fees of any kind—services gratis—we work for glory!"

"Well, then ..." Inspector Béchoux looked distinctly puzzled; worried, too. Barnett smiled guilelessly.

"The fact is, as I was glancing quickly through the fourth letter before passing it to the general, I saw that it stated Christiane Veraldy had from the outset told her husband of her past! Consequently, the banker was fully cognizant of his wife's former love affair, and knew that she had a child! Yet he deliberately neglected to inform the police of these facts. This he did out of jealousy and in the hope that his silence might bring Jean Desroques to the scaffold. He knew that Desroques would never reveal the dead woman's secret.

"You will agree that this was a pretty blackguardly thing to do. Now don't you think that, with all his money, Veraldy would be prepared to come down handsomely in order to prevent that letter becoming public property? Don't you think that if some trustworthy, respectable man—Sylvestre, for instance, General Desroques's servant—were to go to Veraldy and offer quite spontaneously to hand over that piece of paper, the banker would be prepared to talk business? I am taking a chance on being right in my supposition, as I was about the police baton, for instance. In fact, just so as to be able to play my hunch I slipped the letter into my pocket!"

Béchoux groaned. It was all wrong, of course. And yet, it seemed only fair that Barnett should reap some reward for the exercise of his special deductive skill. The laborer is worthy of his hire. And if the innocent were saved and wrongs were righted, what objection could there really be to those "commissions" Barnett habitually extracted from the pockets of the guilty parties in a case?

"*Au revoir*, Barnett," said the inspector, shaking hands again. And at the back of his mind lurked the certainty that next time he had a knotty problem to tackle he would be quite ready to compromise with his scruples and call in Barnett's invaluable aid.

"*Au revoir*, Béchoux," said Barnett. "I shall be ringing you up in a day or so, I expect."

"What about?"

"You'll know all in good time," and Jim Barnett was off and away.